A Life of Illusions

by

DeDe Ramey

Dalton Skies

The Wild Rose Press, Inc.
PO Box 708
Adams Basin, NY 14410-0708
Visit us at www.thewildrosepress.com

Publishing History
First Edition, 2025
Trade Paperback ISBN 978-1-5092-6082-9
Digital ISBN 978-1-5092-6083-6

Dalton Skies
Published in the United States of America

Dedication

This book is dedicated to everyone who has helped me become a published author.

Chapter One

Two Years Earlier

Failure was not an option. He had to save her. Spying her silhouette in his headlights as she ran toward the waiting plane, he barely got the car in park before he bailed out and took off after her.

What had she heard? Did she know she was in danger?

Agent Kale Grey's heart felt like it was trying to break free from its confines as he raced toward the airplane. His holstered gun scraped against his side under his jacket. The smell of jet fuel assaulted his nose, but as he drew closer, everything faded. His sole focus was getting to her in time. To reach her before she boarded the plane and was gone forever.

The lights of the plane illuminated the area around it. He could see her clearly as she climbed the stairs to the Cessna. Her long, strapless, water-colored dress she'd worn in the pageant only hours before, brushed the steps behind her. Tendrils of her sable-colored hair lifted with the wind. "Victoria, stop! You're in danger." He immediately remembered she spoke very little English, so he repeated it in French. Her head jerked. Fear danced across her features, and she lifted her dress to pick up her pace on the stairs.

Kale reached the bottom, and pleaded, "*Arrête s'il-*

te-plaît, tu es en danger."

Arriving at the landing, she turned. "*Je suis en danger? Peut-être, de vous.*"

Shocked at her declaration, he shook his head. "No. I'm not the one after you." Slamming his eyes shut, he sighed, "*Non.*" His French wasn't bad, but his desperation was getting the best of him, and he stumbled through the words as he replied in French.

Her voice was thick with accusations. "*Est-ce que j'ai l'air d'un imbécile? Tu as menti. Vous ne faisiez pas partie de la sécurité.*"

"*Non.*" No. He definitely didn't think she was an idiot. She proved she was highly intelligent at the pageant, and she was right. He hadn't been totally honest with her. He was a security officer, but not part of the pageant's security team. Nevertheless, he'd gotten notified that someone was trying to abduct her.

A man with dark hair wearing an untucked dress shirt stepped forward along with an older man with silver hair and a beard. Who were they? He moved his foot up to the next step. The older man darted his gaze to the beauty queen, then back to Kale.

"Take another step and I'll drop you," the younger man yelled in perfect English.

The roar of the engines engaging drew Kale's attention, and when he returned his gaze, his heart stopped, seeing the glint off the barrel of a pistol. He wanted to tell her to put the gun away, except the deafening whir of the engines made any discussion impossible.

She wouldn't shoot him, would she? Although she seemed aloof at times, he saw a different side of her when he talked to her at the café early one morning.

2

There, she seemed like a different person without the beauty queen mask. They'd talked for hours. She was relaxed; open; engaged. She never appeared to be scared of him. Why would she think he was the one after her now?

The engine noise increased, letting him know he'd run out of time. Before he could stop himself, he lunged at her. The deafening sound of the exploding gun rang in his ears. Pain filled his chest as the air escaped his lungs. His feet flew out from under him, and his hands flailed, grasping for anything. Tumbling down the stairs, he slammed into the tarmac and darkness engulfed him.

****

Present Day

Kaleb woke, gasping noisily, like the oxygen in the room had been removed. His eyes popped open and darted around, as he tried to remember where he was. A dim light breaking through his window had shadows dancing on the walls. Absentmindedly, he rubbed at the spot on his chest where the bullet hit him.

Covering his eyes with his hand, he gulped trying to steady his pulse. "Shit," he groaned, moving his hand into his hair and digging his nails into his sweaty scalp. The nightmare always seemed so real. He thought he was past them, since he hadn't had one in a while. Bekah, his friend, who was a counselor, had given him some techniques to use. They were somewhat odd, but they had helped until recently.

He claimed the nightmares were from a car accident he'd had, because the true story was classified. Although the accident was also traumatic, it never gave him nightmares like losing Victoria had. He hadn't saved her. He'd failed the mission.

It seemed cut and dried when the folder arrived on his desk. Locate a missing French scientist. He'd had very little information to go on, and every lead so far was a dead end.

She wasn't his target, just a happy accident that turned into a real crime. And one that he would probably never know the outcome.

His job was considered low engagement, gathering information. There were other branches that assisted, handling the infiltration and extractions, although it seemed, with each assignment, the engagement and danger had become more prevalent. He'd been well trained for those moments and was damn good at his job. It didn't bother him until he was facing down the barrel of a gun, with a woman he was attracted to at the other end. He decided, when he woke up in the hospital, he wasn't that in love with the adrenaline rush he got from working at the agency anymore. And it led him to the decision to walk away and return to Arkansas with the case still unsolved.

Sitting up, he threw his legs over the side of the bed, then stood, trying desperately to make them work. His whole body hurt.

Slowly, he inched his way up the hallway to the kitchen. Flipping on the light, he winced from the glare then timidly glanced at the clock. Four fifteen. His brother, Joe, had scheduled him to work at the gym at five. *Might as well stay up.*

Pressing the button on the coffee grinder, he flinched at the noise, then breathed in the scent of the fresh ground beans that would pull him from his groggy state. Soon the espresso machine was dripping the dark brown potion into a small cup. His mouth watered with thoughts of how it would taste.

After a quick shower, he polished off some toast and espresso, then grabbed his helmet and headed into the garage where his motorcycle sat waiting for another adventure.

The security light flipped on. A screeching eagle gleamed from the fiberglass gas tank of his racing bike. It was an impulse buy, a moment of weakness after he returned to Arkansas.

Not that he didn't have the funds. He did. However, he always prided himself for being smart with his money...most of the time. Yes, his family owned a plane, a yacht, and had recently purchased a helicopter. They were business purchases. The bike was his, and the regret was minimal.

When he had problems fighting off the demons that invaded his thoughts, taking a ride on his bike helped him silence the voices. Feeling the wind battering his body reminded him how fortunate he was to be alive and healthy, with a great family and a great life. Not everyone hits the lottery in life like he did. He also knew how quickly it could be taken away.

He'd always been a bit of a thrill seeker; an adrenaline junkie, enjoying all that life had to give. Now though, it took on a different meaning. He knew his next breath wasn't guaranteed. Recent events had made him aware of how precious life truly was, and he treasured every moment.

Gravel crunched beneath Kaleb's tires as he pulled his bike to a stop and cut the engine. Light from inside the gym spilled out into the parking lot. He could see his brother, Kameron, better known as Joe, sitting behind the counter. It still felt surreal and brought a smile to his face.

He'd only known his brother for a little over a year.

After his car was clipped by an eighteen-wheeler, resulting in a fiery crash, he only survived because of a good Samaritan.

The day of the car accident, he had no idea he'd been rescued by his own brother. It wasn't until later, when Joe contracted an illness and needed the rare blood type that Kaleb had, that their relationship was revealed. *Life is unexpected sometimes. Like getting shot. Nope. Not going there.* "We aren't playing this game today, Victoria," he murmured under his breath and tapped the shield on his helmet with his fist.

He'd been on the case for two years and had spent almost the same amount of time trying to get her out of his head.

Some cases were simple, self-imposed exile situations, much like what he, at first, expected this one to be. The more he researched the case though, the more it seemed to take him down a rabbit hole that became stranger the deeper he went.

When Victoria Granier came into his life, she added another twist, and he had no idea how she played into the case, or even if she did. The only thing he knew was, as he delved into her case, one missing person's case turned into several, with no leads.

Dropping the kickstand, Kaleb slid off the bike and lifted his helmet from his head, setting his dark curls free. The crisp air of early morning prickled his skin as he yanked open the door and set his gaze on Joe, whose eyes immediately widened in confusion. "Early? Seriously? On your birthday?"

"Don't get used to it. I couldn't sleep."

"Sorry about making you come in, man. I would

have stayed if I could, but I need to get to the job site. We have three houses to get completed by the fifteenth, and the rain from last month put us behind. I initially tapped Tyler to come in, but he's sick."

Joe was a talented contractor, and since joining the family, he'd started his own company. But being the kind of person he was, he still worked a few hours for his buddy, Cody, at Twenty-Four to Life gym. Since Cody took over the business, it had taken off. Tyler was a new hire. His background in physical therapy was a huge asset to the gym.

"Damn. Must be bad. He's always here. It's no big deal, though." Kaleb stepped behind the counter. "Are you going to make it tomorrow?"

"Are you kidding? I wouldn't miss a chance to kick your ass."

Normally, Joe's jabs initiated a sparring of words, but the unexpected visitor to his dreams had put him in a foul mood. "Geez. I love you too, bro."

"Don't get your shorts in a bunch."

"Did I mention, it's my birthday. I'm allowed…and don't start singing. I've heard your voice. It ain't pretty. Unlike mine."

Joe gripped his chest. "You wound me. And trust me, you aren't much better, baby brother."

Kaleb had a love hate relationship with the nickname Joe had bestowed on him in the past few months. He pushed Joe from his stool. "You know, your wife's sarcasm is rubbing off on you, and I'm not sure I like this new version. Go. Make yourself useful somewhere else."

Joe picked up his water bottle and keys then ducked his head under the counter. "How's work going?"

Kaleb was a bit confused by the change of subject. His family owned an oil and gas company, and he had long known that he would one day follow in his dad's footsteps, running the company. His dad had been bringing him to the office and teaching him about the industry since he was in diapers. All his secondary education was in preparation for joining the company. Although his little detour with the government nearly got him killed.

Since returning to Dalton, he'd shadowed in different areas of the company to get a good feel of the operation, even out in the field. "It's going. Haven't gotten to do much except lay the groundwork for the new program. I'm finally building my team, though."

"What's your new title again?"

"Environmental and Safety Director."

"Isn't your degree in environmental management or something?"

"Yeah. One of them."

Joe shook his head. "Right. I forgot you are a freak of nature, with your big brain." His eyes darted as if looking for something. "Well, give it some time. I'm sure Dad will have you meeting yourself coming and going before you know it." He tapped the counter as he walked away, and added, "I need to check something in the office."

Kaleb scanned the gym, taking in the handful of patrons in various stages of their workouts, then turned his attention to the computer to see how the traffic was overnight.

From the corner of his eye, he saw Joe approaching. A loud pop went off, and Kaleb flinched as a rain of confetti drifted over him. Voices from all over the gym rang out in an off-key chorus of *Happy Birthday*. Kaleb's head whipped around. All eyes were on him. Fingers of heat crawled up his neck into his cheeks. He returned a glare to Joe, who tossed the confetti cannon at him and walked to the door wheezing out the finale of the song while laughing.

Rising from his seat, Kaleb growled, "You son of a—"

"Happy birthday, baby brother," Joe said, continuing to laugh as he pressed his back to the door.

Kaleb grumbled and grabbed a handful of confetti from the counter and threw it at him. As hard as he tried though, he couldn't keep the smile from spreading across his face.

Chapter Two

Eden's eyes drifted to the rearview mirror for the thirtieth time. The black sedan had been following her turn for turn for several blocks. She was fairly sure a man sat behind the wheel, but his face was shadowed. There was no way anyone would recognize her. Still, coming to this small town was either going to be the dumbest idea she ever had, or possibly the smartest. Time would tell.

After another turn, she pulled into a parking space on the side of one of the old buildings. People were coming and going, so she felt sure he wouldn't make a move if he was following her. He drove past, and Eden realized the guy was older than she expected. A snicker escaped when the thought crossed her mind that she could probably take him in a fight. She let out an audible sigh. Maybe he was lost.

She closed her eyes and tilted her head back trying to steady her heart. The constant feeling of eyes on her was wearing on her patience. She hated the fact that she had lost all control of her life.

Wiping her eyes, she groaned as she realized how short the time was that she actually felt like she had control. Her mom had always dictated her life. Now though, she'd trade living in a constant state of panic for her mom's heavy-handed reign. Any minute, someone could grab her and haul her off to who knows where. She only hoped that this move would remove her from their radar. Although, it could very well put her in the middle of their crosshairs.

Her eyes lifted, and she took in the area around her. Ornate structures rose in front of her. Worn buildings that probably held generations of stories surrounded her. Most looked like they had been brought back to life. A few still needed some love. Her gaze landed on a narrow two-story red brick building with white trim. Wood covered the large picture frame window. She wished she had the money to breathe life back into it. Maybe make it a music studio. She could almost picture it as she stared at the old storefront and smiled thinking about sharing her love of music with others.

Exiting the car, she scanned her surroundings to make sure no one was watching her. It was sad that this had almost become routine.

From the day she arrived in Dalton, she started familiarizing herself with the different nuances the town held. It was smaller than her hometown of Charleston, but still had the modern conveniences. She'd driven through the downtown historic district a couple of times. It was her favorite part, and today she decided to explore it. The area reminded her a little of Charleston, and the town square looked like something out of a romance movie with wide sidewalks that had flowering trees in planters and streetlamps with hanging baskets. In the center, a pretty white gazebo sat on one end, and the courthouse on the other. People filled the outdoor seating, visiting with each other. Life seemed serene and peaceful.

She had no idea how long she would be staying in Dalton. With nowhere else to go, it didn't really matter.

Although, if she didn't find Kale soon, she would need to find a job, because the money she'd saved from bartending was quickly running out.

Eden's thoughts drifted back to her last memory of him; his body motionless on the tarmac as the airplane stairs lifted. She still got a sick feeling thinking about what she'd done, even though she kept telling herself she had a right to not trust him. He lied to her. Still, she questioned whether he was the one trying to abduct her, even though Adam called him by name. Why? What was the reason? Was he connected to her father?

The look on his face when he chased after her wasn't one of malice. He appeared panicked. And yet something made her pull the trigger. That moment haunted her.

She was taking a huge risk coming to Dalton to find him. He might be the one who set the plan in motion to abduct her, and she had no idea what her next move would be if he wanted to finish the job. She was hoping that wasn't the case. Banking on it even, because he was her only hope. The only one who had the skills to help her. And if he refused, she was out of ideas.

From the information she'd found on him, she knew he worked at his family's oil and gas company in Fayetteville, and lived in a small town just south, named Dalton. She wasn't surprised when she couldn't find his home address online.

She'd gone to the corporate office but was told he was out. Confronting him at work wasn't the best idea anyway, since she didn't know how he'd react. Instead, she decided to scope out the area he lived in and see if she could catch him around town.

Walking along the sidewalk, she perused each shop, committing the locations to memory. Displayed in the window of a kitschy clothing boutique was a pair of distressed jeans and a cute lavender shirt, with the words "Retro Ruby" in glittery red letters. Too bad the store was closed. She would need to check it out later.

Spying the storefront she saw earlier, with the boards covering the windows, she crossed the street to get a closer look. Faded lettering on the glass front door read Williams News Stand. Shading her eyes, she peered through the dirt caked glass, trying to get an idea of what the place looked like. One side had an old wooden and glass counter. Tipping up on her toes, she tried to look above the board on the window, but it left the rest of the room in darkness.

"It's been shuttered for a few years."

Eden yelped as she jumped and clutched her chest at the sudden intrusion. Gathering her wits, she eyed the two women behind her, both holding cups in their hands and decadent desserts.

"Oh my God, I'm so sorry," one woman said with a tinge of humor and a sly smile.

Heat invaded Eden's cheeks recalling the very undignified noise she'd made.

The smile slowly disappeared on the woman, and genuine concern replaced it. "I apologize. I didn't mean to scare you."

Eden waved off her concern. "It's okay. I'm just a bit jumpy." She added a chuckle, but even she thought it sounded fake.

"Are you looking at the storefront for a business?" the woman asked hesitantly. "I…we own the shop next door, and I know the owner of this place. They've been looking for someone to lease it."

She let out a sigh. "I'd love to. Except I'm not from

13

here. I'm just being nosy."

"Oh. Well, you're welcome to be nosy in our shop." The woman pointed. "We have lots of interesting pieces."

Eden glanced at the sign on the corner that read, "Rare Finds Designs," then back at the two women. "Sounds like my kind of place."

"I'm April, by the way," the woman said as she walked up to the bright yellow door, steps away from the boarded-up store. And my talkative cohort is Kaysi."

Kaysi rolled her eyes. "Not like I had an opportunity to speak."

Eden took in their similar features, wondering for a moment if they were sisters, then something about Kaysi made her do a doubletake. She seemed familiar. Kaysi lifted her hand hesitantly and Eden grasped it trying not to stare. "I'm Eden."

April turned, and unlocked the door, then flipped the sign that said, "Back in fifteen minutes." Eden stepped inside, followed by Kaysi. A delicate floral smell immediately greeted her. Vibrant colors popped on a sign that said "Design Center" sitting above a large glass-topped desk. Her gaze jumped from item to item as she wandered through the shop's inspiration rooms.

Kaysi walked past her and said, "Let me know if you have any questions."

Eden quickly turned to her. "I love this place."

A smile burst onto Kaysi's face. "Thank you. I do too. We've only been open about three months."

"There are so many unique items. I could spend hours in here taking in every piece. And I love how you have everything arranged and displayed as if you are visiting a beautiful home. I could walk in and say, I want that office,"—she motioned with her hand—"and it could be recreated in my home."

"Exactly. We set it up that way to help stimulate ideas. I try to utilize as many of the local artists as possible in our designs. We have an incredible amount of talent in Arkansas and the surrounding states."

"Obviously. The whole atmosphere is so warm and inviting with the big fireplace and exposed brick."

"I'm a sucker for the aesthetics and vibe of old buildings. I guess you are too since you were peeking in the windows next door."

"A little bit, I guess. Dreaming too."

"Oh?"

"I was thinking it would make a great music studio."

"You're a musician? Like in a band?"

Eden held in a laugh knowing that Kaysi probably thought she was into heavy metal with all her tattoos.

"I am. Not in a band. I'm a musician."

Kaysi's phone chimed and she reached in her pocket to retrieve it.

"My friend Jenna's husband is in a band," April said, joining the conversation as Kaysi stepped away with the phone to her ear. "They play around this area."

Chewing on the side of her lip, Eden tried to hide the smile, after confirming her earlier thought.

Laughter pulled Eden's attention out a picture window to a group of guys walking by. As her eyes bounced from one to the next, she couldn't decide which one was the best looking. Then her gaze stalled on one. Was he wearing a crown? Seriously?

"How long will you be here? Maybe you can catch one of their shows. I think they are playing next weekend."

Eden was only half listening. Her eyes were still drawn to the guy wearing the crown as he disappeared up the street. He was at least her age or older, with long shaggy curls…wearing a crown. She shook her head and chuckled. Maybe it was a bachelor party or something.

"Do you want me to get you the details?" April's question sucked Eden back in and made her realize she hadn't quite caught the gist of the conversation.

"I'm sorry, what?"

"I can find out where Cody's band is playing next weekend if you think you will still be in town."

"Oh. Sure. It would give me something to do."

"How long are you here?"

Eden had no clue how to answer her. It depended on how long it took to find Kale. "Not sure yet." Eden's curiosity was getting the better of her, and she wondered where the crowned prince was headed. As April texted on her phone, Eden glanced out the window again. She didn't see the group anymore and let out a disappointed sigh.

Kaysi rejoined the group. "Ben said they are grabbing something to eat at Flame Masters, then heading home."

"Our men," April explained.

"Should we join them for dinner?"

"Nah. I've got a few more things to finish before we close." April's phone buzzed, and her face brightened as she made eye contact with Eden again. "Jenna said Cody's going to be playing at Chug Bar and Grill next Saturday in Diamond Springs. It's just south of here. They start around nine. If you can make it, you can sit with us. There's usually a pretty good group of us."

"Okay." She glanced out the window again, not

quite knowing why. "Thank you for inviting me, and thanks for letting me check out your store. I love it. I will have to stop back by when I have a little more time." She didn't want to keep them from closing, and she kind of wanted to see if she could find her prince. It was stupid. He was probably long gone.

She waved goodbye and stepped outside to see if the group was farther down the sidewalk. There was no sign of them. Spinning in place, she gazed across the street to the park and scanned the area. Nothing.

The rumble of her stomach had her strolling up the sidewalk in search of something to eat. Her eyes landed on a sign that read "Hanson's Deli." A sandwich sounded perfect. She opened the glass door, and her nose was hit with the smell of fresh baked bread. Placing her order at the counter, she turned, scanning the room for a seat. There were none. No big deal. She could eat in the park.

The man behind the counter handed her the order, and she weaved her way through the tables, opened the door, and slowly continued down the sidewalk.

The sound of a piano stopped her in her tracks. "On My Mind All the Time" began, and she picked up her pace. A smile crossed her lips. The story told in song seeped down into her core and she started to sing. God, there was just something about music that evoked a response from deep within her, flipping a switch and making her body move on its own accord. Her mind went back to the boarded-up shop. She had no idea if she could teach her love for music, or if it was just something innate within her. It would be fun to find out though.

She strolled a little farther down the sidewalk, and the smell of smoked meat hit her senses. Above some saloon doors was a sign. Flame Masters.

A loud burst of deep laughter pulled her attention to a group of guys in a booth next to the window. One was wearing a crown. *Found you. Now what do I do. Nothing like stalking a stranger.*

Spying an empty table, she sat in a chair out of his view and started to pull her sandwich from the sack, but a young brunette woman in a Flame Masters T-shirt appeared and quickly let her know the tables were outdoor seating for restaurant guests. A bit embarrassed and annoyed that her covert plan was thwarted by the spunky brunette, she apologized and stood, shoving her sandwich in the sack. Remembering her sunglasses, she rummaged through her boho bag until she found them, and put them on. Her eyes landed back on the dark brown curls under the jewel studded crown. He glanced out the window and smiled a wide toothy smile. Her heart slammed into her ribs. *It can't be.* Unsure if her legs would hold her, she paused and adjusted her bag, then slowly walked past the window, glancing at him from her periphery. Was it him? Could she be that lucky? Or possibly unlucky?

Chapter Three

The saloon doors flew open, and Kaleb stepped inside like he was in an old western movie. Clanking silverware and voices filled the restaurant as well as a scent that was something akin to what heaven would smell like if he had anything to do with it. Flame Masters was a hive of activity with the waitstaff weaving in and out of tables resembling a well-choreographed dance, carrying trays of food and drinks.

Joe, Cody, Ben, Malcolm, and Brant filed in behind Kaleb like his posse, and a brunette with a long ponytail bopped up to the counter. Grabbing several menus, she batted her eyes at Kaleb and tilted her head, then eyed the guys behind him. "Six?"

"Yeah."

She immediately turned and escorted them to a booth by a picture window. "I hope this is okay."

He nodded and slid in with everybody else. After handing them menus, the hostess disappeared.

"So, what else can we do to celebrate the birthday boy besides feed him?"

"I say get him drunk!" Cody returned.

Kaleb shut him down. "Not happening."

"Yeah. Not happening. Last time you had that bright idea, he threw up all over my truck and to this day, when it gets hot, I can still smell it."

"Would you guys like something from the bar?" The

brunette had returned, and her question had the whole table busting out laughing.

Cody wiggled his eyebrows at Kaleb, then his gaze landed back on the hostess. "What do you have on tap?"

"We have a Haines Summer IPA, Cheeky Armadillo Summer Pilsner, TopHops Wheat, also a Prairie Fire Porter, Pine Thicket Pale Ale, and Holland lager."

Cody's eyes widened. "You have Pine Thicket on tap?"

"Yeah."

"I'll take that." He eyed Joe. "That's the little microbrewery in Alabama I was telling you about?"

"I thought it was Mississippi."

"No. I found it when Jenna and I went on vacation to Gulf Shores before AJ was born. The owner, Joey, gave us a tour. He was absolutely hilarious. Had a thick southern accent and wore these crazy colored glasses. After the tour, he gave me a complimentary flight. Trust me, their beer is delicious. Some social media influencer found the brewery, and posted about it, and it suddenly became a hot commodity."

"Make that two," Joe added.

"Three," Ben said with a show of fingers.

"Four," Malcolm chimed in.

"I'll take a half and half tea," Brant said.

Kaleb opened his mouth to order then stopped, remembering the previous conversation. Cody's brow arched, and Kaleb narrowed his eyes, throwing mental darts at him. A flash of red drew Kaleb's attention out the window to a woman. Her dark-chocolate colored hair was drawn to one side and braided. Large plastic framed sunglasses covered her eyes. Intricate colorful tattoos filled her arms and legs.

She slung a large bag over her shoulder and turned slightly, like she might have seen him. He smiled. Something about her took him back to a breakfast café in Canada two years ago. It couldn't be her, so what was it about this woman that made him think of Victoria? The way she carried herself, maybe? Wearing a bright red tank top and white frayed jean shorts, she was sexy as hell. He continued to watch her as she disappeared. *Geez, I need to get a grip. Not only am I having nightmares about her, now I think I'm seeing her everywhere.* He cleared his throat, and his eyes landed back on the hostess. "I'll take whatever they're having," he said motioning with a wave toward Cody and his brother.

"Challenge accepted I see." Cody chuckled.

"Cody. I swear to God, if you get him drunk, you are driving his ass home."

The hostess smiled. "I'll get those orders in. Your server will be with you shortly." With a flick of her ponytail, she turned and strolled away. As soon as she was gone, Kaleb's eyes darted back outside where he'd seen the woman, and his mind wandered into the far reaches of the past once again. He spent most of his time there wondering what he could have done differently. Why'd she seem so scared of him? Why'd she turn on him? The case still plagued him. It was like trying to play a game without directions. He felt so close to figuring it out but was missing some key pieces.

It was a last-minute assignment. Through a deep dive on Victor Chalemaare, the missing scientist, they found his company had invested a large sum of money in an international pageant being held in Montreal, Canada. Their mission was to gather information on how the scientist's company was associated with the pageant.

Kaleb didn't mind the mission. He enjoyed being in a room full of gorgeous women. They were fascinating creatures, and he never seemed to have a problem finding company with them. He liked all shapes and sizes and ethnicities. As long as they were interesting to talk to and could make him laugh, he was game.

There was an abundance of women who could hold an intelligent conversation with him at the pageant. After all, that was part of the criteria, along with beauty and talent. Unfortunately, once he laid eyes on Victoria Granier, his brain seemed to disengage, from the other women, from the mission, and from his surroundings, which was unfortunate since it caused him to stumble in front of her. Not the first impression he'd hoped for.

The rest of the week was spent talking to anyone who might have a tidbit of information on Victor Chalemaare, while also inconspicuously keeping tabs on Miss Granier. Any chance he got, he made himself present in the same vicinity as her. And when he found her sneaking out of the hotel early one morning, he decided to follow.

She was fresh faced, and had a colorful scarf wrapped around her messy bun. A pink T-shirt topped printed pajama bottoms and still, as stunning as she was, she was hard to miss.

He'd gotten up early to chat with the hotel manager who had played a part in bringing him onboard as security during the week of the pageant. They were wrapping up their conversation when she appeared. Following her at a distance, he chuckled when she stopped at a little café a block away. The rabbit food they were feeding the contestants must not have been her thing. Needing coffee, he sauntered in and was wrestling with what he'd say to her when she surprised him by asking him to sit with her.

She seemed so different than the woman behind the heavy makeup and evening gowns. She was thoughtful when she spoke—genuine, not rehearsed. She listened intently to him, probably because French wasn't his primary language, and laughed easily at his playful jabs, returning them just as fast.

Her vulnerability surprised him the most. She did well hiding it, but his training made him hyper aware of the people he was with, as well as his surroundings…most of the time.

He'd been mesmerized the moment he saw her. She was intriguing, and she'd completely bewitched him by the time they parted. He hoped they might have an opportunity for another early morning encounter. Their short time together was not nearly enough.

As hard as he tried, he was unable to get close to her the rest of the week. Nor the night of the finale. She'd been crowned the winner. All eyes were on her.

When he'd gotten notified of a plot to abduct her, shortly after the celebration, he knew he had to locate her quickly and keep her safe. He failed and quite possibly caused her abduction.

It wasn't his fault completely. She didn't trust him and boarded the plane. He misjudged her though, and she disappeared. And that was his mistake. A huge catastrophic mistake.

He still questioned what, or who gave her the idea that he was going to abduct her. It was the million-dollar question that had haunted him since he returned to Dalton and put the brakes on his clandestine career. Nothing about her abduction made sense.

Since moving to Dalton, Kaleb focused on finishing his engineering classes that he had put on hold while working for the agency.

He'd never considered making his government job his career. It was something that had been dropped into his lap, and with his passion for adventure, sounded fun. Although he had resigned his position, he wasn't officially done until the case was closed.

Since leaving the agency, his boss, Quinton Phillips, had sent him to follow up on several leads on the scientist and Victoria. With one dead end after another, the case was shelved a few months back, and he was released from his duties, but Kaleb couldn't let her go.

A loud clap next to him made him flinch. "What the hell, Joe?"

"I said your name like three times, and you continued to stare out the window."

Kaleb rolled his eyes.

"So, are you planning on wearing the crown all day?" Lifting his hand, he touched the plastic crown normally given to the birthday boy or girl when they had their party at Direct Hit laser tag. Joe made sure Kaleb wore his crown while they played. He chuckled. Probably why the hostess gave him a weird look. At the laser tag center, he played it up by using a British accent and ordering people around as if they were his subjects. It amused Malcolm since he was British.

Kaleb always tried to be the life of the party, the one who put on a show or took the dare. It wasn't beneath him to make a complete fool of himself to get a laugh. Why not? But he'd felt off, ever since he woke up in a cold sweat from the nightmare. She shot him, then vanished into the night sky like a shooting star.

"He doesn't deserve it," Cody said, reaching for the crown. Kaleb batted his hand away and adjusted it to make sure it was straight.

"I got high score. Plus, I look the best in it."

"You cheated."

"Bet he'd be singing a different tune if Mitch were playing," Brant added with a snicker.

"Too bad Brandon had a playoff game or he'd of kicked your ass from here to Sunday." Cody reached for the crown again, and Kaleb swatted him.

"Don't touch the crown, peasant."

Cody flipped him off and chuckled. "So, if you didn't cheat, explain how you beat all of us. You don't even own a gun?"

"Who says I don't own a gun?"

"You." Joe pointed a finger. "Oh wait. No. You didn't say you didn't have any guns, you said you didn't *need* any guns because you had your looks and brains."

"True statement. And my charm. Don't need guns when you have all this." He motioned to his face. They let out a collective groan.

"Looks don't account for your high score. So, have you been holding out on us?" Brant chimed in again. "Are you some kind of spy for a government agency? Sworn to secrecy?"

He quickly tried to school his face into a blasé expression, hoping no one noticed the sudden explosion of nerves.

During missions, it was imperative to not reveal anything about his government identity unless it was deemed necessary. His agency had a cover, and so did he. Scanning the faces at the table, his eyes met Joe's, then quickly moved to Brant, and he knew his mental dilemma had taken longer than he'd thought. "Yes. If you really want to know the truth. I am a special agent. I work for a highly classified branch of the government. And if I tell you more, I will have to kill you, or at least make you disappear. I hope you're happy. I've blown my whole undercover persona out of the water." Not one word of his comment was a lie other than the killing part. They didn't have to know that though.

"And how many guns do you own?" Joe placated.

"Did you not hear me? I said I couldn't give you any more information. It's top secret."

"Ballpark it. Fifty? A hundred?" Cody asked. "Or how about any cool gadgets? Listening devices? Cameras?"

He knew they were giving him shit, and if they knew the arsenal he had stored at his place, they would probably hyperventilate.

They were all gun nerds except maybe Malcolm, who seemed too proper to be into guns. Although, he wasn't too shabby at laser tag either, and nobody was giving him shit. Then again, everybody was nice to Malcolm, except Ben, who was engaged to Kaysi, Malcolm's ex. For Ben to tolerate the man was a stretch. But then again, Ben barely tolerated everyone.

Kaleb tapped his fingers and darted his eyes between all the men at the table. "I might have a few."

"You are so full of shit, Kaleb. You know damn good and well you have zero guns in your possession," Joe scolded.

"Not on me."

"Not at your house either."

"If you don't believe me, then why the hell did you ask?"

"Because we all had to pay Ben an assload of money on a bet of where you'd land on the standings."

Ben smirked as he twirled a napkin, then lifted his head. "I was surprised. Not complaining. You got a good eye."

That's what his training officer said too. He even talked of moving him to a different branch. In the end, his brains won out over his abilities.

Chapter Four

The server appeared at the table and dropped off the drinks. "What can we get you this evening?"

"What the hell are you doing here?" Brant blurted, and all eyes shot to him then back to the server.

Kaleb was happy the subject was forgotten, although he was a bit embarrassed for the server. She had big blue eyes, and white-blonde hair. Her blue jeans hugged her curves perfectly as well as the pink T-shirt tied at the waist that sported a "Flame Masters" logo on the front.

"Love you too, sweetheart," the server said sending Brant an air kiss. "Didn't Bekah tell you? I moved here."

"When?"

"Two months ago."

"No. She didn't tell me. Not unusual though. We've barely seen each other in the past six months."

"I quit my job at Peppin Energy. They were being reckless and shady; didn't care how they left a site once they were done, and I couldn't, in good conscience, continue to work for them."

"What made you come here?"

"There was no way I was moving back home. I kind of fell in love with this place and the people. Bekah got me in touch with her grandpa and he rented me the cottage. So, here I am. What's going on with you guys?"

"We're having a little birthday party for the crowned

prince here."

Her eyes shot to Kaleb, and she gave him a smile, then went right back to Brant. "How's Bekah doing? I'm guessing you get to see each other enough, because when we had lunch, when I was moving, she was definitely pregnant."

Kaleb snickered along with the rest of the table.

"I guess you got me there."

Her eyes darted around the table and Brant took notice. "Sorry. Guys, this is Marissa Bellamy. She is the reason I'm sitting here and not in a prison cell right now." They all donned a surprised expression and Brant chuckled. "I don't know who've you've met before, so... this is Cody, Joe, Ben, Malcolm, and the royal birthday boy, and Joe's brother, Kaleb."

Kaleb played up his roll, with a princely salute to his crown. She softly giggled as she held her hands out and gracefully curtsied.

"So, why are you working here?" Brant asked.

"Hopefully it's temporary until I can find something in the environmental field."

Kaleb jerked, hearing her comment. "Wait. What's your degree in?"

"I have my master's in environmental engineering from Texas Coastal Technology."

He patted his body then reached for his wallet. Handing over his business card, he said, "Give me a call."

Marissa studied the card, then lifted her eyes to Kaleb. "You're serious? This isn't a joke?"

"Don't listen to him. He's just trying to pick you up," Joe chided.

"Am not. I told you I'm putting together a team."

His eyes returned to Marissa. "Call me Monday, and we'll set up an interview."

She flipped the card over and flashed him a shy smile. "Director of Environmental and Safety Management at Grayeagle? Aren't you a little young?"

Kaleb shrugged. "Perks of your father owning the company. Call me Monday. I'm serious."

"Okay. Thank you." She glanced at Brant, then paused. "Oh. I guess I need to take your orders, don't I?"

Each of the guys took turns ordering, and Kaleb smiled as he watched Marissa walk away with a spring in her step.

"I swear if you're messing with her to make her your next conquest, your ass is mine," Brant warned.

Kaleb's eyes stayed glued to her until she disappeared, then his focus returned to the table where all eyes were on him. "No. I swear. I'm putting together an environmental team. Ask Malcolm. We're working together."

"He's not lying. We've been approved to build a team to handle the new federal mandates dealing with fracking, ground water, and soil contamination."

"She's got the credentials." Kaleb paused. "You said she kept you from going to prison? How have I not heard about this?"

"Yeah. It's not something I want to rehash right now. Long story short, Marissa was Bekah's ex, Bobby's side piece, and his assistant at Peppin. Bekah found out, and all hell broke loose. Marissa didn't know Bekah was in the picture. Bekah's ex tried to frame me, and now the scumbag is rotting in jail, and I'm not, largely due to Marissa. End of story." Brant glared at Kaleb with a deep groove between his brows. "So, seriously man. She's really nice, and she saved my ass. Don't make her a weekend toy."

"Geez. You make me sound like I'm the Don Juan of Arkansas. I don't hit on every woman I meet. I do have *some* self-control."

"So, you're saying you're all talk?" Cody prodded.

"Well, no, I—"

Joe lifted a brow. "Uh, uh, uh, baby brother. You can't have it both ways."

"I'm selective." If he was being honest, Marissa *was* very attractive, and with an interest in environmental management, he would normally be interested in her. But even though she ticked off boxes in his head, he didn't feel anything. Come to think of it, he'd had a pretty substantial dry spell.

"Can we talk about something other than Kaleb's bedroom habits?" Ben interjected. "I was more interested in discussing how he outplayed us."

"Haven't you figured it out yet? I'm good at everything."

Ben threw his napkin at him. "Shut the hell up."

****

Leaving the restaurant, he said his goodbyes to everyone, and he and Malcolm headed up the sidewalk still discussing the possibilities of Marissa coming on board.

Although they liked to pick on him, he knew he was fortunate to be surrounded by such a great group of guys. He was the youngest of the group, and they put up with his craziness, which was saying a lot. He gave as much as he got. Each one had been the brunt of a prank or two.

The streetlamps blinked on with the setting of the sun. Sitting on the bench, across the street, was the woman he'd seen earlier. The streetlamps shined down on her like the north star. She lounged against the arm of the bench with her knees bent, reading something. Occasionally, she lifted her head and watched the people around her. From where he was standing, he didn't think she could see him.

Malcolm cleared his throat. Kaleb had all but forgotten he was there. They both had been captivated by the same woman.

"You going to make her your birthday present?"

Kaleb studied Malcolm. He seemed flustered. Was he thinking of making a move on her? He hadn't seen him with another woman since Kaysi, come to think of it. The thought of taking away Malcolm's chances with the woman felt wrong, but he needed to find out for sure that it wasn't Victoria. "Maybe."

"O-okay then. I guess I'll leave you to it." Malcolm stuck his hands in his pockets and disappeared up the street.

Kaleb watched him leave. He seemed to have lost some of his confidence since the breakup with his sister, and he decided if the woman wasn't Victoria, he would play wingman for the poor guy and try to get her number for him. Unlocking his car, he tossed the crown on the seat, then, at the last minute, he popped the panel under the steering wheel, retrieved his gun, and tucked it under his shirt.

Crossing the street, he tried to remain out of her line of sight. *There is no way it can be her,* was on repeat in his mind. Taking in her form, and the way she moved, it was like his brain was playing tricks on him. There was something so familiar.

She brushed a few wayward strands of hair from her

face, then lifted her sunglasses to the top of her head and returned her hand to her reader. Her fingers gently tapped the side in a silent rhythmic beat.

Kaleb's heart raced. He'd seen Victoria do that same motion with the menu when they were together for breakfast. *How could she be here? How would she know where I live?*

"I know you're there," she said softly without lifting her eyes. Kaleb went still. *It can't be.* It sounded like her, except she was speaking English. His head was pounding trying to process everything. He was almost giddy that she was alive, sitting in front of him. But how? He had so many questions, and he was so confused. Who was she? Their brief encounter flipped through his mind like pages of a book blown in the wind. Could she have been undercover too?

Sliding his gun from his belt, he held it to his side as he approached her.

"If you are going to abduct me, you don't need a gun. I'll go willingly." Her eyes finally shifted to him. Though her voice was unwavering, her eyes told a different story.

"What the hell? I was never going to abduct you. I was trying to save you."

"And I'm supposed to blindly believe you? Just tell me, did you abduct Adam? How about Bill?"

"Why would you think I was trying to abduct you? And who are the guys you are talking about?"

"Please, put the gun away, and I'll answer you. I'm unarmed."

Kaleb chuckled. "And I'm supposed to believe *you*?"

She shrugged. "Unless you're worried my sandwich

could do bodily harm, I think you're safe." She held up the last little bit of the sandwich and polished it off.

"How the hell did you find me?" he rasped, his eyes scanning the area.

"That's all you want to know?" she asked covering her mouth while she finished chewing.

"No. I want to know everything. Who are you really? Where've you been? Why are you here? And why the hell did you shoot me? I have so many damn questions, I don't even know where to start."

"I'm here, *Kaleb*, because I need to find out if you were the one planning my abduction, and if you abducted Adam. And why?"

"No. I told you; I was trying to save you."

"Then I need your help."

"My help?"

"Look. I know you have questions, but can we please not do this right now. Not here."

"Un-freaking-believable. You shoot me for no reason, then disappear for nearly two years, only to show up here out of the blue, speaking English no less, and you seriously think I'm going to just go home and wait for you to call?"

"No. I'm just asking if we can go some place more private. And for the record, I am sorry. I was scared."

Kaleb snickered at the comment, though when his eyes locked with hers, he could see the hurt they held. How could she seriously think he was the one who was after her?

"I know you don't believe me. Please, just give me a chance to explain." The pain in her voice had Kaleb shoving his gun back into his pants and sitting on the arm of the bench across from her.

"Fine. Start explaining."

"Not here."

"Then where? I'm damn sure not going anywhere with you."

"Please. I need your help."

"What kind of help?" With every word out of her mouth, he bounced from being angry to curious, to worried so fast he was becoming dizzy. "Did you rob a bank? Need a place to stash the money? Hide a dead body that you shot?" With that one he couldn't help but snicker.

She rolled her eyes at his jab at her, then she chuckled. "Nah. He didn't die, thankfully."

And with that, the tension inside him released a little.

"Who are you?"

Her eyes darted around, and she repeated, "Please. Not here."

"Then follow me to my place."

"No."

Kaleb clenched his teeth at her quick response. "Victoria. You are safe with me. I promise. I have more to lose than you, right now. We either go to my place, or chat here. You decide."

Eden rolled her eyes again. "Fine. We'll go to your place."

"Where are you parked?"

"Down the block by the flower shop."

"I'm in the lot across the street." He motioned with his head. "What do you drive?"

"A gray Quete."

"A what?"

"Quete. The little all-terrain vehicles they had in

35

Canada at the pageant. What are you driving?"
    "Don't worry. I'll find you."

Chapter Five

Eden shut the door, closed her eyes, and leaned her head back on her seat. *Deep breath. This is what you wanted.* It was a longshot. She knew she might never find him. But he was her last hope of locating her brother.

Nearly a week of familiarizing herself with the town, trying to come up with a gameplan to find Kaleb, and he walked right into her life like Prince freaking Charming, wearing a crown.

Opening her eyes, she noticed how bad she was shaking as she shifted into drive behind his car. The thought of what she was about to set in motion had her almost unable to focus on the road ahead of her. He was right. He had no clue who she was. Neither did she, really. She only hoped the information she had found on him was accurate.

It had been nearly two years since that horrible night, and it still sent a jagged shard of pain ripping through her heart every time she thought about it. She never thought she could pull the trigger. The moment she did, she knew in her gut it was wrong.

The sky was painted with the pinks and purples of dusk. Headlights bounced off the highway as they wound their way through the forest. Turning down a narrow road, moving deeper into the tall pines, Eden's pulse kicked up, as the last rays of sunlight disappeared within the thickening trees. Darkness wrapped around her. A brief tinge of fear passed through her. Could he be trusted?

She didn't know him. He could be married for all she knew.

They had only spoken at length one time the week of the pageant. But there was something about him. It wasn't just that he was gorgeous. He was. Cover model gorgeous. But it was more the way he leaned in when she spoke and challenged her with his own thoughts. Like he was completely invested in the conversation. It made her think deeper. No one had ever given her that sense of excitement from a conversation. No one had ever acted that interested in her. She believed him…until she didn't.

Staring into his back window, she caught a glimpse of his messy curls, and a chill rushed up her spine. What was he thinking? There was so much she had to tell him. He was taking a chance just as much as she was.

The trees parted and glistening lights revealed a modern structure of wood and rock, metal and glass, carved into a hillside. This was where he lived? Following him around a corner, she watched him pull into a garage and get out of his truck. She parked along the side and stepped out of her vehicle. Twitching his head, he motioned for her to follow him. The flood lights illuminating the outside of the house glowed around him and she could still see the weariness in his expression.

He looked so different from the first time she met him, when his hair was short and platinum. Now, his hair was longer and dark brown. His face was also clean shaven, giving him a more youthful appearance. Those arctic-blue eyes were unmistakable though, and when they landed on her, and he smiled at her through the window at the restaurant, it gave her a glimmer of hope.

Then, when she saw him walking toward her in the park, there was no doubt in her mind, it was him. He had a confident swagger that she found extremely sexy. Unfortunately, seeing him had wiped her brain of anything she had planned to say. Every memory of him flooded her, zapping her of the oxygen she desperately needed to think.

How did he know who she was? She'd changed as much as he had. Gone was the pageant queen makeup, prim and proper clothes, hair extensions, fake lashes, and nails. Most days she was in jeans and T-shirts and very little makeup. She preferred it that way. Over time, she'd used her body as a canvas, adding tattoos to her arms, legs, and torso. She could now look in the mirror and smile at the person staring back at her. She'd found herself in the midst of losing her identity.

Surprisingly, it didn't frighten her when she sensed him watching her in the park. Although she still wasn't sure he hadn't been the one who planned her abduction, she felt oddly relieved, though unraveled, when she found him. He'd had that effect on her from the first time she'd talked to him. She couldn't hide behind the poised façade she'd wear around most strangers. He had a way of throwing her off kilter with the shift of an eyebrow. Something else she found very sexy.

They entered through a small mudroom. Lights flickered on, and Kaleb tossed his keys on the large hall tree beside the door. Eden did the same with her bag. Taking in the sleek modern living space, she paused, feeling the space's warmth wrap around her. The kitchen walls were covered with a rich, slatted maple, surrounding stainless appliances, and gray quartz waterfall countertops. The open dining and living area was covered in soft muted green tones, accented with glass and wood and metal. The perfect balance of modern, with a hint of mid-century mixed in.

"Want something to drink?" Kaleb's voice drew her attention. She glanced up to see him holding up a bottle of beer.

"I'm kind of a lightweight with alcohol. Do you have tea?"

"Tea it is." He turned back to the refrigerator and her eyes drifted again to her surroundings.

"I love your place."

"Thanks. I did some minor updating when I bought it, and my sister and her partner decorated it."

"Do you live here alone?" She could feel the heat creeping up her neck at her not-so-subtle question, but she needed to know. Although the place had a bit more masculine feel, and there was no sign of toys, she couldn't assume. Upending his life was bad enough. She wasn't about to drag a man with a family into her problems.

He tipped his head and let his gaze remain on her, then held his left hand up. "No ring. No wife. Not even a girlfriend." She nodded and quickly turned away, so he wouldn't see how red she figured she was.

Darkness had set in, as Eden settled her gaze out the glass door. She tried to picture what the view would be like in the sunlight. "I bet your view is spectacular."

"It's why I bought the place."

Even though he was being cordial, his voice had an edge. She couldn't blame him. She was surprised he even approached her. She deserved his anger. It hurt to know she'd caused him pain and she still had a hard time forgiving herself. Something told her he'd never hurt her.

But her brother's words kept ringing in her head saying otherwise.

Kaleb handed her a glass of tea and walked past her, pushing the door open leading to a large deck. "Is it too cool for you?"

"No. It's fine." Her body betrayed her words by choosing that moment to shiver.

Grabbing a blanket off the ottoman, he ushered her out first, sliding her a side glance, before he sat on the chaise and pointed at the one next to him.

"So. This is *your* place?"

His eyes studied her for a moment, and she knew his patience had run out. A crease formed between his brows and his voice lowered. "I'm kind of done with the pleasantries if you don't mind. Let's cut to the chase. Why are you here?"

His blunt comment stung. It wasn't unwarranted though. If he wasn't her abductor, which was becoming more probable, she had a lot of apologizing and explaining to do.

Leaning her head back, she breathed deeply, glad he noticed she needed the blanket. The crisp April air filled her lungs, and she hoped it would give some clarity to the chaos currently swarming like mosquitoes in her mind.

When they met at the pageant, she was immediately drawn to him. Though his looks were rugged and imposing, he seemed approachable and warm. She enjoyed their talks, even the brief ones, because he was passionate and animated. She had seen him in serious mode…and in playful mode, and she would pay good money to see that killer smile pointed in her direction again.

Now, although he was still polite, his words were clipped and harsh, and his face was like stone. His eyes threatened to freeze her all the way to the bone. She could almost believe he'd been putting on an act at the pageant since he looked so different and spoke to her in French. But her gut told her it was the opposite.

Her eyes drifted to him. He was now serenely staring at the star filled sky. Sipping her tea, she tried to sort her thoughts. Sitting next to him now felt almost surreal.

"Why are you here, Victoria?" he repeated. The hard edge in his voice gone.

Her head tipped back again, and a yawn escaped. The walls at her motel were paper thin. It sat close to the highway, so every truck that passed sounded like it was barreling through her door. Not that she could sleep anyway, with everything going on in her life.

Covering her mouth with the back of her hand, she replayed his questions. "Like I said before, I need your help."

"Why me? It makes no sense. I'm sure you have plenty of people who could help you. Why would you seek out someone you were scared of?"

"I know it makes no sense. And contrary to what you think, I don't have anyone—"

"You shot me."

"I thought you were going to abduct me. You came at me. What did you expect? Anyway, you were wearing a bulletproof vest."

"And that made it okay." His tone was filled with sarcasm. "Did you even consider that I would be thrown down the stairs from the impact?"

"No," she said, shame gutting her. The moment

immediately replayed in her head. The expression of betrayal on his face still brought tears to her eyes. She blinked and slowly met his gaze. Swallowing hard, she tried to keep her throat from closing. "I'm so sorry. Adam said you were going to abduct me." A tear slid down her cheek. "Like you said, I was scared and confused."

"I can't believe you would think I would do something like that," he said, his tone filled with hurt. "I told you I was there to save you. Who told you I was going to abduct you?"

"My brother."

"How does he know me?"

"He doesn't."

His head hit the back of the chaise as he stared into the sky again. "You aren't making sense, Victoria." He paused and took a drink of his beer, then his eyes swung back to her. "Is that even your name?"

"My name is Victoria Eden Granier...Samuels. I go by Eden."

"And you obviously aren't French."

"You aren't either. You spoke the language very well though."

"We were in Canada. I used it when necessary, not to pretend to be someone I wasn't."

She gave him a sidelong glance, feeling the sting of his words, then returned, "Oh right. Explain to me then, agent Grey, why your name was not on the security list?"

Kaleb pursed his lips. "Touché. I have a good reason."

"As do I," Eden triumphantly stated, trying to keep the smile at bay. Point one for the beauty queen. Ex beauty queen. "Actually, I'm part French, so I have dual citizenship. My dad was…is French. My mom lived in France for quite a while. I was born there and raised in South Carolina." She gave him her best southern accent and saw a twitch of his lips. Then a soul stealing smile slowly crawled across his handsome face. His eyes finally made it to hers, and she thought she saw a glimmer of the playfulness she remembered return.

Chapter Six

"You surprised me when you first spoke in the park," Kaleb said letting a chuckle escape. "I saw you walk by the restaurant, and I swear I knew it was you then, but the tattoos threw me off. When I was leaving, I noticed you in the park, and I had to know."

"What gave me away?"

"You started singing."

"I did not."

His smile spread into the beautiful grin she remembered, and she returned his with one of her own.

"Yeah. You did. Not out loud. Your lips were moving, and you were tapping your finger on your reader."

She glanced at her hands making sure her fingers were still.

"It's a nervous habit. I picked up on it when we were at breakfast."

She chewed on her lip, surprised at his comment, because he was right. Anytime she got anxious or bored, she would fill her thoughts with songs. Music was her sanctuary. It calmed her spirit and was the only thing that quieted the chaos that constantly filled her thoughts. That was until she met Kale...Kaleb. He gave her an outlet and even responded to her philosophical theorizing when most people's eyes would glaze over.

Fighting a giggle, she again recalled her favorite

moment when he tripped over one of the awards signs the first night of preliminaries. God, the look on his face, the minute their eyes connected, was heart stopping. He had a goofy grin, and those piercing sky-blue eyes directed right at her. She felt horrible for him even though he laughed. And try as she might to maintain her composure, she failed to keep her giggles at bay. Then, to find out he was part of security, she admittedly wondered if he was qualified. "Who are you? I mean, I know you work for a security company, just not the one affiliated with the pageant."

"Don't you think I should be the one asking the questions?" His head jerked. "Wait. *Now* you believe I work for a security company?" His guard was back up. "Victoria—"

"Eden."

"…Eden, stop playing games and tell me what the hell this is about. You come barging back into my life expecting me to rescue you from God knows what you are involved in, and you still haven't told me anything, other than you need help. It's been nearly two years, Victoria—" his eyes slammed shut "—Eden. Two years of searching for you. I didn't know what happened to you. I was worried you'd been killed."

He searched for me? After what I did? Why? She knew then he was telling the truth, and it made what she did that much harder to come to grips with.

Her head fell back on the chaise as guilt took a bite out of her heart. "I'm so sorry. I didn't…" Swinging her legs over the edge of the chaise, she locked eyes with him and her emotions stormed in. "I shouldn't have assumed you'd just drop everything to help me after what I did to you. I truly am sorry, Kaleb." His eyes

46

snapped to hers, and she quickly turned away and stood, as new tears streamed down her cheeks. "I shouldn't have come." Moving to the door, she was stopped when his fingers latched around her wrist.

"Stay." His hand dropped, as he took a deep breath and sat up. "I don't know who you are," he growled, "or how you know my name. But I damn sure need to find out."

Turning back, she met his gaze, then he looked away.

"I told you the truth when I said I worked for security at the pageant. I just didn't elaborate." She waited for him to explain. He nodded for her to sit. "I worked for a company named Summit Security. The hotel hired me."

"I know. It's a government agency."

"How do you know?"

"A hunch."

"A hunch?"

"I checked the security protocol sheet the first night of the pageant after I found out your name. Your badge said Grey. When I checked the security sheet, your name wasn't listed. I figured there was a simple explanation. But later, that lack of information came back to haunt me. I realized the lies you told were only the tip of the iceberg."

"Care to elaborate?"

She lowered herself onto the chaise again. "Well for starters, your name isn't Kale Grey. It's Kaleb Grayeagle. You're part of a wealthy oil family in Arkansas that recently held a charity fundraiser to benefit the National Center for Missing and Exploited Children."

Kaleb bolted up and faced her. "How the hell do you know that?"

"I listen. Sometimes, maybe when I shouldn't."

"Eavesdropping."

"Not purposefully. Accidentally."

"Explain."

"At the banquet, the first night after prelims, I noticed you were there, and I wanted to officially introduce myself to you. Let's just say, your grand entrance made an impression on me. After dinner, I went looking for you and found you outside the ballroom on the phone. You said, 'this is Kale' and something about behind the scenes information. I felt bad about eavesdropping, so I went back into the room. Later I found you and introduced myself, as you know."

"You didn't get all the information you just spewed from me saying my name was Kale."

"No. It was my first clue, since your badge at the pageant said Grey. When we saw each other at breakfast, we talked about my training, remember? I told you I used hiking as part of it, and you mentioned something about a place called Devil's Den.

"When I started searching for you, I typed in Kale Grey and a bunch of links popped up. After adding the word security, and doing a bit of digging, I found a Summit Securities press release, dated two weeks after the pageant, stating an Agent Kale Grey had been killed in the line of duty. It threw me at first, since it was based out of Maryland, and we met in Montreal, and you spoke French. Then I realized that, with a security job, it wasn't a far reach to think you would travel and were multilingual.

"I absolutely lost it when I thought I'd possibly

killed you. I wasn't trying to kill you, just get you away from me. I swore I saw you wearing a ballistic vest at the pageant. You weren't supposed to die.

"When I searched for more information, I found thousands of people linked to that name, and I needed to narrow it down. Then I remembered you mentioning Devil's Den. I found out it was in Arkansas.

"As I continued wandering down my rabbit hole, I typed in Kale Grey and Arkansas, and an article popped up about a charity dinner hosted by the Grayeagle Foundation. Not the correct spelling, but the photo that was with the article caught my eye. There was a Kaleb Grayeagle in the list of names beneath it. When I took a closer look, even though you had changed your appearance, there was no question. I had found you. And you were definitely not dead, because the photo was taken a few months ago. Which led me to believe you worked for the government, since they had faked your death.

"The article said you worked for your family's oil corporation, based in Fayetteville. After digging a little more under Kaleb Grayeagle, I found a student with your name at University of Western Arkansas in Dalton."

"Shit." Kaleb fell back onto the chaise, resting his elbows on his knees, as his fingers dug into his hair. "That was too easy."

"That's who you are to your family. Still doesn't tell me what you were doing at the pageant playing a security guard. Want to explain that?"

"Not until you stop with the cryptic crap and tell me what is going on."

She could hear the frustration in his tone, but she knew she was getting to him. "I'm sorry. I don't mean to be cryptic. I'm just having trouble organizing my thoughts. The truth is, I was at the pageant to get information on my dad. His company is one of the sponsors and—"

"Wait." Kaleb's eyes widened, and he quickly sat up, studying her before responding, "You're not talking about Victor Chalemaare, are you?"

"Yes."

Kaleb stood again. "Hold the phone. You're telling me, your dad is Victor Chalemaare?"

Eden slowly nodded.

"Holy shit! Your name—"

"How do you know Victor Chalemaare?"

"Kind of the reason I was at the pageant too—" he said motioning with his hand "—and you being here just got way more interesting."

The immediate change in his demeanor had a smile forming, until she revisited his words. "Great. I think?"

His hands threaded through his hair, and his eyes met hers. "So, tell me about your dad. Have you been in contact with him? Is he part of the reason you're here?"

She rubbed her forehead, as she looked away trying to figure out where to start. "It's a long story." A sigh escaped. "Don't know the guy actually. I was told my dad was Louis Granier, a soldier who was killed before I was born. That's what I believed, until a few months before we met. I got an unexpected package in the mail filled with a bunch of documents. One was a birth certificate for Victoria Eden Granier Chalemaare, with my birthdate, and my mother's, Patrice Samuels, name on it. There was a stack of medical reports, and things like my ACT and SAT scores, some of my academic and athletic accomplishments, pageant titles, and my acceptance letters to a few Ivy League schools. I was completely confused.

"A letter was attached, from the guy who sent it, claiming he was my brother. He said he had found the papers after his mom died in a car accident. His birth certificate said his name was Adam Phillipe Granier Chalemaare. He had been told he was Adam Phillipe DiMari and, like me, his father was a soldier who had been killed before he was born. His mom's name was Colette DiMari."

"So, Victor Chalemaare is your real father."

"I'm assuming. And there was one other file he found. It was another daughter. Her name was Eva Renee Granier Chalemaare." Her mom was listed as a Monique Dubois.

"Granier?"

"Yes. I thought that was my dad's surname, and my mom gave me her maiden name after he died. I'm guessing it's Victor's middle name, maybe?"

"No." Kaleb paused, and Eden got the feeling he knew more, but remained silent. Then he asked, "Has he found your sister?"

"No. At least not while I was with him."

"You met your brother?"

"Yes. He was the one who was on the airplane along with Bill. He included his e-mail and phone number in the packet of information, so I contacted him. He said he was raised on Prince Edward Island in Canada. When his mom died, he was looking for her estate information and found this box locked in the filing cabinet. He told me he immediately started searching for me and Eva, who lived in London."

"So, you contacted him and then met?"

"No. Do I look stupid?"

"No. You said—"

"Trust me. I was freaking out, looking through the amount of information this guy had on me. Or rather, his mom had on me. My mind went into hyperdrive. Why did she have this information, and how the hell did she get it? What did it all mean? Was this guy who he said he was, or some crazy catfish lunatic? Then, as I skimmed the information again, I realized the only way she could have gotten some of this information, was from my mom. She was the only one who had it. But why?"

"Did you ask her?"

"No. I thought about it, then decided against it. The more I rolled everything over in my head, the more it bothered me. I don't have the greatest relationship with my mom anyway. I moved out of the house when I went to college, and never looked back.

"She pushed me. Had me in everything from music lessons, to dance and sports, and to be honest, I was tired of the constant running and learning and doing. I needed a freaking break.

"I loved singing. That's what I would have done given the choice. Except I didn't have a choice. And then she kept entering me in pageants."

"Not your cup of tea?"

"No."

"Was that the reason for the tattoos?"

"One of them."

Kaleb lifted a brow in question. "And the other?"

"Hiding in plain sight."

Chapter Seven

Pinching the bridge of his nose, Kaleb tried to stave off the exhaustion he felt from the long day, and from trying to wrap his brain around Victoria's…Eden's story. There were so many things that didn't make sense. "Are you in danger?"

"I'm not sure."

"Not sure?"

"I told you, it's a long story."

"I'm not going anywhere."

She took a sip of her tea and rubbed her eyes. Kaleb knew she was probably more tired than he was, if she'd been on the run, but if there was any chance that she was in danger, he needed to know. The more information he could get out of her, the more he could relay to his team, and the more likely he could keep her safe. He knew she wasn't trying to be evasive. She was nervous, which made him even more concerned.

"I e-mailed my…"

A noise stole his attention, and he bolted up. His mind went back to her "*Hiding in plain sight*" comment. What if she was being watched? Were they followed? He reached for his gun. It wasn't there. "Shit."

"What's wrong?"

Slowly moving away from her, he trained his eyes on the darkness where the noise came from. Quieting his voice, he said, "Go inside, and lock the door."

"Why?"

"Just do it," he said in a harsh whisper.

She slowly stood. "I'm not leaving you out—"

"Damn it, Vic…Eden." In two strides he was on her, grabbing her wrist, and tugging her in the direction of the door. Sliding it open, he pushed her inside and ground out, "Lock the damn door," then slid it closed.

His eyes took in the area as he carefully headed up the few steps to the rise behind his house, and he wondered why the security lights weren't triggered. Spying a decent sized stick on the ground, he retrieved it, hoping it would at least keep the assailant at bay long enough for him to get the upper hand.

A rustling sound next to the house had Kaleb slowly approaching a row of hedges. The security lights kicked on from his movement, and he scanned the area where the noise appeared to have come from. Nothing. Slowly moving around the back of the house, he stopped when he heard a tiny squeak. Beneath the bushes, he saw a white ball of fur. It squeaked again, and Kaleb stepped closer. The kitten, barely old enough to stand, stared up at him and squeaked again. Kaleb picked it up and continued surveying the area. The tiny furball surely wasn't what made the noise. He'd seen cats in the area. Maybe the kitten's mom was around. It could have gotten separated from the litter. After several minutes of searching, he still came up empty…other than his new friend. The kitten clung to Kaleb's shirt. "Where's your momma?" With one more sweep of the yard, he headed back to the house.

His eyes locked on Eden sitting in his leather chair. He tried the door and was happy to find that Eden had listened, and chuckled when she was slow to rise and unlock it for him. "Everything secure, Agent Grey?"

"Yes. I believe I apprehended the assailant." From behind his back, he produced the tiny ball of fur and watched Eden's face fill with rapture.

"Oh my gosh, Kaleb. She's adorable." Snatching the kitten from his hand, Eden gently laid it against her chest. It let out a squeak and Eden snuggled it closer.

"I don't know what to do with it. I was thinking the noise might have been the kitten's mom, but I didn't see her anywhere, and I'm worried it's too young for food."

"Give me a minute and I will see what's on the magic box." She sat back down in the leather chair with the kitten still clinging to her.

Kaleb stole it back and pressed it against his chest. His thumb rubbed against its head.

"Hey!"

"What? I found her." He pulled her away and checked. "Yeah. Her. I think."

"Fine."

Kaleb lay down on the sofa and continued to pet the kitten that had closed its eyes and started to softly purr.

Staring at her phone, Eden confirmed, "It says if she has teeth, she should be okay to eat soft food."

Kaleb gently lifted the side of her mouth. "We have teeth," he proclaimed. "What we don't have, is cat food."

"I can go get some."

"I'd feel better if you stayed here."

"Why?"

"You said you didn't know if you were in danger. You're safe here. And since it's late, you can sleep in the guest room, and we can pick up where we left off in the morning."

"Oh, that's sweet of you, but no. I'll be fine.

Besides, I don't have any of my stuff. The motel isn't that—"

"Motel? You're not staying at Edge of the Ozarks, are you?"

Eden nodded.

"Then you really are in danger."

"It was the only place I saw in town."

"You would have been better off staying in your car. No. You are not going back there. Not that Dalton has a high crime rate, but I'm surprised that place hasn't been condemned."

"It's not that bad, and the man running it seems nice."

"Yeah, I saw that in a movie once. It didn't turn out so well for the woman." Kaleb stood. "Why don't we both go get the kitten some food. Then we can stop and get your stuff."

"I didn't say I was staying, Kale."

"Kaleb. Look, Eden, I can be pretty stubborn, so you might as well quit arguing with me."

"Well then, Mr. Grayeagle, we have something in common. I can be stubborn too. I've been here over a week, and nothing has happened."

"And nothing will, because you aren't staying there another night. We are going to go get the food then your stuff. End of story."

She turned and marched through the kitchen toward the back door. "I can take care…" Her head darted from side to side, and she spun around. "Where's my purse?"

"I didn't want to take the chance you had a gun, so I put it away for safe keeping."

"Give it back."

"Tomorrow."

"Now. Or I'll call the cops." She yanked her phone from her pocket and held it up.

"I know the cops," he said with a grin. "Small town."

With an eye roll, she folded her arms over her chest and let out a frustrated huff. "Fine, but only for tonight."

"We'll see."

"No. No, we'll see. You aren't going to control my life."

"Not controlling. Protecting."

****

"Okay. I think we have her taken care of for the night," Kaleb said, as he finished setting up the litter box. He might have gone a little overboard on the kitten supplies. Who knew Dalton's modest grocery store would have such an array of pet supplies.

When his eyes met Eden's, she still had a bit of a scowl. She wasn't lying when she said she could be stubborn. She still wanted to argue with him at the motel, even though he'd shown her how easy it was to get into her room without a key. He practically had to carry her to his truck. "Grab your stuff and follow me. I will show you your room."

Leading her down a dark hallway, he opened the door and flipped on the light. Pulling a blanket from the closet, he set it on the foot of the bed. "In case you get cold," he said, then pointed. "The bathroom is across the hall."

She continued to stand in the doorway.

"Is there anything else you need?" She barely shook her head. His eyes captured hers for a split second, and the scowl was replaced with something else that had him quickly looking away. He couldn't handle tears.

"Goodnight, Eden."

He headed back up the hallway, trying to escape the current flowing between them that felt like a massive undertow dragging him back toward her. The more she pushed, the more he wanted to engage and test her. But it was late, and they were both at the end of their patience and needed sleep. He hadn't slept well in a couple of days, and the day was busy. He knew he needed to be on his A game with her. Hopefully things would be much clearer in the morning.

Yanking his T-shirt over his head, he jumped at the sound of her timid voice. "You wouldn't by chance have a T-shirt, or something I could sleep in, would you?" She had removed the band from her hair, and it fell around her face in soft espresso waves. Even tired, she was stunning. "My shampoo spilled, and most of my clothes will need to be washed."

"Let me see what I can find." The thought of her in his shirt with nothing else on had his body vibrating. He needed sleep, and that visual was the last thing he needed right before he collapsed in his bed.

Rummaging through his drawer, he retrieved a T-shirt that seemed fairly new. He turned and nearly knocked her down. Wrapping his fingers around her bicep, he caught her before she hit the floor. "Sorry. I didn't expect you to be right there." He shoved the shirt at her, and she held it up. It was going to swallow her. Even though she wasn't short, he was well over six feet tall. He could picture it hanging off one shoulder, and barely covering her silky legs, and...*Nope, probably not going to sleep again tonight.*

"Thanks," she said, barely above a whisper.

He nodded, because he currently couldn't get his

brain to form words. As she stepped outside the door, he closed it.

****

Breathing deep as his body came to life, Kaleb barely lifted one eyelid to see the bright numbers on the clock before rolling over, hoping to let sleep consume him again. Why was he even awake at two thirty in the morning? The sound of breaking glass gave him his answer. Eden's words "*hide in plain sight*" immediately lifted the fog in his brain.

Reaching behind his nightstand, he pressed a button. The top slid forward, and he lifted a pistol from its case.

A dozen scenarios raced through his mind as he silently stepped out of his room and pressed his body against the wall. The house was bathed in a dark gray glow from the moon, leaving strange shadows that threw Kaleb off in his groggy state.

Another thump let Kaleb know someone was definitely in the house, and his pulse rate jumped, realizing the assailant was between him and Eden. Steadying his breath, he slowly lifted the gun and peeked around the corner into the living area. Nothing. Carefully sliding his hand up the kitchen wall, he flipped the light switch, as he aimed the gun. Eden shrieked, then stumbled. Her feet tangled with the broom in her hand. Kaleb dove for her, and a sharp pain set fire to his foot. His arm wrapped around Eden's mid-section, keeping her from hitting the floor.

"Shit!" He spun around, with his body going rigid from the pain, and set her on her feet, just outside the shattered glass on the floor.

"Oh my God, Kaleb. I'm so sorry."

Remembering the gun still gripped in his other hand,

he set it on the counter. "What the ever-loving hell, Vic...Eden. I nearly shot you."

"I couldn't sleep so I came out to get some water. I thought I could see since there was some moonlight. When I reached for my glass, it fell and broke."

Kaleb carefully stepped around the bar, sat down on one of the stools, and lifted his stinging foot.

"Let me see." Eden reached out to take Kaleb's foot in her hands, but Kaleb batted her away. "Stop! Let me see." With one hand wrapped around his ankle, she lifted her other hand to keep his flailing arm at bay. He tried to yank his foot from her, but it only made her tighten her grip.

"Don't touch my fu...foot," he growled through gritted teeth. His eyes met hers, and she bit her lip gripping his foot harder, and he realized just how strong she was. And determined.

A smirk skated across her lips. "You're ticklish?"

His eyes shut, and he let out a heavy breath, preparing for the torture that he knew would ensue. To his surprise, it didn't. She took one look at his foot, and her eyes darted around the kitchen. Grabbing a paper towel, she folded it and dabbed at the blood, then gently removed the shard of glass that had embedded itself. "Do you have a first aid kit?"

"Under the sink in the guest bath."

Resting his foot on the other barstool, she said, "Hold the paper towel on it," then disappeared up the hallway. He lifted it and examined the small hole continuing to bleed.

She appeared moments later, carrying the first aid kit, and hopped up on the stool, then held out her hand. This time, he didn't fight her. "I think I got all the glass," she said, examining his foot again. "I need to clean it out and bandage it though." Filling a cotton ball with peroxide, she dabbed it on the cut, and he flinched. "Sorry." The feel of her breath as she blew on his sensitive skin sent chills racing up his leg. His shirt, that she had put on, gaped at the neck as she leaned forward, continuing to dab at the cut and blow.

He peeled his gaze away. "It doesn't burn," he said, his voice straining from the sensation. "It's just cold."

Eden continued to alternate from dabbing and blowing on the cut, and Kaleb writhed and tried to drag his foot away when he couldn't take it anymore. Her eyes tipped up to him, and she pursed her lips. "I'm almost done, I promise." Amusement laced her voice, and he knew she was getting way too much joy out of making him squirm. "There," she said, as she pressed the adhesive to his foot. "It's stopped bleeding I think, but I can't guarantee it, since it's in a bad spot."

He shook his head while he yawned. "Thank you. You didn't have to do that."

"Yes. I did. I made the mess, and you got hurt." She reached for the broom. "Go back to bed. I'll get this cleaned up. I'm sorry I woke you."

****

Kaleb couldn't remember the last time he'd slept past sunrise. The sun lit up the forest outside his window. Glowing numbers on his clock read seven fifteen. He stretched and slowly sat up. The peaceful stillness of the house had him wondering if his house guests were up. Pulling on a pair of red sweatpants, he checked the kitten's bed. It was empty. His heart skipped, as he checked around the room, wondering if the tiny creature was hiding. When he couldn't find her, he went to Eden's room. It was empty too.

Striding up the hall, the early morning incident played in his memory with each step on his sore foot. The surprise on her face when he flipped on the light was burned into his memory as well as those pursed lips when she was taking care of his foot. He'd left her to clean up her mess and went back to bed. "Damn. Did she find her purse and leave?" he said under his breath. *I'm going to be pissed if she took my kitten with her.* He carefully limped back into the kitchen questioning why he was so irritated with that thought. A moan from the living room, broke the silence. Eden lay curled up on his sofa. Her head was propped up on a pillow, with the kitten snuggled at her chin. Tendrils of her deep-brown hair crossed her face. Her lashes were pressed against her porcelain skin, and her lips were barely parted. His shirt was wadded up around her, sitting below the swell of her breasts, revealing her toned stomach and legs that were enhanced by a pair of bright pink, lace panties. Colorful tattoos wrapped her arms, torso, and one leg. *Shoot. Me. Now.*

She had his favorite fuzzy blanket cuddled in her arms like a stuffed animal. The more he stood and stared at her, the more he wished he could be the blanket.

He studied the tattoo of musical notes on a spiraling staff, set in pillowy water-colored clouds that wrapped around her ribs, and he wondered if it was a song.

While he worked as an agent, he'd held off getting tattoos. Thought they'd make him too easy to identify. But once he returned to Arkansas and met his brother, Joe, who had quite a few pieces of art on his skin, all bets were off. He'd already turned several parts of his body into works of art. Hers, however, were intricate.

Detailed. Nearly three dimensional. He needed to quit staring, or at least cover her with the blanket, but he couldn't quite get his body to move. She was so peaceful and so…beautiful. A living, breathing work of art.

Her phone buzzed on the table beside her, startling her. She quickly raised up and grabbed it. Kaleb suddenly felt like a cornered animal. When she noticed him, she jerked again. He did his best to act nonchalant and asked, "Why are you sleeping on the sofa?"

She sat up and tried to brush her hair out of her eyes. It didn't work. And God, she was even beautiful with bedhead. Yawning, she asked, "How long have you been standing there?"

"Thirty minutes," he immediately responded with a smirk. Eden blanched at his comment, and Kaleb chuckled. "I just got up. I noticed the kitten was missing, so I went on a search and rescue and found you out here holding her hostage."

Trying once again to tame her messy hair, she dug her fingers into her scalp and threaded them through the tangles. She didn't notice how much skin she was revealing, and Kaleb still couldn't tear his eyes away.

He shoved his hands in his pockets, trying to quell the heat currently racing south. "So, I'm asking again, why are you sleeping on the sofa?"

"When I finished cleaning, I went to my room and lay there, trying to go to sleep, which didn't happen. Too much craziness, I guess; like you pointing a gun at me."

"Now you know how I felt."

"Touché," she said, throwing his word back at him.

"At least I didn't pull the trigger."

She rolled her eyes. "No, you didn't, and I told you, I'm sorry. I'm beginning to believe I'll still be apologizing when I'm sixty. Do you want me to finish my story, or not?"

"Please continue."

"Anyway, after lying there for a while, I decided to get up. I snuck into your room, got the kitten, put a little food in her bowl, grabbed my clothes and threw them in the washer, then when she was done, I put her in the litter box to see if she would go. After I had curled up on the sofa with her, my phone rang. It was Adam. When I answered, there was silence, and then it went dead."

"Adam?" He knew he'd heard her say the name last night, but it was too early in the morning to connect all the dots.

"My brother." She lolled her head. "Part of the saga. Let's not go there yet."

"Was that him who called just now?"

She chewed her lip and sighed. "No. Just a reminder to move the clothes. She started to throw the covers off and realized they weren't covering her. Her gaze darted back to Kaleb who quickly averted his eyes, and she wrapped the blanket around her.

Kaleb headed into the kitchen and started the coffee. "Why don't you get dressed, and I'll make breakfast."

"How about you get dressed," she pointed her finger to his bare chest, "and I'll make breakfast."

"Seriously?"

Slowly standing, she made sure the blanket hid her previously uncovered body. "What?"

"You're not okay with me parading around *my* house shirtless, but it's okay for you to be in barely-there lace panties?"

"I have no control over what the stupid blanket does while I'm asleep. And for the record, I'm fine with you parading around *your* house without a shirt on. I was just trying to be nice."

Grabbing the blanket, he said, "Don't disparage The Snoop." He paused and tipped his head as he studied her. "You don't think I can cook."

Eden rolled her eyes.

Kaleb was getting a kick out of annoying her.

"I never said that. It has nothing—"

"I'll have you know, I'm a damn good cook."

"I'm sure you are. I was—"

"My sister says I make the best coconut pancakes she's ever tasted."

"That does sound delicious. I'm sorry. I didn't mean—"

The sudden timidness in her voice had him worried he'd pushed a little too far, so he wrapped an arm around her shoulder. "I'm just playing. But I really can make great coconut pancakes."

"My mom showed me how to make authentic French crepes."

Kaleb tried to stifle a smile. That did sound good. "Okay. We'll both get dressed. Reconvene in the kitchen in fifteen. Cook our asses off and get to the bottom of this never-ending story."

"Deal."

Chapter Eight

Eden leaned against the bedroom door shaking her hands out, hoping to calm the horses currently stampeding through her chest. Those penetrating crystal-blue eyes left no question about what he was thinking when she realized he was staring at her. Yes, she was not quite covered up. Not her fault. But he looked like he was seconds away from having her for breakfast. She was seconds away from letting him. She had to remind herself what she was there for.

The moment she spoke to him in the park, she wasn't sure she was going to make it out alive. With the gun in his hand, and his eyes not giving anything away, she hoped he felt the same strange connection to her that she did to him when they met. Staring in his eyes, there was no sign of that light-hearted spirit he had at the pageant. Their late-night conversation, and this morning's confrontation though, had her head spinning more than it was when she decided to make the trek to Arkansas.

She could have gone to the police, although she still wasn't quite sure what she would tell them. Yes, her brother and the P.I. were missing. But she wasn't sure if they were missing on purpose or in danger. After the strange phone call this morning though, she felt the latter was probably true.

Sliding into her shorts from the previous day, she

opened her suitcase, then decided to leave Kaleb's shirt on, when she realized she hadn't finished her laundry. It would work until she got a bath. Anyway, she loved the way the smell reminded her of him. It was a clean, almost sun-dried smell, mixed with a healthy helping of his natural scent. She caught a whiff of it when he grabbed her last night, and she had to stop herself from burying her nose in his neck and breathing deep.

Pulling open the door, she stopped mid stride. Her lips pinched together when she heard Kaleb…singing? Quietly making her way up the hallway, she peeked around the corner. His bare back was to her. He was still wearing his red warmups with what looked like a full apron, and he was stirring something in a bowl. He continued to sing, although she had no idea what song, because he only sang bits and pieces. "…tenderness…yeah." His body moved so seductively that she wondered if he had another secret job as an exotic dancer. God, he was every girl's dream. Their discussion the night before, and the way he cradled the kitten in his enormous hands, made her heart flutter, and now he was singing and dancing.

She debated whether she should fan herself or cover her mouth to hold back her amusement, when a loud snicker escaped. Kaleb turned. The expression on his face, and the full view of the apron, elicited a bark of laughter that quickly turned into fits of uncontrollable shrieks and giggles, causing tears to stream down her cheeks.

The apron resembled a carpenter's belt, with several pockets and loops. In the middle of it, it said "You think this looks delicious, you should try the food." And snuggled in the pocket at the top was the kitten, perfectly content. Eden wasn't sure, but her heart might have actually exploded.

Kaleb's head tilted, eyes narrowed, and one eyebrow shot up. *God that brow is deadly.* Yanking his earbud out, he asked, "You don't like my cooking routine?"

"Oh, I love it. I just don't know if I have room to cook my crepes, since you apparently need the entire dance floor."

His mouth twisted in an amused smirk, and he gave her an "oh well" shrug and continued to dance. She chewed on her lip as she became his audience of one. After a minute he twitched his head and said, "Come on. I will try to contain myself to this dance space at the island. I'll even let you have one of the earbuds, if you want to listen to my music."

Eden hesitantly stepped into the kitchen and opened the refrigerator. Staring into it, she tried to put out the fire in her cheeks while concentrating on the ingredients she needed, but she couldn't quite get her brain to focus. Her eyes continually drifted to the distraction of the tanned back muscles in motion, and the sway of the red sweats.

After a long moment, she heard Kaleb's amused voice from behind her. "You actually need something out of there, or are you trying to cool off?"

Heat pulsated through her again, and she swung him a glare. Even with the apron bib covering his chest, it was obvious he knew exactly what he was doing to her, as he stirred the batter, letting the flexing of his muscles draw her in. He was the master at sexual manipulation, especially when he swiped his thumb through the batter and licked it off.

Mercy. She swallowed hard and tried to suck in a shaky breath. It wasn't enough.

His eyes never left hers, and the longer he held her in his spell, the wider his smile became.

"I, I thought you were going to get dressed."

"I thought you said you were fine with me parading around *my* house without a shirt. And anyway, I put on an apron." He gracefully gestured with his hand like he was a display model showing off a prize. With a deep sigh, she rolled her eyes and forced herself to focus on the contents of the refrigerator.

For a guy who was living on his own, his refrigerator was well stocked. The only problem was, everything she needed, eggs, milk, butter, were nowhere to be found. Her gaze moved to the counter in front of Kaleb, where everything was laid out. "Ah ha. You still needing those ingredients?"

"Nope. All yours."

She grabbed the items she needed, along with the flour, salt, and sugar, then searched through the cabinet for a bowl and a pan, and started mixing the ingredients.

Peeking at Kaleb, she noticed he'd returned his earbuds to his ears and was swinging his hips to the silent tune, although he'd yet to start singing again. She was curious what type of music he was listening to, so she tapped him on the shoulder. Bad idea. Very bad idea. He jumped and spun around. The mixing spoon he was using flew up, and batter jetted across the kitchen, slapping the side of her face and neck as well as anything in its path. The stunned look on Kaleb's face probably matched her own, but soon transformed into a goofy, fake "I'm so sorry" grin. He popped his earbud out and calmly asked, "Can I help you?"

She grabbed a towel from the counter, let out a loud sigh, wiped the pasty goo from her temple, then giggled.

"You said you would let me listen to your music."

He took the towel and wiped a smudge from her chin. "Oh." Tossing the towel in the laundry basket, he turned back to Eden and held out one of the earbuds, then drew it back at her recoil. "Better idea, since sharing earwax suddenly seems gross." Kaleb removed his phone from his pocket and set it onto a dock on the counter. The guitar's reverb poured out of the speakers, and "Yours Every Morning" began to play. Kaleb's head bounced to the beat, and Eden began to sway.

They each returned to their creations, singing and dancing as they prepared breakfast. Occasionally, she peeked at him out of the corner of her eye, and smiled. Gone were the lines of irritation that were etched on his face the night before. This was the man she remembered from their encounter at the pageant. She was now certain she'd made the right decision when she risked everything to find him.

Kaleb grabbed his coffee, tipped his head, and they moved through the living room. Eden stepped out onto the deck, then turned when she noticed Kaleb didn't follow. He'd set his coffee and food down, wadded his blanket up by the door, and snuggled the kitten in the middle. He was a true anomaly, goofy and fun loving, and yet worked for the government. The two didn't seem to belong together.

She'd always thought of the secret government agencies as the stoic unwavering type. That was not Kaleb at all. He was obviously intelligent, had a broad knowledge of current events, and he knew when to be serious. But she got the feeling he'd much rather be in the great outdoors, enjoying what life had to offer, than be in a suit.

He was nicely dressed when she met him at the pageant, although he seemed more comfortable in the blue jeans she saw him in the night before, or even the sweats he was currently wearing...with no shirt.

Certain things she'd noticed hinted at the money he had, but he wasn't ostentatious about it. His house was a mid-century modern design, carved into the side of a beautiful, wooded hill. It had obviously been renovated, with updated technology, yet retained the mid-century style which fit him. She glanced over as he set his plate aside and wiped his mouth with his napkin. The spark that was glinting in his eyes minutes before was gone.

"So. Your brother? How long has it been since you heard from him?"

"Not since he went missing."

"You think he was abducted?"

"Yes." His question made her stomach sour. "It's why I'm here. He and Bill both went missing about a month ago." She let out a sigh.

"And who is Bill again?"

"His name is Bill McGuire. He's the private investigator my brother hired to find out about our dad."

"And whoever has them is coming after you."

"I guess."

"No, 'I guess.' That's probably who tried to abduct you at the pageant." Kaleb took a drink of his coffee and continued, "Tell me again about your brother and how all this started."

"His mom died in a car accident, and he was searching for her financial information, and in the process, he found these files that basically tracked our lives."

"And you have those files with you?"

"Yes. It's all copied onto a thumb drive." She set her empty plate down. "Anyway, when I got in contact with him, he said he'd looked up Victor Chalemaare. Apparently, he's considered one of the most brilliant minds in the world. He's won several awards for his research in genetic modification and immunology, including the *Medaille de Prestige*. Many labs and facilities all over the world are utilizing his research, although some of it is controversial. Not long after Adam found the files, his mom's house was broken into and ransacked."

"Yeah. The controversy was something Summit Security was working on with his disappearance."

"Adam and I as well."

"So, you and this brother. You've met?" Kaleb asked as he stared out at the scenery.

"At that time, we hadn't. He lived in Toronto. Worked for a commercial building firm and was doing his search from there. I was in Mississippi. We had been researching our dad together over e-mails and video chat for a couple of months. Adam suggested flying to Paris where Victor's company is located. He thought maybe we could meet with him and get some answers but found out there was a special clearance for entry into the facility. Shortly after that, Chalemaare was reported missing.

"Adam hired Bill, the private investigator, to see if he could come up with anything tying the paperwork Adam found to Victor's disappearance. Victor was supposed to be a keynote speaker at a conference in Mumbai. Bill found evidence that he checked into the hotel where the conference was to be held, then vanished.

Chapter Nine

"Everything Bill found about Victor seemed legit," Eden said as she continued to retell the story. "Yes, there was some controversy because of his research in genetics. But it was all legal, and it seemed like his work was primarily in immunology. Nothing, other than his name, tied him to the paperwork.

"And, of course, at the time, we couldn't prove that's what the break-in at Adam's mom's home was about. The police said when deaths are made public, it's not uncommon for the estate to get burglarized. Adam said, even though the place was torn apart, things like the TV and electronics were still there.

"Right before Victor was reported missing, I came across information on the Trinity Elite International pageant. It's touted as one of the top pageants in the world. Victor's company had been sponsoring it for several years. Another confusing element to this whole story, although the pageant raises huge amounts of money for children's medical research, so that could be the connection. I'd been in a ton of pageants growing up and decided to put in my application, figuring if he'd been a part of the pageant for years, we might at least get some answers. I got accepted as the contestant representing France."

Kaleb broke in, "Why did you apply to be the representative for France?"

"Two reasons. One, I figured I had a better shot representing France over the U.S. because there would be fewer applicants for France. Two, being that my dad is French, the company is French, and the pageant is headquartered in France, I thought it would be easier to gain their confidence and therefore, maybe get more information. Plus, I was fluent in the language."

"Good call. So did you find out anything?"

"Nothing," Eden said letting out a frustrated breath. "I talked to several people affiliated with the pageant. Even those in charge of sponsorship, and all were tight lipped about the company."

"I didn't get much either."

"Right. You said you were there to get information too."

"Yeah. We were brought in by ICMP after Chalemaare went missing."

Eden cut her eyes to Kaleb, confused. "ICMP?"

"International Commission on Missing Persons."

"Why were you brought in?"

"Let's just focus on you right now. So, after you won—"

"That's where everything went off the rails. After the banquet, Lena, my hostess, escorted me back to my room. We weren't allowed to have our phones with us during the pageant, so I grabbed it once we got back to the room to see if Adam had gotten in safely. I noticed several calls and messages from him updating me on his arrival. His last message had been sent only a few minutes earlier, and said that he'd gotten to the hotel, but I needed to call him immediately. When my hostess left the room, I called. He said they wouldn't let him into the hotel because there had been a security breach. That's when he told me that he overheard the security guard say someone was after me. He said he had a plane waiting and told me to run."

Kaleb nodded. "All the security guards got notified of the possible planned abduction, and I was heading to your room when I saw you exit the elevator across the lobby. By the time I caught up to you, you were climbing into the cab. I took one of the hotel security vehicles and went after you." Kaleb stood and picked up Eden's empty plate. "More coffee?"

"I'll get it." She stood with her cup in hand and followed him into the house.

Kaleb rounded the island. "Okay. So, you're going back and forth in e-mails and on video chats with a guy you never met. And you weren't the least bit concerned that he might be the one wanting to take you? It's a classic scenario. Gaining the victim's trust, then putting them in a panic situation and making them think they are the hero, then the victim runs right into their arms. You didn't think he might be dangerous? Especially since he had a plane on standby?"

"I know I probably should have, but no. I trusted him. We'd talked enough over the months that I felt like he was being truthful with me. You, on the other hand...I kept playing everything over in my head. If someone were going to take me, it was either going to be by surprise, which was unlikely with all the security around, or it would be someone I felt comfortable with, like you said. Someone who'd befriended me. You'd done that. And Adam said he heard your name over the security guard's comm. So, when I saw you running across the tarmac, it scared me."

They strolled into the living room after refilling their

cups. The kitten wobbled across the floor and Kaleb lifted her and carefully sat down on the sofa. Eden tucked her leg under her and did the same.

"Where'd you get the gun?"

"Bill."

A dip in Kaleb's brow had her responding to his unasked question.

"He had a hip holster."

Kaleb remained quiet as his expression darkened. He was replaying the shooting, and her chest squeezed.

"I'm so sorry, Kaleb. Everything happened so fast."

"I get it. I *was* the logical answer. I did lie. It's part of my job."

"So. You work for the government, right? You lie for a living." She leveled her eyes with his and lifted an eyebrow. "You're a spy?" Kaleb's eyes darted away, and she knew she had him.

He gazed up at her through his lashes. She smirked, and he lost the fight with a smile. "You aren't going to leave this alone. Are you?" he questioned, bouncing the tassel on a pillow in front of the kitten.

"Not on your life."

"Shit. You don't know what you are asking." He paused and pursed his lips then slid his gaze back to her. "Fine. The Summit Agency is a branch of Homeland Security. We specialize in national and international recovery of people with advanced intelligence who may pose a threat to national or international security."

"Victor Chalemaare is considered a threat to national security?"

"Yes."

"You think he's dangerous?"

"Maybe not him per se, but think about it. People

like Chalemaare, or anyone who can alter the pathway of history is a threat. The highly gifted scientists, engineers, and tech gurus see things differently than the average Joe. Now, think about what would happen if they had evil intentions, or their knowledge got in the hands of someone who did. It could be devastating. My team provides security for those who might have to put themselves in a less-than-optimal situation and work to recover those who have gone missing."

"Are there a lot?"

"More than you'd think."

"How did you wind up getting that type of job?"

Kaleb chuckled. "Career day at college. You know where they have all the booths set up? I had some time to kill before my next class, so I was trolling the tables to see what goodies they had to pull the students in, and I saw this one table with a banner that said something like, 'Are you the best at everything?' I was like 'hell yeah.'

"I walked over, and they had the coolest shit. They had sunglasses that had these mirrors on part of the lenses so you could see if anyone was tailing you, and pens that had hidden USBs and flashlights. Anyway, the guy started talking to me and asking questions about whether I liked adventure and excitement. I thought it was going to turn into a recruiting thing for the military. I was all ready to take my cool toys and book it, then he asked if I was good at talking to people. I told him I was. He asked how I did in school and if I had any computer skills. When I told him I had graduated high school early, was working on my second master's degree, and was barely nineteen, he got real interested and set up a time for us to have lunch the next day."

"You had a master's degree at nineteen?"

"I started taking college courses at thirteen. I was a hellion in elementary school. One of my teachers suggested I get tested for the gifted program. Once I passed, they adjusted my curriculum, and that kept me engaged until I got into junior high. The gifted teacher suggested I take the ACT, and when I scored really high on that, I was allowed to do concurrent enrollment. I had my bachelor's degree at sixteen, and I was accepted to an engineering master's program at the University of Maryland."

"Wow. What are your degrees in?"

"Master's degree in chemical engineering, a master's degree in petroleum engineering, and I just finished my Master of Environmental Engineering. What about you?"

"I studied osteopathic medicine at William Carey in Hattiesburg. I took a break after my undergrad though."

"Why?"

"Not sure it's what I want to do." Her mind drifted back to the boarded-up store. "Plus, all my focus is now on figuring out what the hell is going on, and who I really am." She took another sip of her coffee. "So, what happened when you went to lunch with the spy guy?"

"He told me he checked my background, and I was exactly what the agency wanted. He said I was intelligent, outgoing, and good looking." Eden rolled her eyes at Kaleb's cheesy grin. "The job was more along the lines of gathering information. Not engagement in gunfire. The danger was still there, but it was low level. And yes, I was undercover."

"Undercover. Spying."

"Undercover."

"You used an alias and gathered information. I'm sure you planted recording devices, and trackers, and had glasses that took photos too. You're a spy. Grey…Kale Grey."

Kaleb chuckled. "Was. And I plead the fifth."

"Did you ever have to kill anyone?"

"There are different teams within the agency. My team specializes in the investigative portion. The other team specializes in infiltration and extraction. There have been instances where things didn't go quite as expected and they overlapped. We were trained for that." It didn't get past her that he didn't exactly answer her question. But she figured it wasn't something he liked talking about, so she didn't push.

"You said you aren't doing it anymore though?"

"After this case, I'm done. It's not what I wanted as a career. From the time I was little, I knew I was going to help my dad with his company. It's been part of my family's legacy since the turn of the century."

"So why did you take the job?"

"Why not? It was a fantastic opportunity. I traveled the world and socialized with the rich and famous. Very few people will ever get to have the experiences I did. Why not take a few chances and live life while you can."

"So, what made you quit?"

The boyish expression his face held, talking about the once in a lifetime opportunity, suddenly faded and Eden feared she knew the answer when he didn't respond immediately.

"It was me. Wasn't it?"

Chapter Ten

Leaving the agency was bittersweet. Kaleb had learned valuable skills he would utilize for the rest of his life.

Quinten Phillips, his boss, put on a no-nonsense air most of the time. The bond that Kaleb developed with him from their time working together turned into a mutual respect. He was a mentor and more importantly, a friend.

In the time that they'd been tapped for the assignment, the case of the missing scientist had been the catalyst for many migraines as they tried to reason out what limited evidence they'd found from their investigation. It had morphed from not only a missing scientist, but also a beauty queen, and the discovery of other possible victims.

The somewhat straightforward missing scientist's case turned into one hopelessly tangled web. At least now they knew one thing. Somehow, the beauty queen was connected to the scientist, and Kaleb felt certain the others were too.

Eden's head was set on a permanent swivel, taking in all the old buildings of the University of Maryland. The campus was nice, especially in the spring when the cherry trees were in bloom. A part of him missed it. He hadn't been back since they had decided to put the case on hold.

The brisk April wind shocked his senses, and Kaleb folded his arms as he followed Eden up the sidewalk, past the old buildings that held so many of his memories. She stopped in the middle of a grove of cherry trees. "Take my picture." The way her eyes were lit with excitement, and the unhindered smile she possessed, had him reaching for his phone. The wind picked up. Pieces of her raven hair blew across her face along with some of the cherry blossoms, and it appeared the universe wanted to present him with the perfect moment.

It had been warm in Arkansas, and Kaleb wanted to be comfortable on the plane, so he chose to wear cargo shorts and a gray polo, but now he was thinking he should have opted for a hoodie. Eden stressed for ten minutes over what to wear before settling on a pair of black leggings and a soft green shirt. She said she wanted to make a good impression. She could have worn a stained T-shirt and ripped jeans and still been gorgeous.

Trekking across the courtyard filled with blossoming trees, and planters filled with tulips and daffodils, Kaleb reached in his pocket when he felt the buzz of his phone. Quinten.

—*ETA?*—

—*Crossing the courtyard. Be there in a few*—

Bounding up the steps at Rexleigh Hall, his senses came alive as he tugged the door open and was hit with the smells of the Food Court. Not much had changed in two years. There were offerings in just about every cuisine. His stomach reminded him they'd skipped lunch.

—*Gonna grab a bite to eat*—

—*I'll be here*—

When Kaleb filled Quinten in on the sudden reappearance of the pageant queen and briefed him on some of the information she shared, his boss had asked how soon they could make it to the office. He had a feeling that would be his response. Quinten needed all the details and preferably from Eden herself.

It had only taken him a few minutes to get his sister, Kaysi, set up with the kitten. Getting the company plane secured and finding a pilot was a different story. If he hadn't needed to go over all the information with Eden, he'd have flown them there himself. That was one of his loves. Once they had a departure time set, they packed overnight bags and headed for the airport. Kaleb hoped he'd get a chance to pilot the flight home. It depended on how long the meeting took.

After making a quick stop for a late lunch at his favorite Greek deli, they headed up a drab, beige hallway, devoid of any décor, except a plan of escape poster. He shoved his key card into a metal slot next to a door with a bright white sign stating, "Authorized Personnel Only." The buzz and snick of the metal door gave them access to a dimly lit, stagnant stairwell. They jogged up two flights of stairs and Kaleb slid his key card into another slot, finally gaining entry to a large open room, filled with desks holding multi-screened computers. A low murmur of voices could be heard as he let the door click behind them.

"Bout damn time, Grey," a large man with jet black hair and light mocha skin hollered across the room. He'd been on assignment the last time Kaleb stopped in, so it had been a while.

"He looks familiar," Eden whispered.

"We both were at the pageant. He worked as the hotel's concierge. He's the one who got me to the hospital after…"

Eden's eyes met his, and he realized just how haunted she was by the incident. He let his words drop. It was time to make peace with what happened.

Kaleb closed the distance with his partner, and they wrapped each other in a manly hug. His partner's eyes fell to Eden as they backed away. "Ian Prescott, this is Eden Samuels." Ian's friendly expression turned to one of confusion.

"Have we met?"

Kaleb moved behind Eden and held his hands up over her head like a crown. "Does this help?"

Eden rolled her eyes and elbowed him in the stomach, causing him to double over. Ian's eyes darted between them as he busted out laughing.

"I was Miss France, Victoria Granier—"

"Oh! You won! Wait. Didn't you sho—"

"Yes." Kaleb broke in. "Long story. The reason for the visit today. Phillips didn't brief you?"

"No. But to be fair, I got here about five minutes before you showed up. There is probably something in the pile on my desk."

"I'll try to fill you in after our meeting."

Ian nodded, then held a finger up. "Did you hear my news?"

"No. I've been kind of out of the loop."

"I'm out. Going private. An old military buddy of mine has joined up with a guy who has a security and technology company in Colorado. Thought I would jump in at ground level and see where it takes me."

"What will you be doing?"

"Pretty much the same stuff. Technology research and development. Security."

"That's right up your alley then. When are you making the jump?"

"Depends."

"On?"

Ian pointed at Eden. "I'm not leaving my partner high and dry. You know that. Phillips has me on another assignment right now, but if this is getting ready to bust open, I'm on it."

Another voice rang out across the room, and Kaleb saluted a pretty blonde.

As they made their way over to her, Eden whispered, "She's gorgeous."

"Yeah. Don't let that fool you. She is a badass with a capital B. Thank God I'm on her good side.

"Fancy meeting you here," the woman said with a huge smile.

Kaleb leaned in for a quick hug. "Thought we'd stop in and make sure you guys weren't goofing off. This is Eden Samuels. Eden, this is Kat Fleming. We are headed to visit with the boss man, so we better not keep him waiting."

"Catch me up later."

Kaleb waved bye to Kat and latched onto Eden's hand as he weaved through the sea of cubicles. His heart ticked up being back in the bullpen. Although there were a few new faces, he recognized several he'd worked with, and each acknowledged him. He would have to make time to chat with them before they left.

"She seems nice. Is being a ten on the hotness scale a requirement to work for your organization?"

Kaleb chuckled at her comment. "Not a requirement, but unfortunately our society puts a lot of clout on appearance, and when you are trying to get information in the circles our targets usually run in, people tend to talk to people who are attractive quicker."

Memories flooded of different assignments he'd had, and yeah, he had to concede, it felt surreal at times, rubbing elbows with dignitaries and the richest of the rich, while he was undercover. Even though his family was wealthy, they had nothing compared to some of the people he dealt with. A small part of him would miss the adrenaline rush of solving the cases.

The massive white screen on the wall across the room was lit up with a map. He was too far away to see the location, but it was a sure sign of a mission. He knew, with the information they were about to divulge, the screen would be lit with a different location very soon. Their case would no longer be on hold.

Walking past several desks with a few people staring at their computer screens or on the phone, Kaleb led Eden up a short hallway and rapped on yet another metal door. Within seconds the door swung open and a large, well dressed black man emerged.

Grabbing Kaleb's hand, he said, "Agent Grey," then patted him with the other hand and pulled him into a hug.

"Just Kaleb now."

"I'm still holding onto that letter, hoping you will reconsider."

"You'd have to resurrect me from the dead."

"Done it before." Kaleb chuckled at his boss' statement. He was sure it was probably true.

It had been years since Quinten had recruited Kaleb to work for Summit. To most, Quinten Phillips was a professor in Information Securities at the University of Maryland. To Kaleb, Quinten was the director of a highly classified government agency, dealing with the most intelligent people on the planet. Quinten reached out his hand. "And I'm guessing you are Miss Samuels?" She nodded. "Nice to meet you. Quinten Phillips."

Kaleb knew the minute Eden's beauty queen persona emerged. Her back straightened, her shoulders squared, and she locked eyes with Quinten as she took his hand.

"Eden. The pleasure is mine. Kaleb spoke very highly of you."

"As you."

"Oh, I'm sure he had quite a lot to say about me. I don't think he's forgiven me yet."

Quinten gave her a hearty laugh as he ushered them into his office and motioned for them to take a seat at a large round table. Grabbing some folders from his desk, he scooted a chair out and had a seat. Shoving one of the folders to Kaleb, he pointed, "Victor," then pointed at another that he slid to Eden, "Victoria." Kaleb felt Eden stiffen. This was routine for him when he was working an assignment. It wasn't for her.

"Any new updates on Victor?" Kaleb asked.

"Nothing substantial. I'm hoping the information Miss Samuels provides might give us the break we need." Quinten's eyes traveled to Eden. "At least we have one case put to bed...somewhat. I'm anxious to hear your story. Would you mind me recording your statement?"

Eden shook her head.

Kaleb drew Quinten's attention. "As I said on the phone, there are possibly two others to take her place, and I haven't gotten her whole story yet."

He opened Victor's file, and Eden dragged the file on herself to her. "We only knew you as Victoria

Granier," Kaleb interjected when Eden saw the file heading. "Your application for the pageant said you were born in Paris. You listed it as your home. But the address you gave was for *Souvenir Précieux* storage facility."

"The address I used is where my mom said my dad's parents lived. She stayed in contact with them—" confusion etched its way onto her face "—or someone, I guess, since now I have no idea if Louis Granier is even a real person. I never met any of my grandparents."

She continued to thumb through the papers in the file, as her eyebrows slowly drew together.

"As you can see, we had very little to go on." Quinten explained, "The college you had listed didn't have any record of you being a student as Victoria Granier."

"Oh crap. I can't believe I didn't consider that."

"If the pageant had done their homework, I don't think you would have been chosen, because you were basically a ghost. An illusion. My thought is, they didn't need to do their homework when they saw your name."

"What's my name got to do with it?"

"We'll get to that. What do you know about your true identity?"

"I'm not sure anymore. Both of my birth certificates state I was born in Paris."

"Oh. Do you have the files?" Quinten interrupted.

She nodded and reached for her purse, revealing the small thumb drive. "I also brought all the papers that Adam gave me, including his letter, if you need that."

"Yes." Quinten took the thumb drive from Eden as well as the papers. "I'll scan the files in a few minutes. Why don't we get your statement, Miss Samuels, and see if we can piece this all together."

Eden fidgeted in her chair, and Kaleb noticed the apprehension in her expression. She was still trying to remain disconnected, but he could see the scared little girl starting to surface.

His hand found her knee, and he squeezed hoping his touch would calm her nerves. Instead, the charge that ripped up his arm and through his body threatened to stop his heart. He quickly lifted his hand, only to have her entwine her fingers with his. He reached up with the other hand and rubbed the spot on his chest wondering if he'd been shot again.

"When you're ready you can start," Quinten instructed.

Chapter Eleven

Eden turned her panicked gaze to Kaleb. In that moment he saw how truly scared she was. She needed him. And there was something about her that he needed too. He just didn't know if he'd ever have a chance to figure out what it was.

"Okay. Um. Well, I guess what started it all was when I received a large package in the mail while I was in Mississippi for college."

Kaleb stared at the files, his mind drifting to their discussion the night before and that morning, while she recounted the events. It had been two years of wondering if she was still alive. Two years of few leads, grasping at every straw possible, and never getting anywhere.

He tried to tell himself she wasn't the reason he agreed to remain on the case unofficially. It was simply because the case was still unresolved, and he wanted to see it through. It pissed him off though when Quinten had spoken about shelving the case in January because the leads had run cold. She hadn't been found. What if she was hurt? What if she was being held captive? Even if it was the worst-case scenario, and she was dead, he wanted to find her, to bring her home to her family, and give her a proper burial.

Shelving the case didn't mean they were giving up, just moving their focus to cases with more active leads. Still, she hadn't been found. He couldn't let her go. He continued to search. Continued to dig. And when he'd finally thought he'd come to terms with possibly never finding her, the dark-haired woman materialized like she walked right out of his dreams...or nightmares. And now, with every word she spoke and every squeeze of her fingers in his, he knew she had become his obsession, and he had no clue how he was going to stay away from her.

"I was terrified when my brother told me about the attempted abduction. He said he overheard one of the security guard's comms say the assailant was named Grey. Then, I saw him running toward me at the plane, and I knew he wasn't part of the pageant security. He'd been so friendly when we'd spoken and interested in everything about me. He was the obvious answer. And when I saw the gun under his jacket, I panicked.

"I saw Bill's gun in his holster, and I took it. I didn't want to shoot him, but he lunged at me, and the gun went off. It all happened so fast. They pulled me into the plane and raised the stairs, and we were in the air before it even registered what I'd done."

"I understand how you could make the assumption," Quinten agreed.

"I got the transmission that there was a possible planned abduction," Kaleb added, "although I never received the transmission that claimed I was the abductor. Whoever was responsible had to have known I wasn't with the pageant security and pushed the suspicions off on me."

"Where did you go?" Quinten continued to question.

"To my brother's home in Toronto. When we got there the place had been ransacked like his mother's home. Bill took us to his place until we could figure out what to do next."

"So, why didn't Adam go to the police with the information?"

"Bill didn't want to clue anyone in to where I was, since we were still in Canada. At least until we knew more about what happened. Also, we weren't sure what was going on, other than our father was kept a secret. I mean, is that a crime? Is any of this a crime? I still don't know that Adam and Bill have actually been abducted. As far as the pageant abduction goes, we had no idea if that was tied to Victor or not.

"When Adam initially contacted me, all we wanted was answers. His mom never said a word to him, nor my mom to me."

"What has your mom said?"

"I haven't spoken to her. We aren't on the best of terms. She lorded over my life for eighteen years. I was her puppet, performing, and parading, and competing, at her request, until I finally had enough, and pushed back when she wanted me to go to an Ivy league school. I left and didn't look back."

"What did you study in college?"

"Osteopathic medicine. But I only completed my undergrad. I was uncertain about continuing, so I moved off campus to save money and got a job as a bartender, then I got the packet from Adam."

"How'd he find you?"

"My campus address was in the paperwork, and the package was forwarded. I moved off campus in January and I got it in March with the letter. When it arrived, I was dumbfounded. His mom knew my entire life, including my medical history."

"What did the letter say?"

"It said his mom had died in a car accident, and when he was searching for her estate papers, he came across the files. He said he thought he was my brother. It took at least a week for me to decide to e-mail him. But I figured, what was the harm? He knew every detail about me."

"You corresponded only through e-mail?"

"No. We chatted through social media. At some point he gave me his phone number and we started texting and video chatting."

"So, you had a good idea about who he was before you met him."

"Yes. We were well acquainted with each other by that time, and both invested in solving the mystery. I'd read his and Eva's files." She paused, taking a deep breath.

"Eva. Your sister."

"Yes. It just made no sense why his mom would have my file, or Eva's, other than we all had Chalemaare listed as our dad. I live in the U.S. My mom works for a pharmaceutical plant in South Carolina. Adam is in Canada. His mom was a doctor. Eva is in London. Her mom is a professor at a university. I mean, we are from all over the world. How do all of us tie back to a French scientist?"

"Good question. So, how long has your brother been missing?"

"About a month. After his place was ransacked, we were certain it was tied to the files, but still didn't know how, or if the abduction attempt was connected. Adam still hadn't heard from Eva, so we decided we needed to see if we could find her. When we got to the address in London, the door was ajar. We snooped around a little but couldn't tell if someone had broken in and taken her, or possibly left and didn't get the door closed."

"And you said Eva shared the Granier name with you."

"Correct."

"Did Agent Grey fill you in on what we found on the Granier name?"

"No." Eden's chocolate-brown eyes swung back to Kaleb.

"Damn. I'm sorry. I meant to say something last night but with everything that has happened in the past twenty-four hours, it slipped my mind." He leaned back in his chair and settled their laced fingers in his lap.

"You mentioned earlier it might have been how I got into the pageant. What did you mean?"

"After your attempted abduction, we dug a little deeper into the pageant itself. There was another Granier that had been a contestant. Juliette Granier won the pageant twenty plus years ago. After an appearance on a talk show in France, she disappeared."

"Seriously? Do you think that's why someone was wanting to abduct me? Was she ever found?"

"No, she was never found, and we have to assume there is a connection," Quinten filled in. "She wasn't the only one either. So far, we've found five who've won and disappeared, and we feel certain there are more. Since the pageant is international, the abductions have been harder to track because the contestants were from all over the world. Some were abducted years after they won."

Quinten leaned back in his chair. "And did you know Chalemaare has a website?"

"Au-dela`de l`existence?"

"You are familiar with Beyond Existence?"

"Yes. I found it when I was digging into Victor's background. It's an interesting concept. A virtual MENSA think tank. Adam and I both set up accounts before the pageant. Bill had us abandon them after the attempted abduction and created a new profile on his computer."

"There may be some people that went missing from the website," Kaleb added.

"What makes you think that?"

"The feed. I saw several posts of people searching for others who'd been on the site. I thought it was an algorithm issue until a guy I talked to quite a bit disappeared. And it's not like just anyone could get into the site. You had to jump through hoops, and to your point, be a part of MENSA."

"So, you and your brother were both on the website?" Quinten questioned.

"Yes."

"There has to be something we are missing. It's odd how they have it set up."

"In what way?"

"Like you said, it's designed to be a think tank. However, there is no organization. There's no way you could glean any information. Too many people are discussing too many topics."

"Have you been invited into one of the focus chats?"

"Like private messages?"

"No. They are private chatrooms. I was invited into one after I posted about how the medical field is becoming more proactive on health."

"What did you say in your post?"

"Honestly, I don't remember. The lead post was

about how many dangerous illnesses had cropped up in the past few years, and I responded. Someone messaged me, inviting me to their focus group." Pausing for a moment, she tipped her head to Kaleb. "Some of those you think are missing may have gone to a focus group."

"True."

"That's something we will need to look into."

"So, after the pageant—"

"Bill started searching for Eva and investigating what happened at the pageant, figuring it had to be an inside job. The only leads he found were what security had gotten initially."

"And what was that?"

"Apparently one of the hotel staff overheard two pageant security guards talking to a woman with the pageant about taking me. He said it sounded suspicious and didn't line up with the schedule he'd been given, so he went to the coordinator of the pageant, asking about the schedule, and they confirmed his suspicions."

"We received similar information and were able to pull security footage, although it didn't help because of where they were standing."

"Do you think they were after me because of my connection to the other Granier contestant?"

"That was our initial suspicion. With this new information, it could be your connection with Granier or Victor Chalemaare, or, hell, both of them for all we know." Quinten sat back with his arms crossed across his chest. "So, you guys stayed in Canada?"

"Until Bill decided we weren't getting anywhere with the investigation."

"Do you know Bill's last name?"

"McGuire. Adam said he was a retired police

detective who taught the criminal law class he took in college. When Chalemaare went missing, Adam hit him up for help."

"So, he had no ties to Mr. DiMari's family?"

"I don't believe so."

"And he quit his job at the university and left his life behind, to go on this man hunt?"

"No. The pageant was in June, and Bill wasn't teaching any summer classes, so when Adam asked if he wanted to tag along to Montreal, he agreed since I was trying to get information about Victor. It was supposed to be an overnight trip. I never thought I would win the pageant or have someone try to kidnap me.

"Once the ball had been set in motion, he was all in. His wife passed away several years ago, and his kids were grown, so I guess he was up for the adventure. We trusted him. I mean, he was in law enforcement at one time and—"

Quinten jotted something on the paper and then leaned back against his chair again. "I get that. I'm just trying to follow his train of thought. Sometimes those who you think are helping with the situation turn out to be the problem."

"Bill was primarily following Adam's lead. When Adam thought we should get closer to the action and go to France, Bill was not on board. Once the leads dried up from the pageant abduction, he agreed. We rented a small flat in Paris, close to the research facility. Adam kept an eye on the facility, Bill continued digging through the paperwork, and I went to work as a bartender at a pub."

"A bartender?"

"I already had experience working in Mississippi.

We hoped we might get some workers from the facility, since it was close by. Add in a little alcohol and they might start spilling the information we needed. And they did. I had been there a couple of months, when several men came in talking about the research lab expanding. It caught my attention because Chalemaare was still missing. So, who was making the decisions?

"Adam found the company they had contracted with for the expansion, in an article on the internet, and was able to secure a job with them. His background is in commercial construction, so it worked out perfectly. They started construction about eight months ago.

"One night he came home saying he overheard some men leaving the facility, talking about something called *Récolte*, and having to make a delivery there. They were going to meet at some marina the next day."

"A marina?"

"Yes. I can't remember the name. Adam wanted to follow them. I told him to wait and talk to Bill, who had left to follow a lead he'd found about someone with Eva's name on a college roster. I thought he'd agreed. Adam went to work and never came home, and Bill didn't either. When I hadn't heard from either of them for several days, I got scared. I tried calling them and neither answered. My brain was going a million miles an hour with different scenarios, and I needed to separate myself from my current situation. I had some money saved up, so I flew back to Mississippi. I hit up a friend, that worked at the bar I worked at before, and she let me stay at her house until I could figure out what to do."

Chapter Twelve

"What made you search for Agent Grey?"

"I'm going to be honest, my ability to think clearly after everything that happened was not great. I figured if Kaleb were the one who'd planned on abducting me, he might have also been responsible for Adam's, and maybe even Bill's disappearance."

Quinten's brows rose.

"I thought if I found him, I might be able to reason with him. I know it sounds crazy, and before you say anything about how stupid the plan was, I had serious doubts about Kaleb being the one who wanted to abduct me in the first place.

"Even though Adam said they called him by name on the comms, something struck me about what Bill found when he did his investigation. Two security guards and a woman were suspects. I never saw Kaleb hanging around any of the other security guards. He chatted with different people here and there, but never the same person that I saw. When he found me at the plane, he was by himself. None of it fit with what was reported. So, I figured if I found him and he wasn't the abductor, maybe he could help me, because when everything started spiraling out of control, he was the only person I could think of to turn to.

"I searched for his name online, and I found the agencies' obituary for him. I was horrified that I might have killed someone. I continued searching with the information I had for him, and with a few key pieces he provided in one of our conversations, I found him. And he was very much alive."

Sitting forward, a crease formed between Quinten's eyes. He stared at the papers he was thumbing through as he rubbed his mouth. "Damn. How did they get your medical records and test scores?"

"It had to have been my mom. But would she even be able to get all those medical files?"

"Many medical groups put information in e-files for the patient to be able to access. There is quite a bit of information tied to several blood tests and physicals. Why did they do so many physicals?"

"My mom said it was necessary for sports."

"I've only heard of physicals being required once a year maybe, and it never involved blood tests."

"She was kind of a health fanatic."

"Did you ever get sick? Break a bone?"

"No illnesses that sent me to the doctor."

"Broken bones?"

"No."

"Do you wear glasses? Have you had braces?"

"No glasses. Yes braces."

Quinten flipped through page after page and finally sat back, rubbing his neck. His eyes darted between Kaleb and Eden. "Let me wade through these files and Miss Samuels' statement and connect some of the dots.

"The call from your brother might have been an attempt to track your location. Don't know if they were able to trace it or not. Your phone will need to stay here. To keep you safe, you need to find a place off the grid until we can get an idea of what we are dealing with."

****

So much had happened in the past twenty-four hours. Eden hadn't had time to completely process it all. Heck, she hadn't really processed the last two years. Most people would think she made the story up. An unknown father, brother, and sister? An attempted abduction? And what did she have for it? More questions than answers. The biggest one was why? Why did Victor Chalemaare hide his paternity? Or did he even know? And why had someone tried to abduct her?

Staring out the window as they returned to Dalton, Eden watched as the old buildings passed by, including the boarded-up building she'd peeked into. People milled around in front of the stores chatting and having a good time under the glow of the streetlamps. She remembered finding pictures of it on the internet, decorated for the holidays. Lighted garland draped from streetlamps. Trees were lit with tiny white sparkly lights, and festive decorations adorned every storefront. The boughs of the pine trees were covered in snow. A perfect winter wonderland.

"Do you guys get a lot of snow?"

"Not a ton. We usually have maybe three good snowfalls." Kaleb's eyes drifted to hers. "Why?"

"Just curious."

Pressing a button on his steering wheel caused the screen in the center of the dash to light up, and Kaleb clicked through a list of names before tapping one.

"Hello?"

"Hey. We're back in town and we're coming by to get Aurora."

"We?"

Kaleb's eyes widened and he mouthed "Oh shit!"

Clearing his throat, he continued. "Yeah, I have a friend with me."

"Is this why you needed me to keep your kitten?"

"Kind of. I'll explain later."

"If you need some time alone you can leave her with me for a while. Or if she needs a good home, I can keep her. She loves Comet, and he needs a friend."

"No! Aurora is mine, Kase." The panic in his voice had Eden's eyes darting again, and she chewed on her bottom lip trying desperately to stifle the giggle that was erupting. A snort escaped, and Kaleb immediately glared at her. Her hand flew up to cover her mouth, trying to keep the giggles at bay, and Kaleb's attention turned back to the conversation.

"Besides if I let you have her, Ben would make her a barn cat, and I can't handle that."

"Geez, Kaleb. I swear, you are worse than a woman sometimes."

Eden stifled another snort, and Kaleb's eyes narrowed, but there was no malice behind them.

"Aurora huh? When did she get that name?"

"It just came to me. She is like the Aurora Borealis; appeared out of nowhere and no clue where she came from. Did she do okay?"

"Yes. She was perfect. Even went to the bathroom outside while I had her at the shop."

"Oh. Dang. I forgot about the litter box. I guess I need to get an extra one."

"She did fine."

"Great. Well, we are nearly there, so we'll see you in a little bit." Kaleb disconnected and let out an audible breath. "Well crap!"

"What?"

"Things are going to be a little tricky. My mouth kind of betrayed me. So how do you want to play this? I can't really tell them that I'm protecting you from the baddies, because they don't exactly know what I've been up to the past few years. They just think I'm taking extra-long in college. So…college friends?"

Eden chewed on her lip and stared out the window picturing how their story could have started. "What about, we met at a party. I was visiting a friend, and she brought me along. Your friend Mark and my friend Lindsey knew each other, so they started talking, and you didn't want me to feel awkward, so you started talking to me and found out we both liked…hiking. You told me all about the great places to hike around here. We stayed in contact through social media, and I told you I was coming to Arkansas, so you invited me to come stay with you, because you promised to take me hiking."

Kaleb chuckled. "You made all that up on the fly?" Eden shrugged. "You need to go to work for the agency. We are always trying to come up with plausible back stories when we go out on missions."

"That would be fun."

"Yeah. If you don't mind getting shot."

"Geez! How many times do I have to apologize?"

"I'm just picking on you. I forgive you." He paused. "So why did you come to Arkansas?" Eden lifted her brow in confusion. "The story. Why are you visiting Arkansas."

"Oh! Um…I manage a bar outside of Hattiesburg, and we have a sister bar in Fayetteville that we acquired, and I'm doing interviews."

"Damn. You're good at lying."

"Thank you. I think."

"Bar's name?"

"I'll need to research that. Can I borrow your phone?"

He pulled out his phone and handed it to her.

Tapping the screen, her eyes darted to Kaleb, and a twinge of uncertainty pinged in her chest.

"Passcode is soar."

Her throat tightened, and she could feel the moisture at the corner of her eyes. He trusted her. Finally.

"What? I love to fly." His comment made her realize she hadn't moved and quickly tapped in the code and began to scroll.

"I can't find anything in Fayetteville. How far is Mountain Ridge from here?"

"It's about twenty miles east."

"Perfect. Whoa Nelly's bar and grill changed hands a month ago. So, let's go with that."

"You're really getting into this," Kaleb said with a smirk.

"You said we needed a story."

"I'm going to let you talk to my sister. Maybe you can handle her rapid-fire questions."

"Is she bad?"

"Interrogates anyone she thinks I'm interested in."

"Do you date a bunch?"

"I used to, I guess. Not so much anymore."

"I'm sure you have no problem getting any woman you want. Did someone break your heart? Mess up your winning streak? Heaven forbid, turn you down?

"You and my sister will get along famously."

"Sorry. I didn't mean—"

Kaleb shook his head and waved her apology away. "It's okay. I did date quite a bit when I was in high school

A Life of Illusions

and got kind of a reputation. I didn't know how to navigate a relationship. Hell, I'm still not sure. That's what I thought dating was for. Test the waters. So, I dated. A lot. And I had a great time.

"In college, I dated some, but joining the agency ended that. There is a strict policy of no fraternizing with targets or co-workers. And since I was going out of town all the time, and mingling with different people, the job was just not conducive to dating."

"You and that pretty agent never dated?"

"Kat? Hell no. She's beautiful, yes. But, like I said, she's scary as hell. I've seen her in action. She's ruthless. Best person to have your back on a mission, but I pity the poor guy that decides to date her. I'd hate to see what would happen if he pissed her off. Plus, the policy is in place for a reason. It's important to be able to fully trust your partner when you're on a mission because you don't know when your life might hang in the balance. Even though our jobs usually weren't dangerous, we had to stay focused. We had to be prepared in case the mission went south." His eyes drifted, and with the solemn expression that had taken over, she could tell his memories had stolen him from her again. It seemed they both had memories that haunted them.

Shaking his head, he cleared his throat like he knew he had spaced out. "Anyway, after I came back to Arkansas, I started shadowing my dad. Then, after I met my brother, I started helping at the gym and his construction company. So, I was too busy to date." He paused, and when his eyes finally locked with hers, she saw a hint of sadness. Was he regretting his choices? "Did you date?" He shifted in his seat nervously, making her wonder if he was worried about her answer.

After a moment to replay his comments, something struck her memory. "That's right. The article I found about your family's charity event talked about your brother being kidnapped as a baby."

"Way to avoid the question." He chuckled. "Yeah. He was kidnapped and sold, and my parents were told he was killed."

"Oh my God, Kaleb. I can't imagine what your parents went through. How horrible."

"The funny thing is, he'd been living less than thirty miles away the entire time. The people who adopted him contracted with our company as custodians."

"So, how did your family finally find him?"

"He got sick and needed blood, and I'm one of the only people in the area, besides my mom, that has his rare blood type, so when they took my blood, they ran some additional tests and voila, I have a brother."

"That's such a tragic but amazing story. I hope I get to meet him and your family one day."

"Well, you are about to meet my pain in the ass sister."

"You don't get along?"

Kaleb tipped his head back and forth. "We do, for the most part. She loves getting into my business though. You'll see when you meet her."

When Kaleb dropped the kitten off at the store, Eden realized that one of the women she'd met the day before had to have been his sister, but she didn't know which one.

"So, now, back to the question. Did you date much?"

"Oh. Right." She wasn't avoiding the question before. But after playing their conversation about his dating history over in her head, she was nervous about what his reaction would be and decided to take "the less information the better" approach. "Not much."

"Not much, meaning…"

So much for keeping it vague. She let out a heavy sigh. "My mom didn't allow me to date." Her mind stole a moment reflecting on the arguments she had with the woman, and frustration reared its ugly head. "That was another point of contention."

"She didn't allow you to date at all?"

"No."

"Did you ever sneak out?"

"No," she said shaking her head shamefully. "I wanted to. But there was this nagging need for her approval. Then, when we fought over my college choice, I gave up." The warmth of Kaleb's fingers threading through hers sent tingles up her arm. "I was tired of her making me feel like I wasn't enough." His fingers tightened. She peeked over to see his glacial blue eyes darken under the streetlights, his bladed jaw clenching in anger. Not anger. Rage!

Chapter Thirteen

Even when he first approached her in the park, he didn't seem exactly angry, more like irritated. The expression Kaleb held now was new to her, and she didn't like it at all. Especially since she was the cause. It didn't scare her. It was just an expression that should never cross his face. He was too happy. "Well, that was way too much sharing." She giggled, trying to lighten the mood and squeezed his hand back. He loosened his grip some but kept his hand within hers. "I went on some casual dates in college. Nothing serious. My classes were brutal, so the dates were few and far between."

"So, you're questioning being a doctor now? To be honest, I figured you'd do something with music." His question had her hoping that he had moved on, but the expression on his face, although softened, still held an intensity.

"I don't know, honestly. The doctor path was another way my mom manipulated me. She was into nutrition and exercise. I give her credit, though, it's probably why I never got sick." Her thoughts went to the little shop on the square. Her dream. "I don't know what I want to do with my life. But sounds like you do." She paused. "Oh my gosh. Where is my brain? You have a job. You don't have time to—"

"It's fine. Trust me. My buddy Malcolm has my back. We cover for each other. I've called on him to cover for me quite a bit between school and trips, and I've done the same for him. I'll call him if Brant's friend gets back in touch with me for an interview. I'm sure he will be happy to take over."

"Who? What interview?"

"I was made Director of Environmental and Safety Management recently, and I'm in the process of building my team. There was a girl that waited on me and my friends at the restaurant, and she is an environmental engineer."

"How'd you find that out?"

"She's a friend of Brant's, one of the guys I was with."

"And I'm guessing by your expression she's pretty."

"Yeah," he said a little too enthusiastically. "I think she will be a great addition to our team if she is as intuitive as Brant says she is. And she seems nice. She's one of those girls who've been told they're pretty, but not quite sure they believe it."

"Oh." A twinge of jealousy stabbed her as Kaleb's comment about his company's policy played through her mind. She was his target. Off limits. She knew it was stupid to have any ill feelings against someone she'd never set eyes on. She needed to get over it. Although thinking it and convincing her heart were two totally different things, especially when he kept doing things like holding her hand.

Obviously, neither her heart nor her face got the memo quick enough, because the minute she uttered that single word, loaded with all the feelings, Kaleb's face went from somewhat content, to perplexed, and he blurted, "No, no, it's not like that. This works out perfectly, because Malcolm needs a special someone in his life. My sister kind of took his heart on a ride then sort of stomped on it. And it was pretty much my fault."

And just like that, her tattered heart was mended back together. Playing back his comment, she questioned, "Your sister?" She thought about the ladies she met the day before. Even though one scared the life out of her, neither seemed the type to play with a guy's feelings.

"Yeah. Malcolm joined the company through a foreign internship. He was a grad student from the university of Southampton in England. Not long after he started, he developed a crush on Kaysi. It took him a little while, but with a little nudge from me, he finally asked her out. As the semester came to an end, he decided to submit his application to stay on with the company. I think mainly because he wanted to continue his relationship with Kaysi. Not long after he was hired permanently, she ended it. I don't think he's gotten over it."

"So, you're playing matchmaker?"

"I know I shouldn't, because I'm kind of the one who put Malcom and Kaysi together, and I shouldn't have. They weren't right for each other."

"Gasp. Have we found something you aren't good at?"

"Don't judge me. That was my first attempt. There's a learning curve."

Eden laughed. "Seriously though, isn't that a bit dangerous in the workplace?"

"Oh yeah. But that's what makes it fun." He gave her his boyish grin that sent sparkles into his eyes laden with mischievousness.

He turned down a desolate road that was barely wide

enough for two cars to pass. After traveling past a brick house with a black metal fence surrounding it, and then a large barn, the road turned to gravel, and Kaleb continued on. Curiosity set in.

"Where are we going?"

"To pick up Aurora. Kaysi took her home."

"I like her name, by the way. It fits." She glanced down at her hands and realized she was still holding his phone, so she handed it back to him and he set it in the cupholder. "Do you think you got it?"

"What? The story?" His lips pursed. "We met at a party. I was hanging out with Mark, you with Lindsey. They got cozy, so we started talking. We both like hiking yada yada. Stayed in touch. You are doing interviews at a bar your owners acquired named Whoa Nelly, which by the way, is hilarious, and I need to take you hiking."

"Perfect."

Two houses came into view. The garage door was open on the nearest house, and as they parked, Eden could hear the shriek of some kind of machinery as she opened her door.

They both stepped out of the truck and Kaleb said, "Ben must be working on some of his art. You should see it. The guy is seriously talented." He rapped his knuckle on the door and Eden suddenly remembered she hadn't told Kaleb her secret.

"Oh, by the way, I met your sister yesterday."

His head jerked to her as the door swung open. The quiet dark-haired woman with light blue eyes, stood in front of them holding Aurora to her shoulder like a baby. A large, long-haired silver dog stood next to her. The big bright smile that spread across her face revealed the similarities between Kaysi and Kaleb. *That's why she seemed familiar.* It was obvious she was Kaleb's sister. Then her eyes widened as she took in Eden.

"Hey, Kaysi," Kaleb said anxiously. She waved him off and turned to Eden.

"Oh my God, it's you."

Eden nodded.

"I'm Kaysi, if you don't remember," she said leaning in for a hug.

Eden was careful since Aurora was kind of squished between them.

"So, you know my brother?"

"Eden just told me—" Kaleb started but Kaysi was already dragging Eden into the house.

"Come on in. Ben's miffed at me because I 'tricked him,' his words, into being a model for our shop's website. I found this beautiful leather sofa with matching chair and ottoman at this little shop up near Branson, and it came in late yesterday. It has that perfect cowboy feel, so I told him I needed to unpack it and get it out on the floor, and I needed his help. All true." She leaned in conspiratorially. "I really want it for this place. The leather is so soft and comfortable. Anyway, I had him sit on it to see how comfortable it was, and I took a quick photo to show him how good he looked sitting on it. I figured it might help convince him later. The photo turned out amazing and was perfect for RareFinds website, so I told him I was going to use it. Now he is sulking in his shop."

"He's mad because you made him a model?"

"I know." She pulled out her phone and clicked on the photo. "He's perfect. You would think he would be strutting around."

"Wow. You're right. With him in his cowboy hat

and his boots propped up on the ottoman, he is perfect. So, do you think you'll get it?"

"I haven't dropped that bomb yet. I always like to discuss big purchases, because he thinks more logically than me. I'm a bit impulsive. But even though my little plan backfired, I think he'll see things my way."

"Might as well set up a delivery, Kase. You know he can't say no to you."

She looked off toward the shop. "Let me get him."

"Kaysi seems sweet," Eden blurted after she left the room.

"I am," she called back.

"She's got the hearing of a bat, too," Kaleb added comically. Eden snickered and shook her head. It was obvious Kaleb was close to his siblings, even if they picked on each other. A sigh escaped. Being raised as an only child was often lonely, and the idea of having a brother and a sister, regardless of how they came to be, made her excited.

Kaysi returned with a not so happy bearded man who currently had noise cancelling earmuffs around his neck, safety goggles on his head, and sawdust sprinkled like snowflakes in his strawberry blond hair and beard. "This is Ben," Kaysi said smiling from ear to ear. "Ben, this is…"

"Eden," she filled in when Kaysi's eyes lost their focus, and she paused. "Eden Samuels." Ben shook her hand and then his attention moved to Kaleb.

"Did Kaysi tell you she's wanting to keep the kitten?"

Kaleb's head shook violently. "Yep. And it's not happening."

"I told her no."

113

"Yeah, we know how much weight your 'no' carries when it comes to her. I've mastered the art of 'no' with her."

"Please, Kaleb. She loves me." Kaysi gave him her best pout and Eden snickered.

"She loves me more."

"Don't give in, man. I already got her a dog."

"Shut it, Ben. You fell in love, too."

"We have Comet. We don't need a damn cat."

"Kitten, and don't act all grumpy. Who put their flannel shirt in their cowboy hat earlier so she would have a soft place to sleep?" Ben rolled his eyes.

"I'm not caving, Kaysi." Kaysi's lip stuck out and she snuggled Aurora up to her neck. Kaleb shook his head and let out a sigh. "I will grant you Auntie visits. Will that work?"

"I guess." Kaysi turned away and carried the kitten into the living room.

Kaleb grabbed Eden's hand as she followed Kaysi, leaned in, and whispered, "Abort! Abort! Bad idea. Bad. Idea. We need to grab the kitten and run."

Eden returned quietly, "We can't just leave." She continued walking and sat down.

"So, Eden—"

"I warned you," Kaleb sang out of the corner of his mouth, then reached around Kaysi and took Aurora, placing her on his chest as he sat down in an adjacent chair. Ben snuck in behind Kaysi and slid under her as she began to sit, so she sat in his lap, then he wrapped his arms around her and kissed her on the neck.

"Who are you, and what are your intentions with my brother?"

"Kaysi. Could you be a little less—"

"Can't I be excited? You haven't brought a girl home in forever, and suddenly you are trying to hide that you guys are together." Her eyes turned to Eden. "How long have you been together? Why have I not met you before? Well, before yesterday."

"Oh, we're not...I mean—"

"She just got into town."

"Don't tell me you flew out to get her because I will know that's a lie. April and I met her yesterday."

Before he had time to explain, Eden decided to forge ahead with the little ruse. "I'm visiting. I have some interviews in Mountain Ridge—"

"She's a bar manager."

"How did you guys meet?"

Kaleb's eyes cut to Eden's, and she hoped he remembered their story.

"We met at a college party in Maryland. I was hanging out with my friend Mark and...what was your friend's name?"

"Lindsey."

"Yeah, Lindsey. Eden was in town visiting from..."

"Mississippi."

"Geez. You guys are like watching a tennis match." Kaysi pointed to Kaleb. "Go."

"Mark and Lindsey knew each other and ditched us after a while, so we started talking. I don't know how we got on the subject, but I told her about some of my hiking adventures."

"Oo, I know," Kaysi said lifting her hand. "I know. Because you never shut up about them. That is literally the only thing you talk about."

"Is not." Kaleb feigned irritation.

Eden chuckled remembering their conversation

about Devil's Den. Kaleb eyed her and she wondered if he was thinking the same thing the way his brow shot up. Then he turned back to Kaysi.

"Do you want to hear the story or not?"

"Oh, sorry. Please continue."

"Anyway, I told her if she ever made it to Arkansas, I could take her on some sweet hikes. A few months later I get this friend request on one of my social media pages. It's her. We kept up with each other, and she messaged me a few days ago saying she would be conducting interviews at a bar in Mountain Ridge and asked how close it was to me. I told her it was about twenty minutes and offered my place for her to stay, so she didn't have to drive back and forth from Fayetteville, because we all know the motel here needs to be condemned." Kaleb side eyed Eden and she wrinkled her nose.

"Company pays my travel. But honestly, I hate hotels. So, I jumped at the offer."

"Yeah. You haven't seen how he lives yet. Or have you? You might reconsider."

"I think that's our cue to leave."

Eden stood and waited for Ben to help Kaysi off his lap then she hugged her. "It was very nice meeting you. I hope I will get to see you again before I leave."

She lifted her eyes to Ben and noticed him eye her with a bit of a scowl, which made her uneasy. *What's that about?* Brushing it off, she smiled, only for him to walk away.

"How long are you here for?" Kaysi asked, pulling her attention back.

"Not sure. A week for now, unless we don't have any prospects, then I will either stay longer, or possibly come back. Depends on what the owners want."

"Great. Hopefully we can get together next weekend when Cody's band plays."

Eden glanced at Kaleb, trying to gauge his reaction, and when he didn't respond, she returned her attention to Kaysi and said, "That sounds like fun."

Chapter Fourteen

They turned up the narrow road and headed into the hills above the town. The lights of the sleepy little village flickered in Kaleb's rearview mirror. Ahead of them, darkness allowed for a beautiful view of a star filled sky. A backdrop to his place in the woods. As the garage door slowly lifted, his phone buzzed in the cupholder. Quinten's name flashed across the screen.

—*call me*—

He glanced over at Eden who appeared to be nearly asleep. Her head slowly turned, and she noticed the phone was still glowing.

"It's Quinten. I need to take this. Go ahead and take Aurora inside and get her fed. I'm going to call him and see what information he has."

With a nod, she stepped out and shut the door, and he watched as she opened the door to the mudroom. Something seemed off, and he couldn't put his finger on it. A feeling of dread took over as his thumb hovered over the screen of the phone. What was he missing? He was having a hard time focusing because of his house guest.

A shriek from inside the house had him bailing out of the truck and racing through the mud room, the call a distant memory. A dark figure ran through the living room and out the open sliding door, vaulting over the railing of the second story deck. Kaleb slammed into the railing in time to see the shadow disappear into the forest.

Turning, he scanned the room, taking in the mass destruction. Eden was nowhere in sight. "Eden?" The lump forming in his throat, threatened to cut his oxygen off, when his call was met with silence. His pace picked up with each panicked footstep. "Eden?" *Did they hurt her?* His eyes shot to the front door. Locked. A noise behind him had him bolting toward the kitchen. Circling the island, he found Eden, with her knees pulled tight against her chest, and her arms wrapped around her head, tucked snugly against her lap. Leaning over, he softened his voice so he wouldn't scare her and said, "Eden?" Her head lifted, and she launched herself at him. He barely had time to catch her. His arms circled her as he stood and tightened his grip, relief washing over him.

"Oh my God. Oh my God," she screamed and began to sob. Her body trembled as he held her and gently caressed her silky hair.

His lips brushed her temple over and over again, and he whispered, "It's okay, I've got you," as he tried to soothe her. Her body finally relaxed, and her feet found the floor. Backing away, he brushed her tears away and stared into her eyes. "Did they hurt you?"

"I'm okay. He just scared me. I was putting food down for Aurora, and he grabbed me from behind and held me by the throat. He said something about the files. I told him I didn't know what he was talking about. You came in, and he ran."

Kaleb's eyes and hands moved to her throat, examining it, but he couldn't see anything in the dim light. He tugged her back into his arms and couldn't help kissing her hair again. She felt so good, he didn't want to let her go.

A thump behind them had them both jumping back, and Kaleb quickly dragged Eden back to the mudroom. He reached the top shelf of the hall tree and pushed up. With a click, the entire unit opened to reveal a secret room. The walls were lined with different types of weaponry. He might have a few guns. If his brother only knew. Moving his hand down, he hit a button on the second shelf. The bottom opened and he retrieved another gun.

"How'd they get here so fast? The call from Adam was international," she whispered.

"Get inside and hit the lock. Do not come out unless you hear me. After ten minutes, if I don't come get you, call Quinten." He reached in his pocket and handed her his phone as she hesitantly stepped inside the room. "Do you remember the passcode?"

She nodded, and his hand reached up to flip the light switch. Nothing happened, so he grabbed the phone and turned on the flashlight.

"But you—"

Without letting her finish, he closed the door. He knew what she was going to say. He wished she would quit arguing when he was trying to protect her.

Lifting his gun, with only the light of the moon draping everything in a silver glow, he carefully made his way into the kitchen, scanning the area for movement. Boxes and cans of food lay scattered on the floor.

Quietly moving through the living room, it was a similar scene as the kitchen. Nothing was left in its place. His sofa and chair were shredded. Books were strewn across the room. Lamps were toppled along with the coffee table and end tables.

Pressing his body against the wall, he tried to figure out where the sound had come from. Moving from room to room, he scanned each, taking in all the damage. When he came to the laundry room, Aurora was hopping out of the litter box. He'd forgotten about her being there with all the excitement.

The smell wafted to his nose, and he grimaced. Could that have been the noise? He moved past the laundry room to Eden's room. His teeth clenched, seeing the wreckage. Her suitcase was in tatters along with her clothes. The bed was flipped, pillows destroyed. He took a deep breath. They knew where she was. *How the hell did they find her so fast?*

Once the house was cleared, Kaleb returned to the secret room and knocked. "Eden. It's me."

The door slowly opened. Eden wrapped her arms around his waist, and he pressed her tight against him. "I was so scared," she said into his shoulder. "You could have died."

"Not likely unless dirty cat litter can kill."

She giggled as he stepped back, taking a good look at her, checking her neck again using the flashlight on the phone.

"Are you sure you're okay?"

"I think so." She moved away from him, and he immediately missed her warmth. "I don't understand how he could have gotten here so fast."

"Even if the number was international, it doesn't mean they were outside the US," he said as he placed the gun back in the box and shut it.

"I know. He had an accent though."

Kaleb's eyes narrowed. "What kind of accent?"

"British, maybe."

"I'll make sure to tell Quinten when I call him. Right now, we need to get out of here. They know you're here. The place is trashed, and it looks like they cut the power to the main security system." He closed the door to the room and headed to the kitchen. Eden followed. His eyes searched for the white ball of fur.

"Aurora?" Eden sang out.

Kaleb was surprised she knew what he was doing, and laughed at her for believing the kitten would already know her name, until the ball of fur padded around the corner.

Eden picked her up and started gathering her food and supplies. As she lifted the food dish, she sighed. "I'm so sorry, Kaleb. I can't believe I didn't notice when I came in. I guess I was focused on getting Aurora fed and didn't check my surroundings."

"Not your fault. They destroyed everything, including your room."

Eden gasped. Her eyes locked on Kaleb. The food landed on the counter. She pushed Aurora into his arms and bolted up the hallway. When she reached the doorway, her entire body deflated. "No, no, no, no." Quickly entering the room, she gathered her tattered clothes and lifted the mattress. Feathers from the torn pillows floated into the air in her frantic search.

Panic flooded her face as she dug through the goose down. "Shit." She crawled across the floor to the other pillow that was in similar condition to the first one. Her hand swiped through the feathers and tears slid down her cheeks.

"What are you searching for?"

"My money. I had it in—"

"It's in the safe. I found it on the floor before we left."

"Oh my God! Thank you. That is everything I have." Her words sliced through him like a knife.

"Was there anything in here that you had at the pageant? Anything that you have held onto."

"No."

"Where are the crown and sash?"

"I left them behind when Adam told me to run."

"The dress?"

"Left in Canada."

"So, you have nothing on you or in your purse that might be traceable?"

"Not that I can think of. Bill was concerned about being tracked, so he had us dump everything when we moved to France. The only thing I held onto coming here was the phone, the thumb drive, and the papers."

"No computer?"

"No. I used my friend's when I got back to Mississippi."

"Car?"

"Bought it before I came here. Paid cash. The bill of sale is with the money. My other one got impounded when I didn't retrieve it after the pageant."

"Okay. We still need to leave it for now. They could have put a tracker on it. We'll take my truck." Kaleb exited the house and Eden followed. When they were pulling away, Eden took a shaky breath. Kaleb eyed her and saw tears glistening on her cheeks. She had been so strong through it all, but her façade was starting to crumble.

"I can't believe I was so stupid."

"What do you mean?"

"We got new phones when we went to France. I never thought about the fact that if he got captured, they could track me down with his phone. I kept it in case he was having to stay hidden and needed to contact me. It was such a stupid mistake." Her head hit the back of the seat. "They were in your home. They probably know who you are."

"Don't worry about it."

"It's my fault though. What are you going to do?"

"I'm going to call Quinten and update him on what is going on, and we are going to get it figured out."

Back on the highway, Kaleb punched a button on his steering wheel and the screen on his dash lit up and chimed.

"Did you change your mind about Aurora? If not, I don't want to talk to you."

"You wish. I need a favor."

"You already asked for a favor today. You only get one."

"Dock me next time. This is urgent."

"Okay. How can I help?"

"I need to use Ben's guesthouse. My house needs some repairs."

"What happened?"

"Busted water pipe. Flooded everything. It's a disaster over there right now."

"Have you called Joe?"

"Why? I need a place to stay right now, not the stuff repaired. Plus, he's got that huge project going with the spec homes and the side job at Poppi's. Yeah. Let me add one more thing on his plate so he can meet himself coming and going. I'm sure April hasn't seen him in weeks."

"Oh, trust me. She's seen him. And won't shut up about how they—"

"Lalalalala. Not listening."

"When do you need it?"

"Now. There is no way we are going to be able to stay there."

"You know most of the furniture is gone in the guesthouse, right? Ben's been selling it off or getting rid of it."

"Don't care. We'll make do, until I can get the repairs done."

"Would you rather go to Poppi's house? There's still some work needed, but the downstairs is done, and we are staging it."

"Nah. We have Aurora, and I don't want to run the risk of messing up the stuff you might need to sell. The guesthouse is fine."

"Okay. I will have Ben run by and make sure there are fresh sheets on the bed before he gets the animals settled for the night."

"Thanks. We will be there in a little bit."

Kaleb disconnected and was about to say something when Eden asked, "Who's Poppi?"

Chapter Fifteen

Dalton had weathered its share of tragedies in the past few years. Kaleb's family had been on the receiving end of some of them. It had only been a few months since Kaysi was accidentally caught up in a murder that had nearly taken her life. "Poppi was the old man who lived next door to Ben's family, the Corbett's. He was like a grandfather to Ben and his sister Jenna. Right after Ben and Kaysi started dating, Poppi was murdered."

"Seriously?"

"Yeah. Poppi named Ben as the benefactor in his will."

"What's wrong with his house?"

"They set fire to it, and the land, trying to hide the evidence. Kaysi got caught up in it and nearly died in the fire. Ben saved her. But that's another long story."

"Oh my gosh."

Pulling up to the house, Kaleb scanned the area. They were on the back side of Ben's property. A thick line of trees blocked the houses from the highway. They were out of sight.

Eden carefully got out with Aurora attached to her shoulder. "Let me carry something." Kaleb handed off his computer bag, then proceeded to retrieve the rest of Aurora's food and supplies.

Pushing open the door, he quickly scanned the area, even though he was fairly sure they were safe. He thought they were safe at his place, but he was wrong.

There was very little furniture other than the essentials. The floral sofa was probably something left behind by Ben's grandparents. He figured it was only there because Ben didn't have time to take it to the dump. There was no way he would be able to sell it. A brown reclining chair sat next to the sofa and deserved the same fate as the sofa. Holes were worn into the arms, and Kaleb wondered if it even reclined anymore. There was a Formica table, and two mismatched wooden chairs pushed up against a wall, opposite a small kitchen, that luckily still had a refrigerator and stove.

Turning up the hallway, he found the main bedroom. It was adequate size with a small, attached bathroom. Kaleb turned to leave and slammed into Eden, who he hadn't noticed was following him. Aurora squeaked and Kaleb lifted her from Eden's shoulder. Her tiny claws pulled at Eden's shirt. Placing the kitten on his shoulder, he slid a glance to Eden who had her lips tightly pressed together and her brow furrowed. "What? I haven't gotten to hold her all day. She needs her daddy."

Eden tried to hold her glare, but Kaleb could tell she was fighting a losing battle with the giggles, so he polished her off with a cheesy grin. A very unladylike snort exploded from her. His job was done.

When they found the second bedroom behind the kitchen, Kaleb's heart landed in his throat. The room was empty. He quickly moved to the third bedroom that was equally bare.

"I can sleep on the couch," came Eden's voice from behind him. His eyes landed back on the sofa in the living room.

"It might fold out into a bed." Kaleb made his way

back up the hall behind the kitchen and into the living room. Lifting the cushions, he noticed a handle. "Bingo!" He tugged on it and with each tug the sofa moved. He tried lifting it straight up, but it only lifted the sofa. "Damn it." Retrieving his phone from his pocket he punched Kaysi's number.

"Yeah?"

"Is there a trick to this bed in the sofa?"

"No."

"I can't get it to work."

"That's because it doesn't. It's broken."

"Shit."

"It's okay. I can sleep on the couch," Eden reiterated.

"You guys can't sleep together?"

"Kaysi, she's a cli…friend."

Kaleb swung his eyes to Eden. He didn't want to make her sleep on the sofa. But he didn't want to either. The thing looked hard as a rock and half of him would hang off the end. Kaysi's suggestion would solve everything, but he had no clue how he would broach the subject, or whether she would even consider it.

"I have a blow-up bed, if you want to use it."

"You do? That would be perfect. I'll run over there and get it."

"Okay. I will be here."

"I'm going to run next door," he said as he ended the call. "Kaysi has a blow-up bed we can borrow."

"Okay. I'm going to get a quick shower."

"All right. I'll be back in a few minutes."

The crisp April breeze had just enough bite to have Kaleb wondering where the spring temperatures went. It was warm yesterday. A pin prick at his collar reminded him that he had a passenger. He grabbed her and put her against his chest, rubbing her tiny head with his thumb. "We keep bouncing you around, don't we?" The ball of fluff squeaked like she knew exactly what he'd said, and the corner of his mouth lifted. "Hopefully, it won't take too long before we get you settled back in your nice comfy house." He stepped up to the door and tapped his knuckles a couple of times.

Kaysi quickly yanked open the door and her eyes went straight to Aurora. "Gimmy." Her fingers flexed with the word.

Kaleb turned away.

"No kitten. No bed."

"Damn, Kaysi." He rolled his eyes and gently tugged Aurora away from his shirt and handed her over. "Resorting to extortion I see."

"Hey. Whatever it takes." She ushered him in and pointed. "I have the bed over there, and I tucked a pillow and some more sheets in the bag. You are all set." She turned and met Kaleb's eyes for a long moment. "I like her, Kaleb. She seems sweet."

"Kaysi, I—"

"I know things haven't been exactly easy since you came home. I noticed you weren't yourself, and honestly, I've been worried about you. I don't know if something happened in Maryland, or if it's been all the craziness lately, and I didn't want to pry. I figured you would eventually talk to me if you needed to. I just wanted to tell you that I'm glad you are opening yourself up again."

He eyed her for a minute. She could be a little much sometimes. So could he. But, at the end of the day, they were all they had growing up, and no matter how much they bickered and fought, they were there for each other when things got tough.

He wrapped his arm around her and squeezed. "Thanks. I'm sorry if I've been hard to deal with. I've had a lot on my mind with school, and this new position, and…" His phone buzzed in his pocket, and he quickly retrieved it. Quinten. "Sorry, Kase. I need to grab this. Maybe we can get together soon and catch up."

"Let Eden know if she needs anything she can stop by."

Kaleb nodded, threw the strap of the mattress bag over his shoulder, and shut the door. Clicking the button on his phone, he spoke quietly, "Give me one second." Pushing the door open, he snapped his fingers and motioned for Kaysi to return Aurora. She stuck her lip out and his eyes widened, letting her know he meant business. She reluctantly put Aurora on his shoulder. He placed his hand on the kitten to get her adjusted, then waved as Kaysi shut the door.

When he was out of earshot he continued. "Sorry about that." His boss knew to be patient when calling, until the agents could get to a secure location that was private. Still, Kaleb always hated leaving his boss hanging. "I'm sorry I didn't get you called back. We had a visitor when we got back to the house. He attacked Eden. Asked her about the file. She said he spoke with a British accent. He took off when I came in."

"Is she okay?"

"Yeah. Just a little rattled. He tore the place apart. I'm at my sister's fiancé's guesthouse."

"Is it secure?"

"Yeah, I think so. It's pretty remote. Eden said she doesn't have anything with her that they might be able to track, so I think we will be fine until we can get a plan together. What have you found?"

"I have my theories after going through Miss Samuels' papers. And if I'm right, we have a much bigger problem than a missing scientist."

"Care to share?"

"I think Miss Samuels and her brother and sister are somehow part of Chalemaare's research."

"Shit. That was kind of the direction I was thinking too. And that means her mom is in on it." He paused, his thoughts clouding with different questions. "What could it be for?"

Kaleb set the bed inside the door and took a quick peek around. Not seeing any sign of Eden, he flipped on the porch light and took a seat in the rocking chair. His stomach soured at the information his boss shared, and the myriad of scenarios swarming his mind.

"I have no idea. But I am betting these papers opened up Pandora's box, and it's why Chalemaare's missing along with Miss Samuels' brother and possibly her sister. She is the loose end. It has to be someone within Chalemaare's circle behind this, or Chalemaare himself, because I'm betting the minute they saw Granier on that pageant paperwork she became their target. Not saying she didn't win the pageant fair and square, but regardless, I don't think they were going to let her leave."

Trying to keep his voice low, he said, "I can't believe I didn't catch wind of that when I was doing my investigation at the pageant. But then again, I have no idea who was part of the plot to abduct her, and who wasn't." He sat back in the rocker and rubbed his eyes. "But if they knew who she was when she applied, why did they let her go through with the pageant? They knew where she was."

"Did they? She had a fake address on her application."

"True."

"And to your point, I doubt everyone associated with the pageant was involved with the plot to abduct her."

"Also true. So, what do you need me to do?"

"We need to do a deep dive on the website. Get into one of the groups Miss Samuels talked about. See if there is a connection there." Quinten paused, and Kaleb heard him let out a long breath. "There is something else I need to make you aware of."

The uneasiness in his voice put Kaleb on alert. "Okay?"

"Because of the number of active cases we are working, we are stretched pretty thin. I've already got several of our agents out on other missions, and our other team is tied up in Honduras. Agent Scott is passing his case off, and then he's heading your direction. He's already researching the area around Chalemaare's facility, to locate possible places that can be reached by boat. If those guys who her brother overheard were going to make a delivery, it might not be that far from the main facility."

"I agree."

"I'm working on getting you a more secured location, but it might take some time. Are you sure you're good?"

He stared out into the darkness, noticing the twinkling stars. What was he supposed to say? He had no idea if they were good or not. He was still a bit wound up that someone had torn up his house. But Quinten had never left him hanging. He knew he'd do everything in his power to assure their safety.

"Yeah. Unless we come across some other way she was tracked, we should be safe. I'll admit, it was unnerving that they found her so fast. Eden said that call from her brother was an international number."

"It was."

"So, I'm sure they pinged her location when she answered, but from what she said, it didn't sound like she was on the phone long enough for them to zero in on it, so how'd they figure out where she was? And how'd they get someone there that fast?"

"Good question. And we have a thousand more that need to be answered before we can put this case to bed."

"I think we are safe for now. If we need to get away, I've got some places we can go, and trust me, no one will be able to find us. The only problem is, there is no cell service."

"Just be careful. Don't let your guard down. Chances are, they haven't gone far."

"How long before we have backup?"

"Not sure. Possibly a week. Maybe two." Kaleb's stomach bottomed out. He'd never been on any mission without a team in place. Then again, he'd never been in a situation quite like this one.

"It may take longer to untangle this web."

"I hear you. Honestly, this one worries me."

"How so?"

"I'm not liking the direction it's taking. Too many unanswered questions. Too many pieces scattered. More people missing."

Rubbing the back of his head, Kaleb let out a heavy breath. "I'll get with Eden on the computer to see if we can glean some information from the website."

"Sounds good. I will contact you when there are any updates."

"Copy that."

Chapter Sixteen

Kaleb pocketed his phone, leaned back in the chair, and stared up at the sky that currently looked like someone spilled a container of glitter. It never got old. The air smelled fresh, and there was a chorus of crickets and cicadas around him. It wasn't such a bad place to be.

"She's on the run?" The voice spilled from the darkness like the wind had spoken.

Kaleb flinched so badly Aurora dug her claws into his chest to hang on. "Shit, Ben. You nearly scared the life out of me." He appeared like a ghost, out of the blackness on his horse. Kaleb's mind immediately went into hyperdrive. *How did I not hear him? How much of the conversation did he hear?* "Where'd you come from?"

"I was checking on the animals. I knew that pile of bullshit you fed Kaysi about her being a college friend was a lie. What the hell have you gotten yourself into?"

"Nothing you need to worry about."

"Like hell. You aren't a stone's throw away from us. How do you expect me to protect Kaysi if I don't know what the hell is going on? And if you aren't willing to tell me, then you can pack up and get the hell out right now."

"Don't worry, Ben. I am on it. You're safe. We're safe. It's all good."

"So good you are asking about backup."

"How much of my conversation did you hear?"

Ben slid off his horse, Dash, and wandered over to the chair next to Kaleb. Breathing deep, he focused on the sky. "You know, I think you have some secrets you are keeping from your brother and sister and all your friends. I've suspected it for a while. All those trips you kept taking couldn't have all been business trips. And when Kaysi went missing, I overheard you on the phone calling in reinforcements, and I wondered then who you'd called."

Ben lifted his chin and turned his head, meeting Kaleb's eyes.

Kaleb could see the concern etched on Ben's face. "Ben. Trust me, you don't need to get involved. I've got it handled."

"Doesn't sound like it. Sounds like that little lady in there blew into town with a whole lot of trouble that she dropped on your doorstep. Now, whether she instigated it or not, I don't know. She obviously knew you from somewhere, or she wouldn't be here. The question is, where exactly? Is she part of this investigation you were talking about?"

Kaleb took a deep breath and let his head fall back onto the chair. He was so focused on Eden not catching wind of his conversation, that he didn't consider someone else overhearing him. "Ben, I—"

"You're family, Kaleb. Family helps family."

"So, tell me what you heard."

"Enough to suspect that you're not just my fiancée's goofy brother. And you're probably closer to what you told us at dinner yesterday. And if that's true, you better damn well come clean, because one, I need to know how dangerous you are. How many people are after you right now? How many people have you killed? And two, how the hell did you get your ass into that kind of work?"

Kaleb's eyes bore into Ben. What if he told him? He'd obviously overheard way too much of the conversation. And he was right; they were family. It could be several days before Quinten could get them into secured housing, and there was no back-up coming any time soon other than Ian. So, he really could use the help. Chances were good that whoever had ripped apart his house was hanging out in Dalton. If he was being honest, he had no idea what they were up against. Phillips' admission that he was concerned raised major red flags.

That being said, it was still his choice to join the agency and to risk his life. Not theirs. He needed to keep them safe.

Standing, he pushed open the door, set Aurora down, then closed it. His gaze locked on the concern in Ben's eyes. He searched his brain for some semblance of the truth without giving everything away and came up with nothing that Ben wouldn't see right through. There was too much going on in his head for him to even focus. "Are you sure you want to know the truth?"

Ben scratched his stubbly cheek. "Let me think—"

"Smartass. I don't know what my sister sees in you," Kaleb scoffed, but his smirk told the truth. Sitting, he leaned forward, letting his elbows rest on his knees, and stared at the worn wood and peeling paint beneath his feet. "I don't have anyone after me right now that I know of. Eden's a different story. As far as killing people? I don't like thinking about that, and you don't want that answer. My job was primarily fact finding. That doesn't mean I didn't get into some situations that warranted using force." His gut tightened thinking back to the missions he'd been on, and those he would rather forget.

Ben's expression never wavered, but his voice was a low growl. "Kaysi's never coming to your house again."

Kaleb raised a brow, wondering if Ben was being serious. He was such a hard read. He'd rather not pick a fight with the man, so he nodded and went on. "And as far as how I wound up in this line of work? It's kind of funny, but it happened in college. I was hired by a government agency to protect those who may pose a threat to national security and gather information when they went missing. While I was working a mission, I met Eden, and soon after that, she disappeared."

"You're a federal agent?"

"I *was* a federal agent. I left a couple of years ago."

"So, what is she doing here?"

"Right after she disappeared, I made the decision to leave the agency, but the case I was working on when I met Eden was still unsolved. Add to it, Eden's disappearance, which I felt somewhat responsible for, and I just couldn't abandon it. So, I told my boss I would work on the assignment until it was resolved."

"But she's no longer missing. Case closed."

"She wasn't the assignment. She was an add on. At the time, we didn't even know if the two were connected. Now, we do."

"So, what was the assignment?"

Kaleb knew he was treading into dangerous territory. Their missions were top secret for a reason. "Find a missing scientist."

"Okay. And this missing scientist is connected to your lady friend?"

Kaleb sat back in his rocking chair and

contemplated how much he should share. Since Ben had started dating Kaysi, he had become like a brother. He knew if he told him everything, his sister would know, and word would spread. But he also knew, those who would be told were his family. The people he trusted most. Every one of them would lay down their life for him and he would do the same. Letting out a deep breath, he began.

****

Ben's eyes widened. "She shot you?"

"Yeah. Her brother overheard one of the security guards name me as the assailant, and he told her, so she knew exactly who was after her. Or at least she thought she did. She hit me in the right side of my vest. It threw me off balance and down the stairs, which knocked me out. My partner pulled up right as it happened. I spent a day in the hospital in Montreal then flew back to Maryland. It would have been a whole different story if I hadn't had my vest on."

"Damn, Kaleb. So, now what?"

"As long as you're okay with it, we'll hang out here. It's remote enough that I think we're safe. My partner should be here in a couple of days, then we can come up with a plan."

"Seems like they hung you out to dry."

"The case was shelved a few months back. Leads had gone cold. Other cases needed to take precedence. Agents were moved to those assignments, so we are kind of in a holding pattern until some of the agents can get free."

"How long will that take?"

"Don't know. It kind of depends on the other cases."

"You and Eden are basically sitting ducks."

"I hope not. I'm hoping they won't be able to find us out here."

"Still, I'd feel better if—"

"Ben. The problem is, the more people I have get involved, the more blood I have on my hands. If anything were to happen to any of you, it would be my fault. I'm the one who chose this career and the risks involved. Not you, or anyone else."

"No matter how secret your life was, Kaleb, your family was never completely safe. You gotta know that. The only way you're going to keep them safe now, is to let them know what you're dealing with. You can't let them go into this blind. They deserve to know, so they can be prepared. And the more prepared we are, the easier it will be to protect you and Eden."

"It's not your battle to fight, though."

"Why don't you let us make that decision."

****

Eden sat on the sofa, with a feather dangling from a stick, letting Aurora bat at it. Kaleb barely spoke to her when he went inside after talking to Ben. He went straight to the bathroom to get a shower and think.

The squeak of the floor caused her to turn toward him, and her mouth betrayed her by dropping open.

It wasn't that he was unaware that women thought he was attractive. They were rather obvious sometimes. But there was something different about Eden. She wasn't into flattery. All her words and actions were genuine, like the stunned look on her face. His eyes dipped to her mouth again, and damn, her teeth were digging into the plump flesh causing his brain to misfire.

Droplets of water clung to his shaggy hair and cascaded down his bare chest, which made it hard to tug his T-shirt on. It was also a bit tight. Eden's eyes were still fixed on him when he got the shirt pulled down, and he fought a chuckle. After shaking his hair a couple of times, he threaded his fingers through it to get it out of his eyes. She finally returned her attention to the kitten, and started dangling the toy again, although Aurora had given up and was curled up asleep.

"Is she playing with it?" he asked as he walked to the sofa.

"She was. I think she likes it."

Pressing his hands on the back of the sofa, he leaned over. "Where did you get the T-shirt and pajama pants?"

"I'm betting the same place you got your sweats, since they hit your mid-calf and appear a bit tight in…" she motioned around his hips "that whole area." Drops of water from Kaleb's hair landed on Eden's arm and she tipped her eyes up to him. His white T-shirt was almost soaked through. "Did you even dry off?"

Kaleb took the opportunity to shake like a dog and scatter droplets everywhere. Aurora lifted her sleepy head and ran for cover behind Eden, who pushed against his damp chest to move them away from the splash zone. Kaleb chuckled as he stepped back and retrieved the air bed.

"I wonder why Ben left all the clothes in the chest."

"Probably his emergency stash when he gets in trouble with Kaysi." He slung the bag over his shoulder. "Speaking of Ben, remind me after I get the bed aired up, that I need to talk to you."

"What about?"

"Let me get this set up, and I will tell you."

Kaleb plodded up the hallway. The day was catching up to him. He still wasn't sure spilling his secrets to Ben was the right move. It felt like he added more weight to his shoulders instead of lightening the load like he'd hoped. And he had no idea how the rest would react if he let them in on what was going on.

Rolling the bed out on the floor, he plugged in the pump and watched it rise.

"Are you hungry?"

He peered over his shoulder and saw Eden leaning into the doorframe. The way the fuzzy Christmas themed pajama bottoms hugged her hips, and her breasts filled out the T-shirt she had knotted at her waist, had him clenching his teeth, so his mouth didn't hang open like hers had earlier. He repositioned, hoping she wouldn't catch on to the dilemma he had quickly happening down south, but by the smirk on her face he'd already been outed. He slid his focus back to the bed. "Is there anything here to eat?"

"There's plenty of beer in the fridge. Some freezer burnt meat that I think at one time was a roast, maybe. Don't think that's a good idea. I've found some mac n cheese in the pantry if you're interested. The good stuff, with the gooey cheese."

"I thought you were Miss Health Nut."

"My mom was the health nut. I was the rule follower. I like eating burgers and pizza like everyone else. And on occasion, I have eaten the good mac n cheese. You gotta do what you gotta do when you're a poor college student. And tonight, we have limited choices."

"Bachelor's kitchen. Most single men would rather grill, not cook."

"Here, definitely. Yours, on the other hand, was stocked like a professional chef's kitchen."

"Because I like to cook."

"You seemed like you were having fun. Honestly, I wasn't sure if it was genuine, or you were just putting on a show for my benefit because you thought I called you out."

"Maybe a little of both. But yeah, I enjoy it. My mom loves to cook, and she made sure to teach me some cultural dishes before I left home."

"Oh? What's her heritage?"

"Our family is Osage Indian."

"Really? That's very cool. What's your favorite dish?"

He scratched at the scruff on his cheek which reminded him he needed to shave. "Well, I do like to grill, so I would say I make a decent smoked salmon and frybread. It's actually something my grandma passed down."

"That sounds delicious."

"You're not getting it tonight. I'm game for mac n cheese though."

"Gotcha. But I'm calling raincheck on the other."

"Okay." He continued to inflate the bed, still feeling her eyes on him as she stood in the doorway, and he knew the moment she walked away. The lightness she brought to the room vanished, and the weight he felt returned. He was so tired.

When the bed was fully inflated, he made it up with the sheets Kaysi gave him, then lay on it to make sure it had enough air. Aurora appeared at the side of the bed, and he lifted her onto his chest. Her tiny claws dug in as she purred, and the quiet rhythmic noise calmed him. His eyes drifted closed.

Chapter Seventeen

"Kaleb?" The beautiful melodic voice drifted through the nothingness and called him back to life. Breathing deep, he opened his eyes to see Eden kneeling beside the bed staring at him. Her hand lifted from his shoulder and tucked her hair behind her ear. "Sorry to wake you. The mac n cheese is ready."

"Okay," he said roughly, still blinking through the fog.

"Are you okay?"

"I'm fine. It's been a long day."

"All right." Her voice was barely above a whisper, and something in her eyes bothered him. She moved to stand, but he latched onto her wrist, and she swayed before her body crashed into his. The hair she had tucked behind her ear dropped over her eyes. He gently tucked it back again, revealing an expression of sadness.

"I lay down to test out the mattress and fell asleep. I'm sorry if I worried you."

"It's okay."

"No, it's not. None of this is okay. I know it hasn't been easy, and it probably scares the shit out of you. I see you trying to put on a strong front, like nothing is wrong. You don't need to with me though. I'm not going to let anything happen to you. I promise." Her eyes searched his and quickly filled with tears.

"Who's going to protect you? You've already risked

your life trying to protect me, and I don't know what I would do if something happened to you. I was—"

"Nothing," his thumb wiped away the tears, "is going to happen to me. And if you think this is your fault, get it out of your head. It isn't."

He'd hoped his words would bring her some comfort, but the tears only came harder. He circled her with his arms and tugged her to him. God, he hated when she cried. Something within him broke every time, and he could feel his own eyes threatening to fill with tears. His lips met her temple, and the fresh powdery smell of her shampoo filled his nose. It was intoxicating and immediately ignited a need. Another kiss brushed her silky cheek, and she lifted her head, just enough for her tortured gaze to meet his for a brief second, before they dipped to his lips. That was the only invitation he needed.

Slowly closing his eyes, he tightened his arm around her and brushed his lips to hers. Guilt immediately washed over him, and he quickly backed away. He knew it was wrong to kiss her even before he stepped over the line. It was against protocol. But beyond that, she was fragile. The last thing he needed to be doing was making advances on her with everything going on in her life. But as tired as he was, and the feel of her in his arms, it was too much for his self-control. He'd been fighting the desire since she walked back into his life. Hell, probably since their breakfast chat at the pageant.

Opening his eyes, he could see her innocence behind the tear-filled lashes. Her earlier words whispered in his thoughts. *"My mom didn't allow me to date."* He backed away even more, then delicate fingers wrapped his cheek, and she pulled his mouth to hers.

In an instant his entire body became electrified.

Every place their bodies connected stung like pin pricks. His mind had been wiped of the chaos of their current situation. All that he was aware of was her and how perfectly plush her lips were as she pressed kiss after kiss against his.

Moving slowly, he brushed the seam of her lips with his tongue, relishing their softness, preparing, in case she granted him entry. Her palm gently caressed his cheek as her fingers tangled in his curly mess, then she jolted back suddenly, breaking the spell and sending a knot of panic to his gut, until he heard a tiny squeak, and Aurora's furry head appeared at her shoulder.

"What the hell, Aurora?" He had to chuckle when she squeaked at his scolding. Eden laughed, so he figured he'd forgive her this time. Anything to see that beautiful smile that made Eden's eyes light up back in place.

She grabbed the kitten and held her up, trying to give her a scowl, and failing horribly. Her eyes shifted to his. "Are you hungry? The mac n cheese is getting cold."

He let out a disappointed sigh. She leaned in and gave him a light kiss on the side of his mouth, then backed off the bed and disappeared up the hall. Kaleb sat up and tried to stand, but the bed gave with the weight of his body. Awkwardly, he leaned forward and rose to his full height and stretched, then shuffled to the kitchen, continuing to taste her on his lips.

Eden set out some plastic bowls and cups along with a couple of printed napkins. "I'm going for rustic chic. How'd I do?"

Kaleb chuckled. Her southern raising was peeking out, and he found it adorable. He liked it much better than her proper pageant dialect. "Wonderful ambiance."

He filled Aurora's dish with some food, since she

didn't get to eat earlier, before he scooped up a helping of dinner and sat down across from Eden. She'd pulled her hair up in a messy bun and reached up, fiddling with it.

"Stop."

"Stop what?"

"Playing with your hair. You look amazing."

"Right," she scoffed.

"No. You do. You look comfortable. Relaxed."

She glanced at her noodles then peered at him from below her lashes, and the hint of a smile bloomed on her face. Kaleb's heart faltered. He wasn't lying. She did look amazing. The tortured expression that haunted her features earlier had faded and was replaced with something Kaleb hadn't seen before. Her dark chocolate-colored eyes were almost black beneath her long lashes. Her cheeks were a light crimson, and her teeth dug into the corner of her lip with a smile that held a mischievousness. Or was it desire? Did she like the kiss? She didn't pull away. At least, not until Aurora interrupted them. Just the thought had his pulse pounding.

"Not discounting anything that has happened, but right here, right now, I'm not too bad. So, I hate to ask, because I'm sure it will alter my contentment, but what's next? You said you had something to tell me."

Kaleb's thoughts quickly shifted to the conversations he had with Quinten and Ben. He knew her beautiful smile would disappear. Nothing about either of the conversations was going to make her happy. There was no way he could keep it from her though.

"I talked to Quinten. He's got some of the agents and ancillary teams out on different assignments, so we are going to need to stay here." Eden nodded, and the smile didn't fade. Unfortunately, that was the easy part. "Also, while you were in the shower Ben came by. He overheard my conversation with Quinten, and I had to fill him in on what was going on."

Her eyes darted. "He knows you're a, a…spy?"

Kaleb chuckled at her covert whispered comment. "An undercover agent."

"Again. Tomato tomahto. Call it what you will. He knows?"

"Yes. And he thinks it would be best to give everyone I'm close to a heads up. This involves you as much as it does me, so I need to know what you're comfortable with me sharing."

"What did he hear? I'm guessing he knows I'm not here to interview for the bar?"

"Yeah. We didn't sell that as well as I thought we did. Still thought it was a great story."

"Thank you."

"But he said he knew something was up anyway, and when he was on his way back from checking on the animals, he overheard my conversation with Quinten."

Eden sat back in her chair. "That was what that glare was for."

"Excuse me?"

"When we got ready to leave, Ben shot me this look, like he was angry with me."

"Honestly, that's just Ben. He basically wears a permanent scowl. And trust me, there have been times I've wanted to take his head off, but Kaysi loves him, and he follows her around like an adoring puppy. You watch, within the next couple of weeks, that leather furniture will be sitting in their living room."

"They make a cute couple," Eden said donning a smile that Kaleb knew was just for his benefit.

"I'm sorry about this. I know it's probably not something you were ready to divulge—"

"No. It's not that. It's the idea of bringing others into something I don't even have a good grasp on. I understand where Ben's coming from, and I agree with him. Your family needs to know about what we are involved in. Whoever it is that is after me probably now knows that was your home. So, I'm sure they are trying to find every detail on you. Which means, they will know who your family is, and where they are."

"Good point. I told Ben I would call him tomorrow, and we could set up a time to get together."

"Was there anything else? Did Quinten get a chance to go through the papers?"

"Yeah," he said on a deep sigh, "He did." Swallowing hard, he tried to come up with the best way to share the information since it was going to be difficult for her to hear.

She sat back in her chair and crossed her arms. "I see your wheels turning. Don't try to sugar coat it for me."

The chair squeaked as he tried to get more comfortable. God, he hated doing this. "Quinten thinks you were somehow being used in your father's research. With all the medical reports, that's the only plausible answer."

She dropped her eyes to her hand and picked at her cuticle. Her mouth twitched and moved. Her eyes lifted slightly, and she swallowed. He could see her quickly trying to apply the coat of armor she hid behind. But she was failing.

Her lips pursed and one tear slowly trickled down her cheek. Kaleb reached over and grabbed her hand. She lifted the corner of her mouth. Her lips quivering as she fought back the tears. When her fight was gone and the tears flowed freely, he stood, pulling her up with him. His arms wrapped around her. "I'm sorry. I shouldn't have just blurted it out. I didn't mean to make you cry. Talk to me."

His hand rubbed against her back, and he pressed a gentle kiss into her hair.

"He's right," she whispered.

"Who? Quinten?"

Eden nodded and lifted her head to meet his gaze. "It all fits." She slowly stepped out of his embrace and cast her eyes to the floor.

"What fits?"

"You may not have gotten a good look at the documents. There is no reason anyone, even a parent, should have that much medical information on their kid, unless the kid is sick or it's for research. Some of those medical papers didn't make any sense to me, so I'm sure they had something to do with the research." Her eyes searched, and more tears came. "Oh my God, Kaleb. My mom…my mom…What if the stuff she did to me was for research?"

"Like what?"

"Remember me telling you how hard she pushed me," she said, glancing back his way. "It was like I could never quite meet her expectations, like she was pushing to see how much I could handle, before I would break. I had to be the smartest, most talented, most athletic. And if I wasn't, she would add to my lessons. There was no praise for doing well. No proud mom moment.

No…love.

"She wasn't necessarily mean, but she wasn't affectionate." Her words faded back into a whisper as she spoke, and her eyes finally lifted to capture his.

The more Eden talked about her mom, the more he hated her and what she did to Eden. Who would treat their kid like that?

"Adam said his mom also pushed him, but they were close. I don't know about Eva, other than what was in her paperwork." She paused, and Kaleb was about to speak when she continued. "Why, though? Did he say what he thought it was for?"

"No. I don't think he knows. He wants us to try to get into some of the chat groups on the website, to see if there are any possible clues. There may be some key words that play into who is invited into the different groups. Do you remember anything about what happened?"

"Not much. There was a post about all the dangerous viruses that had recently appeared. Some studies and articles that were posted caught my eye, because I had taken a class on infectious diseases. I commented about genetic immunities and building your immune system naturally."

"What does that even mean, natural and genetic immunities?"

"Natural immunity happens when you're exposed to a virus or illness and your body builds immunities, sometimes without you ever feeling sick. Genetic immunity is when something within your makeup makes you immune to a disease. You can be exposed repeatedly, and you never get it."

"Like you don't need the vaccine?"

"No."

"Dang. That would be cool. I hate shots." That got a small chuckle out of her, and he was thankful for the glimmer of hope.

"Do you want me to try and find the post?"

"Later. We'll have to come up with new usernames. It shouldn't be hard to get back in. I'll spoof the IP to keep us from getting tracked. But not now. It's late."

Chapter Eighteen

Eden tried to stay focused on what Kaleb was saying, tried to stay engaged, but her mind was firing off so many thoughts all at once, she felt like she was going to pass out. Her entire evening had been filled with thoughts of him. The expression on his face, when she found him staring at her after she woke up, like he wanted to eat her alive, flashed through her thoughts, and then the completely tranquil look he had when he was sleeping. God, even when he slept he was gorgeous. His mouth was slightly open, and it took everything within her not to put her lips on his, just to see what he felt like. And when she woke him, his dark lashes parted and he studied her, questioning. His eyes held something she couldn't put her finger on, but somehow it gave her hope. And then it happened. The kiss. That moment that would forever brand her heart and her lips.

Now though, all the moments that made her heart tumble were overshadowed. They waged war with the words that threatened to filet her heart completely to pieces.

The idea that her mom was a willing participant made her sick to her stomach. Her whole life, she'd tried to be perfect; meet all her mom's expectations; make the grades; win the games; learn the routines or pieces of music. Or parade around in a bikini, in front of leering eyes, only to be met with criticism.

To know it might have all been for research wasn't only confusing, it was humiliating. She wasn't performing for her mom's lofty desires, but some demented science experiment, like she was nothing more than a glorified lab rat. It made her feel like she was somehow less than human. If Adam's mom hadn't been killed, would she have ever known?

Every piece of her life was quickly fading into a transparent fog of uncertainty. She had no idea what was real. Who was she really?

"Eden?" She lifted her gaze, and Kaleb's concerned expression stared back at her. How long had she been washing the pot in her hand. She ran it under the water and set it on the towel.

"I'm sorry. I'm still trying to process everything."

"Don't apologize. It's a lot. I know."

"I just wish I knew why." She ran the lid under the water and set it next to the pot on the towel. Her life played out in her mind, flipping through one event after another, and she couldn't keep the tears at bay, realizing that all the effort she put into trying to please her mom was a waste of time.

Kaleb plucked the rag from her hand, set it across the faucet, then dragged her to him. "Don't go there. I can see it on your face. It's not worth it."

His arm snaked around her back, and his other hand dug into her thick hair and pressed her head to his chest. The way he gently cradled her made the tears come harder. No one had ever comforted her, or cared for her, like he did every time she lost it. And it had been a lot the past couple of days.

Overwhelmed and scared, she questioned every decision she'd made. Her thoughts and emotions were a jumbled mess. She'd always prided herself on how she'd mastered the impenetrable, porcelain doll image she portrayed. The epitome of poise, she could field any question with quick, decisive answers, and remain in complete control of her emotions.

And yet, with Kaleb, no matter how hard she tried to hide from him, he saw her for who she truly was, the scared, hurt, and overwhelmed little girl. By now, she figured he would have had enough and sent her packing. But here he was, treating her like she was some kind of precious treasure. His hand stroked her hair, and his lips tenderly pressed to the crown of her head. Was this what being loved felt like?

"I tried so hard to please her and—"

"Shhh. She's not worth your tears."

"She's all I had. I wasted twenty-two years of my life trying to do everything right...for nothing." The more she compared the way Kaleb treated her to her mom, the angrier she became. Finally, the rage simmering in her gut erupted, and she twisted out of Kaleb's arms. "I hate her!" Wrapping her arms around her waist, she let the fury spew from her. "You're supposed to love your kid." Her tear-filled eyes slid to Kaleb, who was helplessly watching her breakdown. Her chest tightened, and her breaths became labored. "Who the hell uses their healthy kid for research?" Her body shook uncontrollably. Tears streamed down her face. "Did she get paid for the research? Was that why she did it? For the money? Was I a means to a comfortable living?" she questioned with a sardonic edge.

Kaleb reached out. "Eden, please. Don't torture yourself over this woman."

As she paced, consumed by memories, her legs

started to feel unstable, but she kept going. "How much was I worth? A hundred thousand? Two? Or maybe, I was a bargain at fifteen grand." The world started spinning around her, and she couldn't quite get enough air. She'd had panic attacks before, and she knew she was moments away. "I just wanted her to love me. I just wanted to feel…wanted." Kaleb reached for her as she stumbled, but she didn't take his hand, so he lunged forward, latching onto her wrist and cocooning her within his arms.

She collapsed and let him hold her full weight.

"You are wanted…and needed. More than you know."

"Sure. Maybe as a lab experiment." She hiccupped the words as the painful sobs spilled out of her, leaving her gasping. Kaleb picked her up, cradling her like a baby, and carried her to the sofa.

He tucked her into him, snuggling her against his chest as he confessed quietly, "No, Eden. By me."

His body slowly began to rock. "I got you. Focus on taking some deep breaths." His lips brushed against her temple and tenderly pressed into her hair, and he quietly hummed as she tried to steady her breath and regain her composure.

With each kiss, each sweet note he hummed, it was like he was somehow erasing the dark thoughts one by one. Focusing on the melody of the music, she let it work its magic. The pain that had consumed her moments before subsided. Her breathing evened out, and she settled into him, letting his warmth surround her. After several minutes, she asked, "What song is that?"

"There When You Fall."

"I don't think I know that song," she whispered, her

throat feeling raw.

"It's by Tailgate Party."

"Can you sing it for me?"

"No. That's not happening," he said, with a soft chuckle.

"Why? You have a great voice."

"I'll play it for you sometime."

Slowly, she sat up. Kaleb cupped one cheek and wiped the tears with his thumb as she wiped the other. His eyes were glassy when she finally lifted her gaze to his, and guilt again flooded in. *He doesn't deserve all this.* "Kaleb, I'm—"

"What kind of music do you like?"

She tilted her head, wondering if he was trying to distract her or if he really wanted to know. "It kind of depends on my mood. Recently, I've been listening to some of the new country music."

Kaleb's eyebrow arched. "Country?" he questioned with humor. "I honestly didn't peg you as a country girl."

"What do you listen to?"

"You heard some of it when we were making breakfast."

Her mind drifted to him dancing and singing, dressed in his red sweats and the apron with Aurora snuggled in the pocket. The corner of her mouth tipped up, thinking about how comfortable she was with him.

She hadn't felt that comfortable in her own skin before. No make-up. She'd barely ran a comb through her hair, and yet every time she peeked at him while she was cooking, he was staring at her like she was a big slice of chocolate cake. For a moment she wondered if every morning would be like that with him.

It was so odd. He had so much energy and this

wistfulness about him, yet all that energy had a way of making her feel strangely peaceful.

"I tend to stay mainstream, and maybe throw in some southern rock."

She barely comprehended his comment and had to repeat it back in her head. "No country?"

"Very little. They're all too sad for me. I don't like the tears in my beer cuz someone kicked my dog songs."

A light giggle escaped at his exaggerated southern drawl, and little by little his distraction was working. Music always did. "You need to listen to some of the new songs like…" her mind shuffled through the artists she loved. "Like…"

"See. You can't come up with one that isn't sad."

"Give me a—"

Her words were cut off with a kiss, completely catching her off guard. Not that she hadn't thought about their previous kiss a million times by now, but in that moment, her mind was still working through her playlist, so her body stiffened. And by the way Kaleb quickly backed away, he must have felt it.

Red flooded his tanned cheeks, and he started to speak, but she knew what he was about to say by the uncertainty on his face. "I'm—"

"Don't." She put her finger to his lips to stop him. "Don't apologize. It just surprised me." She moved to her knees to face him and pressed her lips to his cheek, then another to his jaw, then whispered, "I love it when you kiss me."

"Oh good." The nervous laughter in his voice had her raising up and taking in his boyish grin. "I was beginning to wonder." Still smiling, he lifted his chin and captured her lips again. His hand wrapped the back of her neck as his fingers caressed her hair, and he gently moved her head to deepen the kiss. She gladly let him. Their tongues didn't battle; it was more like a well-choreographed dance. There was no awkwardness, no effort. It was all a give and take in perfect sync.

He let out a growl that vibrated through her and set her skin on fire. No one had ever made her feel so wanted, so cherished.

Every sweep of his tongue was filled with tenderness, building a storm of desire that had her body begging for more. His fingers massaged her hair, and she slid closer, hoping he would take the hint, but he continued slowly savoring her, then with one last brush of his lips to her mouth, he backed away, leaning his forehead to hers. "I'm glad you love it when I kiss you, because it's quickly becoming one of my favorite things to do," he said breathlessly.

"Then, then why'd you stop?" Even to her ears, she sounded desperate, and an inferno burst from every pore of her body.

"Oh, if you only knew," he said with a strained breath, and squeezed his eyes shut. She wondered if he wasn't expecting those words to escape.

"What do I need to know?" The tinge of frustration and confusion in her voice had Kaleb's brow drawing together. All the boyish joy evaporated.

His hand reached up and brushed the hair from her face. "I had to."

"Why?"

Grasping her hand, he brought her fingers to his lips and kissed them. "Because if I hadn't, I wouldn't have been able to stop myself from taking it farther, and that's not what you need right now."

"What if it's what I want?"

"It's what I want too. Trust me, stopping was about the hardest thing I've ever had to do." He raised up, and just the small distance he added between them felt like a mile. "But I can't do that to you, Eden. We are both too keyed up. You're hurting, and I want to be here for you," he pulled her into his arms again, "to hold you and give you whatever you need. But not that. It would just be an emotional release right now. Okay? I would feel like I was taking advantage of you. And that's the last thing I want to do."

Studying his face, she remained silent, letting his words sink in. He was right. She was so overwhelmed she couldn't even think straight. He was having to protect her from herself. She swallowed trying to dislodge the boulder settling in her throat.

His eyes shifted, and a little bit of the boyish smirk he had the first time she laid eyes on him reappeared. And in that one moment, she knew beyond a shadow of a doubt she was treading into dangerously deep waters.

She never believed in love at first sight, but now she wasn't sure. Thinking back to the moment she heard the crash of the sign at the preliminaries, her heart stumbled when their eyes met. She remained stoic, emotionless, until a sheepish grin filled his face, making his sky-blue eyes twinkle. It ripped apart every shred of control she had. She had never been so captivated by anyone.

Even when she thought he'd betrayed her, she didn't want to believe it. She couldn't. He still held her heart captive. Adam and Bill thought she was just traumatized by the attempted abduction when she couldn't stop crying on the airplane. That was only part of it. The thought of what she'd done to him ripped her heart from her chest and felt like she'd lost a part of herself. She cried for him, and because of him, for what he might have done to her, and what he made her do to him.

Now though, after experiencing what it might be like to be wanted by him, a realization set in. He would protect her at all costs. She'd thought about it earlier, when he said he'd protect her, how selfish it was of her to put him and his family and friends in danger. Now more than ever she knew she wasn't worth it. She didn't deserve what he was willing to give her.

It had been a huge mistake to search for him. As devastated as she was when she thought she'd killed him, it would be even more if he sacrificed himself to protect her.

A knot settled in her stomach as dread took hold. She had to let him go. And she needed to do it now, because the longer she stuck around the harder it would be.

She sat up and brushed the hair from her face. Taking a shaky breath, she closed her eyes and let the words fall before she chickened out. "I need to leave."

"Leave? To do what?" Concern immediately filled his voice and had her swallowing the prickly boulder that was now firmly implanted in her throat.

Her eyes met his and immediately filled with tears. Biting her lip, trying to stave off the onslaught she knew was coming, she shook her head and whispered, "I-I can't stay here with you." Backing away, she added, "I should have never come; never dragged you, and now your family into this. I don't think I could live with myself if anything were to happen to you or your family."

Kaleb sat up more and gently tried to move her

around to face him. She knew making eye contact would only break her heart more than it was already, so she fought him, even though it was almost laughable against his strength. His knuckle wiped away her tears and then he growled, "Look at me." The sobs burst from her, and she covered her eyes.

He held firm as she moved to stand, throwing her off enough that she opened her eyes, then quickly slammed them shut again. His finger pushed her chin up. "I will sit here all night, Eden."

She finally lifted her watery gaze, and warm tears blazed a trail down her cheeks once again. It seemed crying was all she was capable of doing now.

"You didn't drag me into anything." She couldn't stand the sadness in his eyes, and her focus moved to the fireplace across from them. "If you will stop and think for a second, I was already on the mission to find Victor Chalemaare when we met. And I'll still be working that assignment whether you leave or not. But to be clear, you're not leaving. That's not happening. I will arrest you if I have to."

"Arrest me?"

"You shot a federal agent. You don't think that carries a punishment?"

"You wouldn't do that."

"Try me. I will not lose you a second time."

Eden's head whipped back to him at his words. Her response was barely audible. "Lose me?"

"Yes. Lose you. I know it sounds crazy, but the minute I laid eyes on you, it was like everything came into focus. The more I was with you, the more I needed to be with you. By the time the pageant ended, I was trying to come up with ways to see you again.

"When I saw you on the tarmac, I thought you were walking into a trap. I had no clue what you'd been told or what they were going to do to you. I was panicked. My mind played through every worst-case scenario imaginable. And when I got back to the states, I would not let myself believe you were gone. I followed up every possible lead, even if it was a long shot. And when I saw you that day in the park, I was so relieved that you were alive I could hardly breathe. I know I barely know you. But it doesn't seem like it."

Funny. That's exactly how she felt.

Chapter Nineteen

It was well past midnight when they headed to their respective bedrooms. Kaleb was drained both physically and emotionally, and it took everything in his power not to follow her into the bedroom, crawl in next to her, and pull her against him. But he knew where it would lead, and he meant what he'd told Eden. As much as he wanted her, she didn't need that in the state she was in. So fragile. Instead, he let her take Aurora, after she argued that she had more room. She was worming her way into his psyche. He couldn't make himself tell her no. Lucky cat.

With most women, no matter how beautiful they were or how well they held a conversation, he was able to keep himself closed off. He would be polite and charming, but at the end of the day, they were simply an acquaintance. Even those who were elusive, who were fun to chase, and gave him a challenge, didn't hold his interest for long.

Eden was different. He was comfortable with her. Even when he found her in the park and had his guard up, the moment she spoke, he felt his whole body relax. It was like walking into his childhood home.

From the first time they met, there was an almost tangible force that drew him to her. And the more he was around her, the more she piqued his interest. She was beautiful, yes, but she was so much more. She had so many facets, and he felt like he'd only skimmed the surface.

Yanking his T-shirt over his head, he dropped it on the floor then plopped on the edge of the bed to shuck his warmups. The bed immediately folded around him, and he fell backward as it continued to give way. "Damn it." Reaching up, he plugged the pump back in and had a sinking feeling he knew where this all would lead. Once the bed was inflated again, he reattached the fitted sheet, yanked his pants off, and climbed in, hoping the exhaustion would quickly consume him before the bed did. Breathing deep, he closed his eyes and tried to clear his mind of the chaos. And as his body relaxed, his thoughts drifted to visions of her.

****

Reaching for his phone, Kaleb was blinded by its light as he clicked it on. It was four in the morning. So much for sleeping. It was the third time the bed had tried to smother him. He let out a defeated breath and rolled over, trying to escape the suffocating confines, only to get tangled in the sheets that had come untucked and wrapped around him.

Dragging the blanket from the sea of bedding, he slowly stood and wandered out to the living room. A crocheted pillow sat in the recliner, so he tossed it on the sofa and lay down. It was lumpy, and his feet hung over the arm, but he figured it beat sleeping on the floor. Not by much though.

****

Pin pricks of pain radiated up his stomach and chest. The silence gave way to a murmur, then a squeak, as he returned from his comatose state. His nose filled with a buttery scent, and he finally lifted his heavy eye lids to see his cream-colored fur ball staring at him. Her little paws kneaded his left pec, and she let out another squeaky meow. His large hand wrapped around her as he sat up. A moment passed as his senses began to respond, and a sweet melody had his head turning toward the kitchen. His eyes locked on the beautiful creature that had been in his dreams and nightmares for the past two years. Eden swayed as she sang softly "love so hard you feel like you're flying..." unaware she was being watched. Though the lyrics didn't sound familiar, her voice was smooth as melted caramel. Every time he heard her sing, it brought tears to his eyes. This time was no different. And now, he noticed an ease about her that she didn't have when he confronted her days ago.

Her hair was pulled half up with large chunks hanging loose, framing her face. Her raspberry-colored lips were still moving, even though she'd gone silent as she focused on the meal she was creating. The pajama pants she borrowed swallowed her, but she had them cinched so they sat on her hips, and the T-shirt was tied to where it lay tight against her ribs, leaving her belly on full display. A very taught belly that was adorned with a purple crystal crown in her belly button the last time he caught a glimpse of it. The colorful tattoo peeked out slightly from beneath the shirt.

Smelling the distinct scent of bacon, he realized the sound he'd thought was running water when he woke was bacon frying. Bacon that was not in the refrigerator last he checked. Had she gone to the store? What time was it? He tried to stand and quickly realized the lower half of his legs were asleep. Different sleeping arrangements needed to be made if they were spending another night in the house.

He cleared his throat. "Hey," he rasped, getting her attention.

"Oh. Hey. I didn't wake you, did I? I was trying to be quiet."

"No. Aurora was trying to do some sort of acupuncture on me." Finally getting the feeling back in his feet, he stood and slowly shuffled to the kitchen. "Smells amazing. Where'd you get the food?"

"I got hungry, so I knocked on Ben and Kaysi's door."

Dragging his fingers through his messy curls, he asked, "What time is it?"

Eden turned to check the clock on the microwave and Kaleb's eyes tracked hers. "Nearly nine."

"Wow! Okay. That late. And yet I feel like I haven't slept at all."

"I was surprised to see you on the sofa. Was the bed not comfortable?"

"The bed was great until it tried to murder me. And after the third time of waking up on the floor with the sheets and rubber wrapped around me, I decided to cut my losses."

"You can have the bed tonight. I can sleep out here."

"No. I'll get something figured out."

"I bet if I asked Kaysi would let us stay with them."

"No. I love my sister, but no."

"Or I could sleep over there and you could have the bed."

"No. I'd feel better if I had you here, where I can keep you safe."

"I wouldn't be that far away. And Ben and Kaysi would be there."

"I don't want to drag my family into this any more

than they already are."

"Oh. Speaking of which. You might want to go ahead and eat and get dressed. Everyone is showing up here in about thirty minutes."

****

And they just kept coming. Every time he'd shut the door behind someone, another would push it open. Probably wasn't the best idea of Ben's to send everyone to a house that had limited places to sit. Not only were his brother and sister there, his friends, along with all their significant others, and even a representative of the local law enforcement were also. Did he really want to do this?

"Dad's at work, so you will have to explain whatever this is that Ben felt the need to gather us all together to him later." It was still weird hearing his brother, Joe, calling their dad, Dad. It hadn't been that long ago when their worlds collided, and Joe was dropped into their lives. "What is going on anyway?"

Kaleb's eyes scanned the faces of the people he'd grown to love. Some who'd been a part of his life since he was little, and others since he returned from college, broken and hiding secrets he thought he'd never reveal. He was wrong. It was time for him to come clean.

Eden snuggled up beside him, cradling Aurora against her chest. And like he did while she gave her statement, she threaded her fingers through his, releasing her energy into him. The warmth of her chocolate-brown eyes calmed his racing pulse.

"Everyone, this is Eden," he began, keeping his eyes fixed on hers. "I met her at a pageant two years ago," his gaze finally moved to his audience, "when I was on an undercover assignment."

"Assignment for college?" Joe questioned.

"No. While I was working as a federal agent with homeland security."

Joe's hand flew up. "Whoa, whoa, whoa, wait. Back up. Undercover...federal...you're a spy?"

"I would like to go on record to say I called it first," Brant interrupted.

Kaleb slow clapped, then rolled his eyes. "We are called undercover agents."

"I knew you couldn't have been that good of a shot without having some experience," Cody added.

"And you've been doing this how long?" Joe continued to question, his voice still filled with confusion.

"I was hired when I was like eighteen or nineteen. They showed up on career day at the university."

"You gotta be shittin' me. Like set up a table and said, 'Hey, want to come work for us as a spy?' " Mitch chimed in.

"Exactly."

Joe's eyes widened. "Jesus. Well, that explains a lot."

"What do you mean?"

"Your ability to shoot. Your place that lights up like Fort Knox when it gets dark. Your crazy skills on the computer. You taking off in the company jet, and now the helicopter, all the time. I was getting worried you were out in Vegas blowing your trust fund."

"Some of those trips were a mix of business and pleasure. Most though, were company related. Oil and gas, I won't lie though, a few were to follow leads on the case involving Eden that needed to be addressed immediately."

Kaleb began laying out what little information he could give pertinent to the investigation. Enough to satisfy their curiosity and keep everyone safe, but not enough to compromise the case itself. When he finished, he met the eyes of each person, wondering what their response would be. Joe pushed off the wall and strode toward him. Kaleb braced when his arms lifted from his side. As easy going as he usually was, he still hadn't quite gotten used to Joe's hugs. Every time he hugged him, it felt like a volcano erupted in his chest, and it was hard to keep the emotions from spewing everywhere.

Joe's massive arms enveloped him, and he squeezed a little too hard, then leaned down and growled low enough where no one else could hear, "At some point I'm going to kick your ass for doing this, especially to Mom and Dad, but right now, I'm here for you. Whatever you and Eden need, I've got your back, baby brother." That's all it took, and he could feel the warm wet tears slide down his cheek. Damn him. "You know that, right?" Kaleb could only nod. "You're crying, aren't you?" Kaleb shook his head. "Bullshit." Joe chuckled, which had Kaleb doing the same.

"Do you have a description of any of the suspects?" Mitch's voice had the pair giving each other a hard pat then breaking apart. As discreetly as possible, Kaleb wiped his eyes, then his gaze met Mitch's, and he shook his head.

"They were smart enough to take out the security cameras and lights."

"So, you're saying they aren't amateurs," Brant added.

"Not in the least bit. But I wouldn't expect them to be. Victor Chalemaare, the scientist who is missing, is considered one of the most brilliant individuals in the world. He has won accolades throughout the world for his genetic research and is one of the creators of a highly acclaimed think tank website that gathers exceptionally intelligent people in all different areas. We've been working this case for two years and haven't gotten very far, until now. Whoever is behind this, whether it's Victor or someone else, has the best working with them.

"My team hasn't been able to hack into his website, and we have access to some of the most cutting-edge technology out there. Plus, it's not like we are slouches at Summit Securities. You have to be MENSA qualified to be accepted."

Chapter Twenty

Mitch crossed his arms over his chest. "So, what you've shared is all we have to go on."

"It's all I can give you right now. The information is classified. Telling you this much is already a breach. I'm going to get onto the website this afternoon and see if I can gain access to any of their private group chats. I honestly think it holds the key to this entire case."

"Let me have the link, and I will get my guys on it in Little Rock too."

"Get with me before you leave, Mitch, and I will write it down." Kaleb dug his hands into the pockets of his jeans. "I guess that's it. You've got the whole story. Or at least all I can tell you."

"Oh, that's far from it," Cody chimed in. "We need to come up with a plan. No matter how safe you think this place is, you can't stay holed up here forever. Since we all have places we need to be, let's figure out a time this evening we can meet back up."

"My shift is done, so I'm good with whatever," Brant quickly responded.

"Can we do seven?" Cody continued.

Everyone nodded.

Kaleb felt uneasy with the direction the discussion was going. "Guys I appreciate…everything. However, this meeting was to let you know what was going on, to keep you safe, not get you involved. It's against company pol—"

"Well, it's happening. We don't let family fight battles on their own." Joe's eyes narrowed. "You should know that by now."

"I'll get my guys over to your place to search it. See if we can get any prints and do a sweep for devices," Mitch stated.

"What about us?" Jenna piped up. "What can we do?"

"One thing I need you to do is check out Aurora. We found her in the bushes by the house. She seems okay. We got her some soft food, and she's eating it fine." Jenna scooped up Aurora from Eden's arms and sat down in a chair to examine her.

"Ben, can you get with your dad to make sure the gate gets secured when we leave?" Kaleb's eyes swung to Mitch's voice, then April laid her hand on his shoulder.

"Until they get things cleared over there, where you can at least retrieve some stuff, you're going to need to hang out here, and that means you guys need some supplies," April stated. "You said you guys only came with a change of clothes, right?"

"Yeah, I'll give him a call. He should be back up at the house by now. If he doesn't answer, I'll make sure it gets done."

"How about when we get off work, Bekah, Jessi, and I run to the store for groceries, and you and Kaysi shop for clothes?" Jenna suggested.

"Good idea and—"

Conversations were buzzing all around him, and he felt like his head was going to spin right off his neck. "You guys don't—" He tried to cut in but realized it was a waste of words when it came to April. When she set her mind to something, it was going to happen.

April added, "That will give us girls something to do while you guys handle the man talk."

"What about Eden?" Kaysi chimed in.

"She's coming with us," April exclaimed.

"I don't—"

"You're coming with us."

Eden's gaze questioned as it landed on Kaleb, then it was April's, daring him to confront her, until Eden ended the who blinked first competition. "I think I better stay here," she said in a quiet voice, and Kaleb could hear it shaking.

"Okay," April chirped, obviously trying to lighten the conversation. "You're about Bekah's size, so we'll go shopping, and if we can't find anything, we'll raid her closet. As you can see, she has fabulous taste."

"I don't have that much money. I—"

"Shut up and let us help."

Jenna stood and handed Aurora back to Eden. "She seems to be in good shape. I'd bring her in in a couple of weeks to start her on her vaccinations."

"Okay. The plan right now is to reconvene here at seven," Cody broke in.

"Let's meet at the bunkhouse," Ben quickly suggested.

"Okay. I need to get back. Seven at the bunkhouse. Anything else?" Mitch questioned.

The group started moving around, and Kaleb met his eyes and shook his head. Mitch turned and grabbed Jessi's arm as she stood. "You good?"

"I'm fine." She rubbed her hand over her barely visible baby belly and squeezed in closer to him. He laid his hand on top of hers. Her head twitched. "Did you feel her?" She quickly moved her hand and placed his on her stomach. "She kicked." His eyes locked with hers, and a smile lit up his face. "There." The smile was replaced with a grin.

Jenna's mouth dropped open. "Oh my gosh. Did you say 'her?' Are you guys having a girl?"

"Yes. We found out yesterday." Jessi bounced on her toes, unable to contain her excitement.

"Another little Georgia girl," Bekah added.

Mitch rolled his eyes. "Lord, I hope not."

Jessi backhanded him. "Mitch."

"Love her to death, babe. You know that. But one of her is all I can handle. Two would send me to an early grave."

Cody moved over to the bar. "I'm putting us all on a group text." Within minutes all of phones began to buzz. Kaleb's chimed and buzzed, and he jerked in confusion, then slid his phone out of his pocket. It chimed again, and a number he didn't recognize lit up. A burn filled his chest and moved into his gut as his pulse ticked up. His eyes darted to all the faces in the room, and he moved out of earshot as he clicked the button.

"Hello?"

"Hey," a sweet female voice chirped. Kaleb wracked his brain to figure out if it sounded familiar. It didn't. Was it someone he'd dated? Why in the hell were they calling? This was the last thing he needed. He didn't want to be rude, but what could he say that wouldn't give him away. His inner dialogue was interrupted when she let him off the hook.

"This is Marissa Bellamy. Brant's friend?"

His eyes closed, thanking God that he didn't have to

fake knowing the woman on the phone. "Miss Bellamy." He cleared his throat and called on his professional voice. "Good to hear from you."

"Well, it's Monday, and I love a good steak as much as anybody, however I'm getting tired of smelling like one."

Kaleb chuckled at her comment. "So, I'm guessing you're ready to interview at Grayeagle?"

"Yes, I am. I already filled out the online application."

"When would you like to come in?"

"I was hoping we could schedule something tomorrow afternoon. I'm off work."

"I already have a full schedule, so I will need to pass you off to Malcolm. He's part of my team. Are you okay with that?"

"I'm good with whatever you need me to be good with as long as I get a chance to interview."

"All right. Let's say one o'clock? I'll check with him and text you the confirmation. Sound good?"

"Sounds great."

"Perfect. Talk to you soon."

He dropped her call and clicked on Malcolm's number. It rang several times before Malcolm answered.

"Yes?" Malcolm barked.

That wasn't the response Kaleb expected out of him. He was always professional and composed. It immediately had Kaleb concerned. "Everything okay?"

It took a minute for Malcolm to respond. "Forgive me. I'm…I'm buried up to my ass in this environmental research audit. It's going to take forever to get through it. When you come in tomorrow, we need to sit down and figure out the best strategy to tackle this. I'll be glad when we get some help, because there is way more here than I was expecting."

Kaleb took a deep breath. He hated that he was dumping everything on Malcolm. He'd already left him high and dry today and was about to turn it into indefinitely. He hadn't even had the opportunity to discuss it with his dad and had no idea how he was going to broach the subject. "Well, do you want the good news first or the bad news?"

"You aren't coming in tomorrow, are you?"

"I'm going to be out of pocket a little longer."

"How long?"

"Not sure."

What happened?"

"Busted water pipe. The whole house flooded."

"Damn. Okay. Do you have a place to stay until it's fixed? I have an extra room if you need it."

"Thanks. I'm good for now. Just dealing with trying to get it all cleaned up and repaired."

"Are you sure? Please tell me you aren't staying at that hell hole they call a hotel."

"You should know me better than that. Listen, I'll try to come by tomorrow and pick up some of the files."

"Okay. Let me know when."

"I will. Now for the good news. The girl I gave my card to at Flame Masters called. She filled out the online application. Would you have time at one tomorrow to interview her?"

"You want me to conduct the interview?"

"Yeah."

"Wait. This isn't some elaborate ruse to set me up with this woman, is it?"

"No."

"Man. Seriously. I—"

"I swear."

"And you've checked out her application. She's qualified?"

"No. I haven't. You will have to retrieve it from the server. But she said she had a master's degree in environmental engineering and worked for Peppin Energy."

"That's all well and good, but you have no idea what kind of employee she was."

"Brant vouched for her. He said she was the reason he wasn't sitting in jail. I think that says something."

"Yeah. It says she's a decent person. Doesn't say she's a good employee. Do you know why she isn't at Peppin Energy anymore?"

"She said she quit because she didn't like the way they did business, and they weren't following environmental standards."

"And you believe her?"

"Dude? What's your problem? You were there when we talked. I thought she seemed fine at the restaurant."

"Nothing. I just have a ton of shit going on, and now I have to go over her application, and interview her, and—"

"Never mind. I'm sorry I'm putting all this on you. She just had tomorrow off, and—"

"No. It's fine." He let out an audible breath. "If she checks out, I'll hire her and get her in here. Maybe she can help with the audit material."

"It will take a couple of days to get through HR, but yeah, that can be the first thing you delegate. In the meantime, I'll try to swing by and pick up some of the files."

"Don't worry about it. As long as you aren't trying to play matchmaker again, I think I can handle everything. You have enough on your plate with the flood."

"I'm sorry, man."

"No worries. So, did you get the number of the woman in the park?"

"Who?"

"The woman you saw in the park?"

He'd nearly forgotten that Malcolm had seen Eden. "Oh. No. She just resembled someone I thought I knew. When I got closer, I realized it wasn't her."

"Ah. So. What time is the interview?"

"At one tomorrow."

"Okay. Yeah. I don't have anything pressing other than the audit material, so consider it confirmed."

"Perfect. I'll let her know."

He texted Marissa after finishing the call with Malcolm and returned to see everyone leaving.

As Ben walked out the door, he fixed his eyes on Kaleb. "I'm going to be in my studio this afternoon if you need anything."

One by one his friends filed out until Kaleb and Eden were left alone. Resting his elbows on the counter, he let out a loud breath and stared at the empty room still revisiting what had just happened. He appreciated the quiet that had overtaken the house. His emotions were on overload, and he questioned whether he'd done the right thing by telling them. Never in his wildest dreams had he considered that his brother and friends would take this as a call to arms. It was just supposed to be a meeting to inform them so everyone could stay safe. His brother's words rang in his ears. "We don't let family fight battles on their own." He didn't relish the idea of putting others in harm's way, but if he was going to, he couldn't think of anyone he would rather go into battle with more than the men who just walked out the door.

Chapter Twenty-One

Arms snaked around him from behind. Her head leaned against his back. "Are you okay?"

It was worth it. She was worth it. He slid one of her hands up and kissed her palm, then tugged her from behind him. "I am now." Squeezing her into him, he dug his fingers into her mahogany strands. Her head slowly lifted, and her coffee-colored eyes pierced his heart with the emotion they conveyed. He swallowed back the desire that had engulfed him and closed his eyes, reciting all the reasons he needed to back away and keep his distance.

She was part of the mission, and he didn't need to complicate things. Getting involved with her would cause him to lose focus. Plus, she had enough to deal with. But when his lashes parted, all he could see was the need in her eyes that flicked to his lips then back up. All he could feel was that innate energy they shared from the moment they met. And he couldn't move. Her mouth opened slowly, allowing her soft pink tongue to peek out, wetting her lower lip, followed by her teeth scraping against the plump flesh, and it incinerated any ability he had to restrain himself.

He lowered his head and dared to let his lips graze hers. Just the slight touch made his body stiffen, and a hunger surged through him so intense he could feel himself shaking.

Chancing the feel of her lips once more, he captured her mouth and immediately became lost in her, intoxicated by everything that was her. Gently lifting and settling her on the counter, he moved to cup her face, tilting her head as he ran his tongue along the seam of her lips, requesting entry.

She opened, and he plunged deep, seeking to memorize every nuance of her taste. Sounds of her soft whimpers escaped, and he swore it was the sweetest sound he'd ever heard, knowing it was him who made her do it.

All the troubles and plans and thoughts of the assignment evaporated until the only thing left was this exotic creature that held his heart in her hands. She had enchanted him, cast a spell on his heart that he never wanted broken.

His hands skimmed her body and pressed against her butt, scooting her into him as he continued to pillage her mouth. She returned his kisses with the same intensity, her fingers tugging at his curls.

He knew where it was leading and that it was probably a mistake. But he was hopelessly addicted. He wanted his hands on her, needed his body pressed against hers, and no matter how much his mind told him to stop, he couldn't.

From the moment he laid eyes on her, there was a palpable force that drew him to her. And when she disappeared, the pain he felt wasn't only from being shot, but from losing her. Now, she was sitting in front of him, and he still wasn't sure she was real.

She rocked her hips against him, causing a groan to erupt from deep inside his chest, and she smiled against his lips. Dropping kisses across her cheek, he moved down the delicate skin of her neck and gently tugged the collar of her T-shirt aside so he could run his lips along her collarbone. It had her gasping and fisting his shirt, yanking it up.

He loved the feel of her hands tracing his ribs as she pushed his shirt up. He needed to remove the barriers between them. Raising up, he pulled his shirt over his head then his hands went to the hem of her shirt, sliding it up. Her arms raised and he slipped it off and tossed it aside.

His lips reconnected with her neck, and she lolled her head to the side as he lapped and kissed his way back up to her mouth. God, those lips. They framed her wide toothy smile, accenting only one of the perfect features her face held, and every time they pressed against his skin they sent a shockwave through him that threatened to stop his heart.

He leaned his forehead against hers with his eyes closed as he tried to steady his breath and regain some control. Things were happening so fast, and the way she was responding told him she probably wanted it as much as he did, but his dad taught him to never assume. His thumb tenderly brushed against the sensitive skin above her bra, and he cleared his throat. "Eden?"

"Hm?" she responded on an unsteady breath.

"Are you okay with…this."

She nodded.

"I-I kind of need you to say it, please." The desperation in his voice caught him off guard, and Eden softly giggled. His eyes popped open, and heat coursed through his veins, and he was practically vibrating as he waited for her answer.

Her fingers threaded in his hair, and she lifted her

eyes to meet his. "Take me to bed, Kaleb."

The words barely crossed her lips before he lifted her off the counter and was moving down the hallway. He dumped her on the bed, and she shrieked as she bounced. Her eyes met his as he unsnapped his jeans and lowered the zipper. Her beautiful smile appeared, and he wiggled his eyebrows.

"Oh, dear God, maybe I should rethink this," she said, laughing with the back of her hand pressed against her mouth.

"Oh no. We had a deal. You agreed to it."

He reached in his back pocket, retrieving his wallet, and pulled out a purple metallic packet. Tossing it on the bed, he laid the wallet on the nightstand and stepped out of his jeans. When his pants were puddled on the floor, he started working on her jeans, laying soft kisses on her belly as he worked the snap and zipper. Shimmying the fabric down her legs, he revealed a pair of skimpy, black lace panties that matched her bra, and another piece of his self-control evaporated.

With her pants on the floor next to his, he let his gaze drink in everything that was Eden. From her unpainted toenails to the intricate tattoos displayed on her tanned legs, to the soft rise of her hipbones that he couldn't stop himself from pressing a kiss to, she was what his fantasies were made of.

His eyes rested on her flat stomach that was moving rapidly, then shifted to the fair-skinned mounds, that pushed against the lacey fabric of her bra. His body trembled, and he again gave into his need, brushing his lips along her delicate skin, and noticing the goosebumps rise with every swipe of his tongue. Continuing up to her rose-colored lips that were perfectly parted for him to capture, he sucked on the bottom one, then the top, before backing away so he could memorize her lightly freckled nose, hooded caramel eyes, and finally her dark sable hair, dusted with golden highlights. She was exquisite.

****

Goosebumps raced over her body every time she got a glimpse of him. Her stomach filled with butterflies when he was close enough that she could smell his chocolatey cologne, and she shivered when he spoke in that sweet smooth tone that warmed her like a shot of expensive rum. Now, she was struggling to breathe.

With every stroke of his tongue, every graze of his fingertips against her over heated skin, her body sparked to life, one flicker at a time. Her heart was beating so fast it felt like a thousand hummingbirds inhabited it.

His movements were urgent and needy, but he wasn't rough. He was almost reverent the way he drank her in with his eyes, the way he gently caressed her skin, the way he took his time with her. It had her head spinning and her blood about to burst from her skin.

Lifting her, he unclasped her bra and flung it behind him, then his mouth was on her sensitive peak. Her body writhed, and her head slammed into the pillow as she let out a strained moan.

"Do you like that?" he asked as his mouth moved up her neck, and his fingers danced along the lace of her panties.

"Yes," she said in between gasps. His lips found hers again, and he pushed against the last scrap of material covering her. Backing away, he continued to stare at her as he slid them down her legs. Then dragging his fingers along the inside of her calf, he hovered over her, taking her mouth with his while his hand explored.

He was too far away. She wanted to feel him pressed against her. The heady urge exploded throughout her body. Her hand slowly skimmed along his pulse point, down his chest to his stomach, and around to his butt, gently coaxing him to her. His eyes closed, and he took in a deep shuddered breath then opened them again. This time, they held something different, something that had her whole body going rigid. Distress? Apprehension?

He let out a breath. "Eden…Are you still…a virgin?"

Letting out a relieved sigh, she tucked her lips between her teeth, trying not to give away her secret.

The corner of his mouth lifted into a sheepish smirk. "I need to…you said you haven't dated…and I'm kind of…"

He was so flustered. It was truly adorable, but she felt kind of bad, so she shook her head, letting him off the hook. "No. I'm not."

Relief washed over him, and he chuckled.

"Were you worried?"

"Hell yeah, I was worried. It hit me what you'd said about not dating, and I don't want to hurt—"

She lifted up, wrapped her hand around the back of his neck, and brought his lips to hers. He didn't have to know it was only one time, and it was less than enjoyable. He'd already changed her mind in that regard.

His hand skimmed down her neck, taking her breast in his palm. She could tell her distraction worked. All talk was a distant memory. She rolled her hips and could feel his muscles constrict.

He rose up momentarily, searching for the packet he threw on the bed earlier. After locating it, he discarded the empty wrapper and settled between her legs again. His lips quickly pressed against hers, and he raised up on his elbow letting their eyes connect while he caressed her hip and entered her slowly. She knew immediately why he was worried. He was not small. She bit her bottom lip, trying to keep any pained noise from escaping. Truth be told, it was the oddest feeling, a cross between agony and euphoria.

He stopped his movement. "Am I hurting you?"

She quickly shook her head.

"You don't have to lie, Eden." He brushed some hair from her face. "If I'm hurting you, I'll stop."

"No," she yelped. "Please."

"I'll take it slow and try to be gentle, but damn, you're tight, and it feels really good. You gotta promise, though. Tell me if I'm hurting you."

She nodded. "I promise."

"You haven't done this much, have you?"

She figured he already knew the answer.

"That obvious?"

His eyes remained on hers for a moment before they dropped to her lips and then he captured them. His fingers combed through her hair and tugged as his hips rocked into hers, slowly. The pain dissipated, and the tingling sensation that was making her fingertips dig into his back rocketed. Her legs wrapped around his, and she began to move against him. "Does it feel okay?"

"Y-yes," she said, breathless. This was all so new to her. He was slowly sending her entire body into a frenzy.

His mouth found her dark pink nipple, and his hand slid down to her hip adjusting her just enough to plunge deeper.

Heat shot through her, and a new sensation began to

build. It was like he'd already mapped out exactly what she needed. Her body moved on its own, and she could feel herself beginning to spiral. Moans that sounded foreign to her were escaping with each panted breath.

His teeth scraped against the tender skin below her ear, and he breathed, "Time to go, babe."

His fingers dug into the flesh of her hip, and he let out a primal growl as he plunged deep over and over, sending a jolt to her core that had her exploding with surges of ecstasy. "I, Kaleb?" Her eyes slammed shut as wave after tortuous wave of pleasure washed over her, causing her body to shake uncontrollably and her breaths to come in short bursts. Kaleb's head buried into her shoulder as his body jerked against her, and he let out a strained grunt. Warmth spread within her, and Kaleb suddenly stilled, then quickly rolled off her.

"Shit!"

Chapter Twenty-Two

Eden's eyes flew open hearing the panic in his voice. She backed away, tucked the sheet around her, and sat up. "What's wrong?"

Staring up at the ceiling, continuing to breathe erratically, Kaleb draped his arm across his eyes. "Kind of had a malfunction."

"Malfunction?"

"Eden. Please tell me you're on some kind of birth control."

Only then did it dawn on her what happened, and she understood Kaleb's panicked state. She had never considered birth control, figuring she would cross that bridge if she got into a serious relationship. The one time she had sex, they used a condom, and it hadn't failed. This moment with Kaleb had been so unexpected and spontaneous, her mind was so far gone that she was glad he was clear headed enough to think about protection, even if it didn't work, because she sure wasn't.

"Eden?"

When was her last period? Was it a week ago? How long had it been? Was it before she arrived in Dalton? "No," she finally responded, still trying to pinpoint the date. The thought of her getting pregnant overwhelmed her. The last thing she wanted to do was make him feel trapped. "If it would make you feel better, we can go to the pharmacy and get the day after pill."

"That's not up to me. It's your body."

"No. We are in this together. You should have a say so."

"Tell me how you feel first."

"Honestly. My mom raised me to be a bit phobic of chemicals. She used natural treatments for colds and stuff and didn't give me any medications unless it was absolutely necessary. That was one of the reasons I didn't get on birth control."

"Okay. So, I think the day after pill is a no."

"It shouldn't only be my decision though. How do you feel about it?"

"I'm fine with it."

"But that means we are taking a chance."

"I know."

"It hasn't been that long since my last period, and I'm fairly regular."

"I'm fine with whatever happens."

"But what if I get pregnant?"

Kaleb's grin spread wide. "Then we'll have the best-looking baby on the planet."

Eden giggled. "Be serious."

"I am. If you are okay taking the chance, so am I. Are you?"

"I-I guess so," Eden conceded, her voice still sounding unsure, even to her. Kaleb stared into her eyes again, and she tried to put on a brave face, but she could tell he didn't buy it.

"God, I'm sorry."

"Kaleb. It isn't your fault. These things happen."

"Not to me. I've never had anything like this happen." He scooted out of bed and headed for the bathroom to clean up.

Eden continued to pry. "Not with any of your *dates*?"

"I said, I dated a lot. I didn't say I slept with all of them. And no. I've never had this happen before."

The shower turned on, and she couldn't help picturing him under the spray of water. His body was a masterpiece. The minute she laid eyes on him in his naked glory she couldn't tear her focus away. His bronze skin gave definition to the hard packed muscles of his stomach and the V at his hips. Veins wrapped his arms that were decorated with detailed tattoos. He wasn't overly bulky, just enough to show that he took care of his body.

Sitting up, her eyes drifted to the half-opened door of the bathroom. Her feet hit the floor, and she padded across the room and peeked in. From the mirror, she could see Kaleb's reflection. His movements as he slid the bar of soap over his chiseled muscles had her hypnotized. She chanced another step farther into the room. He stood with the water sluicing down his face and over his body. Cupping his hand, he sucked some water into his mouth then spit it out as he slid his fingers through his hair. Every movement he made was erotic and had her sucking in a shuddered breath as she glanced away. Then, as she returned her gaze, she saw him staring at her with a halfcocked grin on his face. He opened the door, inviting her in. She took a hesitant step. He held out his hand to steady her as she joined him. The minute the door closed, his mouth was on hers.

****

Her eyes slid to the large window, and she watched the branches of the tree sway in the wind as her mind drifted. She couldn't quit thinking about the hunger in his eyes. How desperate he seemed to have her yet handled her so carefully. She was a bit sore since they spent the entire afternoon exploring each other, but she'd never felt so wanted and cherished.

He walked back into the bedroom, still naked after getting them both some water. Handing off her glass, he slid back between the sheets. She loved the fact that he was so comfortable in his skin. Taking a drink before setting her glass on the side table, she mulled over a comment he made earlier. "Can I ask you something?"

"Anything."

"How long has it been since you've…"

One eyebrow curved and a crooked smile lifted his lips. "A while. How about you? I'll be honest; I was kind of surprised when you said you had."

Eden noticed the time on the clock next to the bed and took off for the bathroom. "How long is a while?"

"Evading the question?"

Truth be told, she was.

"I haven't, since before the mission," he called back after a minute, just as she shut the door.

Stepping into the shower, she wasn't sure she heard him correctly. *Before the mission? He hasn't had sex in two years? Why?* She quickly rinsed off, because she had to find out the answer. After she toweled dry, she returned with the towel wrapped around her, feeling a bit self-conscious. It was silly since she spent the afternoon with him naked. She wished she could be more like him and parade around uninhibited. He flung the covers back inviting her back in, so she complied and mirrored his position.

"Did you say you haven't been with anyone in two years?"

"Geez. Why does everyone think I sleep around? I do have scruples."

"I didn't mean to imply that. I was just surprised. You're very attractive, and I'm sure you have had your share of opportunities."

"A few. Like I said before though, I was busy with the assignment, then working and going to school, so I didn't have much time to date."

His words left her feeling hollow. She wanted it to be because of her. It wasn't.

"So, you didn't answer my question."

"What was that?"

"How long has it been for you?"

She'd hoped he would have forgotten. It wasn't something she was entirely proud of. "It was only the one time, and that was back when I was a sophomore in college."

"And?"

She pulled the sheet up a little more as heat crept up her neck, seeing a smirk spreading across Kaleb's face. She dropped her eyes to the sheet unable to take his gaze any longer.

"Eden?" Alarm saturated her name. She glanced at him through her lashes then back down to the sheet. "No one hurt you—"

"No. Nothing like that. It was kind of a science experiment," she softly confessed, before she lost her nerve.

Kaleb let out a deep breath and chuckled. "A science experiment? Okay, this just became very interesting."

Her face felt like it was about to catch on fire, and she didn't know if she should explain or not. He was already laughing. But somehow his soft chuckles made her want to tell him her whole life story. "When I went to college, I had a little more freedom than I did at home. I didn't go crazy, mind you. Never went to keggers or anything like that. The program I was in was very tough, so I tried to keep my head screwed on straight.

"Sophomore year I was paired up on a project with this guy in my advanced biology class named Kenneth. The professor gave us a short period of time to complete the project, so I went to the library to do some research and found Kenneth already there. We got to talking and decided to grab some pizza and work on the project at the house he shared with some other guys. He was nice, a little bit awkward like me, so we got along okay. "

"This sounds fishy already. Some guy you barely know invited you to his place and you blindly went along?"

"We were partners in biology class. I lived in a ten-by-ten dorm room, so there was no place to work on the project."

"Dorms have communal areas."

"Yes, but everyone is noisy, and the tables are always being used for games and stuff. Anyway, the house was right off campus, and his roommates were all gamers and barely noticed us, other than someone requesting a slice of pizza. We handed it off and went into the dining room. During our brainstorming over the project, we somehow got on the topic of dating. He said he liked this girl in one of his other classes and wanted to ask her out. Then he went on to say how inexperienced he was and figured he'd be shot down right out of the gate. That led to him confessing that he was a virgin. I didn't want him to feel weird about telling me, so I said I was too and that it was nothing to be embarrassed

A Life of Illusions

about. He said guys are expected to be experienced, which, I guess, in some ways, is probably true. I think most girls want a guy to take control.

"So, the more we talked, the more we danced around the idea of being each other's first to kind of get the awkwardness out of the way. I admit, I was kind of questioning everything when we decided to do it, but once it happened, I'm pretty sure he was telling the truth."

"So, you had pizza, worked on the project, and had sex?"

"No. The sex part was a different day. We did the whole date night, so he could get comfortable in case she accepted his invite."

"You were his practice run."

"I guess you could call it that. And he was mine too."

"Did he get the date?"

"Yes. Although, I didn't ask about the afterward. I really didn't want to know."

"I have three words for you."

"Oh geez. What?"

"You got played." Kaleb sing-songed the words and laughed. "At least he had the decency to feed you first."

"I honestly don't think so. I saw the girl he was interested in."

"Did he introduce you?"

"No. He pointed her out."

"You got played. She could have been anyone."

"Trust me, the whole entire date night was one big awkward moment after another. He seemed very inexperienced."

"Oh. No. I don't doubt he was inexperienced. I

doubt there was another girl. He found himself partnered with this stunning woman, and he was smart enough to come up with a story that tugged at her heartstrings."

"You really think he was playing me?"

"Who brought the idea up; you or him?"

"I don't remember."

Kaleb immediately lifted an eyebrow.

She closed her eyes, remembering the conversation. "Okay. Maybe it was him."

"I'm just surprised he didn't hit you up for another date."

She fell back on the pillow, giggling at the memories. "He did. Like maybe a month after we had finished the project and hadn't spoken for a while. He came up to me after class and asked if I would like to split a pizza, then had the audacity to grin. I asked him about the girl, and he said she turned out to be a little too crazy for him to handle."

"Yeah. Gotta give the man props. He had you hook, line, and sinker. I'm guessing you turned him down?"

"Oh yeah. Once was enough for me."

"Not as spectacular as our time together?" Kaleb's fingers danced over her belly under the sheet, then traveled up to her breasts.

Eden rolled back onto her side, and she let out a soft laugh. "No. Not even in the same universe. You left a much better impression about the whole thing. I was kind of worried there was something wrong with me after the first time."

"Why is that?"

Was he honestly going there? Heat crawled up her neck, thinking about what he was asking. His eyes were on her, waiting for her to continue. She chewed on her lip, trying to figure out how to say it. "I never…"

Her eyes met his, and she hoped he wouldn't make her go on. His expression softened, filling with understanding. "He didn't let you finish?"

She shook her head.

"But you've had an orgasm before, right?"

Tucking her lips between her teeth, she shook her head sheepishly. "Again, I thought there was something wrong with me."

"Oh my God." Kaleb chuckled and donned a huge grin. "Well, I am very glad I had the opportunity to change your mind." He leaned in and placed a chaste kiss on her lips then backed away. "Now, you have two options. We can continue to work on changing your mind, or we can actually work on the case."

Chapter Twenty-Three

Changing her mind was quickly becoming one of his favorite things. However, all good things must come to an end, and as much as he hated it, he needed to get his head back in the game. Opening his laptop, he plugged in the web address for Beyond Existence and tried to focus as he scrolled through the posts, but all he saw was a bunch of letters. His mind continually drifted back to her.

He'd never had anyone consume his mind, body, and emotions so thoroughly. The way she touched him and felt in his arms; the way she smelled like fresh gardenias; and the sweet noises she made absolutely snapped every thread of self-control he had. And God, the way she kissed him. He'd had nice kisses before, but nothing compared to the way it felt when she let her control slip and the passion take over. It was like he provided the air she needed to breathe.

Her desperation had nothing though on the overwhelming hunger he had for her. He wanted to devour her so badly his entire body was trembling. He tried to be gentle, tried to take it slow so he didn't hurt her, but he couldn't stop himself. The need for her was too intense.

She appeared from the bedroom wearing a teal-colored crochet halter top that revealed her toned stomach, and a pair of brown flowy pants. Her long, dark hair was pulled back in a low ponytail draped over one shoulder. Nope. There would be no way he could concentrate with her in his line of sight.

"What are you doing?" Her voice had a bit of humor in it, and he wondered if she could see what she was doing to him.

"Checking to see if there are any posts on the website that I could respond to, that might pull me into one of those chat groups you talked about. But I can't seem to focus with you standing there."

A smirk slowly curled her lips, and she sauntered over to him and wrapped her arms around him from behind. Her fingers threaded through his curls, and his head fell back as his eyes drifted shut. God, her touch was the perfect drug. It had the ability to remove every ounce of tension in his body.

He lifted his head and began to scroll again, not quite knowing what he was looking for.

"Wait. Stop. Go back."

"What?"

"I recognize that screen name. TheAnswer. I think they are one of the moderators of the group I was in. They were the one who initially posted the question I answered that got me the invite."

"How long ago was it when you got invited to the group?"

"I don't know. It's been quite a while. Let me see if I can pull up my account and find out."

"You can't log into your old account."

"I know. I'm going to do a search and use yours to look at it."

She scooted into Kaleb's seat and typed in her screen name.

"No," Kaleb said under his breath, when she pulled up the profile, and stepped away from the chair he was leaning on.

"What? What am I missing?"

His eyes connected with the screen again and read the name. "ImposterSam...You're not missing."

Eden turned around in her chair. Her face was full of questions, and Kaleb couldn't help but smile.

"What in the hell are you talking about?"

"Do you remember talking to someone named 'K?' The username was 'Skyhigh.' "

Eden's eyes widened. "Oh my gosh. That was you?"

Kaleb nodded. "I guess we can mark Sam off the list of missing persons."

"Wait. I looked for you when I got on under Bill's screen name, but it showed you had stopped posting."

"I didn't get on much once I got the mission for the pageant because I was getting a plan together. I rarely posted anyway and very seldom responded to anyone else's posts. I mainly researched and engaged with questionable posts. Then you 'Sam' disappeared."

"Was I questionable?"

"No. If I remember correctly, you posted about a trail you'd hiked."

Eden laughed. "Maybe so. I remember posting about my training regimen. I found some pretty hiking trails in Mississippi. Who knew that would be what captured your attention. Oh wait, your sister said that is all you talk about."

"You know what is funny?"

"What?"

"I never knew you were a girl. This whole time I thought Sam was a guy."

"I played it that way, hence the name 'ImposterSam.' I wasn't there to get guys to slide into my DMs. I figured if I didn't give away that I was a girl, I would be left alone. I guess I didn't consider a hiking fanatic."

"What can I say. I like the great outdoors."

"If you haven't noticed, I do too." She glanced back at the screen. "Aren't you worried that since they have my information they'll track your IP address?"

"I was on the company computer before and I signed up with a new screen name and spoofed the IP. We should be good."

"Okay."

Her finger continued to scroll through post after post. "Geez. I wish there was a way to search for specific posts. It would make it so much easier."

"Are you sure it's them?"

"Almost positive."

"Then let's see what is on their profile."

She tapped their screen name into the search bar, and they both groaned when "private account" popped up in bold black letters. "Damn. Dead end."

"Not necessarily. It's a name we need to check. Let me see if I can find the post we saw earlier." Eden stood and threw her hair over her shoulder as she leaned over Kaleb, who'd taken the seat. A hint of her floral scent cascaded over him, and he took a moment to breathe deep. His finger scrolled through posts he had seen before, hoping to come across the post that Eden had zeroed in on. "Is this it? You said TheAnswer, right?"

"Yes. That's it. What does it say?"

"*An estimated eight million babies are born worldwide every year with some form of birth defect. And the number is growing. Why, with all the cutting-edge scientific research, are the numbers so high?"*

"See. Now, if you answer the question, you might get invited into a group. I have no idea how people are chosen though."

"What should I say?"

"Your best chance would be to at least agree with them."

He sat back, folded his arms over his chest, and stared at the screen, trying to get inside this person's head. Reading through the question a couple of times, he finally typed out a response. *With all the genetic advances and in utero surgeries available, you would think the numbers would go down.*

"How does that sound?" His attention slid to her, and she nodded. Reading through the question again had his thoughts going back to earlier in the day and the "malfunction." What if she did get pregnant? The thought had his heart racing.

He was barely twenty-five, and his life had been on hyper speed, chasing one adrenaline rush after another for as long as he could remember. He'd never seriously thought about what it would be like to get married or have a family. He'd never even been in a serious relationship.

His dating life was much like his life in general. It moved at breakneck speed. He went from one girl to the next, never remaining too long. He was far from being a virgin, but never had sex with anyone just for the physical release. There had to be a connection. The problem was it never lasted. Sometimes it was his decision and sometimes hers.

The connection with Eden was instantaneous.

Everything about her fascinated him. When she disappeared, finding her became his obsession. And now that he'd found her, he didn't want her to leave his sight. He wanted to take care of her, protect her, and keep her safe. That's what had him currently feeling like the room was closing in on him. The idea that their feelings could somehow be associated with the case and nothing more set a bomb off in his gut. Would the connection disappear once the case was solved? What if she didn't want a relationship? She'd been through so much. She was in an emotionally fragile state. What would that mean if she did get pregnant? The thought had him sucking in a deep breath wondering if he was really ready for what might come.

He didn't lie to Eden. He was fine with her decision. If she was pregnant, he would do whatever she needed him to do to make sure she and the baby were taken care of. He'd held AJ, Cody's son, as a newborn, and he had to admit, the thought of him and Eden having a baby gave him an indescribable feeling of elation and panic all at the same time. He knew they would be able to navigate through it. His fear was she wouldn't want him there.

"Kaleb?" Her sweet voice called him back from the far recesses of his mind, and he wondered how long he'd been staring at the screen.

"Huh?" He glanced up at her and then back to the screen. "Sorry. I was trying to figure out other possible ways to find out who 'TheAnswer' is," he lied.

"It's okay. I was thinking you should refresh the page to see if you got a response."

He did as she asked, and a bright red check showed up in the little blue envelope at the top of the screen. His pulse rate ticked up with the feel of Eden's hand tightening on his shoulder. He clicked on the check and the message opened.

It simply said, *'If you would like to learn more about combating birth defects, join our group.'*

Kaleb's finger hovered over the blue highlighted link, and he wondered what he would find behind the veil. As his finger tapped the pad, he noticed Eden dragging the other chair next to him.

Just as he was ready to delve into the posts on the chat, there was a knock at the door. More like a banging. Eden attempted to stand, but Kaleb threw his arm out holding her in place.

Chapter Twenty-Four

Peeking out the window, he quickly headed to the door and opened it. April, along with Jenna and Jessi, crowded the door, arms loaded down with bags. "There's more in the car," April stated as she pushed past Kaleb and set the groceries on the counter."

"Did you buy out the entire store?"

"Hey. We want you to be taken care of."

Eden moved into Kaleb's spot as he exited the house with April.

"Where's Kaysi?" he asked as they descended the steps.

"She is closing the store up then heading over." April reached into the trunk and handed off more bags. "So, is she a client, or is there more going on?"

His mind played back their afternoon, and he sucked in his cheeks to fight the smile tugging at his lips. April stopped and stared at him with her hands on her hips. "Oh my God, Kaleb. I know that look, and as long as I've known you, it's never crossed your face."

"What?"

"You like her."

"I've liked girls before, April. I've got lots of girl friends."

"Not like this. Trust me."

She wasn't wrong. At this point, that was not quite the word he would use, although he wasn't sure what he currently felt after the recent realization, so he chose to keep his mouth shut.

"She seems cool. She said she's a musician."

"When did you talk—"

"When she was at the store. She was fawning over the boarded-up building next door. She said she would love to have a music studio there. I told her I knew the owners."

The smile he was fighting spread across his face as he pictured her. Every time he had his music playing, her eyes would close, her body would move, and then she would sing. It was like the music took possession of her soul, then radiated out of her. And her voice was angelic. A music studio seemed like a far better fit for her than being a doctor. "Yeah. She has an amazing voice, and I think plays a couple of instruments."

They headed back into the house with their arms loaded and set everything on the counter next to the bags that Jenna and Jessi were unloading. "Oh. Backseat has clothes," Jenna commented quickly, like she had just remembered. Kaleb turned to the open door.

Eden jumped up. "I feel like I'm doing nothing. I'll help."

Aurora decided to see who came to visit and put on a show by hopping sideways as she came into the room from the hallway.

"Oh my gosh. Who is this little furball?" Jessi squatted down and lifted her in her hands.

"You didn't see her earlier? That's Aurora," Jenna said adding a few strokes to her head.

"She is adorable and so soft." Jessi let her crawl up to her shoulder.

"That's her favorite spot," Eden confided, following

Kaleb out the door.

Opening the back door to the SUV, he was stunned at the number of sacks and luggage that were crammed in there.

"How long are they expecting us to stay?"

"Obviously longer than *I* expected to." He started handing her bags and dragged out two large suitcases.

"April wasn't lying when she said that they want to make sure we are taken care of."

"All those ladies in there are absolutely the best people you could have in your corner. Don't tell them I told you that." He winked at her. "I gotta keep up my image."

She giggled. "I definitely got that feeling when I met April and your sister at their store."

As they entered the house all the girls stopped talking, and Kaleb tilted his head. "Secrets are no fun. Secrets are for everyone," he sang in his best little kid voice, as he walked up the hallway and set the luggage down in the bedroom. Eden followed, dropping her bags. Laughter floated into the bedroom.

When they entered the kitchen, April piped up, "I was telling them how fun it would be to have Eden's music studio next door."

"Oh. That was a pipe dream. I have no money."

"There are ways around that." April's eyes shifted to Kaleb, and she winked. His heart thudded with what she was implying with that one wink. Eden's eyes then turned to him, and he felt flames dancing up his neck to his cheeks.

"What would you do with it?" April asked. "I mean, if you were able to buy it?"

"I don't know." She chewed on her lip, and Kaleb

could tell she was formulating her vision. Tilting her head, she said thoughtfully, "That front area would be perfect for a waiting area and maybe a coffee bar. And I would love to have a stage to have small performances. Some rooms for lessons. And maybe even a small recording studio would be cool. But again, I, I'm—"

"Guys. Eden is from Mississippi. Let's focus on the case before we get too far ahead of ourselves." As he walked back out for the next load, Eden again followed him, and he remembered something she'd said in the interview with Quinten. "You said you stayed with a friend when you came back from France. What happened to your apartment?"

She stared off in the distance; her voice sounding melancholy as she spoke. "I lost everything." She squinted as her gaze returned to him. "Not that I had much in the first place. I went by the complex after I got back to see if they might have stored my stuff somewhere. They said they had to file an eviction after there was no response to the letters they sent about late payment."

"So, you're homeless." The thought put a rock in Kaleb's stomach. He'd never wanted for anything in his life, and he had no concept of what it would be like to have no place to call home.

"I mean, I figured they kicked me out. I disappeared for two years. It didn't come as a surprise. And again, I didn't have much. I moved from a dorm. Most of what I had was furniture and decorations my friends were getting rid of. Still, it was mine, and it kind of stung when they said they had gotten rid of everything."

"I can imagine." They walked back in the house with their arms loaded down and took it to the bedroom.

"We tried to think of everything," April said when she appeared in the doorway. Eden stared at all the bags. "Anything that doesn't fit, shove it in a sack and we'll go through it later." She pushed away from the doorway. "We got your kitchen set up. Kaysi is bringing food from Flame Masters, so whenever you guys decide to head over is fine."

Kaleb's phone chimed. April stepped back and headed up the hallway. "Thanks, April."

Eden jerked her thumb over her shoulder, letting Kaleb know she would walk them out, leaving Kaleb in the room alone. He hit the button, and a deep voice spoke before he could utter a word. "I'm on my way. About to cross over into Tennessee."

Kaleb let out a breath, and a tiny bit of tension unwound from his shoulders. "Thanks, man." Ian had been his partner on several assignments, and although he knew everyone he worked with had his back, he and Ian had almost a sixth sense about each other. They knew each other's moves. Having him there gave him an added sense of security.

"You have anything for me?"

"Did Quinten tell you about what we came back to?"

"Yeah, he did. You're secure for now?"

"I think so. The property backs up to the highway, but there's a thick ridge of trees in between. And there are quite a few acres around us. Do you have an estimated time?"

"I'd say late tomorrow afternoon."

"When you hit Dalton, call me. I'll bring you out to our location."

"Copy that."

Now was the hard part. He hadn't even had time to

let Quinten know what had occurred. "Listen. My family and friends know what's going on. I was on the phone with Quinten, and my brother-in-law overheard the conversation and called me on it. With the situation we are in right now, I felt it best to tell them since you're my only back up."

"You're in a tight spot. I get it. This hit at the exact wrong time. We could use some extra hands, and maybe we can gain a few more recruits when we're done."

Kaleb chuckled. Another reason he got along so well with Ian. He kind of reminded him of Joe the way he took everything in stride.

"I doubt that, but you never know. We have a couple with military backgrounds and one on the police force. I'm about to head over and try to put together a gameplan. Honestly, I have no idea where to start. I'm flying blind."

"We'll get it figured out. Just stay focused. You have always been able to keep a cool head." That was when he could detach himself from the assignment. There was no way that would happen now.

"Yeah. When we have a team, maybe. This is different. Even though I think we are secure, it's not like when we know we are."

"Dude. Where is this coming from? You've never been afraid of anything."

Ian was right. Kaleb usually went in guns blazing. Not this time. "I don't like not knowing who we are battling. Usually, when we have an assignment, there's solid information, a concrete plan, so the danger is reduced to a minimum. But we don't have a clue what we are up against, and we've already been hit. They've already gotten to Eden."

Ian let out a loud breath. "It's her, isn't it?"

"I. She's—"

"Don't try to bullshit me, man. You know better than that. I noticed how you acted around her at the pageant." The line went silent for a long minute. "We'll keep her safe."

Kaleb knew Ian would do everything in his power to make that happen. "I know."

"We're going to put this bullshit behind us."

"Then we'll ride off into the sunset."

"I don't know about you, man. I'm riding off to Colorado. Gonna be strapping on some skis and pointing them south on a mountain of white powder. The only way it could be better is if headquarters was on a beach somewhere."

"You'll have to tell me all about your new adventure when you get here."

"I'll let you know when I hit town."

"Sounds good."

He disconnected the call as he strolled out of the bedroom. Eden was sitting at the small table with the laptop open. Everyone was gone. It was quiet. He walked to the refrigerator and opened it. The shelves were full of all the necessities and then some. He wouldn't have expected anything less with April heading up the crew. April had been a part of his life since he was young. Although she and Kaysi annoyed the hell out of him most of the time, he knew she would be there in a heartbeat if he needed her.

"Was that Quinten?" Eden asked peering up from the computer.

"No, it was Ian. Agent Scott. He will be here tomorrow."

"Is he going to stay with us?"
"Yeah."
"Then we better find a bed."

Chapter Twenty-Five

It'd been over an hour since everybody had gathered in Ben's studio. Eden sat listening to the discussion between Kaleb and all his friends and family. She was officially overwhelmed and on the verge of tears from the moment they arrived. She'd never been around a group of people who cared for each other the way they did. Their sole goal was to protect her and Kaleb at all costs. The sergeant had already set up rotations with his officers for patrol. And although Ian would be staying with them as protection and help with the case, all the guys were talking about taking turns hanging out at the ranch, as well as some of the girls, to keep her company. And if there were a breach, there was a plan in place where they would help Kaleb and her go off grid.

Kaleb appearing a bit annoyed as Kaysi slid the trimmer up the back of his head. Joe had suggested it would be easier for Kaleb to move about town without being detected since they resembled each other so much. Eden couldn't help feeling a twinge of pain as each of his beautiful brown curls fell to the floor. But the more Kaysi continued with the cut, the more Kale Grey emerged. The only difference was the color of his hair. Her eyes bounced between Kaleb and Joe, and she was surprised she didn't see the resemblance before. It was unmistakable now. Although Joe was a bit bulkier, they could easily pass for each other with the right clothing.

It was all so surreal. She thought back through the past two years and marveled at how complicated everything had gotten. In some ways she'd wished Adam had never contacted her, but then she may have never known she had a brother and sister, or that her mom was part of some secret research program that she was an unwilling participant in. And if Adam hadn't contacted her, she would have never met Kaleb.

Kaysi removed the cape, and Kaleb dusted himself off, then ran his fingers through his much shorter hair as he stood and moved to a chair next to Eden. She reached up and ran the back of her fingers against his short hair, then leaned in. "Hello, Agent Grey." He winked in response.

Glancing around the room, she suddenly realized, with all that was going on, she hadn't noticed her surroundings. Stacks of wood filled open shelves on the wall. Different machines took up space in one area, and large worktables in another. The sweet scent of sawdust and varnish filled the air. Ben's artwork sat in different stages of finish around the studio. There was no doubt he was talented.

The more she was around him, the more she saw the soft squishy teddy bear inside the growly exterior, especially when it came to Kaysi. He adored her. And she knew Kaysi felt the same way.

That could be said for each one of the guys in the room and their special someone. In the short period of time that she'd been around them, there was no doubt about the commitment and love between each of the couples. It was an atmosphere vastly different than the one she grew up in and had her wondering if she would be able to offer that kind of love to anyone.

She let her eyes settle on Kaleb again, who smiled, but it was laced with concern. She wondered what was in store for them. He squeezed her knee, and she immediately wrapped her hand around his to fend off the panic taking over. The uncertainty of the future seemed to be growing by the millisecond, and it felt like a dark ominous cloud above them. A thousand questions held her consciousness captive, and she didn't even notice she'd disconnected until the sound of her name broke through the haze. "I'm sorry, what?" She wasn't even sure what had been said, or who had said it. Heat filled her cheeks as her eyes made contact with those around her.

"Kaleb said you got into a group on the website. Did you notice anything odd?" It was the sergeant who'd ask the question.

Kaleb leaned in and whispered, "Are you okay?"

It was all she could do to keep her body from shaking uncontrollably. She'd let the mask she normally hid behind fall away with Kaleb. It was time to put it back in place and suck it up for the audience. "I'm fine. Just tired." She pasted on a smile but could tell Kaleb wasn't buying it for a second. As hard as she tried to shove her feelings down into the dark recesses of her soul, it was becoming harder and harder.

Thinking about the question, she turned to the sergeant. "We answered a question posed by one of the members named TheAnswer. I think they might be a moderator. I remember seeing the name before, and they always pose questions that seem to get quite a bit of exposure. The question they posted had something to do with the increasing number of children born with birth defects amid cutting-edge research. We responded and got an invite within a few minutes. I only had time to glance at the group before we had to leave. It looked like it had about a hundred people in it. Several people were discussing birth defects that had happened in their families."

"Nothing odd?"

"Not that I noticed. I mean, Chalemaare is a genetic scientist, so it would stand to reason the website would lean heavier on that area."

"What was the goal of the question? Why did they want to get people into the group?"

Eden sat back in her chair and thought about what Mitch asked. "Well, the basic question was 'why isn't science and technology reducing the number of birth defects and diseases.' And since the website is a think tank, maybe they are searching for other like-minded scientists to do Chalemaare's research."

"Maybe. But something tells me it's not that simple, taking into consideration what has happened to you and your brother. Keep digging."

After another hour of discussion, Eden lifted her eyes to see Kaleb yawn. She knew he was probably exhausted and hoped the meeting was ending. She didn't particularly like being the topic of discussion, even if they were trying to help. It was her fault they were possibly in danger and having to come up with a plan.

A tug on her ponytail had her jerking her head away and immediately twisting in her chair. Kaleb's bright smile shined down at her. "I was wondering if you were planning on camping out here, or if you might want to walk me home, to keep me safe."

Her eyes darted around to see everyone standing. She rose from her chair, and Kaleb's hand pressed against her back as he leaned in. "It's going to be okay."

"All these people are putting their lives on hold and possibly in danger for me. They barely know me."

"They know me though, and if you're important to me, you're important to them."

The funny thing was, they had already become important to her too. Kaysi bumped her shoulder, and Eden lifted her head. Kaysi's eyes were glued to Ben as she spoke. "If they want a fight, they won't know what hit them until it's too late. Don't you worry." Then she turned to Eden. "These men have had each other's back in fights before, and they haven't lost yet. And we women are pretty badass ourselves. We've all been through fights of our own, and we're still standing." A crooked smirk lit up Kaysi's face. "We've got you."

"Thank you," was the only thing she could manage as Kaysi wrapped her in a hug, and a warmth passed through Eden that blurred her vision. Then each of the women took their turn, giving her a hug before they left. As the door closed from the last one, she smiled, and tears pooled in her lashes and streaked her cheeks.

Kaleb came up behind her, wrapped his arm around her shoulder, and kissed her temple. "Like I said, it's going to be okay. I promise."

"I've never felt so loved in my entire life," she whispered.

Kaleb dragged her into his chest. "I like to hear that."

"Is she okay?" Kaysi asked, as she threw away the remaining trash from dinner.

He nodded, rubbing his cheek on the top of her head. "A little overwhelmed." His head lifted and he placed another soft kiss to her forehead. "Ready to head home?"

Home. It truly was beginning to feel that way. The thought of leaving Dalton had her heart sinking. Still, there were too many variables to assume things would work out to where she could stay once the case was solved. She wished she could. In a perfect world, she would. And she would buy the abandoned brick building and have a music studio there.

Kaleb's hands cupped Eden's cheeks to lift her eyes to his.

"Let's go home," she said, hoping her wish would somehow come true.

****

From the opened door of the bedroom, Aurora came bounding toward them and stretched. Kaleb picked her up and cuddled her close to him. Eden spied the sacks and luggage still piled on the bed. She dug through a couple of them and was surprised, seeing everything from toiletries to bras and panties, to cute cocktail dresses, that had her wondering where they thought she'd be wearing them. They thought of everything. But all she wanted to do at the moment, was put on a comfy T-shirt and crawl in bed. Kaleb had disappeared. So, after stripping out of her clothes and pulling on one of his T-shirts, she took a deep whiff of his scent and quietly strolled up the hallway.

Kaleb had the feather toy and was playing with Aurora.

"Where'd you go?" she asked, opening the refrigerator and plucking a stem of grapes from the bag.

"I figured Aurora was hungry."

She sat down on the sofa opposite him. "I don't know about you, but they have me clothed for every occasion, including fancy cocktail parties."

"I figure April raided Joe's closet for me. Though I'm hoping she didn't raid his underwear drawer."

Eden winced at the thought. "Me too." She chewed on her lip and tapped her fingers against her leg while she tried to think of the best way to ask the question that had been on her mind since they got home. "I got everything moved off the bed. I'll put it away tomorrow." She paused to see if he was going to react to her comment. He continued to bounce the toy in front of Aurora. He didn't even make eye contact with her, so she went for the straightforward approach. "Are you going to be long? I don't want to go to sleep without you." At that, his eyes lifted, and a mischievous smile slowly formed on his oh so kissable lips. A hint of fire ignited in his icy-blue irises.

"Are you asking me to *sleep* with you?"

Rolling her eyes, she pinched back the smile that his comment caused. "Well, you haven't slept in two nights and—"

"Three."

"What?"

"It's been three nights, but who's counting."

"Why didn't you sleep—"

"I had a nightmare."

"Oh. Well, even more reason to have you sleep with...sleep in the bed with me."

"Are you sure that's the only reason? That you want me to have a good night sleep?"

"Well... no. I—"

"The problem is,"—he rose from where he was sitting and closed the distance between them, snaking his arm around her waist—"I don't know that I could sleep with you in bed with me. I don't seem to have much

219

control around you." His fingers pushed her hair off her shoulder, and his lips came down at the base of her neck and worked their way up, nibbling and sucking. Cupping his hand at her chin, he softly grazed her cheek as his eyes met hers. "See?"

"Please? Can we at least try?"

His lips brushed against hers, nibbling at her bottom lip, then her top. Her breath halted. God. She knew she was playing with fire, but she didn't have much control around him either. She loved his hands on her.

He leaned his forehead against hers and breathed heavily. "If that's what you want, I guess I could try," he hesitantly conceded, feigning the weighty sacrifice he was making.

A toothy grin burst onto his face, and she realized he'd had her begging him to sleep with her. He was such a mess. She couldn't help but giggle at his antics. She stepped back, and as his hand dropped she laced her fingers through his and tugged him behind her. He stopped and released her hand. "I need to make sure Aurora uses the bathroom. I'll be right there."

She dodged several of the bags and flipped on the lamp. Folding back the covers, she fluffed the pillow, then crawled into the cool sheets. Kaleb appeared in the doorway with Aurora clinging to his shoulder. He set her in her little bed, yanked his shirt over his head, then started to remove his jeans. The way the low light hit him every dent and curve of his body was highlighted and shadowed perfectly, and Eden couldn't drag her eyes away.

"You keep staring at me like that, and this innocent arrangement is going to go south very quickly."

"It's just, you have a perfect body; like a living

sculpture."

"I was thinking something similar about your intricate tattoos. You're like a living canvas. You had an excellent tattoo artist. And as far as your body goes, I think you're perfect. And by the number of awards I saw in your file for all the pageants, I would say others feel the same way." He slid under the covers, propped his cheek on his hand, and dragged her to him. "And I like it because it fits so perfectly with mine."

Aurora let out a tiny meow, and Eden felt the bedspread tug a little. And then again. A little furry head appeared over the edge of the bed. "Aw. Do you feel left out?"

"She didn't like being left here all alone."

Eden rolled over with her back to Kaleb and pulled the kitten to her. Reaching over, she clicked the lamp and threw the room into total darkness. Kaleb's hand slipped over her waist and tugged her close, then his finger brushed against Aurora's head before resting on Eden's belly, and it sent a flood of emotions through her.

****

Tiny meows tore Eden from her dreams and immediately caused a wave of anxiety to invade her body. Was something wrong? She picked Aurora up and quietly tried to scoot out from under Kaleb's protective grasp.

"Where are you going?" he groggily said behind her.

"Aurora is meowing, so I thought maybe she was hungry. I'm sorry I woke you."

"Do you want me to get up with her?"

"No. Go back to sleep." She leaned over and placed a gentle kiss on his scruffy cheek, then moved off the bed.

Out in the kitchen, she poured Aurora some food and yawned as she leaned against the counter. The clock on the microwave glowed three fifteen. Aurora dug into the food like she hadn't been fed just a few hours before. Eden closed her eyes and immediately popped them back open, realizing there was a distinct possibility that she could fall asleep standing up.

After finishing her food, Aurora took off around the corner to where her litter box was. "Good kitty." With another yawn, Eden stood, preparing to pick up Aurora when she was done with her business and cart her back to bed. Aurora surprised her, darting up the hallway at full speed. When she got to the end, she raced past Eden and into the living room. Eden leaned her head against the wall, not even close to being ready to play like Aurora was. She slowly shuffled into the living room and found Aurora batting around the feather toy that was hanging off the sofa.

A creak of the floor had Eden glancing over her shoulder to see Kaleb coming toward her in his boxer briefs. She had to blink to make sure he wasn't just a dream.

"What are you doing?" He leaned over the back of the sofa and placed a soft kiss on her neck.

Nope, not a dream. "Aurora thinks it's time to play."

"I guess she slept the whole time we were gone, and now she's awake." He brushed the hair off Eden's neck and then began to massage it. She lolled her head to the side so he could get at a specific spot that was stinging. "Do you want to go lie down? I can play with her for a while and wear her out."

"No. You need to get some sleep. I'll let her play for a little bit, then I'll come back to bed."

"Are you sure?"

"I'm fine. You get her next time."

The minute his hands left her skin, she felt an emptiness, like his presence somehow made her whole.

Thirty minutes later, she decided she would try going back to bed. She carefully lay down, trying not to wake Kaleb, then snuggled Aurora under her chin and pulled up the covers. Kaleb's large hand gently pressed against her stomach and scooted her until she was snug against him. Her body relaxed, and within minutes she was drifting off to sleep.

****

Please tell me it's a dream. The squeaky meows had her peeling her eyes open once again. The room was still bathed in the soft gray darkness. She took a deep breath and tried to sit up, but Kaleb tightened his grip.

Rising to his elbow, he kissed her shoulder. "Don't. I got her," he said in a gravelly voice, then reached over and lifted Aurora into his arms. Eden rolled over and watched his back flex as he sat up. She lifted her hand and lightly ran her nails over his pronounced muscles. He flinched and leaned back, bringing his mouth inches from hers. "Don't move." His lips grazed hers, and he sat back up, then stood and tugged a T-shirt he retrieved from the floor over his head.

The light outside the door flickered on, and she heard him moving around the kitchen. Within a few minutes, she felt the bed give, and she slowly rolled over and opened her eyes.

He leaned in and lifted his hand to move her hair. "The little one is taken care of, and I have the coffee brewing."

"What time is it?" She sat up, turning on the lamp

beside the bed.

"A little after six."

"I wonder what is going on with Aurora. She usually sleeps through the night."

"Don't know."

"What if she's sick? I know Jenna checked her, but maybe something's wrong."

He patted her leg through the covers. "The way she was eating, I doubt seriously she's sick." His eyes met hers and he chuckled as he tilted his head. "Is this what having a baby is like?"

She wanted to laugh with him, but the comment sent a firestorm of panic through her.

Chapter Twenty-Six

The fear that spread across Eden's face echoed through Kaleb. "Eden? Are you having second thoughts?"

"Why? Are you?"

"I asked you first."

Her eyes studied him, and dread settled in his stomach as a thought passed through his mind.

"I'm scared."

"About what?" He sat back, bent his knees, and wrapped his arms around them.

Eden sat up more. Her focus zeroed in on her hand, smoothing the covers. She was nervous. His gut soured. Tears glistened in her eyes as her jaw worked back and forth. Waiting for her words to come, Kaleb could feel himself holding onto the tiniest bit of breath he had left in his lungs.

"I've already dropped a bomb on your life, and I'm scared you're going to feel trapped with a baby."

He stared at her, fear evident in her eyes, then he turned away, battling his thoughts. He didn't want to influence her decision, but after they'd initially decided not to do anything when the condom failed, he'd gotten used to the idea and was actually excited. The thought of what she might be considering now sent a lump into his throat. "Just please promise me you won't get rid of it," he said quickly, his voice breaking. "I know we talked about the day after pill, and it's your decision, Eden, I'm not—"

"I could never do that to our baby. I'm—"

Kaleb took a deep breath, relief replacing the tightness in his chest. "Eden. First off, it takes two. You didn't make me have sex with you, and we used protection. It just…failed. It wasn't your fault or my fault. I have to admit though, even though it wasn't exactly planned, I've been excited about the idea of having a baby. And as far as 'the bomb' you dropped; you need to quit making yourself out to be the bad guy. I'm glad you came to me. Like I said before, I was already working on the case, and honestly you did me and my agency a favor. We were at a standstill, and you gave us a bunch of new leads to follow."

Eden gazed at him through her lashes, and he could see a spark of light replace the darkness from moments before, but a tear still trickled down her cheek. "You have?"

"Have what?"

"Been excited about the baby?"

"I can't say it hasn't scared me some too, but I think that's to be expected."

Turning away she said, "You know when I told you I was a bit phobic of medications?"

"Yeah?"

"That was only half the truth."

She peeked at him, and he raised a brow. Then her head turned back to him. Her voice was barely above a whisper. "I liked the thought of having a baby…with you. You would be an awesome daddy."

A deep laugh rose up his throat. "Why do you say that?"

"The way you treat Aurora. She is so lucky that you found her. You have been so sweet with her."

"So have you."

"Well, if she keeps me awake like last night, she will see a different side of me."

"I doubt that seriously."

"You haven't seen me sleep deprived."

"Uh. What about right now?"

"Oh yeah. I guess you have."

"Are you ready for some coffee and breakfast?" he asked patting her leg again and moving to stand. She quickly fisted his shirt and tugged him off balance, causing him to fall into her. Their noses collided, and he jerked back wincing and rubbing the tip of it.

"Oh my gosh. I'm sorry," she said, smiling and doing the same.

He leaned forward, moving her hand and nuzzling his nose against hers, then laid a soft kiss on it. "The pain is worth it, if I get to have you for breakfast."

She raised up to brush her lips to his, igniting a fire in every cell of his body. With her fingers rubbing his now shorter hair, he pushed her to her back and slid under the covers, then pulled her body to his. She let out a breathy whimper as he pressed himself against her, letting her feel what she did to him. Her hand gently rubbed the stubble of his cheek, then traveled down his bare torso to his briefs and hesitantly brushed against him.

He loved her innocence; how timid she acted with her motions. There were no preconceived notions of what she was supposed to do when it came to exploring the different nuances of sex. It was all new to her. He wondered what she would do if he gave her free rein.

Even though she'd technically had sex, she might as well have been a virgin. She'd never truly experienced having a sexual partner, and he loved being her first. It gave him a rush of pride knowing he'd given her her first orgasm, and something inside him made him want to be the one to give her her last. The thought of what that meant should have terrified him, and maybe it would later. Right now, it didn't.

He rolled over and dragged her on top of him.

"What are you doing?"

"What? You initiated it."

"I did not."

"Oh yes you did. I asked if you wanted breakfast, and you attacked me."

"Oh. I guess—"

"So, get with it. I haven't got all day. Ravage me."

"You. I—"

"Babe. Do you have things you'd like to try?"

Her eyes darted away, and her skin added a rosy tinge. "That right there tells me you do. And I'm here for it. Anything. My body is yours to do with what you will. If you want to ask about something, ask."

"I'm afraid you—"

"Eden, I'm going to let you in on a little secret. When it comes to sex, just about everything feels amazing."

That shy smile that she very rarely revealed, formed on her face, and she gathered her T-shirt with her fingertips and lifted it over her head, revealing another pair of barely there, shimmery, ruby-red, lace panties. Red was his favorite color. She tossed the shirt onto the floor. Just the motion had his body responding, and he sucked in a breath through gritted teeth.

His hands grabbed her thighs and pressed her against him, hoping to satisfy his need just a little, but the moan that she released and the fire that ignited in her hooded eyes made it worse.

Her fingers brushed against his bare skin as she scooted his T-shirt up past his ribcage. He raised his arms, and her fingers glided over his muscles as she removed the shirt, then immediately moved down his body, dragging his boxer briefs with her. A mischievous glint in her eyes had him bringing the soles of his feet to the bed. "What? Don't you trust me?"

He raised up on his elbows. "Not with that look on your face, I don't."

Her hands rubbed up and down his calves. "But you said your body was—"

"Not my feet."

"You said anything." Part of him wanted to see what she would do. However, even the thought of her hands on his feet made his body clench.

"Eden, I don't think you appreciate how ticklish my feet are."

"I didn't tickle them when I found out you were ticklish."

"That's because I was injured."

"Trust me. I think you might like it."

His eyes leveled with hers.

"Close your eyes."

There was something in her voice. He lowered his head to the pillow, placed the back of his hands over his eyes, and slowly released the muscle holding down his foot. And waited. Nothing. After a minute, he covertly peeked out of one eye and realized she'd disappeared. A noise came from the bathroom, and she returned carrying something. Her gaze tipped up. "No peeking."

Covering his eyes with his arm, he resigned himself to his fate. His body stiffened preparing for the torture. Hearing a click, he then felt her hands on his ankle as she lifted his foot, and her thumbs dug into his arch, rubbing in small circles. The pressure she applied was almost painful, but it quickly began to release the tension he'd felt.

The oil she used had a sweet scent and was warm against his skin as she continued to massage different spots on his feet then worked her way up his legs.

"How does it feel?"

"Amazing. Where'd you get the oil?"

"I guess your sister or April got it. It was in with a bunch of the toiletries they brought." He chuckled. They were trying to play matchmaker. He didn't mind it though. Not when it felt this good.

Her hands traveled up his thighs, and she moved over him, straddling his legs as she placed more oil on his torso and spread it over his chest and abs, then worked her way over his shoulders and down his arms, then back up again.

He moved his arm up and opened his eyes to see her lips barely parted, her brown eyes not quite visible beneath her long lashes.

"Don't peek."

"I like watching you."

"You'll make me embarrassed."

"Why? You're good at this."

"Yeah?"

"Yeah. I told you. It feels amazing."

"I took a class in college. Several of us would set up in the commons and give massages before finals."

"Don't tell me that. It makes me jealous."

"Jealous?"

"I don't like picturing you doing this to someone else."

Her fingers pressed against the short stubble of his hair, and she brought her thumbs to his temples then rubbed along his cheek bones and back up.

"This is only part of what I want to do."

That piqued his interest. "Oh. What else?"

"Close your eyes and you'll see."

He did as he was told, and she gently massaged his neck, then her warm lips pressed against his skin over and over. His mouth curved into a smile as she placed a chaste kiss against his lips, then across his cheek, to the lobe of his ear, where she bit down and tugged, which shot an electric jolt through him causing a groan to crawl up his throat.

Letting go, she lightly licked and sucked along the pressure point, down to his collar bone, and along his shoulder. Pin pricks erupted with every brush of her lips.

She continued across his chest, licking and sucking, and his body writhed with the feel of her hot breath and mouth all over him. Opening his eyes, he watched as she continued, lashes pressed to her cheeks, hands kneading his warm skin, and her pink tongue lapping at the oil glistening on his stomach. Sweet torture.

He could feel her breaths becoming labored as her hands moved lower, exploring, touching him, making him twitch. And just when he thought he was going to hit his breaking point, she moved up his body and pressed her lips to his. The rich vanilla flavor of the oil filled his mouth as her tongue swept in. She was letting go of her inhibitions. Letting the moment take her, and

Kaleb was glad he was along for the ride. No longer timid, her body moved against him at a frantic pace, her fingers dug into him, and moan after sweet sensual moan shredded his control.

"Eden." He gulped as he tried to fight off the overwhelming sensation. "I need to be inside you... now."

She slid off him, hurriedly shedding the thin piece of material separating them, while he fumbled for the condom. Once in place, he pulled her back on top of him.

Bringing her hair to one shoulder, she gave him a crooked smirk, then leaning in, she brushed her nose with his, letting her mouth hover, teasing him as she licked his bottom lip.

Lifting his chin, he threaded his fingers into her hair and captured her mouth fully, delving deep, unable to hold back any longer. She pulled away and slid down his body until he rested at her entrance. Her eyes tipped up and locked with his as he entered her, then closed with a flutter of her lashes.

Wrapping his hands around her butt, he nuzzled into her hair and pressed her against him as she began to move. His need for her consumed him. She smelled like the sweetest lavender, tasted like a decadent candy, her skin was as soft as the finest silk, and the whimpers that came from her sounded like a church chorus at Christmas.

Her lips grazed his neck, and she sucked on the tender skin below his ear, again causing his whole body to constrict. His hands slid up her body, and fisting her hair, he slammed his mouth to hers in a fevered kiss. A kiss that was not merely a kiss. It was a sharing of souls, of promises...of forever. He knew, in that moment, beyond a shadow of a doubt, he couldn't live without her.

She suddenly pulled away and pushed against his chest, sitting up, and the motion sent sparks up his spine, edging him dangerously close to his release. "Eden…"

He was cut off by her cries. Her legs tightened at his hips, hands fisted on his chest, and he watched as she came apart before his eyes. It was the most beautiful sight he'd ever seen, and he couldn't hold on any longer. He grabbed her thighs and thrust deep inside her, letting the waves of pleasure engulf him.

Leaning forward as her labored breathing began to even out, she planted soft kisses along his jaw, then finally his lips. "Now, aren't you glad you trusted me?"

****

They sat in the weathered rocking chairs on the porch while Eden opened the computer. Kaleb leaned over, reading the comments as Eden slowly scrolled down the page. Nothing seemed out of the ordinary. Just a few questions and discussions about how to combat the rising number of illnesses and birth defects in children. One post from TheAnswer asked the question "*Do you think the government is putting too many regulations on genetic research?*" Several comments followed then another question. "*How far would you go to ensure you had a healthy baby if you knew you were predisposed to a disease?*" The question had him wondering, if Eden were pregnant, what they'd be willing to do.

As she scrolled through more comments, an uneasiness settled in his stomach.

"Oh my God, Kaleb. These people are talking about genetic editing."

"Okay?"

"Altering DNA."

"I got that. Isn't that what Chalemaare specialized in. "

"His research is in treating genetic disorders… sometimes in utero. It's after the defect is found, or at least that's what I thought. This is altering genes to preempt diseases."

"And that's bad?"

"Genetic altering isn't all bad per se. Discoveries for eradicating diseases is commendable. Everyone wants cancer, multiple sclerosis, ALS, and other diseases that take the lives of our loved ones to disappear. But genetic altering is also extremely controversial, because it gives birth to designer children. You want a boy predisposed to be tall, with brown hair and brown eyes? Boom. You got it. It's like html coding."

"Do you think that's what Chalemaare was doing?"

"I have no idea. But that is where this moderator is leading the discussion. Also, remember you telling me about having to protect the highly intelligent, so they didn't fall into the wrong hands? This," she pointed to the screen, "this could be devastating in the wrong hands."

Chapter Twenty-Seven

Kaleb's phone chimed. He stood and dug it out of his pocket. Malcolm. "Hey, man, how'd the interview go?"

"She never showed." Malcolm's irritation was evident, and Kaleb couldn't blame him.

"What? Seriously?"

"Are you sure you said one?"

He stepped to the side of the porch and leaned on the railing. "Yeah. I confirmed with her for one o'clock." He knew Malcolm had his plate full because of him, and the last thing he needed was to be wasting his time. Feeling the fingers of anxiety crawling up his spine, he straightened. His hand perched on his hip, and he let out a frustrated breath as his fingers threaded through his shorter hair. "I'll call Brant and see if he's heard from her. Sorry about that. I know you're buried."

"Yeah."

"I'll let you know what I find out."

"Fine," he snapped back, and disconnected.

Kaleb stared at his phone feeling guilty at the work he'd heaped on Malcolm.

"What's wrong?" Eden's voice came from behind him.

Without glancing up from his phone he answered, "Miss Bellamy didn't show up for her interview with Malcolm." Lifting his phone to his ear again, he leaned against the railing and pinched the bridge of his nose.

"You guys okay?"

Kaleb would have chuckled at Brant's concern if he wasn't so annoyed at the situation. "Hey. Yeah. We're fine, but have you heard from Miss Bellamy? She didn't show up for her interview today."

"She didn't?"

"Nope. And Malcolm has his hands full with the environmental audit, so he's a bit pissed."

"I think Bekah talked to her earlier. Let me call her, and I'll have her call you."

"Okay. Sounds good." He pocketed his phone and turned to Eden. "Damn. I had my hopes up with her."

"For a woman for Malcolm?"

"Well, yeah, that too. She said she had a master's in environmental engineering. And she already had some oil and gas experience. I was hoping she would be a good addition to my environmental team."

Ben pulled up in his pickup and hopped out. "Brought the bed over from Poppi's."

"Great." Kaleb trotted down the steps as Ben released the tailgate. Eden set the computer on the table and helped carry the railings for the frame. Within a few minutes, the bed was set up. A rumble had everyone turning to see an unmarked delivery truck heading toward them. Kaleb's eyes quickly took in his surroundings, preparing a plan in case things went sideways. He gently nudged Eden behind him. "What are they doing out here?"

Ben rolled his eyes. "Apparently, I'm getting new furniture."

A wave of relief untied in his chest, and he let out a bark of laughter.

"Keep your mouth shut," Ben growled.

"I'm not saying a word," he said, trying to stifle his amusement.

Ben climbed in his truck and drove it next door, and Kaleb and Eden watched from the porch as the leather sofa and chair were unloaded along with the ottoman. Kaleb's phone chimed again. Brant. "So?"

Eden opened the door and held it for Kaleb while they walked inside.

"Bek said Marissa sent her a text message asking about what outfit to wear, and then another one that she was on her way to the office around twelve. She tried calling her, but she didn't answer," Brant rattled off.

Eden mouthed *"what happened?"*

Kaleb moved the phone away from his mouth and said, "She's not answering her phone?"

Eden's eyes widened.

"I'm going to call Mitch to see if there have been any reported accidents."

"Good idea."

"If she calls or texts you, tell her to call Bekah. She's worried."

"Absolutely."

He hung up and his eyes met Eden's. "Brant is calling Mitch to see if they have had any accidents reported."

"'Oh, I hope that's not the case."

"Me too."

"I'm going to make the bed." Kaleb nodded and Eden took off up the hallway with a tiny furball in hot pursuit. Seeing Aurora prancing behind her helped lighten the mood, but only for a moment. Something had the hairs on the back of his neck tingling. He'd been in secret service long enough to have a sixth sense when something was about to go down. It was like an ominous fog had rolled in. *Come on, Ian, I need you to call.*

He reached inside the refrigerator and wrapped his hand around the cold neck of a bottle, hoping a beer would calm all the questions firing off in his brain. What the hell happened? The last thing he needed was to have someone else disappear. He was hoping Marissa's disappearance would be easily explained. There was little chance it was connected to Eden's case, but his brain was on hyperdrive trying to figure out how it could be.

His phone buzzed. *About damn time.* Expecting to see Ian's message to come and get him, Kaleb was surprised when an unfamiliar number appeared. He let out a frustrated breath and clicked on the number. A photo appeared of a bloodied man, and he immediately recognized him as Eden's brother. "Shit!" Sucking down a swig of beer, he stared at his phone with a million more questions forming. Dread flooded his gut. How was he going to tell Eden? He took another drink, breathed deep, and tried to lock down his nerves so he could figure out his next move. At least he was alive.

His eyes darted around, searching for the computer. He stepped outside and grabbed it off the table, then sat down on the sofa, and opened his text messages on the computer to see if there was anything that could give him any clues as to where the photo was taken. Nothing.

His phone buzzed again.

—Bring Eden to Drake Field at six pm this evening and her brother will live. You will know where to go when you get there—

Shit. How did they get my number?

—*How do we know it's him?*— He fired back. —*That photo is dark. Could be anybody*—

A minute passed, and another photo popped up on the computer screen. This time, Adam's bruised and bloodied face stared into the camera. A gasp came from behind Kaleb.

"Oh my God. Adam." Eden's voice shook. Kaleb slammed the computer shut and stood. "That, that's Adam." Tears were already filling her lashes. "Where did you get that photo?" She pointed to the closed laptop as she rushed over to the beat-up coffee table, flipped it open again, and sat down. "Why did you hide it from me?"

"I just got it. Someone sent it to my phone." He held it out to show her.

"That, that's Adam's number. How'd they get…" her question died as she scrolled back and saw the text. "They know I'm with you?" Horror filled her face, and she swallowed hard as she read through the messages. "He's in Dalton?" Her watery eyes darted to his, and she bolted from the seat. "You need to take me to the airport."

"That's not happening." Kaleb pocketed his phone and grabbed her from behind.

She turned in his arms, trying to get away. "They're going to kill him," she bellowed.

He held tight, making her focus on him. "That's not what they said."

"Yes, it is."

"No." He reached up and gently tucked some loose hair behind her ear. "Listen to me, Eden. I've worked cases like this. They will play with words to manipulate you into doing what they want. Adam is their bait."

"What if you're wrong? What if they really want to kill him?"

"Eden. I know what I'm doing. This is my job." He slid his phone from his pocket. "Give me a minute." She rolled her eyes in frustration and stormed off.

Scrolling through his contacts, he stepped outside and pressed the phone to his ear.

"Gallagher."

"Hey, Mitch. It's Kaleb."

"Now what? I've got everybody in the state searching for Miss Bellamy."

"What have you found?"

"Not much."

"Damn. I hate adding to your workload, but I just got a text message from Eden's brother's phone. There were a couple of photos of him. He's been roughed up."

"How the hell did they get your number?"

"I have no idea. Hang on."

Kaleb moved the phone from his ear and tapped on the screen. "I sent you the photos and a screen shot of the text with their demands. If they have my number, I'm worried about what else they know."

"Got 'em. First picture doesn't have much to go on. The second one, we might be able to use a program to sharpen the blurred background."

"They're using him as bait. They aren't going to do shit to him. I'm thinking he's just as valuable as Eden to them, and they're using him as leverage to get her."

"They did a number on him, that's for sure. So, you think this guy is in Arkansas at the airport? He disappeared in France, right?"

"Yeah, somewhere outside of Paris a month ago. I'm not certain he's here, but they're making it sound like he is. I'm wondering why. If they had him and his phone all this time, why wouldn't they have baited her before now to get her to come out of hiding?"

"No telling. Let me get some of my guys over to the airport and do some investigating. See what I can dig up. Give me her brother's name again."

"Adam DiMari. If they are there, they came in on a private jet. Drake Field is the executive airport north of Northwest Regional."

"I'm familiar."

"Do you think we need to get out of here?"

"No. Stay put. The ranch is gated, and you have Ben right there keeping an eye on things. Just make sure the entry gate is secured. I know Will tends to leave it open."

"My partner is supposed to be arriving today. He's going to be staying with us."

"Even better."

"So, what have you found so far on Miss Bellamy?"

"She contacted Bekah about noon, and there is video of her car pulling into the parking lot at corporate and her exiting her car, but she didn't log into the electronic sign in. She just vanished."

"So, she was there and never made it into the building?"

"Yeah, the video footage shows her pausing after getting out of the car, then walking out of camera range. There was no sound, so we don't know if she was talking to someone or she saw something. We're trying to track down possible witnesses now."

"Okay. Let me know if you find anything." He paused. "Can you update the group?"

"Yep."

Kaleb pocketed his phone, and it buzzed again.

Glancing at it, figuring it was Mitch's text to the group, his breath halted when a video popped up from the same number as before. He stared at the screen taking in every nuance, then played it two more times before forwarding it to Mitch, with the words,

—I still think they're bluffing—

—Heading over now—

—That's at a hangar. We have one over at Drake Field. I'd start there—

—I guess that answers whether he's here or not—

—I'd say so— His phone chimed. *—got a call coming in. Keep me updated—*

—Will do—

"It's about damn time, man. Where you at?"

"Flame Masters."

"I'll be there in about fifteen."

"Take your time. Waiting on dinner."

"All right."

Traipsing back inside, Eden was nowhere in sight. Mulling over his next plan of action, he plodded up the hallway, dread gnawing at him. There was no way he could show her the video. She was already too wound up.

As he turned the knob on the bedroom, he found Eden leaning over a suitcase filled with clothes. Her back was to him, but he knew she heard him come in. She chose to ignore him. The sniffling let him know why. He slowly approached her and wrapped his hands around her wrist, pulling her into his arms. Burying her head in his chest, sobs wracked her body. "I can't let him die because of me."

"Eden." He spoke softly, lifting his hand and letting his fingers thread through her hair. "I know what I am doing. I called Mitch. He's on his way to the airport now to check things out."

She raised her head, and her watery eyes held a mountain of pain. "They will kill him if I don't go. They already beat the shit out of him."

"I'm telling you. They won't kill him. He's their leverage to get to you. You responded exactly how they'd hoped." He could see she wasn't hearing him, so he decided to try a different tactic. "It's better that we keep you away from him, because they are using him for bait. Once they have you, he may no longer be useful, and then who knows what might happen to him. So, in order to keep him safe until we can find him, we have to keep you hidden."

"How can you be sure?"

"Nothing is guaranteed. But I've dealt with situations very similar. I've been trained in hostage negotiations, abduction, and kidnapping. It's what I do. I need you to trust me."

"I do trust you, but I'm scared. He's my brother."

"I understand. If anything were to happen to Joe or Kaysi, I'd burn the world down to save them…and you. I think this is the right move though. It would risk both of your lives if we caved to their demands."

"That's the other thing I'm worried about. They contacted you. How'd they get your number?"

"I have no idea. But let's not worry about me. Let's focus on keeping you safe and solving this case, okay?" It did gnaw at him that they had somehow gotten his number. Eden's brother wouldn't have had it. And evidently, they knew his family had a hangar at Drake Field. He kissed Eden on top of her head and held her until her tears subsided. His hands slid to her cheeks, and he lifted her chin. "Now. Do you want to take a ride with me? I need to pick up Ian. He's at Flame Masters."

****

Kaleb hopped out of the pickup, and anyone getting a quick glimpse of him would have sworn it was Joe. He had on a pair of worn jeans and a cotton, button down with the sleeves rolled. Both were stained with paint. His cap was on backward, and a pair of aviators shielded his eyes.

He stepped inside Flame Masters, and the hostess appeared at the counter as he shoved the glasses to the top of his cap. Waving her off, he said, "I'm hunting for someone." Searching the area, Kaleb caught sight of Ian, sitting at the bar, deeply engrossed in the game on the big screen.

Taking long strides, he didn't dare try to sneak up behind him. With their training, Ian would have him in a choke hold on the floor in seconds, so he slid onto the stool next to him and tried to steal a fry.

"I'd hate for you to lose a finger," Ian growled.

"Eh. It's on my left hand, I can deal."

Ian kept his head down over his food only lending a side glance to Kaleb, then his eyes tracked up and down his attire.

"A bit of a disguise."

"Ah." Ian nodded. "Any updates?"

"We have a lot to talk about. I'll show you when we get to the truck."

Ian's eyes lifted to the bartender, and with two fingers he flagged her over. "I'm ready to tab out." Picking up a fry and dredging it in ketchup, he took a bite. "I have some interesting information to share with you too."

A Life of Illusions

"Let's get back to the house."

The ticket was dropped off, and Ian laid some cash on top of it, then stood and headed for the door.

Chapter Twenty-Eight

Eden sat up, hearing the door to the truck open. She lifted the cap she had pulled down over her eyes.

Ian did a double take as he opened the passenger door. His aviators he had pushed up on his head slid down onto his eyes, and he push them back into place and smirked. "Hi, honey, I'm home," he said as he hopped in. She rolled her eyes at his comment, and he continued. "I can't believe you're still hanging out with this lowlife."

Eden snorted at Ian's joke. "He's holding me hostage." She tried a bit of humor, but the reality was, she was a hair's breadth from losing it completely.

Kaleb dug his phone from his pocket, unlocked the screen, and handed it to Ian.

"Where'd you get this?" he asked after viewing the photos.

"Whoever is after Eden sent them to me."

"How?"

"Haven't figured that out yet."

"Damn. Who the hell is this poor dude?"

"That is Adam DiMari, Eden's brother."

Ian bounced between the two photos for a moment, then the video started to play. A bright light reflected off a cement floor, then the camera panned up to Adam, who was tied to a chair with a gag in his mouth. He was bleeding from his nose and a cut on his head. As the camera continued to pan, it stopped on the gun pointed at Adam's temple. The light glinted off the barrel, then the screen went black.

Eden sat stunned. "Wha-what was that?" she blurted before her throat closed down completely.

Kaleb glanced back at her as he started the truck. "Shit. Eden, I'm sorry. I got it right before we left."

She yanked the phone out of Ian's hand and sat back, staring at the screen as it played again. Fury filled her. "You didn't want me to see this. Don't lie to me, Kaleb."

Kaleb turned, giving her his full attention. He remained silent for a long minute, not breaking eye contact, then his jaw ticked. "Fine," he said through gritted teeth. "I didn't want you to see it, because you were already so wound up and upset from the photos that I thought it would upset you more, and I already had Mitch heading to the airport."

"And you still don't think they will kill him? Adam has a gun to his head."

"No, Eden. I didn't think they would kill him. And I was obviously right. It's after six, and they would have contacted us by now if they followed through with their threat. If we haven't gotten any update by now, he's not dead. Mitch is supposed to get back with me once he does a complete sweep of the hangars."

"He's bait," Ian broke in.

Eden had almost forgotten Ian was even in the truck with them.

"That's what I told her. They're trying to lure her into their trap."

Eden turned the volume up. She could hear Adam breathing hard against the gag. And then there was a whimper.

"Wait. Play that again," Kaleb rushed out. Eden hit the button. "Did you hear that?" His eyes darted to Ian's.

"Sounded like a woman."

"Damn it." He turned back to Eden. "Find Mitch Gallagher's contact and call him, then hand me the phone."

Eden did as Kaleb asked, and after handing the phone off, Kaleb put it on speaker. "Gallagher."

"Mitch. I think—"

"They were here. Found traces of blood in one of the hangars."

Eden gasped.

Like Mitch knew what she was thinking, added, "Not enough to constitute someone being shot. They are nowhere to be found now. We did a thorough search."

"And I think they may have Marissa Bellamy," Kaleb added.

"What the hell gave you that idea?"

"Eden watched the video with the audio turned up, and you can hear a noise in the background. It sounds like a woman whimpering. I'm betting it's Marissa Bellamy."

"How does she fit into all this, though?"

"It has to be me. They know I have Eden. I'm sure, since we disappeared they are staking out places they'd know I would be."

"But how would they know she's connected to you?"

"How the hell do I know? How'd they get my number? None of this shit makes any sense. What I do know is we need to figure it out now, or it's going to blow up in our face."

What evil had she unknowingly brought with her to

Dalton? Eden's heart raced. In the short time she'd spent in Dalton, she'd caused the destruction of someone's home and an innocent woman's abduction. What next?

"Settle down. We won't get anywhere if we let our emotions run the show."

"I don't like feeling like they have the upper hand. There are too many unanswered questions, and we can't come up with a game plan when we don't have answers."

"I get it. We aren't going to get anywhere if we don't keep a cool head though. Now, since there is no obvious connection between Miss Bellamy and Miss Samuels, I'm thinking she was in the wrong place at the wrong time. Plain and simple. The good thing is, at the time they made the video she and Miss Samuels' brother were still alive. You haven't gotten any other communication from them?"

"Not since the video."

"Okay. And I'm pretty sure we know where the video was made. We'll wrap things up here and continue the search for Miss Bellamy, in case you're wrong."

"All right. Keep me in the loop if you find anything."

"Will do, and you do the same."

Kaleb disconnected the call. "Let's get back to the house. We'll call Quinten once we're on the same page."

"I'll be right behind you." Ian opened the door. Kaleb waited for him to get in his car before he pulled out.

Eden climbed into the passenger seat, overwhelmed with what was unfolding around her, and let her frustrations fly. "I can't believe you kept that video from me," she seethed.

"Eden, I got it right before we left. I shot it off to

Mitch, who was already headed to the airport. It wasn't going to change anything, other than make you more upset. You would have fought me more about taking you to the airport, and I wasn't going to do that."

She remained quiet, trying to rein in her emotions that were threatening to consume her.

"I'm right, aren't I?"

Closing her eyes, she leaned her head against the headrest. She knew he was right. It didn't make the thought of Adam dying any less painful though.

He then added, "I'm going to do everything in my power to get your brother back, but that doesn't include risking your life to do it. Are we clear?"

She continued to stay quiet.

"Are we clear?"

This was such a different Kaleb than she was used to. This forceful, leave no room to argue attitude was something new. And something about it stoked a fire in her. He wanted to protect her. But he didn't understand that she wanted to protect him too.

Crossing her arms as desperation set in, she took a deep breath. "Things are just getting more screwed up by the minute. First, I put you in danger, then your family and friends, and now some poor woman."

"I told you, this is—"

"Not my fault. I know what you told me, Kaleb. However, it doesn't make me feel any less guilty."

His phone chimed in the cupholder, and "Dad" popped up on the dash. Tapping the screen, he answered. "Hey, Dad."

"What the hell is going on? I just got back in town. Police are swarming the office saying some woman got abducted and you and Malcolm are nowhere to be found."

And now his dad was jumping down his throat. He still hadn't spoken to him about his side hustle with the secret government organization.

"Malcolm may be with the police. The woman was supposed to be meeting with him for an interview, and she didn't show up. Her car was found in the parking lot. She never made it inside."

"Where were you when all this was happening?"

"I had some personal business I had to deal with, so Malcolm agreed to do the interview."

He was trying to sound matter of fact, but as his eyes shot to her when he turned down the gravel road, there was no masking the distress in his expression.

"Okay. Come by my office when you get here tomorrow, and you can fill me in."

"I won't be there tomorrow. I am still dealing with this personal issue. Malcolm is handling everything."

The silence on the other end of the phone lasted longer than Eden was comfortable with, and the line between Kaleb's brows grew deeper as he waited for his dad to respond. "Son. Is everything okay? I know we've been through a lot in the past couple of years, and if this job is too much—"

"No, Dad. It's fine. Malcolm and I are handling it. I'm working on what I can from the house until I can come back in. It's—"

"Kaleb, I know there is something going on with you. I've left you alone because you're an adult now and you're allowed to have a personal life, but—"

The worried tone in his voice cut through Eden. With everything their family had gone through, there was no way his dad wouldn't be worried about him.

"I'm fine, Dad. Really. Please don't worry about me."

"All right. Just know, I'm here for you, son."

"I know you are." They parked in front of the house, and Kaleb left the truck running. "Hey, I need to go, but I will keep you updated with the investigation, okay?"

"Sure."

"And I promise. I'm okay. I will let you know if I need your help."

"I'll hold you to that."

"I love you, Dad."

"Love you too, son."

He killed the engine, and his eyes darted to Eden, like he was suddenly aware that she heard the entire conversation. She chewed on her cheek feeling her eyes burn. "I wish I had that with my mom," was all she could manage before she popped open the door and hopped out, not giving him time to say anything. The feelings were too raw. How could she put him in a position where he might get hurt? How could she tear his family apart again?

Ian got out of his car and hoisted his bag over his shoulder. Kaleb finally exited the truck. She heard him call back to Ian. "Need any help with that?"

She didn't want to stick around and headed straight for the bedroom. Lifting a sleeping Aurora, she propped her on her shoulder and carefully crawled up on the soft covers of the bed, leaning against the pillows. Her mind was reeling from everything that had happened. The video of the gun pointed at Adam played over and over in her thoughts, as Kaleb's dad's voice echoed asking if he was okay. How could things have spun so out of control so fast?

The door opened, and Kaleb tipped his head as he entered. "You okay?"

He sat down on the edge of the bed and ran the pad of his finger along the kitten's head. Eden took a deep breath. "I'm sorry."

"What are you sorry for?"

"Your dad sounds like such a sweet man, and it killed me to hear how worried he is for you. Your family and all your friends are on edge because of me."

"Eden, I don't know how to get it through your head. You're the victim."

"Am I? What am I the victim of? I wasn't abducted."

His eyes widened in disbelief. "Are you kidding me? You would have been at the pageant if you hadn't run, and also the other night if I hadn't come in."

"I feel like I'm causing so much trouble for everyone. I am so scared someone is going to get hurt."

"They are all well aware of the risks."

"I don't want anyone risking their life for me, Kaleb."

"Then I guess you came to the wrong place, because, as you heard, we don't let family fight their battles alone." He leaned on his elbow. "And you're part of the family now. We've claimed you, so you're kind of stuck with us."

"I could think of a lot worse things I could be stuck with."

Kaleb chuckled. "Just you wait. They can be brutal."

"Why do I get the feeling some of the less than stellar treatment might be well deserved."

Kaleb's mouth dropped open at her statement, but then he tipped his head considering it. "Possibly. But you don't have to worry. You're new, so everyone is on their best behavior…well…aside from Ben. But once you've been around them a while, trust me, their true colors come out."

Her lips twitched at his comment, and he pointed his sexy crooked smile at her, causing her to lose the battle she was fighting against hers. He was good at that.

"Now. Ian is waiting to be debriefed, and I'm going to need your help. Are you up for it?"

"I guess." Regardless of how guilty she was feeling, if there was anything she could add that would help them get the case solved without anyone getting hurt, she was willing to do it.

Chapter Twenty-Nine

They returned to the living room. Kaleb set his laptop on the table, and Ian dug his out of his duffle. "Why don't you go first. Who is this woman that you think is on the video?" Ian asked as he swiped his finger across the pad on the computer.

"I was supposed to interview her for a job at our company today. When everything went down, I asked my partner, Malcolm, to do the interview for me, but the woman never showed up. We have her on security pulling into the parking lot and getting out of her car, then she disappeared. There is no way she could be connected to the case. I only met her a few days ago. She's a friend of a friend. There is no reason for them to have her."

"Well, we aren't sure it's her."

"It's got to be."

"And you said that happened today?"

"Yeah. I found out about it around two. Right after that was when the photos of Eden's brother showed up on my phone. I sent Mitch Gallagher, a friend of the family and a police sergeant, to the airport. You heard what he found."

"Anything else?"

"We got invited into one of the groups on the website." He shifted his focus to Eden, who was still standing but moved to sit next to him. "Tell him what you think is going on."

Lifting her focus between the two of them, she felt oddly excited that she was being asked to join in on their secret mission. "We answered a question discussing the increasing percentage of birth defects around the world, and within a short time we were invited into a group chat. The moderator posed several questions dealing with gene altering and its value in the possibility of eradicating certain diseases and abnormalities. Which sounds great. Who wouldn't want to get rid of cancer. But at the egg and sperm stage it's illegal, because it delves into designer babies and the creation of an elite race, along with the possibility it could be used for some kind of warfare. And this discussion was absolutely heading in that direction."

Ian rocked in his seat on the sofa, and Eden saw something in his expression that had a sick feeling quickly taking hold. "What did you find out?" she asked knowing she didn't want to hear the answer.

"The address on your pageant application was of a storage facility, but it wasn't for grandma's estate. It was a cryopreservation facility. As in frozen embryos. And we found a hidden paper trail that led back to Chalemaare."

"Okay."

"As of yet, the only thing we have tying Chalemaare to any children is what Adam produced. Adam's mom was a doctor of obstetrics. A specialist in fertility. So, all these pieces seem to be part of the same puzzle that we have yet to fit together. We were given what was left in her office. It was of no help. I doubt seriously if they were doing anything illegal they would keep the files in the office. And if she had any files or medical records at her house, the ones who tore it apart probably took those.

"We went to Eva's home, and it had been wiped clean. Completely empty. The university said Professor Dubois took a leave of absence. Her office was cleaned out also. No surprise. We have yet to obtain a search warrant for your mom's house. It's coming. As well as the pharmaceutical plant she works at."

"Sounds like you guys got quite a bit done."

"ICMP put some of their people on it."

Kaleb nodded. "Anything else?"

"We found some old photos of Chalemaare, early in his career, and a woman who might have been a partner or girlfriend. We haven't identified her yet."

"So, we are thinking Chalemaare…"

"Still not sure. He could have been delving into genetic editing, and when he got the award for his other research, someone got wind of what he was really doing and decided they needed his research and is holding him hostage. Or he got wind of someone getting too close to the truth, and he went into hiding. My guess is the latter, since we found that paper trail, and someone still seems to be calling the shots at his Paris facility."

"His facility was checked out. All legal, right?"

"Yeah. All legal. The paperwork for the cryopreservation facility was well hidden. We probably wouldn't have found it had Eden not put that address on her application. ICMP is digging deeper now, because where there is one buried trail there are usually more. If Chalemaare's behind all this, he's a sneaky bastard, I give him that. He's connected to many legitimate organizations and research facilities all over the world, so when he tucks one away that may be not so legitimate, it gets buried. Just like Adam's mom's facility. She was obviously connected. But would we have known if Adam hadn't found those papers? No. And I'm sure the paperwork for the facility is somewhere. But I doubt we will ever find it."

"What about *Récolte*, the place Adam overheard the men talking about?"

"Nothing with that name yet. There are a ton of marinas and ports along the coast that we checked. None having that name and so far, we have found nothing with that name connected to Chalemaare."

"Okay. What else do you have?"

Ian picked up a small leather bag that was sitting on the coffee table. "I brought some fun stuff." He unzipped the pouch and laid out the contents. Eden leaned forward. Ian held up a clear piece of plastic with a circle smaller than the size of a dime. "This is a new tracking device that I've been working with MIT on recently. Extremely hard to detect. Works similar to the airlines, using satellites. Download the ID of the patch, peel the adhesive from the back to activate, place it anywhere on the body, and you can track the person just about anywhere. Plus, and this is a huge plus, it has a mic built in. So, we can track the person and hear everything going on around them from thousands of miles away."

"Damn! That's next level."

"Still in the experimental stage, but I figured in this situation better to have it since we don't have the team behind us right now. "I got some prototypes to test right before I left. I want you each to have one. It's important we know where you are at all times." He handed it to Eden and then Kaleb. "They should last for at least five days after applying then the adhesive starts to break down."

"We can put them anywhere, and they should work?"

"I'd say somewhere not covered by clothes would work best. I've already gotten all the trackers downloaded into the computer, so once it's activated, it will notify me, and I should be able to pick up the signal."

"Any word on the cavalry?"

"Quinten is working on it, as well as the safe house, but I think you have a great set up for now. No one would know this is back here."

"I didn't think they would get my number either. Makes me wonder what else they have. That shit is driving me insane. I can't protect my family against the unknown." His words sent a knife into Eden's chest. She tried to keep the guilt at bay, but its noise wouldn't be silenced.

"Let's call Quinten with what we have before it gets too late. And we can see where he is on his end."

Eden figured she didn't need to be in on the conversation, so she wandered into the kitchen, dug the tea out of the refrigerator, and poured herself a glass. She turned to offer them some, but they were already on the phone.

Needing to clear her head, she grabbed her sweater, slipped on her shoes, and stepped outside. Taking a deep breath of the fresh air, she sat down in the rocking chair on the porch, not bothering to close the door completely, in case they needed her for something. The sun was setting. A chill nipped at her nose, and she tugged the sweater tighter.

She mulled everything over in her head and wondered where she fit into the scenario. With the information she had now, she wondered if she was even conceived naturally, or if she was created in a lab. Just some research experiment. The idea gutted her.

Their voices carried, and she noticed Ian had an odd accent. Maybe Australian? A sudden rush of goosebumps filled her body as the voice of the man who grabbed her came to mind. His voice was similar. Shaking, she remembered his hands on her, and she wondered what would have happened if Kaleb hadn't come in. Was he the same man that had the gun pressed against Adam's head? She had no idea if he was even alive now. And what about Eva? She leaned her head back and brought her knees up, wrapping her arms around them. Tears spilled down her cheeks for the millionth time. It was all so overwhelming.

Kaleb's phone chimed and she leaned closer to the door. "What do you mean you got a message?" She stood, hearing the anger in Kaleb's voice, and moved closer. "How the hell did they get your number?" There was a pause before he said, "No, Kaysi. Sit tight for a minute. Let me talk to Ian. I will call you back."

Through the crack of the door, she saw Kaleb tugging at his short hair as he stared at his phone. "Shit!" he roared. Ian ended the call with Quentin and set his phone down. "That son of a bitch contacted Kaysi. Sent her a photo of Marissa with the message, *Last chance. If Eden's not here within the hour, you're next.*" He handed Ian the phone and paced in front of the sofa. "How the hell are they doing this?"

"Looks like they didn't treat her any better than Adam. Are they in the same place as before? Where'd you say it was?" Ian held out the phone and Kaleb took it.

"The private airfield hangars north of the airport." His hand pounded against his mouth and Eden could practically see the fury radiating off him. His family had been through so much already. She couldn't be the reason some other tragedy occurred. Her being here was costing him too much, and she wasn't worth it.

Chapter Thirty

Kaleb's body quaked with pent up energy as his mind flipped through different scenarios so fast he couldn't seem to land on the best laid plan of attack. The pieces weren't coming together. He'd never felt so confused.

"Has your cop buddy requested the flight logs for the charters and private planes arriving in the past few days?"

"That's an excellent question. I bet the son of a bitch has the hostages on one of the planes. Mitch wouldn't have access to search the personal jets unless he had a warrant, but he might be able to get the flight logs." Kaleb swiped his screen and made the call.

"Gallagher."

"Hey, Mitch. We had another contact. This time they texted Kaysi."

"Kaysi? How the hell—"

"Great question. Wish I knew the damn answer. I'm sending you the text. The photo is of Marissa Bellamy. So, we have confirmation on her. She was beaten pretty badly."

"Got it. What does Kaysi have to do with it?"

"About as much as Marissa Bellamy does. I figure it's another scare tactic. From the photo, it looked like they're back in the same hangar, or another hangar at the airport. They gotta have a plane, and that's probably where they've been keeping them."

"Thought of that, but it would take me forever to get warrants—"

"What about flight logs? For incoming private and chartered flights."

"I requested them, but I haven't gotten anything back yet."

"Damn, you're good. Let me know when you get them."

"Not my first rodeo. I'll be in contact the minute they turn them over."

Kaleb's eyes darted around after he disconnected the call. "Where's Eden? We need to fill her in."

"I saw her head out the door earlier. How is she handling all of this?"

"It's been a lot for her."

"So, tell me, how far down the rabbit hole have you gone with her?"

"I'm not quite sure what you're asking."

"She's not just a client, obviously."

"Oh." He could feel the heat creeping up his neck and his fingers rubbed against his chin as it spread.

"I knew when you started talking about her at the hotel, during the pageant, something was going on. But I thought after she shot you she kind of lost her luster."

"I thought so too, until she showed up here."

"And so…" He knew what Ian was asking… If he'd crossed the line. And he had. He'd left it in his rearview mirror many miles back.

His mind drifted back to her body wrapped in his black sheets, setting off the colors of her tattoos. Her lips, a deep plum, bruised from his onslaught of kisses. He could almost smell the deep, rich scent of her perfume, which was like a magic potion beckoning him to her now. "That right there tells me everything I need to know."

Kaleb stiffened. "What?"

"That look on your face gave me all the sordid details I need. I just wanted to know how much I was going to have to cover your ass while I'm here. From what I'm seeing, you're going to be next to worthless."

"Shut the hell up."

Ian chuckled. "Nah. I'm happy for you, man. Never thought I'd see the day when a woman could lock your ass down."

He couldn't help but smirk. "She hasn't locked down nothing."

"I beg to differ."

He had him dead to rights. She'd awakened something within him he didn't even know existed. Even though there was more to the assignment than protecting her, he couldn't seem to make himself care much about it. His focus was her. "You'll understand one of these days."

"I've been down that road before, if you remember. It didn't turn out well for me. I'd just as soon tear off my right arm and beat myself with it than go through that hell again. But more power to you."

They'd shared many stories about their lives during their assignments together. Ian had told him how he and his dad had moved to America when he was going into high school after his mom left them for another man. He fell in love and married his high school sweetheart before joining the marines. After a particularly rough tour, he'd returned home to find her gone, along with most of his money. It devastated him and made him feel like a fool, since his mom had done the same thing to his dad. His dad had even warned him about her, but he didn't listen. In the end, he decided to disappear, and what better way than to become an undercover agent.

"Trust me, when you least expect it, it will happen."

"I'm not holding my breath."

Kaleb stood. "Let me check on her, and then we can compare notes." He stepped through the partially open door, but Eden was nowhere in sight. "Eden?"

He jogged down the steps and around the corner of the house. There was no sign of her. When he returned to the front, he noticed her glass of tea sitting on the side table by the rocking chair.

Pushing the door open, he returned inside and moved quickly, checking the bathroom, then the bedroom, trying not to let the panic consume him. When he still didn't find her, he felt the walls of his chest cave in, rendering his lungs useless. "She's, she's gone," he said weakly.

Ian's head popped up from his computer. "Have you checked next door?"

"No. Good idea." Hope sparked again as he retrieved his phone and tapped the screen.

"Hello?"

"Kaysi? Is Eden over there?" *Please, please let her be there.*

"No. Why?"

"Shit!" He shook his head to Ian. Pinching his nose as the sting reemerged, he breathed out, "She's gone. She went outside while we were talking to Quinten, and I just went to find her, and she's gone. Did you see any cars pull up?"

"No. Let me check with Ben. He just came in."

Kaleb stepped outside again, hoping she was on the other side of the house, but there was still no sign of her.

"Ben said he hasn't seen her either, and he said no one has come on the property. The gate is closed, and he would have gotten notifications from the security cameras."

Without saying good-bye, he clicked out of the call. "Son of a gggrrrrhh!" Throwing his phone against the wall, he seethed. "They got her."

"What did she say?"

"They haven't seen her. Ben's got security cameras to notify him if cars come on the property. He said there hasn't been any notifications but—"

"Why would they have sent the text if they knew where she was?"

"Shit, I don't know. None of this makes sense."

"Let's work with what we do know. No cars came on the property. Which means they would have parked off property and come on foot. And if that's the case they couldn't have gotten very far."

"Unless they parked up on fifty-one. It wouldn't take that long for them to get there."

"Then I suggest we get a move on."

"I'll notify everyone."

Kaleb picked up his phone from the floor. It was still intact. He quickly sent out a group text.

—Eden is missing. No cars are gone, so we are assuming she's been taken. Ben has not received any notifications from his security cameras that any cars have entered or left the property, so they may be on foot. We need all the help we can get—

—Kaysi and I are heading out on horseback up the trail by highway fifty-one—

—*I'll be over in five. I'll take Rubi out along the ridge up by the cliffs*—

—*I'm at a construction site outside of Fayetteville. I'll take the copter up and let you know when I'm close*—

—*Where do you need me? I'm in Fayetteville right now*—

—*Can you go to the airport and team up with Joe*—

—*Done*—

—*I have no idea what we are dealing with, so make sure you're armed*—

"What do we have?" Ian asked when Kaleb's eyes met his.

"Ben and Kaysi are heading out on horseback. Cody is heading over in his jeep to ride along the ridge. Joe and Brant are picking up the helicopter. It will take them a bit to get here, but it might be our best resource. It has the spotlight."

Ian's attention swung back to his computer. "Do you think she left on her own? She wouldn't try to take him down by herself, would she?"

He didn't want to believe it, but with the comments she'd made, he couldn't rule it out. "Possibly. She's been worried that she was putting my family at risk."

Still focused on his screen, Ian responded, "She hasn't activated the tracker yet. If she is on the move alone, she may not want to be found."

"Regardless, I know where she's headed." He glanced at his phone. "It's been what, thirty minutes since the call from Kaysi?"

"A little more."

"I'm going to the airport."

"I'm coming with you."

"I need you to stay here and man base camp."

"Not happening. Get someone else. I'm not leaving you hanging this time."

"Fine. I could use you to help me keep my head on straight anyway."

Kaleb picked up his keys, and they headed out the door. He could practically hear his blood roaring through his body as he climbed into his truck and raced up the dirt road. The moon was full in the night sky and Kaleb was thankful for the little light it provided.

At the entrance to the ranch, he stopped long enough to call Joe. From the background noise, Kaleb knew Joe was already in the air. "Brant and I are heading your way. Should be there in about ten."

Kaleb pulled out onto the road. "Kaysi got a message. They said they would be coming after her, if Eden didn't show up at the airport within the hour. Sent a photo of Miss Bellamy. She was pretty bloody. I'm heading to the airport."

"When I was getting the helicopter, there was a Cessna out by our hangar with its lights on. I hadn't seen it before."

"Good to know. That's where I'll head."

The noise of the helicopter filled the lack of voices, then Joe's voice broke through. "We'll find her, man."

The knot that formed in his throat rendered him speechless. He pursed his lips fighting the sting behind his eyes. Clearing his throat, he finally responded, "I hope we're not too late."

He disconnected the call and found Jenna's number. "Hey, Jen. I need your help," he spouted before she even had a chance to say hello.

"I saw your message. What do you need me to do?"

"Can you be point of contact at Ben's old place? I

need someone there in case Eden comes back, or any of the search crew needs anything."

"Yeah. April and I will head over."

"Thanks."

He hung up just to get a call from Mitch. "I'm heading to Drake Field. I got held up with a wayward cow on Main. They're supposed to have the flight records for me. I've also got a call into Fayetteville police, but our hands are tied regarding searching the planes until we get our search warrant."

"We're headed there too. I've been keeping an eye out on fifty-one behind Ben's, but I have a sick feeling, Mitch. She thinks this is her fault."

"We? We who?"

"My buddy Ian is with me."

"So, you don't think they grabbed her?"

"Maybe not. She might have left on foot. She kept saying she didn't want anyone to get hurt because of her."

"Well, hopefully we will be able to get there before her. How much time do we have?"

"We are pushing an hour right now and we are about five miles out."

"Don't do anything stupid and get yourself shot before I get there."

"I'll try not to."

"I'd appreciate it."

Blue runway lights lit up the night as they approached the airfield. Large hangars filled the landscape. Drawing closer to his family's hangar, the Cessna his brother spoke of came into view. He'd seen a plane similar to it before. It had occupied too much of his memories and nightmares. But what was the plane doing by his family's hangar? The security lights kicked on, and Kaleb watched as Eden jumped out of a utility truck and ran toward the plane where the stairs were down. Someone was standing on the landing, but the door blocked Kaleb's view.

He threw the truck in park and bailed out, running toward Eden. She had a head start on him. "Eden. No!"

Her eyes darted as her foot hit the bottom step and she stopped. "Kaleb, stop. I can't let you put your family in danger."

A flood of déjà vu hit him. Everything from that night came rushing back, and he suddenly felt like he was running in cement. His heart pounded against his chest so hard it rang in his ears, making his head swim and the ground unstable. He blinked, trying to bring everything back into focus, and slowed his pace, hoping to stay upright.

"Please don't do this, Eden." His hand clutched his chest as he tried to suck in a breath that didn't come, and he stumbled to the aircraft.

Footsteps quickly approached behind him, and a voice rang out from the plane, "Call off your dogs, or she's dead." It had him halting in his tracks as his eyes lifted to the landing, and a wave of nausea settled in the pit of his stomach.

Shaking his head, he closed his eyes, refusing to believe what he was seeing. "Malcolm?"

He stood at the landing, with a gun pointed directly at Eden, who remained at the base of the stairs. Memories of the man he called his friend raced through his mind: the first day they were introduced, their in-depth discussions at the bar with him sharing about his infatuation with Kaysi, and his dejected expression when she put an end to their relationship. Kaleb had sat for hours, while Malcolm tried to come to terms with the break-up. He swallowed the lump in his throat as the deep betrayal set in.

Eden's head jerked. "This is Mal—"

His body trembled as fury set a course through his veins. "All the times talking at the bar…I counted you as my friend…And you and Kaysi…" The memories kept coming, and tears streamed down his cheeks as he roared, "You son of a bitch. You lied about it all." Sweat droplets formed at the base of his neck. Rage exploded within him, and he lunged forward. Malcolm's gun swung to him. Eden backed away from the steps, her eyes following the aim of the gun.

"You made it too easy, my man. Two birds. One stone. Money can buy you a wealth of knowledge, and just about anything you want to know. You shouldn't play spy games when your family is well known. And you shouldn't be so obvious with your affections. It only took me a few hours to find out your true identity. Too much information on the world wide web." The gun swung back to Eden. "Now, my darling Eden. Or do you prefer Victoria? The plane is waiting."

"Eden, please. Don't do this." Kaleb's head felt like it was going to explode, and he stumbled again as his chest tightened even more. Ian reached out in time to keep him from hitting the ground. Eden's eyes darted between Malcolm and him. "Please."

Malcolm's gun swung to Kaleb. "Eden. Either you come with me, or I put a bullet in your Agent Grey's head." Kaleb's eyes locked with hers, and he held her gaze as she silently spoke, then with the slightest nod, she turned and headed up the stairs.

Malcolm grabbed her roughly, and she disappeared into the cabin of the plane. "Eden!" Kaleb bellowed, although he knew it was pointless. The stairs started to lift. "Malcolm, you son of a bitch."

He saluted Kaleb, and the door to the plane closed.

Kaleb fell to his knees unable to take a breath. His chest felt like it was tearing apart. Tears cascaded down his cheeks. The roar of the engine increased, and he watched as the wheels began to turn, and the behemoth started to move. Ian kneeled beside him.

Red and blue lights flicked back and forth. Mitch exited his vehicle and jogged to them. "Is he okay?"

Kaleb lifted his head slowly.

Mitch stared at the plane. "She on it?"

Kaleb nodded. The plane was positioned to taxi. A thumping noise rose over the roar of the engine. The wheels of the jet groaned as they came to a stop. Kaleb's head whipped around to see Joe and Brant in a standoff in the helicopter in front of the plane. The phone in Ian's hand chimed. He handed it to Kaleb. "You left it in the truck. I notified everyone about Eden."

Kaleb answered.

"Call them off," Malcolm roared, "or I swear I will take out every member of your family, one by one, and I will make you watch them die."

Kaleb put his hand on the ground with the phone still in it, trying to stay conscious. He raised his chest trying to fill his lungs. Closing his eyes, he swallowed hard. Tears flowed freely. He gave up trying to stop them. Finally, he lifted the phone, and thumbed his way to Joe's number, and clicked. "Let them go," he said weakly.

"To hell with that. I'm not letting this mother—"

"Let them go," he reiterated. "I think Eden might have a plan, and I don't want him to hurt her." With that, he dropped the phone on the cement, and watched as the helicopter backed away and the wheels of the jet started moving again.

Chapter Thirty-One

Tears streaked Eden's face as she stepped across the threshold of the plane. Worry over Kaleb strangled her like an impending storm. He was in so much pain, and she wanted to run to him. The gun Malcolm had pointed at him ended the thought. She needed to keep her head in the game and put an end to this before anyone else got hurt.

She didn't really have a plan when she ran from the house, other than finding a way to get to the airport. That was the only way she could keep Kaleb and his family safe.

The dense pine forest didn't allow for much light as she tried to find her way to the highway. There wasn't much anyway as late as it was.

She knew the dangers of hitchhiking. Not that she'd done it before, but it was probably far safer than what she was about to face. She'd told the man in the utility truck to take her to Drake Field. He opened his mouth, like he wanted to say something, then pinched his lips tight and reluctantly agreed. She figured he was going to question why she was out on a deserted highway late at night. The question never came.

When headlights approached at a high rate of speed as they entered the airfield, she knew it was Kaleb. Seeing him so unhinged, so desperate, obliterated her heart. Realization dawned on her then, why he was so good at calming her when she had the panic attack. He had them too. She wanted to run to him, but she had no clue what her captor was capable of and didn't want him to hurt Kaleb.

The cabin of the jet was very similar to Adam's. At least it would be a comfortable ride wherever they were going.

Seeing a tuft of dark hair in one of the seats facing away from her, she hurriedly moved up the aisle. Adam sat with his hands zip tied to the armrests. A blonde woman sat next to him, her face battered, her hands immobilized in the same way. She appeared to be asleep. A man dressed in black sat across from them.

Adam's head bobbled as he lifted his glassy eyes to Eden's. Bruises and dried blood covered his face. He blinked slowly, and Eden could tell he'd been drugged. "Eden. You shouldn't be here," he slurred. His eyes drifted closed, and she wondered how long it would be before he became unconscious.

She moved some hair away from his eyes, and found it matted together from the dried blood. Her heart ached, imagining what they did to him. "He said he was going to kill you. I couldn't let anyone else get hurt because of me."

"He won't kill us."

"You can't be sure of that."

"We are his survival. He's a vampire."

His remark had her wondering if she should be talking to him right now. The drugs were obviously affecting his mind.

"I'm going to have to ask you to have a seat. The plane is ready to take off," came a voice behind her, and it sent a familiar chill streaking down her spine. The voice of her attacker. She turned to see Malcolm with a smug smile on his face. Moving to take the empty seat across from Adam, she was stopped, when Malcolm grabbed her wrist, and led her to a seat a few rows up, then sat across from her.

"Are you going to restrain me?" she questioned with a bit of an edge in her voice. "Maybe rough me up too?"

His brow rose. "Depends on how much you fight me."

"Why don't you drug me like you did them? At least I can get a good nap in."

The sarcasm laced words surprised her that she could be so indignant with her life on the line. It didn't seem to faze her captor though. He smiled, and even chuckled, then replied, "Maybe after we chat."

"Oh goody. A chat. Sounds positively delightful."

"Good. Then we should get along fine, and I won't have to *rough* you up."

Even though she knew her sarcasm didn't faze him, she suddenly had second thoughts about her attitude. Perhaps she needed to play to his line of thinking. She didn't quite know what his game was yet, but she damn sure had one of her own. If everything worked out, every word that was being said would be overheard, and maybe she could get the information needed to close the case. Patience was the key. Putting on the Victoria persona, she tucked her hair behind her ear and waited for his interrogation.

"So, I guess Adam told you who I was?"

"No. We didn't get that far in our conversation. He was a bit out of it. I know who you are though, Malcolm. How could you do this to Kaleb? He counted you as a friend." The confusion in Kaleb's voice when he saw

Malcolm standing at the top of the stairs, and the hurt in his eyes from the betrayal, made Eden want to destroy the man in front of her.

He nodded slowly. "Yes. I do regret hurting him," he said, like he regretted he didn't bet on the favored football team to win, then his eyes shifted away from her and something different crossed his expression. Maybe he did have a conscience. His jaw clenched and with a bat of his lashes, the smug demeanor returned. "It was necessary to keep an eye on him in order to find you and your brother and sister."

She wasn't buying his excuse or regret, but she had to remain calm so he would let down his guard. Sitting up, she crossed her legs and placed her hands in her lap. "So, are you some kind of bounty hunter for Victor Chalemaare?" Malcolm's brows drew together, and he snorted, then fell into fits of laughter. Eden wondered what was so funny. Her head tipped as she watched him laugh uncontrollably. He tried to speak but couldn't get the words out without getting a case of the giggles. She bit her lip trying to stave off a smile she didn't want to reveal. Unfortunately, his laughter was infectious. It wasn't maniacal like she expected. It was warm and genuine and had her emotions playing chess with whether she hated him or not.

Finally, he gained enough composure to let her in on his secret. "No. I'm your brother...well, half-brother. I'm Victor's son."

His confession caught her by surprise. "Your name isn't—"

"...It's Blair. My mum's."

Confusion bombarded her.

"They met at a conference and fell in love, and he

brought her onto his research team. Things happened as they do, and she got pregnant. They were going to get married, but she wanted to wait until after I was born. When I arrived, it was evident that there was something wrong. After many tests, they found I had a rare form of anemia and I was going to need ongoing blood transfusions to survive."

Eden tried to remain stoic, focusing on the fact that Malcolm had held a gun on her not thirty minutes ago, although his story was compelling and tugged at her heart. She couldn't even imagine having a baby with medical issues and how heart wrenching it would be to know that your baby might not survive.

"My parents, being the researchers they were, started studying the disease. They were already well educated in gene therapy, so they immediately refocused their work to finding a cure for my illness. In the meantime, I was getting blood transfusions every two weeks and on high doses of medications for complications. Even with that, the doctors were not encouraging with their diagnosis, so my parents were highly motivated to find a cure, or at least a treatment."

The more Malcolm spoke, the more her heart broke for him and his mom and dad. Her dad. The thought of the gun wielding Malcolm began to fade into the background a little more.

"After about a year of research, they came up with a possible treatment. It was far from the cure that my dad was determined to find, but by then I was hanging on by a thread. Time was running out. The treatment, if successful, would allow me to go for longer periods between transfusions, which in turn would lessen the severity of the iron overload that my body had to endure with the transfusions. He also hoped that it would help my body start to produce hemoglobin on its own, moving me closer to being cured."

"And our blood was needed?"

"More specifically, *you* were needed." It was something that my parents had discussed in depth before I was born. They knew how controversial it was, so they'd steered clear of it."

"Gene altering?"

"Germline genome editing."

"Isn't that still considered illegal in most countries?"

"Many aspects are. My dad was taking a huge risk, so he moved my mum and me to England."

"So, Adam, Eva, and I are the products of your dad's research and this controversial genome editing? To save you?"

"You are."

"Is that why Adam called you a vampire?"

"He did?" Malcolm busted out laughing again, and again Eden found herself biting her lip to keep from following suit. "I didn't hear him say that, but probably." He took a deep breath. "Bloody hell." He let out an audible sigh trying to compose himself. "You three have been my life blood since you were born."

Eden's mind played through what Malcolm had shared. He'd confirmed what she'd suspected. She wasn't born out of love. But she had so many unanswered questions. "So, is that why you kidnapped us? For our blood?"

"No. Actually, I am no longer a *vampire*," he said with a chuckle. "As of about three years ago, I stopped requiring transfusions. My father's research, and your contributions, provided a cure. My father decided that the research was so valuable that he wanted to continue the study."

"What exactly does your father want with us?"

"You will learn that soon enough. I have shared enough for now, and it's late. We will talk more later. I still have some questions for you. But for now, get some sleep."

"But wait. I kind of know why you have Adam and me, but what about Miss Bellamy?"

"She was a casualty. She heard me discussing Adam's arrival. It didn't go quite as planned, hence the decorations on his face." His eyes darted to the seats in the back of the plane. "In the heat of the moment, I forgot that I could be heard when I was talking through my speaker system in my car, and I didn't notice when she got out of her car until I'd gotten out of mine. By the expression on her face, I knew she'd overheard the conversation. Unfortunately, she knew too much, and let's just say, she didn't want to come with me willingly."

"What's the plan exactly?"

"You're an inquisitive one, aren't you, Eden. It will all be revealed in due time. As I said before, we will have much more time to chat later. Right now, let's get some sleep." He patted her arm like they were good friends, then stood and disappeared. Moments later, he reappeared with a blanket and pillow.

She had to wonder why he was treating her so well, compared to Adam and Marissa. Was it because she didn't resist? "Will they get pillows and blankets?" Malcolm held her stare for a moment. She didn't back down. He flipped around and disappeared again, then returned with more blankets and pillows and carried them up the aisle. She watched as he released Adam's and Marissa's restraints and made sure they were comfortable. A wave of satisfaction washed over her. Whether or not he trusted her, or felt guilty for what he'd done, she had no clue. She would take it as a tiny win. Fluffing her pillow, she leaned it against the window. Her eyes caught a glimpse of the glittering lights far below and wondered where she would wind up.

****

Sleep was a joke. No matter how hard she tried, she couldn't shut her brain off from the visions of Kaleb and the questions that plagued her. She was both mentally and physically exhausted. At one point she tried to talk to Adam, but the large guard sitting in the seat across from him wasn't as cordial as Malcolm with his words.

They'd landed a couple of times, long enough to refuel, then they were airborne again. She had no idea what time it was, only that it was daylight by the time they got off the plane and were ushered into the waiting limousine.

Workers circled the plane and guided it in, then went about their tasks, never acknowledging the fact that there were people who were obviously injured being escorted off the plane into a waiting car. It was strange. How far did her father's influence reach? Apparently, he was well off, having a private jet and a limo pick them up. And when they arrived at the dock, a massive yacht was waiting.

The staff aboard had prepared a meal. It was as if they weren't victims of an abduction, just honored guests. A table was set on the deck. Eden, Marissa, and Adam were led out to the area. They all were a bit shell shocked, wondering when the guards would show up.

They never did, but what were they going to do, jump overboard?

The sound of the water splashing against the hull soothed Eden's frazzled nerves, but only a little. She stared out at the waves and wondered what Kaleb was doing, figuring he and Ian were huddled up, trying to come up with a plan. She hated the idea of putting him in danger even if he was trained.

Crew members brought out salads and a charcuterie board. Glasses were filled with their choices of beverages. Eden was already feeling a bit woozy from the boat ride, so she chose water. Before they sat, Malcolm appeared and joined them.

He motioned for everyone to sit, and his gaze landed on Adam, Marissa, who was next to Adam, then Eden. "Now that everyone has rested and we have this delicious food in front of us, I thought we could get to know each other better."

Eden didn't waste any time. "You said you're cured, so why are we here now?"

"That will be answered soon enough. Tell me about—"

"Why did Victor go into hiding? He was obviously doing things that were against the law long before he went missing."

Malcolm sat back in his chair and crossed his arms. His eyes roamed the faces at the table again before he let out a sigh. "When he received his award for his gene therapy, which had to do with my cure, someone who was close to the program wanted out. The cure was found, and they no longer wanted to be a part of it. Unfortunately, they were one of the founding members and knew too much. Victor couldn't allow them to walk away. When they refused his terms and threatened to expose him, things—"

"It was my mom, wasn't it?" Adam broke in. "Her car accident wasn't an accident, was it? He killed her because she wouldn't stay quiet."

Malcolm's eyes shifted, and Eden knew Adam was right. Out of the corner of her eye she could see the truth set in on Malcolm's face. He didn't have to answer for Adam to know the truth.

Adam chewed on his cheek fighting desperately not to let his emotions get the best of him. She knew that he and his mom had a much different relationship than she did with her mom, and it broke her heart to hear that his mom's death wasn't an accident. A tear slid down his cheek and she reached out her hand to give him strength, and he took it.

Malcolm cleared his throat, evading the question, and moved on. "We hadn't counted on Adam getting his hands on the files so quickly."

"Why did she have the files in the first place?"

"Again, she was one of Victor's close associates going into the research. She was a researcher herself and a doctor. She was also the first to come forward offering to be a surrogate for the program. He trusted her, and she continued to help with the research out of her office in Canada to advance the program."

"Wait." Eden was sure she heard wrong. "What do you mean surrogate?"

"My mom and dad were both carriers of the gene that caused the blood disorder, so for his research, he wanted to use healthy donor eggs along with his genetically altered sperm to create a host."

Hearing him call her and Adam a host had anger

burning her skin. They were lab experiments; nothing more. A mass of cells grown in a petri dish.

"Six eggs were fertilized. Three were viable."

The conversation was interrupted when a delicious main course was delivered by the staff, and everyone waited for everything to be served before continuing with the discussion.

"If surrogates were used, who donated the eggs?"

"Your mom's name is Juliette Granier."

"She was the beauty queen that went missing."

Malcolm tipped his head and hesitated only a moment before answering. "Yes."

Eden's eyes drifted to Adam, then to Marissa, who had stopped mid bite with her mouth gaped open.

"Why are you telling us all this? So far you have confessed that your father's research is illegal, and he's committed murder and also kidnapping."

"Let me ask you a question. How far would you go, if you were a world-renowned scientist with a child who was about to die if you didn't find a cure?"

Chapter Thirty-Two

Kaleb felt like he was about to self-combust. As the plane lifted into the air, he sat on the tarmac, trying to regain his composure. Tears were coming hard and fast, mostly due to his inability to breathe. Another reason for his need to retire from his undercover job. He never knew when a panic attack would hit, although he should have predicted this one.

Seeing the jet and Eden running toward it had reality colliding with his nightmares. The overwhelming pain that filled his chest was like he had taken the bullet full force again. It was crazy how the brain could cause such a visceral response. He'd come a long way since he started counseling. But with the recent turn of events, all bets were off.

Once he was able to take a deep breath again, he carefully stood to his feet and began sharing with Mitch what he now knew about the abductions. It was still hard to believe. He had to give Malcolm credit; he had him fooled, as well as everyone else, it seemed.

Everything about Malcolm's hiring seemed above board. The paperwork that came from the university seemed legitimate. His dad was always careful after what happened with Joe as a baby, and even he was fooled.

Even revisiting all their interactions, Kaleb was hard pressed to find the warning signs. The red flags. It made him sick, thinking about the time he'd spent with him, not realizing it was all a ruse. The thought of him having his hands on his sister had bile rising up the back of his throat, and he instigated it.

When he climbed into his truck to head back to the house and regroup, he got his first bit of good news. "She activated the tracker," Ian said from the passenger seat. "I doubt it will register while she's in the plane though."

"What good is it going to do us then?" Kaleb barked and immediately regretted it when Ian's eyes filled with compassion.

"When she gets off the plane, we will get another ping."

Kaleb's head hit the headrest. "We need to be up in the air now though."

"You don't have a clue where he is taking them."

"They're going to France."

"Maybe. Are you willing to bank on that? I mean, yeah, the research facility is in Paris, but why would he take them there? My bet is, wherever Chalemaare is hiding, that's where he's taking them. Could be that *Récolte* place, and we still don't have a clue where that is."

"I don't—"

"Listen, I know you want to get to her and make sure nothing happens, but unless you want to be chasing your tail from here to France, it's better to follow protocol."

Protocol. Yeah. The last thing he wanted to do was follow protocol. His truck chimed with a call. Joe.

"Hey."

"What's our next move?"

"I'm not sure. Mitch is following me over to the house."

"Let's all head that direction then," Cody said.

"Whoa. Wait. Who all is on this call?"

"We all are," Kaysi responded in the background.

"All meaning who?"

"Everyone who was in the text chat," Ben answered.

"Guys, let Ian and me handle this. This is our job."

"Nope. We'll see you at the house."

The line went dead, and Kaleb stared at his phone, then darted his gaze to Ian. "What the hell do we do now?"

"I don't think we have a choice. We don't know what we are up against, but if what we saw at the pageant, as far as security is concerned, is any indication of what Chalemaare has on his payroll, we're screwed if it's just the two of us."

"They aren't trained, Ian."

"Do they know how to use a gun?"

Kaleb thought back to their battle at laser tag. "Yeah. I've seen all of them shoot, and they're all decent."

"Then I say we use them."

"What about protocol?"

"Screw protocol. We are signing our death warrant if we go into this mission with just the two of us. And if we wait for backup, it might be too late. Who knows how long it will be before Phillips finds us some support. He's trying, but to your point, things kind of went off the rails. We need to put together a plan now and execute it. And we need their help to do it."

"I get that. But they all have jobs."

"They volunteered. It's their call whether they want to join us."

Kaleb pulled up in front of the house and got out. Cody's red jeep sat off to the left, and Ben stood in the doorway as Kaleb plodded up the steps. His whole body hurt. It always did after a panic attack. It was like every cell had been jolted with electricity.

"We're going with you. End of story," Ben announced. The groove between his brow meant he was daring Kaleb to argue. Mitch pulled in and immediately exited the car. Ben hadn't moved and Kaleb hadn't responded.

"Let him in. We need to get to work," Cody hollered from behind Ben. He moved just as Joe drove up in his truck and he and Brant exited. They were discussing something between them, but Kaleb was too busy taking in the scene in the living room to comprehend what was being said. It looked like the bull pen at headquarters. Open laptops covered all the flat surfaces and phones sat beside them.

His eyes zeroed in on Kaysi. She was holding Aurora like a baby against her shoulder as she sat on the edge of the ugly reclining chair talking to Cody and April. Comet lounged beside her. How was he going to tell her that the man she'd had a long-term relationship with was behind Eden's abduction? A hand landed on his shoulder and even without looking he knew it was Joe.

April turned to them. "There is a fresh pitcher of tea on the bar with some glasses."

Kaleb glanced at the clock on the microwave while he poured himself a glass. It was almost ten. Visions of Eden and the last time their eyes met crossed his mind. Something within them told him she had a plan, and finding out she'd activated the tracker brought a smidge of relief. He still wished he could have stopped her. *We're going to find you, Eden.*

As he approached the living room, he found all eyes

on him. They expected him to be their leader, and he couldn't even keep himself from having a panic attack.

What would Quinten do? He took one more swig of his tea and set it on the coffee table next to one of the laptops. "I need to have a word with Kaysi before we begin." She stood and followed him out onto the porch. His eyes darted to Ian who was still on the phone inside the cab of his truck, then they swung back to Kaysi. As much as he loved picking on his sister, it was a gut punch when he made her cry. And he knew it was coming. This was going to suck. "I know who is behind Eden's abduction and who sent you that message."

Kaysi's eyes widened, but she must have seen something within his, because her brows dipped and her voice was hard when she asked, "Who?"

He swallowed and felt his jaw tighten at the thought. "Malcolm."

"Wh-what?" Kaysi's head shook. "No. No, no. Kaleb, come on. He—"

"He was there, Kaysi. I confronted him."

Her face reddened. Tears welled in her eyes. "I-I don't understand. He's been here for what, almost two years." The shakiness of her voice had Kaleb questioning whether he should continue. "He, he—"

Taking a breath, he ran his fingers through his hair and went on. "It was all part of a plan. He was after Eden. At the pageant he saw me talking to her. When she disappeared, my guess is, he figured out who I worked for and knew I would be searching for her. He applied for our company internship, hoping to get accepted and swoop in when I found her. Then she surprised all of us when she showed up here."

Anger flared in her eyes. "So, I was—"

"Probably a way to keep tabs on what I was up to in the off hours."

"That, that—"

"I know. And I'm so sorry, Kase. This is my fault." He wrapped his arms around her and pulled her tight.

"No, it's not. You didn't make him use me."

"Well, I did kind of encourage him. He acted like he liked you."

"He played you."

She was giving him an out from the enormous guilt he was feeling, and he wasn't dumb enough to turn it down. "Yeah, he did." Thinking back, there was no way he could have connected the case to Malcolm. He still had no idea who he really was or what his role was in the case.

His paperwork was all based out of a university in England. That's all he really knew about him other than what he'd told him. And who knew how much of that was true. He knew a little about secret identities.

It was like his real life in Dalton, his safe haven, was another world. But Ben's words came back to haunt him, "No matter how secret your life is, Kaleb, your family is never completely safe," which unfortunately was true. Precautions were taken to keep his real identity a secret, but it wasn't enough. "Anyway, I didn't want to blindside you with the information in front of everyone."

"I appreciate it. I'm glad I broke it off with him."

"You and me both. I'm still not completely sold on Ben…"

Kaysi giggled, "Well, it's a little late for that since we're getting married."

Kaleb shrugged, and after an awkward silence he tipped his head, silently asking if she was ready to join the others. He heard his truck door slam and turned to see Ian jogging up the steps.

"Anything I need to be aware of?"

"Nothing's changed. No backup."

"What did he say when you told him what was about to happen?"

"What could he say? The lead is hot, and we need to move on it. He has no idea when there will be extra hands."

"I hadn't planned on saying anything to anyone, then my hand was forced. Now they are getting involved, and that was not my intention at all."

"You didn't ask them, if I recall the conversation. In fact, you told them we would handle it. So, it's their decision." He knew Ian was right, but the last thing he wanted to have happen is one of them get hurt, or God forbid killed on a mission he was leading, and one they volunteered for.

He stepped back into the house and all eyes were again on him. He scanned the faces of his friends and family, and a lump formed in his throat. What was he doing? He couldn't let these people put their lives on the line.

"We're going."

His eyes jumped to Joe who had echoed Ben's comment earlier. "Guys, I can't ask—"

"You didn't. Now tell us what needs to happen," Cody interrupted.

"But you all have jobs and families."

"And we will handle that. Now, what is the plan?" Mitch offered.

Kaleb eyed him, then his gaze passed over each face with the same resolute expression. They weren't backing down. "Well, I guess the first order of business is heading over to my house to get some gear."

****

Holding his phone as a flashlight, he opened the door to the back of the house. He'd forgotten the mess the intruder left behind after the break-in, and it was made worse, since he now pictured Malcolm at the crime scene with his hand around Eden's throat. The terror in Eden's eyes invaded his thoughts as he glanced in the direction of where he found her huddled on the floor. He let out a low growl. How could he? His jaw flexed as he thought about what he would do to him if he ever got his hands on him. He'd be hard pressed to not leave him with more than a few broken bones.

Heading up the hallway, he entered his bedroom and tapped the button on his nightstand, releasing the top and revealing the hidden drawer. Lifting the gun from its case, he shoved it into his belt and moved back to the living room where he heard voices. The guys had gathered, each with their phone flashlight lit up, surveying the damage.

He'd suggested that Joe and Cody could ride with him and bring back the gear they'd need, but after all the discussion on his birthday about him owning guns, everyone wanted to see what he had for an arsenal.

He passed in front of them and grabbed the top shelf of the hall tree. The latch disengaged, and he tugged the door open.

"Damn!" Cody said drawing out the word. "A secret room and everything."

"It was a butler's pantry and wine storage when I bought the house." He stepped inside, and lights swung left and right, as the guys took in the guns and gear that lined the walls.

"April is never coming over here again," Joe growled as his head swiveled, taking in his collection.

Kaleb laughed, remembering the similar message from Ben. "Ben said the same for Kaysi, but you guys are going to have to deal with it. I'm counting on them fixing this mess."

"Well, I'm coming too, then."

"What the hell are you doing with all this stuff?" Ben pulled a long-range rifle off the wall. "I thought your job was collecting information."

"We're cross trained, in case things go south on a mission," Ian responded, "or we have to be part of the extraction. Every agent is trained and has government issued firearms. We have to be ready for anything we get tapped for."

"It's still hard for me to believe that you lived this secret life."

"By the time we met, I had already walked away pretty much."

"Doesn't matter. You still did it without anyone knowing. I bet you have some crazy stories."

"Yeah, I do. But they're all classified."

"Damn. That's too bad."

Brant examined one of the guns. "They issued you all of this?"

"Not everything. Some stuff is mine." Kaleb grabbed a canvas bag off the floor and started filling it with the guns, ammo, and gear that they would need.

Mitch stepped up beside him. "Do you have comms and vests?"

"Not enough."

"I'll take care of that."

****

He'd already walked the aisle of the airplane at least a dozen times, trying to release some of the pent-up energy. It hadn't helped. His brain was stuck in hyperdrive, and there were no signs of it shutting down any time soon. It had been almost twenty hours since Eden boarded the plane. They had roughly four days left before the tracker started to fail. The group had devised a loose plan, although he wasn't completely comfortable with it. There were still too many variables.

After raiding his gun room, everybody returned to their homes and waited for the call to come. The minute the tracker pinged and they had a location, they would be wheels up.

He was partially right. The tracker pinged in France, although not in Paris. As much as he hated to admit it, Ian made a good call. And after the first ping, it quickly became apparent that they were on the move. Unfortunately, the communication aspect of the tracker, so far, was useless. All they were getting was static. He hoped, once they landed and were in closer proximity, it would clear up.

Now that they were airborne, there would be no way to track Eden and the others until they touched down, and each minute moved them closer to the device failing. Ian handed out trackers to everyone and had them download the app associated with them, then briefed them on how the device worked. That way, anyone could be point of contact, if need be, once they were at the location. Wherever that was. Kaleb just wanted to get there.

He leaned out into the aisle, taking in all the familiar faces, still feeling uneasy for allowing them to be a part of the mission. Although Bekah, Jenna, and Jessi stayed behind in Dalton, Kaysi and April were currently fast asleep a couple of seats back. Kaysi wanted to take Malcolm down herself, and he had no doubt she could, but he wasn't about to put her in that position when he had no idea how dangerous Malcolm was.

Voicing his concern to Ben when Kaysi wouldn't back down, he hoped Ben could talk her out of going. Ben surprised him with his response. "That girl right there is your worst nightmare. She's all sugar sweet, and then she will turn around and rip your throat right out. I feel sorry for Malcolm if she finds him." Then his eyes landed on her, and Kaleb could see the pride on Ben's face.

He reluctantly agreed to take her, figuring they needed someone to man communications. And once Kaysi made up her mind, April was hell bent on going too. Joe tried to protest, but he didn't have a leg to stand on. She said if he could volunteer for a dangerous mission, so could she, and dared him to fight her on it. But as much as he appreciated each one of them for having his back, he had to wonder if they knew what they were getting into.

The minute their wheels hit the tarmac, Kaleb and Ian were on the phone with Quinten to get updates. He had cars waiting for them and had reserved rooms in a nearby hotel so they could gear up.

As everyone exited the plane, Kaleb checked his phone, hoping for a ping. Nothing. His chest burned with regret. He should have fought harder to keep her off the plane. But he realized he was in no shape to fight anyone, and a cold sweat erupted. Would he be able to do what he needed to save her? Or would he be hit with another debilitating panic attack?

He approached the deep blue SUV and reached for the key that had been hidden on the underside of the front bumper, and his phone vibrated. Quickly digging into his pocket, his eyes met Ian's, who was still on the phone with Quinten. Kaleb held out his phone in front of Ian, so they both could see. Tilting it, he saw a black dot, moving on a grid against a blue background.

Ian nodded then spoke into the phone. "We're going to need a boat."

Chapter Thirty-Three

In the distance, Eden saw a portion of a stately compound perched on a hill, rising above a brick and iron barrier. Not at all what Eden had expected when she was helped off the yacht by one of the security guards. The castle-like structure was something straight out of a fairy tale. As they approached, the wrought iron and brick walls stood like sentries around the estate. The massive gate shut, and Eden noticed guards in the spires that rose high above them. "What is this place?" she murmured under her breath.

"*Récolte*," Adam responded quietly.

The grounds were lush, with well-maintained rose bushes and flower gardens. "Isn't it beautiful?" Malcolm questioned. "It was an abandoned prison my father discovered about fifteen years ago, and he's been restoring it ever since."

The car stopped in front of a four-story building with polished stone stairs leading to intricately carved doors surrounded by arched windows. The place was breathtaking.

The door opened. Malcolm walked up, eyed the building, then his eyes turned back to Eden, and her enchanted bubble popped. Her stomach became queasy with the thought of what she might be in for. She wasn't here for a vacation. She wasn't even here under her own free will.

Malcolm's eyes drifted to Adam and Marissa as they joined them. "Shall we?"

Eden glanced at the guard next to her, who bobbed his head, signaling her to move. Adam placed his hand in the center of Marissa's back, and they all made their way up the steps.

Malcolm held the door like they were his welcomed guests, and Eden again felt dread coil in her gut. Now that they'd arrived at *Récolte*, he seemed like the perfect host, welcoming them to their vacation destination. She couldn't quite get a grasp on his odd demeanor. It was all too easy to get caught up in the grandeur of the place, with the massive chandeliers, gold sconces, and large vases adorned with beautiful flowers. Everything you would find in a five-star resort.

"It's peaceful here, isn't it?" Malcolm said almost serenely behind her, reminding her he was there. It was like he was a completely different person than the man holding the gun on her at the airport. She glanced over at Adam and Marissa. Their faces still bore the remnants of their capture. Did he really have the ability to kill someone? Or was he bluffing to get what he wanted? Even though he said they got their injuries from struggling when they were captured, it didn't matter. They were taken against their will. And they'd gotten hurt.

People milled around the lobby going about their day, acting like they hadn't seen the bruises and blood all over Adam and Marissa, nor the armed men guarding them. When they saw Malcolm, did they not see the monster he was? Or were they his captives too?

She shook her head. None of that mattered now. She had a job to do. She needed to get him talking. "So, where are we? What is *Récolte*?"

Malcolm lost the serene appearance, seeming to become a bit irritated with Eden and her refusal to let the question go. After a long minute, he finally answered. "Victor knew what he was doing was in a very gray area of science when he started on his journey to find a cure for me. He knew he had a limited amount of time with his research before the powers that be would become suspicious. So, he went in search of a place where he could have seclusion. This island was isolated in the middle of the channel. It housed a prison and its workers. Once the prison shut down, the island remained uninhabited for several years.

"Victor used his family's wealth, as well as my mom's, along with the money he received for his research and discoveries, to purchase the facility. Then he slowly built it into his main research compound away from prying eyes. He would allow the public to see only what he wanted them to see."

"But if he didn't want to call attention to himself, why did he disappear? He had to know people would search for him."

"Once he'd made the decision to continue his genome research after he'd received the award and his colleague had threatened to turn him in, he had no choice. He knew his associate could handle the Paris lab. He'd basically turned it over to him anyway.

"Since Victor had been active in the company, he couldn't leave without people getting suspicious. So, he and his associate decided to direct the narrative of his disappearance. It was reported he disappeared while he was out of the country in India at an Asian research conference. That way the investigation would be thrown off."

"So, what exactly is he doing?"

"I think it's best to have Victor explain. Would you like to meet him?"

Eden's heart raced at the thought. It had been two years of wondering who he was. She'd seen photos and watched some videos of him accepting his awards, even some French news reports. That still didn't tell her who he was privately.

Her eyes swept to Adam because she knew he was as anxious to meet him as she was, and guilt immediately engulfed her seeing his bruised face and Marissa's blood-tinged hair. Malcolm had been so cordial, and she'd been so focused on finding out information, that she'd completely forgotten the hell they'd faced, and a renewed anger bubbled to the surface toward their captor.

She couldn't show any emotion though. The mask had to remain in place. She glanced at Adam one more time then responded, "Maybe after we've had time to clean up."

Malcolm tipped his head. "Very well. Let me show you to your room." He moved quickly through the foyer and stabbed at the elevator button. The elevator arrived at the top floor, and Malcolm showed them to a three-bedroom suite. "I hope this will meet your approval."

Eden, along with Adam and Marissa, stared at their surroundings that displayed the same luxurious details as the entry foyer.

Malcolm handed off the key to Adam. "The front desk will be happy to assist you if you need anything." Opening the door, he joined the guards waiting for him in the hallway, then disappeared around the corner.

Eden scanned the room more closely, then her eyes landed on Adam's, questioning. "Don't look at me. The place they held me before barely had running water. They'd throw food at me occasionally, and a change of clothes every few days. Probably one of the old prison cells that wasn't renovated."

"If you guys don't mind, I think I will get a shower."

Guilt again spilled through Eden's gut. "Marissa, I am so sorry you got dragged into this."

"It's not your fault. It's his," she said pointing to the door.

There was a feistiness and strength to Marissa. Although she had been quiet most the trip, Eden had the feeling it was due to her taking everything in and calculating a plan more than being scared.

She turned and headed to one of the rooms. When she was out of earshot, Eden whispered, "So, what happened to you? Do you know anything about Bill?"

Adam shook his head. "No. Why? I was going to ask you the same thing. Why didn't you stay with him?"

"He never returned. You disappeared, and I figured you went to the marina, so I waited. After several days, I got scared and left."

"If he got captured by the same people, he wasn't being held in the area I was, as far as I know."

"You don't think he was connected to any of this, do you?"

"No. Why?"

"I was asked if that was a possibility." Eden moved to the kitchenette area and opened the refrigerator, removing two bottles of water. She pushed one to Adam, who took it and walked over to the sofa and sat down.

"By whom?"

"First, tell me what happened to you. Did you go to the marina?"

He leaned back into the cushion and crossed his ankle over his knee, wincing as he moved. "I went to work, and the same two guys I'd seen before were talking to someone in the parking lot. I heard them mention Serein marina, so I texted Bill then headed there hoping I was quick enough to catch the guys with the item before they left for *Récolte*. I really didn't have a plan, but figured if I spotted them, I could rent a boat and follow them.

"When they showed up, a woman was with them. Her hands were bound, and her head was covered. I ducked behind a boat that was docked nearby, then found myself with a gun jammed into my neck. So, I got the same treatment as her, then got to ride on the yacht with the other unwilling passenger. At that point, I had no idea what I'd stumbled into."

"What'd they do with her?"

"No clue. We were escorted off the yacht, and she was delivered to two people while I got taken to the dungeon."

"What happened after that?"

"Mostly, I sat and stared at the peeling paint on the walls or slept. I tried to talk to my handlers, asking them about Victor, but they didn't give up anything, so neither did I when they asked what I was doing. Then one day, they came and got me, put me on the yacht again, and took me to the airport. I still wasn't sure what I had gotten myself into, so when we landed and they escorted me off the plane, I made a run for it as soon as I found the opportunity. I didn't make it far before they body slammed me."

"Are you okay? I mean, you're pretty banged up."

"Yeah. Nothing too serious. It knocked the wind out of me, and I got a few cuts and bruises. Mainly, I'm just sore."

"So, at that time you hadn't met Malcolm?"

"The guards said they were taking me to him. Again, I had no idea who he was, but after I took off they tied me up, stabbed a needle in my arm, and dragged me into one of the hangars. Later, Malcolm came in and introduced himself. Told me about the same thing he told you, I'm guessing. That he is our half-brother and needed our blood to stay alive. So, our dad basically created us to save him. He told me he had located you and needed my help convincing you to join us."

"How did he know we even knew each other?"

"They confiscated my phone. I'm thinking they hacked into it and figured out who I was. I'm sure they went through my text messages, videos, and e-mails, and found you from that."

"I got a call from your phone a few days after I got to Dalton. They were probably trying to pinpoint where I was."

"Malcolm took some photos, then had one of the guards point the gun to my head, hoping you would give in."

"And Marissa?"

"She showed up with Malcolm all banged up and bloody. I heard Malcolm talking to one of the guards. He said she put up a fight." He chuckled. "You've seen how big Malcolm is, right? He's not bulky, but he has some muscle. I would like to have been there to see her try to fight him. I mean that takes some guts."

"She doesn't strike me as one who would just go

peacefully."

"And it's funny, because talking to her, she is the nicest person you'd ever meet." He paused. "So, what made you give in?"

"They sent Kaleb your photos and the video. Then they sent Kaleb's sister, Kaysi, a photo of Marissa and said she was next. I just couldn't let anyone else get dragged into the mess."

"I don't understand. Who—"

"Malcolm was one of Kaleb's friends."

And who is this Kaleb person?"

"You don't remember him? Oh, duh. Right. Agent Grey. He's the agent I shot."

"Wait. I thought he was the one trying to abduct you."

"No. He was trying to save me. He thought I was running into a trap. He thought you were going to abduct me."

Adam's face filled with confusion. "How'd you figure that out?"

"I didn't know for sure until we talked. Turns out, it was all a ruse to find me. Malcolm was at the pageant, although I never saw him. I had applied as Victoria Granier, so I was on his radar. Kaleb and I had spoken several times at the pageant, and he'd apparently seen us together. Once I disappeared, he went searching for Kaleb, found out about his side job, and figured he'd hunt for me. So, Malcolm applied for an internship with Kaleb's family's oil and gas company and waited. He even dated Kaleb's sister Kaysi."

"No. Seriously? What the hell."

"Yeah."

Adam's face grew more and more confused. "Wait.

Back up. You didn't know whether Kaleb was your abductor or not when you went to Arkansas?"

Eden started to explain how she and Kaleb were reunited but was interrupted when a phone rang and startled both her and Adam.

After finding it on the desk next to the TV, Adam answered it. "Malcolm said Victor is not available this evening," Adam announced once he hung up the phone. "He said he will call tomorrow and set up a time when we can meet. In the meantime, we are free to explore."

"Okay. Well…I guess I will get cleaned up and figure out what to do next."

"Can I ask you something first?"

"Sure."

"Your agent—"

"Oh. Yes. Sorry, the phone call distracted me." Eden continued her story of returning to the states and ultimately finding her prince, crown and all, in Arkansas.

"Do you think he—"

She stiffened and shook her head. Adam took the hint. Glancing around to see if she could make out any possible cameras, she walked over to the desk and found a pad and pencil. *Yes. He's coming for us.* She wrote on the scratch pad. *I'm wearing a tracker that can pick up voices. We need to find a way to get outside so we can make sure they pick up our location.* Adam nodded, and she quietly tore the paper off and wadded it up. "Anyway, I'm going to get cleaned up, then maybe we can go explore."

"I guess I will too," Adam responded as his eyes darted between two doors. After a moment, he moved toward one, so Eden chose the other. She could only hope that the tracker was working and Kaleb was on his way. She figured if they could get outside, the signal would be stronger, and even if they were being watched, they might be less likely to be overheard.

Hope. She clung to it like it was the only thing keeping her from an untimely death. And for all she knew, it was.

Chapter Thirty-Four

The stagnant smell was not what she expected when Malcolm opened the door to the building on the other side of the massive courtyard. Unlike the rest of the accommodations that rivaled any top-rated resort, these halls were stark white and were devoid of any decorations.

Two days had passed since they arrived. Warmer temperatures brought out more people to the enclosed garden area. The landscaping was immaculate. Rose bushes and beautiful water features decorated grassy areas, as well as the large tower resembling a lighthouse that sat in the middle. Benches surrounded it. In any other setting it would be considered peaceful. Except nothing about this place gave Eden any peace.

After exploring their accommodations, they found the courtyard and quietly tried to share some information, hoping her tracker would pick it up.

As usual, Malcolm had his guards when he arrived to escort them to their meeting with Victor. It made no sense, since they were left to their own devices before and no one even gave them a second glance. Now, she felt like a criminal being led to their demise.

She peeked at Adam and then Marissa. Both wore solemn expressions as they traipsed up the non-descript hallway surrounded by their guards. The more she got to know Marissa, the more she liked her. And the more she suspected Adam did too. She'd noticed them glancing at each other several times. And then she caught him leaving her room this morning. Of course, he'd explained it away as he was asking her if she was planning on joining them when they met Victor after dinner. His pink cheeks were a dead giveaway.

Her eyes darted around. Each of the four men with them had the same cold blank stare. They'd barely spoken the entire time, other than to give orders. What exactly did they think they would do? Try to kill Victor? They had no guns. Or maybe try to make a run for it? They were on an island, inside a compound, surrounded by a ten-foot wall that was heavily guarded. There was no way to escape. It all felt like a weird dream. One she hoped Kaleb would be the hero in. She couldn't help but wonder if he was on his way.

Windows lined white walls that seemed to go on for miles. People passed dressed in office attire. Three elevators came into view, and Malcolm pressed the button. He peered back at the group and smirked. Once the doors opened, he retrieved a card from his jacket and swiped it in front of the panel of numbers. A green light flashed where the floors were usually displayed. There were no buttons pushed, and Eden's stomach plummeted. Wherever they were being taken was hidden from the world, and she felt sure the tracking device would not be able to transmit the location.

The doors closed, and with a jolt the elevator began to move. She thought they were going down, but she couldn't be sure. The ride was short, and the doors opened to more stark white walls, this time with no windows, and as they stepped off the elevator, there was a distinct antiseptic smell.

Pushing through double doors, they entered what looked like a hospital. A large station on one side held several people dressed in scrubs. The other side was lined with doors. As they made their way up the corridor, another set of double doors opened, and two men in scrubs pushed a gurney carrying a woman who appeared to be sleeping or unconscious. Eden couldn't seem to stop staring. Her steps slowed, and one of the security guards nudged her to continue. *What is this place?*

Malcolm swiped his card in front of a non-descript metal door and with a snick, it opened. A large pane of glass stood to their right displaying a massive room below with several people dressed in sterile surgical attire. A man with salt and pepper colored hair lifted his head and removed the plastic safety glasses from his eyes. Eden recognized him immediately from the photos and videos she'd seen. Victor Chalemaare. Finally. All the time spent wondering who exactly this mysterious man was had come to an end. It was time to meet him. Her father.

A smile tugged at his lips, and he removed his rubber gloves as he moved toward a door on the other side of their room. Adam stepped in front of the girls. His act of protection had a lump forming in Eden's throat. He would fight for them to the very end.

The door swung open, and Victor stepped into the room. Eden suddenly couldn't breathe. He was her father. As much as she wanted to hate him, after what Malcolm had told them she was happy in that moment. And something within her wanted that kind smile he was giving her to be a love for her.

Her eyes bounced between him, Malcolm, and Adam. There was a definite resemblance between him and Malcolm. Adam must have resembled their mom.

They'd laughed one day early on in their relationship as they stared into a mirror, comparing their similarities. At the time, they had thought it had come from Victor, but with the knowledge she'd been given, she wasn't sure now. Would she get to meet her mom? And where was her sister, Eva? Had they found her? She couldn't remember what she'd been told. Had Adam's letter made her run? After reading about her, she felt she already knew her.

"*Bonjour.*" Victor cheerfully said. "*Cést bon de enfin te rencontrer.*" Eden watched, as the groove in between Adam's eyes deepened. He sucked in his cheeks and widened his stance in front of her and Marissa. He wasn't buying Victor's exuberant greeting. She was happy Adam had come into her life.

Victor took notice and his head tipped, then his eyes swung to Marissa who seemed confused. "Oh…um…my apologies," he said, like he'd just realized she was there. "My English is not the best, but it would probably be better. No?"

Marissa was quick to respond. "I had French in high school. That was several years ago though. Not much stuck with me." Eden had to admit Marissa seemed to take everything in stride.

Victor nodded at Marissa's comment and seemed to be amused. Eden wasn't buying it.

"Okay. Well…I'm very pleased to finally meet you. Malcolm has kept me abreast of what has been happening." He paused, like he was expecting a cordial response, but no one felt the need to placate him, so he continued, "I'm sure you have questions, but before I tell you about my research, there are a couple of people I know you want to meet."

Moving past them, Victor opened the door and headed back up the hallway. He swiped his card as he entered the elevator, then held the door for everyone to enter. The doors closed, and he spoke as the elevator began to move. "I hope your stay has been enjoyable. I pride myself on having the best of everything."

Enjoyable? Although Eden was impressed by the accommodations and the food that was delivered for their meals, it didn't make up for being kidnapped at gunpoint. She figured Victor could see her look of astonishment. Adam and Marissa didn't feel the need to speak up either.

As they exited the elevator, the only sound that could be heard was the shuffling and clicking of shoes on the marble floors. Victor opened the door to the courtyard, and Eden immediately thought of the tracking device and wondered what she could say that wouldn't tip anyone off. "Ah. Fresh air." She breathed deep. "That basement is kind of claustrophobic." Adam gave her a barely perceptible nod of acknowledgement, and Marissa chewed on her lip. They knew what she was doing, but from the expression on Malcolm's face, he didn't catch on.

An attractive older woman with silver hair twisted on the back of her head stood by a small pond with a waterfall. Her back was turned to the group. Victor quickened his steps. "Juliette." The woman quickly turned. Her hand flew to her chest, then to her mouth. She moved up the pathway, meeting Victor halfway. Tears were glistening on her cheeks.

"Juliette. *Voici Adam et Eden et leur amie Marissa.*"

Her hand reached up to Adam's cheek, and her

expression turned to concern as she brushed her finger gently against the cut on his eye, then she kissed his cheek. Moving to Eden, she cupped her cheeks and kissed one, then the other. "*Jái attendu si longtemps pour te rencontrer.*"

"It's good to meet you too," Eden said.

Juliette's eyes moved to Marissa, and she grasped her hands. Without saying a word, she leaned in and kissed each of her cheeks. Backing up, her eyes met Adam's and Eden's again, and her hand returned to her mouth as the tears continued to fall.

Movement behind Juliette had Eden's eyes landing on a dark-haired woman slowly rising from a bench by the waterfall. Her eyes lifted to Eden, and Eden immediately knew who she was. Grabbing her metal crutches, the dark-haired woman slowly moved toward them, but Eden couldn't just stand there. She stepped around Juliette and Victor, and a flood of emotions hit her as she closed the distance and wrapped the woman in her arms. "Eva. I'm Eden. Adam and I have been searching for you for so long."

Adam stepped beside them, and Eden backed away so he could give her a hug. "I knew nothing about you until recently." Eden noticed Eva had some difficulty speaking, but didn't remember anything regarding it in her file. It made her wonder what was wrong.

The sweet smile Eva had gracing her face quickly disappeared as the rest of the group joined them. Eden took notice and moved back to the bench Eva had been sitting on previously. She waited for Eva to sit, then she sat next to her. "Adam and I came to find you, but your house was empty when we got there."

"My mother came and got me from school. She said

we had to leave but wouldn't tell me why or where we were going."

Juliette sat down beside her and interrupted the conversation. "It's nice to finally have my children all together."

"You speak English?" Eden asked.

"Some."

"Did you know that you're listed as a missing person?"

Juliette's eyes shifted to Victor, and the hint of fear that skirted across her face didn't get past Eden. "That doesn't matter. I want to know about you."

"So, how involved were you with all this?" Adam questioned.

Juliette's eyes swung to Victor again.

"I'm sure you have many questions, and we will have plenty of time to get to know each other," Victor interrupted. "Let me show you around *Récolte* and explain what we do here." He waited for everyone to gather again before he spoke, "The entrance where you came in is our guest resort. It is fully staffed and," he opened the door, "as I'm sure you noticed, there are restaurants, and stores, and entertainment. Again, I pride myself on having everything available for our guests." He showed them around the lobby and talked up the different cuisines of the restaurants then exited out the same door. "The building across the way that we were in earlier is our research and medical facility. It has a fully functioning hospital."

"What do you need the hospital for?"

"One wing is for our research and the other is a medical spa." He tugged open the door.

Juliette grabbed Eden's hand. "I am so glad we got

to meet. We will talk later. Too much walking is hard on Eva."

Eden fought back the tears as she hugged Juliette and Eva. She already felt such a connection. Adam and Marissa both gave them hugs before they all were ushered into the research building.

"And you own the whole island?"

"I do. Well, technically Malcolm's mother, Louise, owns the island and the facility. It was renovated as an all-inclusive medical spa and resort. I am sure Malcolm has told you my research is highly sensitive so we had to find a way to keep it out of the public eye. The spa was the perfect plan. No questions asked. We take in a small number of patients a year."

"What about the lab?"

"A more public section is dedicated to creating high quality beauty products." He paused, then added, "I think it turned out wonderfully. You will come to realize it's very peaceful here."

His words reminded her of what Malcolm had said when they arrived. Were they trying to brainwash them, like the more they said it, the more it would become true?

"Malcolm said you moved his mom and him to England to protect them from what you were doing. Wouldn't her name on the paperwork for the facility be counterintuitive?"

"I did in the early days. I had to be careful. But when we came up with this plan, it was too perfect to pass up."

Victor punched the button to the elevator, then swiped his card once everyone had entered. As they arrived at the viewing room again, he motioned for them to have a seat.

Eden discreetly glanced at Adam, then at the guards,

and slowly lowered herself in a chair. Marissa followed her, and Adam finally, reluctantly, found a seat. The guards all stood by the door while Malcolm remained with his dad. Her dad. That was going to take some getting used to. She still wasn't quite convinced. The documents could've easily been forged. But something deep inside her told her they weren't. Regardless, when this was over he would most likely be put behind bars, along with Malcolm.

"What you see behind me is our main research lab. Within these walls, we have made it possible for many diseases to be eradicated at a molecular level, and we hope to do that for many more."

"And how are you doing that?" Eden questioned, figuring if there was any possibility that her tracking device was picking up anything she better get as much information as possible.

Victor leaned against the glass, crossed his arms, and took on a relaxed posture. "When I started as a research scientist, I was fascinated with the genetic make-up of human beings; how two people could come together to create a new being that still had pieces of each. I knew early on the minute I had the chance to work in the field I would jump at it. I wanted to make a difference. It bothered me that there were so many illnesses and diseases in the world. So, I worked tirelessly trying to find cures, not just treatments, and I made great strides. However, there was one thing that still haunted me. I was working with illnesses that were already present in the body. I wanted to eliminate them.

"Although my research center in Paris is one of the top labs in the world, I wanted more. When Malcolm was born, I knew it was time. I needed to find answers, and the only way to do that was do dive deep. This lab is state of the art. From the DNA of our patients, we are able to find the weaknesses, the possible risk factors for different diseases, and we can genetically modify the egg and sperm in order to remove the risk."

"You can't completely remove all risk though. And doesn't it create other possible risks?"

Victor nodded at Eden's question. "You're correct. And it doesn't take into account imperfections caused at birth, as in Eva's case, which we have no control over. We haven't perfected everything, and I doubt we ever will, but we are making progress, and more and more diseases are disappearing or being greatly reduced. And others, like Malcolm's, we have found cures for."

Adam sat back in his chair and crossed his ankle over his knee. "Wasn't this research deemed illegal?"

"You already know the answer to that. That's why this facility was necessary. The importance of finding ways to fight the ever-growing number of diseases far outweighs the risks we are taking. Think about it. We are this close," Victor held up his fingers, "to eradicating cancer. Can you imagine that?"

"That sounds all well and good, but at what cost? What exactly are you doing for the sake of science?"

"As I said before, we are creating healthy embryos that are free of the risk factors of many diseases."

"And who are providing the eggs and sperm to create these healthy embryos?"

Eden saw the first fracture of Victor's confidence with Adam's probing question.

"And what exactly do you do with these embryos that you've created?"

Victor shifted and his eyes narrowed, but Adam

didn't waver. He returned the glare with a cool confidence.

"We seek out individuals all over the world who are in good health, who have distinct qualities to give us the best possible outcome. Many people come to our fertility centers requesting help or seek us out through our website."

"And for a fee, you provide them with their designer baby. How do you keep your illegal research under wraps with all that going on?"

"That's not—"

"Don't try to tell me that's not what is going on, because this facility wasn't created just from your magnificent research. It's here because you're collecting a shitload of money from people who are willing to pay a premium to make sure they get everything they want in their kid. I'm willing to bet that is what is really going on here. And I'll go you one further. I'm betting those other donors, the ones you chose not to speak of, are in missing persons files all over the world. Aren't they?"

Adam stood so quickly his folding chair tipped back. "That's why you had my mom killed, wasn't it? You son of a bitch. You'd promised her your lab rats would have their freedom after you found the cure for your precious baby boy. And when you reneged on that promise and she figured out we were going to wind up your prisoners as donors, she wanted out. But you couldn't let that happen because she held all your dirty secrets. So, you killed her."

Malcolm stepped between Victor and Adam, but Victor held him back.

"You figured you'd kill her, grab the files, and no one would be the wiser. Only you didn't count on me finding the files before you. Did you? You do realize they are in the hands of the authorities right now, right?"

Eden sat stunned. Her eyes drifted to Marissa, whose gaze was transfixed on Adam. Oh yeah, there was something going on between them.

Resignation settled on Victor's face. "Although the authorities having those files is not ideal, laymen wouldn't understand what is in those documents, and there is no blatantly illegal activity stated in them."

"But us, and the information we hold, along with the files, is a volatile combination, and that added to the reason why you needed to find us. Isn't it? And now that you have us, you can continue using us as your lab rats, right?"

Victor tipped his head, and Eden felt the hair on her body stand on end as a cold calculated expression filled Victor's face. His eyes locked on Adam, and the words he uttered left no doubt how far he would go to get what he wanted. "You don't understand how important the research is. Second generation—"

"Screw your so-called *research*. What you are doing is a crime. We are human beings, regardless of the fact we were created in your lab."

He nodded to his guards, and they moved in. "I was hoping you would be more compliant, but if this is the way it has to be, so be it."

Eden tore her arm away from the guard as he was trying to seize her. "What about Marissa? She is not a part of any of this. She doesn't need to be here."

"I'm afraid she overheard too much."

The guard reached out and wrapped his hand around her bicep. "So, what? You're just going to keep us locked up forever?"

"That's exactly what he plans to do," Adam responded as his guard was escorting him from the room.

"I think the accommodations are quite nice, actually."

"But we're your children. Doesn't that mean anything?" Eden's eyes met Malcolm's, hoping her words would strike a chord. He averted his attention quickly.

"Let's get some bloodwork, shall we?" Victor stated as he followed.

Chapter Thirty-Five

Kaleb stood at the side of the small yacht and watched the silver reflection of the moon bouncing off the undulating waters. Everything was quiet. There was no drone of the engine. Just the sound of the waves. It would seem all was right with the world, but it was far from it.

While they waited to hear back from Quinten earlier, they'd headed to their hotel to prepare and gear up. He and Ian had gone over the plan plenty of times with everyone. There was no doubt they could execute it. The problem wasn't their ability. The problem was the plan was flimsy at best. There were too many unknown elements. His gut told him they were walking into a possible bloodbath, and they were going to be the victims.

He'd been on rescue missions before and watched how the team worked with precision. He tried to replicate that when organizing the attack. Still, regardless of how well they might be able to execute the plan, these were his friends and family, not highly trained soldiers. Kaleb had always been one to take life by the horns and go all in, but not when it meant putting the ones he loved in danger.

Ian sent up a high-definition drone to get a read of the area where Eden's tracker last pinged. It was a strong signal, and although communication was still staticky, they could make out different voices off and on, which gave them hope that all three victims were still alive. He just wished he knew if there were others, and if so, how many.

The sound of footsteps against the deck had him turning. April had a computer in her hand, and Ian was following her. "From what I'm seeing, we have twelve guard towers along the wall, and one central tower in the middle of the compound. You can kind of see how the buildings are laid out. Almost like an arrow."

After getting the ping from Eden's tracker, they initially pinpointed the area via satellite and found it was an old, abandoned prison. A deeper dive gave them information of a renovation of the site.

Now, with the real time visuals from the drone, Kaleb was able to get a better sense of the layout of the massive structure taking up at least a quarter of the island. He didn't like it. "If all those guard towers are occupied, we're screwed," he said to no one in particular. "Even if we had a helicopter to drop in, there is no way we can get in unnoticed even under darkness."

Kaleb took the computer out of April's hands. He set it on the table and stared at the screen, taking in for the first time what they were dealing with. There was a rise at the north end, which indicated a possible basement or underground bunker, making their mission even more dangerous, but it also could possibly be their point of entry if there were an outside entrance. He flipped over to the infrared transmission from the drone and noticed several people moving around inside the compound. "Looks like we have civilians." Another problem they would need to deal with.

Reducing the drone camera's screen, he scanned the

pictures of the compound that it had taken and zoomed in on some of the buildings outside the compound for possible points of entry. Each appeared to be private homes and businesses.

The more he studied the layout, the more his gut tightened. "Damn!" He shook his head. "Our only chance is to take out the guard towers. We've got Cody and Brant, but they'd only be able to hit, at the most, four towers, and the minute one goes down, the guards will be all over us. It's going to set off a chain reaction." He took a deep breath. "Bring the drone in and let's think."

He stared at the computer screen for several minutes until a low hum drew his attention away. It was too deep to be the drone. He stood and searched the area, spotting a light in the distance. "Shit! What now?" The last thing he needed was to have security from the compound coming after them, or worse, local law enforcement. He thought Quinten had taken care of that, but maybe not. Drawing his gun, Ian did the same, and they ducked under the cover of the yacht.

The light grew brighter, and he realized it wasn't someone approaching in a boat, but a helicopter. His phone buzzed, and when he retrieved it, a smile spread across his face as relief filled his chest. "Kat!"

"I heard you guys were going rogue and might need a hand."

He could barely hear her above the noise of the helicopter. "We could use all the hands we can get. Do you have some to spare?"

"I might be able to provide a few, but it's gonna cost you."

Kaleb couldn't wipe the smile from his face. "At this point, I'm willing to do just about anything."

"How about talking to the boss?"

"Oh. That depends—"

"How many people do you have with you, and who are they?" A deep voice rang through the phone.

"Quinten?" A gust of air escaped his lungs. "I thought you were still in Maryland."

"Not quite."

Kaleb knew what he was doing was way out of line for the agency, but there was no way he was going to stand by and let Eden sacrifice herself for the mission. He'd told Quinten he was going off the books to save her, but he chose the "as needed" approach when it came to divulging the details, and luckily Quinten hadn't asked too many questions. But now it was time to come clean. "Ian and I, and several of my friends who have military experience or law enforcement experience.

"We can't—"

"Before you say anything, I know I'm way out of line. I know the agency doesn't want innocent blood on their hands, but I didn't feel like I had a choice. Eden disappeared, and I couldn't sit back and wait for you to secure help while the window of opportunity closed. My team was ready to go, and they weren't going to let me leave without them."

"Well, you have help now, so they can stand down."

"With all due respect sir, we will not stand down." Joe's voice was respectful but left no room to argue. "He didn't ask for our help. We told him we were helping. He's my brother, and like hell I'm going to let him go in there without having his back."

"I understand that you want to help, but we have highly trained soldiers with us now, who do this sort of thing for a living."

"Let me make this clear. We don't work for you. We know very well what we are risking, so you can choose to utilize us or not, but we are still going in there."

Kaleb's heart stumbled with Joe's declaration. It hit him in that moment what his friends and family were willing to do for him. They were willing to sacrifice their lives to help him save Eden. If any of them didn't make it home, it would devastate him. Quinten knew that too, and that was what he was trying to avoid. He could probably call on different laws and statutes to try to keep them on the boat. It still wouldn't mean they'd listen.

Minutes passed, and Kaleb could only hear the thumping of the rotor blades of the chopper before Quinten continued, "You have no idea what we are about to face."

"I am well aware we are going in blind. We sent up a drone to get a little more of an idea, and we have been formulating a plan. I think there might be a bunker level on the north end, and I'll lay you odds that's where we'll find them. We've also had eyes on other civilians. Possibly more victims." Kaleb glanced around, trying to get an idea of who he'd be working with, when more lights appeared. "So, who is gracing us with their presence this evening?"

"Only ICMP's finest. Four in the water and three in the air."

Now we're talking. He'd worked a few missions with the extraction teams from the International Commission of Missing Persons, and they were extremely well trained. Kaleb was surprised Quinten was able to secure them.

"Once the boats get to me, we'll sync the comms. Have you discussed a plan of action with the extraction teams?"

"You said you've been formulating a plan, so you will be taking the lead," Quinten quickly responded. "We'll take second on air. This mission has been yours from the beginning. I'm going to let you bring it home."

"I'm too close—"

"That's exactly why you need to head it up. You're directly connected. You have the most information and the most to lose. You've got this."

Kaleb swallowed back the panic that threatened to overtake him. He'd taken the lead before. Not in an extraction though, and somehow having Quinten give him full rein over the entire mission felt like a daunting task. Still, he couldn't let the panic win. This had been his mission. It had consumed his life for the past two years. Like Quinten said, he needed to bring it home. "Okay. Stand by."

The boats arrived with their teams, and the lingering feeling of hopelessness that Kaleb had been harboring subsided. This rescue mission was now manageable, and a clear plan started to form in his head. After syncing the comms, he started to lay everything out. "We are going to have to come in hot. There are no dark areas. We have twelve guard towers, with another main tower in the center of the compound, and we have to assume they are all manned. We will clear the civilians in the area first, then once we have the towers secured, we will breach the compound. Tango one is Malcolm Blair. He's considered armed and dangerous. With the information we have gathered, Victor Chalemaare is also considered an enemy, until we know differently."

As he continued to give directions to the teams, the nagging thought kept eating at him. What about the team he came with? He finally turned to Joe, who'd been right there beside him practically the entire time. Their eyes connected, and he noticed the rest of his team standing with him.

"You aren't getting rid of us," Joe said, like he'd read Kaleb's mind. "Remember, we have a stake in this too."

"I know. I just don't want to risk any of you getting hurt. And let me be clear. This mission is, by far, the most dangerous mission I've been lead on. There are a lot of variables here."

"Don't care," Cody chimed in.

"We had a plan coming into this without their help, and it's great that we have them, but we don't need to change course. It just means we have more access and better cover," Brant added.

Ben crossed his arms, drawing Kaleb's attention. "And Kaysi still wants to kick Malcolm's ass."

That got a laugh, but Kaleb's eyes went to Kaysi's. She raised one brow, daring him to cut her out of the plan. Was Ben wanting her to gear up? He'd planned for her to stay on the boat with April and be point of contact. His eyes lifted to Ben, whose expression didn't give anything away, so he turned back to Kaysi. "Kaysi, I want you and April manning the trackers and comms."

"Let her go," Ben rasped. "April has a handle on communication."

Kaleb's wide eyes returned to Ben. "No. Are you kidding me? It's too dangerous."

"She can handle it. She's been through a lot, if you remember?"

"All the more reason—"

"—to let her go," Ben finished.

"Absolutely not. She could get hurt, or even kil—"

"Then it's on me for not tying her to the boat and making her stay."

"Does she know how to shoot a gun?" Kat's voice rang through his phone.

Kaleb knew Ben had been taking her out shooting, so that answer wasn't going to help his case. "Yeah."

"Let her go."

Kaleb took a deep breath. His gut said no. But his head...It wasn't the fact that she was a woman, he didn't think. Kat was one of the best agents they had. She was tough as nails, and her instincts were fine-tuned. So why was he letting Joe go, and not Kaysi? He stared down Ben, while Kaysi slid on a ballistic jacket, and shoved a nine-millimeter in a holster. "Fine. You both are with me."

Kaysi stood, tipped up on her toes, and kissed Kaleb on the cheek, then patted his shoulder as she shoved her earpiece in her ear.

"Damn, girl," April popped off, then tugged her into a hug. "Be safe. Kick his ass."

Kaleb eyed her, then turned to everyone. "Okay. Let's test comms." He tapped his ear. "Return your call."

Each member responded from the teams on the water and in the air. Kaleb found it almost funny the different accents he could pick up.

With him, he had Ben and Kaysi, along with three menacing looking men from Echo team that he'd yet to get the names. Brant and Cody joined Echo team, replacing two of theirs, and would be on overwatch. Joe and Mitch joined Delta team. Ian headed up Bravo. He'd made sure that the teams on the ground force had trackers in place.

Everyone was dressed in dark gray or black to help them remain undetected, with Joe and Kaleb dressing similar in case he needed a decoy.

Scanning the area one last time, Kaleb tapped his comm. "We're go." Flipping his night vision goggles down, he pushed away every thought except saving Eden.

Chapter Thirty-Six

The boats and helicopters moved in under the inky black sky, and moments later Kaleb heard the loud bangs as the smoke grenades went off in the courtyard. The drone moved in.

"All clear on civilians." April's voice broke through.

The helicopters moved into position. Flashes lit up the night sky as missiles streaked through the darkness, and explosions erupted followed by gunfire. The compound illuminated, and tower after tower blew apart as the rockets hit their targets.

"This is air three. Towers one and two are secured."

As each tower crumbled, Kaleb's pulse increased. And finally, the words came.

"Towers secured. Go for infil."

"Roger that." The teams were on the move. Breaching the compound still wouldn't be easy. He expected to encounter more fire power, but with the cover of the smoke at least they wouldn't be easy targets. He and two of the ICMP soldiers were the first to make it inside.

Kaleb keyed his comm as they waited for the others. "Alpha one. We're in." Remaining in the shadows of the wall, Kaleb eased his way toward the building. Two guards appeared and were taken down by the soldiers with him.

Ben's voice came through the comms. "Alpha four.

We're in." His stomach soured hearing his sister's call signal, then seeing her step through the haze. He turned away closing his eyes. He had to focus.

"We have a good read on all of you," April responded.

"Copy that."

"I'm right behind you," Ian added.

"Roger. I'm at the door." A muffled noise behind him caused him to spin around. Another guard appeared out of the shadows with his rifle trained on him, and with a pop, he dropped in front of him.

"You're welcome," came a voice in his ear seconds later.

Kaleb's eyes darted in search of Cody. "Where are you?"

"Hiding."

"Thanks."

Flashes of gunfire pierced the smoke, and Kaleb scanned the area, prepared to pull the trigger.

"Damn. Where are they coming from? They're like a bunch of ants." Mitch's voice echoed through the comms.

"I got eyes on two at your two o'clock," Brant said calmly.

"Copy."

As more gunfire rang through the haze, Kaleb slid back into the darkness. Bravo team joined them then slipped into the building. With a motion of his hand, they split up, heading down opposite corridors.

Kaleb led his team up the desolate hallway acutely aware of his surroundings. Inside, the only sound that could be heard was the squelch of their shoes against the tile floor. Coming to a T in the corridor, he pressed his body against the wall, then seeing no one, he moved forward toward a bank of elevators. The ding of a bell had Kaleb dropping back around the corner, raising a fist, signaling the rest to freeze. The elevator door slid open, and Kaleb heard Malcolm's voice. "Where the hell are they?"

Slowly leaning around the corner, he saw Malcolm on his phone with two guards beside him. As his steps drew closer, Kaleb flattened himself against the wall. His body vibrated as he prepared for the encounter, but Kaysi bounded into the open unexpectedly, plowing headlong into Malcolm, knocking him into the adjoining wall, sending his phone sliding across the marble floor. Kaleb lunged for her, only to have Ben grab the back of his shirt, keeping him in place. Anger flared within him, and his head jerked back to Ben who shook his.

Squaring his shoulders, he raised his gun at the guards who had accompanied Malcom, but they hadn't even grabbed for their weapons, probably still stunned by the hellcat's attack. Ben lined up beside him with the three other men behind them.

Kaysi rammed her knee between Malcolm's legs, bringing a pained groan from his throat as he doubled over. "You messed with the wrong woman, asshole," Kaysi growled. As he slid down the wall, her fingers dug into the back of his head, shoving it down, and slamming her knee into his face. "And that is for hurting my brother, you son of a bitch." Ben elbowed Kaleb and lifted a brow, along with the corner of his mouth. The guards stood stock still with their mouths gaped open.

Blood poured from Malcolm's nose, and he crumbled to the floor. Kaysi stepped backed and smashed her foot into his side, then backed up. Ben quickly moved toward her. The guards stared at Malcolm, writhing and coughing on the floor. Their eyes finally made it back up to Kaysi, then to Ben and Kaleb, questioning.

Ben shrugged. "Ex-boyfriend."

Kaysi's head whipped to the guards, her eyes wild, her chest heaving with fury. The two guards both lifted their hands in surrender and pointed up the hallway. Kaleb tipped his head, approving their silent plea, but kept the gun on them as they passed, then walked over, knelt beside Malcolm, and zip tied his hands.

"Do you think they're bringing back reinforcements?" Ben asked.

"I don't think they want to take that chance with her, but let's not stick around to find out."

"Told you. Worst nightmare."

"I'm not going to ask how you figured that out."

"Yeah. Don't." Ben pulled Kaysi into a hug. "You feel better?" She nodded, although the anger in her eyes when Kaleb helped Malcolm stand told him she still wanted to land a few more punches.

Malcolm rubbed his sleeve under his bloody nose and cleared his throat. "Kaysi, I—"

Ben quickly latched onto Kaysi as she tried to go after him again. "Man. If I were you, I would keep my damn mouth shut. You're in no position to fight back, and not one of us would feel a bit of remorse if you didn't wake up tomorrow," Ben disclosed. "Well, they might a little—" he nodded to their three companions, "—since they don't know you. Although, I bet I could convince them differently if I had a minute."

"Do these elevators go to the basement?" Kaleb asked, pulling him toward them.

Malcolm's eyes darted, but he remained silent.

Gunfire erupted farther up the corridor. "We need to move," one of the soldiers stated.

Kaleb glanced back, trying to remember what he said his name was. Daniel? David? Giving up, he turned back and grabbed Malcolm's bloody button-down and shoved him against the wall with his gun under his chin. "Answer the question." He pushed him toward the elevator and hit the button, hoping it would take him to Eden.

Static filled Kaleb's ear. "I've got some guards on a wild goose chase on the east side." Kaleb recognized Joe's voice. *Stay safe, brother.* "We have them distracted, but they are coming out of the woodwork. Any way we can get some backup?"

"We're on the way," Kaleb heard Cody say through the comms.

A phone chimed just as the elevator doors began to close, and Kaleb quickly put his hand out to stop them. His head whipped around as he tried to determine where the sound was coming from. Ben stepped out of the elevator and located it, putting it on speaker. Kaleb pressed the gun to Malcolm's temple, encouraging him to answer.

"Blair."

"The lab is secure, sir. But we have an issue."

Kaleb was surprised the person on the other end spoke decent English.

"Where's Victor?"

"Gone."

Shit!

"What's the issue?"

"We have elevated HCG levels in one of the new

donors your father brought in."

"Which one?"

"Samuels."

Kaleb's eyes darted to Malcolm. "What does that mean?" Kaleb murmured low and menacing.

"Do you want me to move forward with the procedure?" the voice on the phone continued.

More gunfire erupted. Kaleb disconnected the call. "Take me to the lab," he seethed, his jaw pulsing with rage. "I better not find a hair out of place on her head, or I swear to God, I will end you."

He tapped his comm. "Air one, do you have a copy?"

"Go ahead."

"Do you have eyes on any activity outside the walls?"

"That's a negative."

"I think Chalemaare is on the run. I can't help but feel like there is a hidden escape route." His eyes met Malcolm's and something within them told him he might be right. "See if you can find anything associated with the name Blair on the island."

"Copy that."

Malcolm still hadn't moved even though Kaleb's gun was staring him in the face. A sly smile curled on his lips. "Seems we are at an impasse. You need me to get to Eden."

Every muscle in Kaleb's body was taut with rage. He couldn't believe that only days ago he considered him one of his closest friends. Now, Malcolm's cold gaze held nothing but evil. Kaleb broke the connection, his eyes landing on Malcolm's blood-soaked shirt, and zeroed in on the outline of a small rectangular object in his breast pocket. Pinching it between his fingers, he slid it out. "Well, what do we have here?"

Malcolm didn't answer. Kaleb studied the elevator panel to find a slot that the card would slide into.

"Alpha one, you located the basement?" Ian questioned.

Kaleb keyed his comm. "Negative, but I have tango one, and we may have found a clue."

"What's your twenty?"

"Still in the northwest wing."

"We're coming to you."

Within minutes Kaleb heard Ian's voice. He opened the elevator, and they loaded in. "What happen to him?" Ian asked, lifting his chin to Malcolm.

"His worst nightmare." Kaleb chuckled, tipping his head to Kaysi.

Ian's eyes rounded. "Damn, girl."

Kaysi played shy, and Ben pulled her close.

"Are we about to be ambushed?" Ben interrupted.

"Absolutely." Lifting Malcolm's phone, Kaleb tapped the last number in the list of calls.

"Yes sir?"

"We are coming down, and Mr. Blair is going to be front and center, so unless you want to have his blood on your hands, I suggest you have your men stand down." He clicked out of the call before anything else was said then studied the panel again. Kaysi yanked the card from his hand, and her lip curled into a grimace when she realized it was covered in blood.

Placing the card against the panel, she moved it until the light at the top turned green. Handing it back, she gave him a very satisfied smile.

Kaleb hated to admit it, but he was glad he let his

sister come on the mission. He just needed to make sure she stayed alive.

Ian turned to Kaleb. "You guys go ahead. I'll bring reinforcements." Kaleb nodded and handed him the card.

The doors peeled apart, and as he predicted, soldiers stood with their guns ready. Ian and Kaleb's teams, from ICMP, protected them as they exited the elevator into a medical wing. Kaleb kept his gun at Malcolm's head, pushing Malcolm in front of him, Ben, and Kaysi. The number of guards told him that reinforcements would be needed, but he couldn't wait for them. "Take me to Eden," he growled.

"I don't know where she is," Malcolm hissed.

Kaleb lifted Malcolm's cuffed hands from behind his back, causing him to bend over in pain.

"I swear to you—"

"No!" It was one word. A barely audible scream that filtered into the hallway above the noise as more guards came through another set of metal doors. He'd know that voice anywhere.

Chapter Thirty-Seven

She hadn't seen Victor since he'd dropped them off with a group of his minions dressed in lab coats. Guards had separated them into different rooms, and she was strapped down to a gurney as they drew her blood.

She tried to stay calm and talk to every person that came into the room, but the extent of the conversation only consisted of the clinical instructions they'd give her. Panic creeped in. Where was Kaleb? By her calculations, he should have been there by now. He should have found them. Her mind kept playing through the different scenarios. What if the tracker didn't work? Ian said it was a prototype. Or what if the guards had already...No. She refused to even consider that.

A woman in scrubs came in and hung two bags of unknown solutions from an I.V. tree. Then, rummaging through the drawer, she withdrew several items and walked to the side of the bed where she flipped Eden's arm over, patting it. Eden tried to move away as the woman set the items on the tray. Uncapping a needle, the woman reached for Eden's arm, but she jerked, trying to free it from the restraints. It was no use. The sting of the needle caused her to wince. "What are you giving me? And why?" Terror was setting in, and even though Eden kept peppering the nurse with questions, she remained silent as she connected the first bag. Eden felt helpless.

She tried yanking on her wrist restraints again, but

they were too tight, although it made the nurse lose her grip, trying to connect the second bag.

Loud voices boomed outside her door. They were too muffled to make out what was being said, but it was obvious, there was a commotion. Her heart skipped. Was it Kaleb? Was he here? Her head swam, and she knew whatever was in her IV had to be causing it. Probably the same thing they'd given Adam and Marissa.

A guard burst in and ripped the IV from her arm. He released the restraints and grasped her roughly as he escorted her from the room. Her feet felt heavy, and she couldn't get her eyes to focus, so he practically had to drag her. "Where are you taking me? Where's Adam and Marissa?" He didn't answer her, and she wasn't about to leave without them. Fighting him, she dug her fingers into his grip, and screamed, "No," as she flailed her body against his force.

"Eden!"

Her head whipped around, and tears sprang to her eyes. "Kaleb!" she screamed. He stalked toward her, dressed in black tactical gear. The guard tightened his grip and slammed his hand against a button, opening a pair of metal doors. "No!" she shrieked again as he dragged her down the empty hallway.

The doors flung open. Eden spun, trying to free herself as Kaleb hurled himself at the guard. The force threw Eden to the floor, and she quickly crawled away. Rearing back, Kaleb delivered a painful blow. The guard stumbled and fell to the ground. Kaleb quickly straddled him ready to do more damage, but the guard bucked his hips and threw him off balance then popped up and reached for Eden. Kaleb grabbed him from behind, swept his legs out from under him, and sent him to the ground again. Wrapping his arms and legs around the guard, Kaleb tightened his grip, but the guard was too fast and spun out of the hold, and with a quick move, he stood and yanked Eden back into his side. In one swift motion, Kaleb stood, drew his gun, and pointed it directly at the guard's head. "Let her go, or your brains will be decorating that wall." She'd never heard him with such venom in his voice. A tinge of blood sat at the corner of his mouth. "And don't even think about reaching for your gun. Trust me, I'm faster."

The guard didn't move, continuing to stare Kaleb down. Eden's body quaked as she tried to calculate her next move with her head still feeling foggy. She'd taken some self-defense classes, but none had taught her what to do when she was three beers in.

Breathing deep, she spun around, and with all her force she shoved the heel of her hand into the base of the guard's nose. His grip loosened, and she stumbled into Kaleb's arms. But it only took the guard seconds to shake off her assault, and he barreled into Kaleb.

Eden was slammed into the wall, causing her head to bounce off the plaster so hard sparks fired in her eyes. She crumbled to the floor, her legs unable to hold her.

Kaleb's gun slid toward her across the marble floor as the guard pinned him. She needed to get the gun, but her body felt like a million tiny bees were stinging her, and she couldn't make herself move.

The guard's head snapped back, and Kaleb had him flipped over and was sitting in the middle of his back. He slid a zip tie from his tactical belt and zipped his hands and feet. Then he retrieved his gun. "Are you okay?" he asked, suddenly appearing in front of her. She nodded but winced when a sharp pain drilled into her skull.

"Oh. No, you aren't."

"What did I hit?" She reached up and dug her fingers into her hair, searching for the place that was stinging. Her gut seized when she withdrew bloody fingers, and she coughed.

A low drone of voices was heard seconds before the doors flew open. Joe, Cody, and Ian came through, followed by Adam and Marissa, then Ben and Kaysi. Mitch and Brant were escorting Malcolm. They were all surrounded by eight of the men from the ICMP. Kaleb helped Eden to stand. "Brant, can you take a look at her?"

"Sure. I've got some supplies in my backpack."

"Let's move to a more secure area first," Ian quickly added. "We left most of our teams back there holding off the guards, but that doesn't mean it's forever."

"I have no idea where we are. We could be walking into a trap, or it could be a dead end, and I don't trust Mr. Blair to get us out of here," Kaleb confessed, as his head swiveled back and forth, ready for more guards to come out of the walls.

Kaysi put her arm around Eden, and they moved with the team, making their way up the hallway. Confusion clouded her already groggy head. "I don't mean to sound rude, but what are you doing here? And who are those guys?" she asked pointing at the men in camo BDUs.

"I'm here because I needed closure." She pointed to Malcolm's bloody face. "I got it."

Eden followed Kaysi's finger. "You did that?"

Kaysi lifted her brow, and a satisfied smirk pulled at her lips.

"Remind me never to make you mad."

"The other guys are part of some foreign security

organization that Kaleb's group works with."

Her eyes scanned the group again. She was glad to see Marissa and Adam. They seemed much clearer headed than she felt. The stark white walls were quickly closing in on her. Everything looked the same, with no distinction, and in her drunken state she started wondering if they were moving in a circle.

Finally coming to a T, she eyed their choices. One way was a pair of metal doors, and the other was an open hallway. Kaleb turned toward the wide opening, but quickly backtracked, raising his gun, when the sound of the metal doors unlatching echoed through the hallway. Eden turned and nearly lost her balance. Kaleb and the team waited, ready to open fire on whoever came through the door. It slowly opened, and Eva's eyes widened. Her head swiveled, then settled. "Eden?" Her voice sounded small and shaky.

"Eva, what are you doing here?" Eden blinked, trying to get her eyes to focus, and took a tentative step forward in front of the line of armed men.

"You're hurt."

She reached up to touch the spot again, but dropped her hand, remembering how much it stung and nearly caused her to puke. "I'll be fine."

Kaleb's eyes bounced between Eden and Eva, until Eden remembered he'd not met her.

"This is my sister, Eva. Well, and Adam's too. Oh, and I guess Malcolm's...too." At that Kaleb's head jerked. She put her hand up...signaling she would explain later, then turned back to Eva and asked again, "What are you doing here?"

"Searching for you." Her eyes darted. "Several guards were yelling outside my room. They said somebody had gotten into the compound. I figured it was someone searching for you and Adam and Marissa. When they made a comment about the lab, I came down here to find you."

"Is there another way out?" Kaleb asked.

Her eyes moved to Malcolm, then back to Kaleb. "The safest way is through Victor's." She motioned for them to follow her and turned toward the metal doors. Pulling one open, she stumbled, and her crutches clanked as they hit the floor. Ian lunged forward and caught her before she did the same. He picked up the crutches and made sure she was stable, then released her. She gave him a shy smile that reached her crimson cheeks and led them down another corridor, stopping at a door in the middle of the hallway. There were no markings. It was like every other door, except it had a slightly different handle. No one would have noticed any difference.

Holding the card over the door handle, she waited until there was a click. This time Ian caught the door and opened it. "This will take you to Victor's house. She handed Eden a keychain with a key and fob. "You'll need this. It's from Juliette. She sends her love." Her eyes went back to Malcom, and Eden noticed his jaw tick.

"Wait. I don't understand. "If you could leave, why didn't you?"

"I had no place to go. My mom all but abandoned me. Juliette took me in."

"But what about Juliette? She was able to leave, too?"

"Yes. They gave her access to the island. She knew she wouldn't be able to leave though. Most everyone on the island works for Victor. And if not, he has them in his pocket, so she was scared what he would do to her if she tried to leave the island. Plus, she's been held captive for so long she doesn't know what the outside world holds anymore."

"Come with us," Adam interrupted.

"No. Not now. I would only slow you down, and you're still in danger."

"We will come back for you," Kaleb promised. "How far is it?"

"Less than a mile."

Eden hugged Eva, and when she backed away, she stared at her, easily recognizing their similarities, and relishing the fact that they had already developed a bond.

As they stepped through the doorway, Eva reached for Kaleb. "Stay safe."

He wrapped one arm around her and squeezed. "We'll be back for you. I promise."

Chapter Thirty-Eight

The tunnel was made up of huge square concrete culverts butted together and lit with security lights along the way. Once they were farther in the tunnel and Kaleb felt fairly certain no one had followed them, he stopped and turned to Eden, then pointed at Brant to join them. "Check her head." While Brant brought Eden under one of the security lights to get a better view, Kaleb leaned against the culvert. "Do any of you want to fill me in on exactly what's going on? Malcolm is your brother? And Victor...I mean, I have my suspicions. I'm guessing since he has a house he's not being held captive."

"Malcolm is our half-brother," Adam supplied. "Juliette, the woman Eva was talking about, is our mom. Victor is our and Malcolm's dad, and he is definitely not being held captive. He is attempting to create the perfect species by using people he handpicks as his breeding stock."

"Seriously?" It dawned on him. "Juliette. As in Juliette Granier."

Eden nodded. "He used the pageant to find women who met certain criteria, and at the first opportunity he would abduct them."

Shaking his head, he reluctantly asked, "And the website?"

"To find male specimens and buyers, I'm guessing. And maybe flesh out more like-minded minions to add to his research team," Adam answered.

"That place is huge. How many victims are we talking?"

"Who knows."

"And by breeding stock, you mean—"

"He harvests the egg and sperm, makes the necessary changes, then sells the embryos on the black market to the highest bidder."

"Damn. That's messed up."

"Eden, Eva, and I were his first successful transfers."

"And Juliette?"

"Was his first victim."

"And Victor is your dad."

"Unfortunately."

"And Malcolm is Victor's son—"

"—the natural way," Adam answered for him. "He's the reason Victor started all of this."

Kaleb opened his mouth.

Adam shook his head. "Don't ask."

He was afraid of the answer anyway. In all his years of working with Summit, he'd seen about every scenario possible, but this one had his mind misfiring and his stomach getting queasier by the second.

Staring down at the floor, still trying to come to grips with what they'd stumbled into, he tapped his comm. "Air one, this is Alpha one, do you copy?"

"Copy, but you're breaking up a bit."

"We've found a tunnel, that leads outside the compound, to Victor Chalemaare's home. I can't be sure, but if," his eyes searched the tunnel, "the rise in the compound ran east to west, I believe we are headed west. Can you get eyes on any buildings that might be within a mile of the compound on the west side?"

After a moment, Kat responded, "There are a few."

"Damn it. I don't know what to tell them to hunt for," Kaleb said to no one in particular. "This tunnel could wind up inside his house."

Eden winced as Brant dabbed at the cut on her head.

"He knows there has been a breach, so have them check to see if there are any houses with guards," Brant instructed.

"Air one, are there any locations being guarded?"

"That's a negative."

"Okay. Let's—"

"I'm tracking your location," April broke in.

"That's my girl," Joe's voice rang out as a smile filled his features.

"Send that to Air one."

"Already on it."

Eden moved back over to Kaleb after Brant finished cleaning her up. "You okay?"

"Yeah. At least I don't feel like spiders are crawling all over my head now."

"Are we good?" Kaleb directed his question to Brant.

"Yeah. It's not bad. Maybe could have used a stitch or two, but I glued it. It should be fine."

"You glued my head together?"

Brant's brows raised. "Yeah."

Eden swung her eyes to Kaleb. He chuckled and gave her a quick kiss to her forehead, then moved through the group. "Okay. Let's get moving. It shouldn't be far."

"Alpha One, we have a location."

"Great. What'cha got?"

"There is a house about half a klick ahead."

"Any outbuildings?"

"Negative."

"Copy."

"We will be in position momentarily."

"This is Delta one, we have secured the compound."

"Roger that."

Kaleb let out a shaky breath. He could feel his heart pounding in his chest and tried to relax so his anxiety didn't take over. He had been so focused he'd forgotten about the other teams who were part of the mission.

"There may not be guards surrounding his house but we have to assume he has security. We may be walking into a trap." His eyes flashed to Malcolm. "You know, you've been awfully quiet since we got down here."

"What the bloody hell do you want me to say? I have no way of contacting him. You have my phone, and I couldn't use it if I wanted to with my hands tied."

"What do you think we are walking into?"

"Look. I know you think my father is a monster, but I wouldn't be here if he hadn't done what he did. All he's ever done is try to rid the world of deadly diseases. He's trying to make the world a better place."

"Something tells me if that was all he was after he wouldn't have had to resort to kidnapping."

"And murder," Adam added. Kaleb's eyes widened as his head jerked to Adam then back to Malcolm.

"Murder? Oh, that's admirable," Kaleb mocked.

"His research saved my life. I can't believe you are so quick to judge, with her in her condition."

"What's that supposed to mean?"

Eden's head snapped at Malcolm's outburst. His eyes narrowed, and a sinister smirk formed on his lips as his focus locked on Eden. "Oh! Or maybe Eden is hiding something from you."

Eden stepped up beside Kaleb. "I'm not hiding anything."

"Well, the blood test says you are."

"What blood test?" Kaleb's mind skipped back to the phone call earlier.

Malcolm's focus again moved to Eden. "Come on, sweetheart. Don't play games."

Kaleb turned to Eden. Her arms crossed as she stared off up the tunnel, then her eyes suddenly filled with fear, and he wondered what she was about to reveal. What could she possibly be hiding? Was she sick? Did something happen while she was away from him that she was afraid to tell him? She chewed on her lip, and Kaleb grew more concerned. Malcolm sucked in his cheek with a self-satisfied expression. She had quickly become the most important thing in Kaleb's life, but doubt's venom was seeping into his veins.

"Eden what is he—"

"I'm pregnant." The words rushed from her lips so fast that he wasn't sure he heard her correctly.

"That's it, isn't it?" she asked as she turned back to Malcolm who tipped his head in confusion. "You didn't know?"

Eden shook her head, then her tear-filled eyes finally met Kaleb's. She was obviously scared, and he knew he had to have had a stunned expression on his face because that wasn't what he expected her to reveal. He was preparing himself for a dagger to the heart, but this, this was making his heart feel like a million butterflies took flight.

Eden swallowed and closed her eyes. Tears slid

from the corners as he circled his arms around her. When her eyes met his, he knew she questioned how he felt about it. But he meant what he'd told her back at the house. He was excited.

Pressing his lips to her warm flesh below her ear, he felt her body shiver in his grasp. A smile lifted the corner of his mouth as he quietly sang, "We're having a baby." Eden nodded, but he could feel her body trembling, so he added, "I can't wait."

Finally backing away, he waited as she peeled her lashes apart, then gave her his goofiest grin, and a smile finally formed on her beautiful raspberry-colored lips. She whispered back to him, "We're having a baby."

He nodded excitedly, then remembered the phone call again, and his eyes cut back to Malcolm.

"So that was what they were talking about when they said something about elevated levels?"

"Yeah."

"Then what was the procedure he was talking about?" Malcolm's face paled, and Eden turned to face him. His throat bobbed as he swallowed. Kaleb stared at him, obviously noticing how uncomfortable Malcolm had become. "What were they talking about, Malcolm?" Kaleb stepped closer, and Malcolm averted his eyes. "Answer me," Kaleb demanded.

"To abort the fetus. Okay?"

Bile rose to the back of Kaleb's throat so fast he nearly gagged. He latched onto Malcolm's shirt and slammed him against the concrete wall.

Malcolm stumbled then rushed out, "I didn't give the order."

"That's only because we nearly got our asses handed to us and we had to run."

"That's not true." Kaleb released his shirt. "It's not my call, usually. It's Victor's. They called me because he disappeared."

"What would you have said if we hadn't come under gunfire?"

"I've never had to make the call."

"But what would you have said, damn it?"

Malcolm stared up at the ceiling. "His research is a controlled setting. *He* creates the embryos. *He* chooses. If anyone in the compound turns up pregnant—"

"—the pregnancy is terminated. You would have followed protocol." Kaleb's voice was deadly calm. "And you still don't see him as a monster?" His gaze landed on Eden and drifted to her belly. "That's our baby, Malcolm. No one has a right to take our baby away from us. She's your sister, and that baby will be your niece or nephew. Do you understand? What if it was your child?"

Malcolm sucked in an audible breath, and his eyes darted to Eden's. In that instance, Kaleb saw, for the first time, what he thought was regret. "It didn't happen," Malcolm said barely above a whisper.

Eden stepped forward. "It almost did, though. They had me strapped down. A nurse started an IV. I had no idea what was going on because no one said a word to me. But now I know. The only reason it didn't happen was because Kaleb showed up and a guard came and got me. Tears sprang to her eyes, and Kaleb wanted to rip Malcolm apart. He could tell by Malcolm's expression what she'd said was true. They came extremely close to losing their baby. His head shook as the impact of her words dug in under his skin and he slammed Malcolm against the cement again. "I treated you like a brother, man." His voice came out shaky, so he cleared it and leaned in. "I trusted you, damn it." Malcolm closed his eyes and remained silent. Kaleb drew back his arm, ready to unleash his fury, when someone cleared their throat, and Kaleb stopped.

Joe's hand squeezed his shoulder, and he leaned in. "He's not worth it." Kaleb's eyes met Malcolm's. He released his shirt and stepped back.

"Uh. So, I guess congratulations are in order?" Cody said weakly. Kaleb turned realizing everyone had witnessed the entire conversation, and a rush of heat crawled into his cheeks. How were they going to explain this one? Eden giggled, and the sound immediately penetrated the darkness that had wrapped around him.

"Yeah. I guess so," he confessed sheepishly, finally allowing a smile to appear.

Joe's brow raised.

"Don't start with me. We had a malfun—"

Joe covered his ears. "Lalalalala. I don't need to know. I'm happy if you're happy."

"I'm ecstatic."

Impromptu hugs and pats on the backs were given, until Cody commented, "Does anyone find this really weird that we are in a drainage tunnel with our lives hanging in the balance and we are talking about having babies?"

"Seems like, on stressful cases—" Mitch confided, "—something always comes up to lighten the mood."

"Then I guess this would be a good time to bring up the fact that since we've been crawling around down here, I've pretty much been feeling like one of the turtles," Cody added.

"Where the hell did that come from?" Ben growled.

Brant's hand shot up. "I call dibs on Leonardo."

"Why do you get to be Leo? I'm the designated leader," Kaleb threw back.

"Because I'm Leonardo, and everyone knows, you're Michelangelo." Several heads nodded in agreement.

"Why Michelangelo? Why not Donatello? He's the brainy one."

"Because you're crazy. You go in with no plans, guns blazing, and hope for the best."

"And yet you all are following my orders. So, who's the crazy ones in this group?"

They rounded a slight corner, and a metal door came into view. Kaleb tapped his comm. "Air one, you got a copy? Any updates? We've found the door."

"That's a negative. No activity."

"I sent up the drone," April added, "to get a better view. They do have security cameras but nobody walking around outside."

"Roger that."

"I think Ian is Donatello," Joe added. "He's the one with all the cool gadgets."

"Yeah," Cody agreed. "And Ben is Rafael."

"Why me?"

"Because you're grumpy."

Joe chuckled. "He's not wrong there."

Quinten's voice rang through the comms. "Are you guys seriously trying to decide which turtle you are?"

"Why yes. Yes, we are."

"And of course, you're Michelangelo?"

"Apparently."

"Well, I guess I need to order some pizza then," Quinten added with a chuckle that elicited a round of laughter. After it died down, he added, "Be safe. Bring them home."

"I plan to." Kaleb slipped the key in the lock.

"The security panel is on the right of the door." Malcolm said quietly. "You will be entering the garage. The lights are automatic. The code is twelve twelve ninety. You have thirty seconds."

Kaleb tipped his head, surprised at the information he divulged, then nodded once in confirmation, not knowing if he should trust it. The remorseful expression on Malcolm's face made him believe he could. He was offering an olive branch. It didn't discount the part he'd played in the case, but it would help them none the less.

Chapter Thirty-Nine

Turning the key, Kaleb shoved open the door. The light was blinding. Taking in the surroundings, he noticed several cars that sat on the shiny cement floor. On the other side was an opening with stairs. He pushed Malcolm into the room, while Ian punched in the code to the security system and cut the lights. The security lights in the tunnel offered enough light for everyone to cross the room and gather at the base of the stairs before Mitch switched on his flashlight and shut the door. Kaleb flipped his flashlight on and shined it around at the cars. It gave enough light for him to see the ramp leading to freedom. Malcolm obviously noticed what Kaleb was shining his light on.

"The fob opens the hatch, but it will trigger the security system."

"Do they normally have guards?"

"No. Not at the house. My father has a team of four, that are with him at *Récolte* though, and I haven't seen them today."

He turned back to the group and tapped his comm. "Air one, we need a recovery location."

"Copy. Standby."

"The west side has thick tree coverage, and there is an open field northwest of the property," April informed.

"We can confirm that."

"Copy. Standby."

Kaleb turned back to the group. "Dalton crew, I need you to help get Eden, Adam, and Marissa to the helicopter. Ian, the ICMP crew, and I will finish the mission."

"Not on your life. I'm not letting you do this without me," Joe argued.

Cody stepped forward. "Me neither."

Mitch and Brant said the same.

"Listen. I appreciate you having my back. I do. But I've already put you guys in danger, and I'd rather use your help to get them out of here safely."

"I'll make sure they get to the helicopter. I never wanted Kaysi caught up in the fray, and I know she won't leave unless I do," Ben piped up.

"Okay. We will open the hatch, cover for you in case there is movement, and then my team will move in."

"Sounds good."

"Air one we have five for—"

"I'm staying," Adam interrupted, and Marissa's eyes darted his direction.

Kaleb eyed him. "Correction. We have four for extraction."

"We are in position. Go for extraction."

"Copy."

Kaleb's eyes landed on Eden, and he stepped in front of her. Her eyes were already becoming glassy as she gazed up at him, and he knew the tears wouldn't be far behind. Wrapping his hand around her waist, he tugged her to him and pressed his forehead against hers.

He couldn't have cared less about the mob that was standing around them or how much danger they were currently in. Right now, all he wanted was to feel her body against his one more time. "Don't cry, baby girl. I will be fine," he whispered.

"I'm scared."

"I know." He backed away, yanked the guard's gun that he'd retrieved earlier from his waistband, and handed it to her. "But you're the reason this mission will succeed. Do you realize that? Because of everything you did. You were so brave. I just need you to be brave one more time, and then before you know it, we will be together picking out baby furniture."

Fear and happiness battled in her expressions. "Oh my God, Kaleb. We are going to have a baby. Are we crazy?"

His hands slid to her cheeks, and he stared into her eyes as his thumb stroked her soft skin. "I've done some crazy shit in my life, but this? I think this is about the smartest thing I've ever done, even if it was kind of an accident. Because I don't know that you know this, but I kind of have these feelings for you." A crooked smirk formed on his lips and, just like he'd hoped, a smile she was fighting appeared.

Her tongue peeked out, pressing against her teeth and she whispered, "I kind of have these feelings for you, too."

He couldn't hold himself back any longer, and his lips collided with hers over and over. He couldn't stop. She tasted too sweet, felt too perfect. She was the satisfaction to his insatiable craving. Was this what it felt like to have an addiction? "God, I love you, Eden." The words tumbled out, and he waited for her to become rigid in his arms, but she didn't. The only thing that changed was the smile that formed behind her kisses.

Someone behind them cleared their throat. His nose brushed against hers, and he grimaced, knowing what needed to happen. A knot quickly lodged in his throat. "You go, and I will be right behind you. I promise."

Her eyes shifted to the floor, and she took a deep breath, then nodded. He kissed her forehead, and she tugged him to her for one last kiss. "I love you, Agent Grey."

His thumb hit the button, and a large metal hinged portion of the roof began to move. With one last glance back, Eden, along with Ben, Marissa, and Kaysi, ran toward the opening, with two of the ICMP soldiers at their back. Kaleb held his breath as they disappeared around the corner and knew he wouldn't breathe until he laid eyes on her again. His teeth clamped tight as he tried to fight the sting in his eyes and send an invisible force field around them.

As the two soldiers reappeared, the garage door closed, and the door at the top of the stairs opened. Kaleb signaled to the team to move into a darkened area behind the stairs.

The open door gave enough light for Kaleb to see two men enter the garage from the stairs. They quietly moved about the garage, guns in hands.

Approaching the area, Joe got the jump on one while Brant took the other and made quick work of subduing them.

"Dang it. You guys took away all my fun."

"I thought you were busy with Wonderboy." Kaleb's eyes drifted to Malcolm, who had been so quiet, he'd all but forgotten he was supposed to be watching him. Even in the low light, he could see his shoulders slumped, and complete exhaustion was etched on his blood-stained face. A pang of regret hit him, knowing his friendship was irreparably damaged. He was still having a hard time reconciling that Malcolm was wrapped up in this shit show.

Shaking his head, trying to bring himself out of the chaos taking over his thoughts and emotions, he scanned the room. With the guards' hands and feet tied, he tossed one of their guns to Adam, tucked the other one into his waistband, adding it to their arsenal, then motioned for the team to move.

Cautiously, they headed up the stairs and entered the house through a large state-of-the-art kitchen that flowed into a dining area and opened to an outdoor patio. "Damn. This quest to rid the world of disease pays well," Kaleb whispered over Malcolm's shoulder as he pushed him farther into the house and down a short hallway. Voices echoed, and Kaleb motioned for part of the team to take the other possible entrance.

A large living room came into view. Two men, similarly dressed as the previous two they'd subdued, were engrossed in a soccer game playing on a massive TV screen that hung on the wall.

An older blonde woman, pulling a large suitcase, emerged from a dark hallway opposite the one they were standing. Kaleb released Malcolm and backed away, retreating out of view.

He watched from his position in the kitchen as horror formed on the woman's face when she noticed Malcolm standing in the hallway. "Bloody hell, sweetheart. What happened to you?" She left her luggage behind and raced to his side. "Victor!" she yelled. The two guards quickly joined them. Malcolm had yet to utter a word. Kaleb wondered if it was because he didn't want to confess that he got jumped by a girl. That thought caused Kaleb's lip to twitch. Kaysi's abilities had truly surprised him.

With the sound of more footsteps, Kaleb's gut tightened at the sight of a gray-haired man emerging from the long hallway. Victor. He looked just like the photos they had of him. Behind him, two more guards appeared. *Shit! Two were not going to be a problem, but four might be a little trickier.* He could only hope that there weren't any more.

As their attention focused on Malcolm, Kaleb emerged from his hiding place with his gun lifted. Mitch quickly flanked him. Cody and one of the ICMP guards fell in behind. Victor was the first to notice. His head swiveled, but by then Kaleb had eaten up the distance and the other team had closed in from the other side.

"What is this?" the blonde woman screeched.

"What does it look like, Mother? *Récolte* is no more. It's been seized. But you already knew that, didn't you?" His eyes flicked to the suitcases. "You were just trying to get away before you got caught. Thanks for letting me know."

Victor's eyes narrowed, and his voice dropped to a low menacing growl. *"Qu'aves-vous fait?"*

Malcolm let out a sardonic chuckle. "What have *I* done?" Kaleb's breath stalled in his lungs when Malcolm turned his watery eyes to him. "Honestly? I've done some pretty shitty things, actually." His eyes returned to Victor. "All because of you. But this isn't one of them. It's over. You're done."

"How could you do this, Malcolm? Your father saved your bloody life."

His eyes darted to Adam. "And how many others has he taken?"

"He did it because he loved you."

"Right. He loved me. Enough to leave me behind when the compound was under siege."

"*Toute ma vie a été centrée sur la recherche d'unremède pour toi.*"

"That's bullshit," Malcolm seethed. "Finding a cure for my illness might have started you down this path, but I was just another one of your lab experiments. And once you found the cure, I was no longer needed, so I became another one of your brainwashed lackies that you guilted into doing your dirty work. Yeah. That's real love."

"*Tu as tout gaché.*"

"That's funny coming from you. How many lives have *you* ruined, Father? How many people have you ripped from their families for your grandiose plan? But you don't care, do you? You don't care because it got you this." Malcolm gestured to his surroundings. "If anyone has ruined anything, it's you. You ruined my life. It would have been better to let me die. Because of you, now I'm probably going to spend the rest of my life behind bars. But you know what? I'm taking you down with me. I'm telling them every damn thing you've done."

"You won't get away with this," Victor raged. Kaleb's attention whipped to Victor, hearing him speak English, and in that split second he saw the flash of a gun, heard the explosion echoing off the vaulted ceiling, and felt the force of impact as Malcolm slammed into him and they both fell to the floor. More shots rang out, and Kaleb flinched, feeling the heat of a bullet fly past his head. Moving quickly from under Malcolm's dead weight, he latched onto his collar, dragging him around the corner into the kitchen and tapped his comm. "Shots fired." Red stained the front of Malcolm's shirt. Kaleb ripped it open and noticed pools of blood pumping from his upper right chest. He tore the shirt off, wadded it up, and pressed it against the wound. "Tango one is down. I have a pulse."

"Copy. We're standing by."

"I'm s-so sorry."

A lump stuck in Kaleb's throat. His emotions were at war. He hated Malcolm for what he'd done. Yet the pain in his expression as he spoke to Victor made him want to believe there was a decent human being inside that mixed up mind and forgive him. "Don't worry about that right now; just don't die on me, Malcolm."

His mouth moved but Kaleb couldn't make out what he was saying. Shouts and scuffling had his attention drawn to the other room hoping the gun battle was over. His heart beat in his ears as he tried to figure out his next move. Like an answer to his silent prayer, Brant appeared next to him. "Oh, thank God." Brant dropped to his knees and lowered his shoulder to retrieve the backpack he was carrying. Gently lifting him, Brant checked his back. "Looks like a through and through."

"What's the status? Is everyone else okay?"

"We've secured the premises. Our team is good. We have Mrs. Blair subdued, along with the four guards."

"And Victor?"

Brant took a deep breath. "Deceased."

Chapter Forty

Eden lay on the gurney, waiting for the doctor to return. She'd been poked and prodded enough to wonder if they were doing acupuncture. Her arm stung where she had fought them as they were attaching another I.V. They assured her it was for dehydration.

The ordeal she'd been through had her fighting the panic setting in from being in yet another hospital, and now she was alone. Her skin was crawling. Her mind was racing, and she desperately wanted to leave so she could find out about the team.

She'd left every fiber of her being clinging to Kaleb when she ran from the garage knowing that the fight was far from over for him. She had no idea how she was even moving because she was an empty shell. After reaching the helicopter, the only thing she was capable of doing was praying for his safety. It was a repeated mantra. Even when Marissa wrapped her hand around hers and Kaysi snuggled her into her side, she still felt numb. Her heart had been torn from her chest. She'd felt that feeling before, and there was always one common denominator. Kaleb. And only one reason for it. She loved him and nothing would bring her back to life until she knew he was safe. Until she looked into his eyes. It felt like a never-ending nightmare that only he could awaken her from.

The thick glass door opened, and the antiseptic smell

quickly invaded her nose making her stomach churn. The doctor, who was there when the helicopter landed, entered, rubbing his hands with antibacterial gel. Moving to the laptop sitting on the table, he studied it, then the monitor she was hooked up to. "Miss Samuels?"

Her name sounded wrong to her now. After all she'd been through, she didn't want to be associated with it anymore. "Please, call me Eden." She slowly sat up and straightened her posture even though her body groaned at doing so. Her years of training made it a mindless motion.

"Very well." It struck her as funny that the medical team had all spoken to her in English, but she guessed they were used to tourists. "We have your blood test back," he said. She returned from her musings as he shifted his attention to her. "Are you aware that you're pregnant?" His thick French accent bled through every word calling her back to the compound. A tsunami of panic flooded her.

She wanted to run, but she was still hooked up to all the machines. Her eyes bounced from the doctor to the door. There was no way to escape. The only thing she could do was plead for their safety. "Don't hurt my baby, please." The words came out in a broken rasp. "Please. Please, don't hurt my baby."

The doctor's features filled with compassion. "No, no. No harm will come to you or your baby. You're safe. We are here to take care of you." His words, although well meaning, did little to relieve the panic that now had her heart thumping in her ears. He took a step back, putting more space between them. "I just wanted to make sure you were aware so you could seek prenatal care when you return home."

The added distance allowed her to take a breath but she still didn't trust her voice, so she nodded.

"All of your other tests have come back fine. Your head wound is mild. Just be careful when you wash your hair for the next few days and try to take it easy. With what you've been through, you should expect to be a bit sore for a few days. I will let the nurse know you can be discharged."

The door slid open as she carefully shoved her feet into her shoes, and a young nurse entered.

"I have your discharge papers with your care instructions. Will you need a wheelchair?" the nurse asked as she began disconnecting the IV.

"No. I came in with three others. A blonde woman, a brunette, and a guy with a beard. Do you know where they are?"

"No. We'll check the waiting room."

After getting all the equipment disconnected, the nurse hit the button to open the door, and Eden followed her down the hallway and through another set of doors to the waiting room. She scanned the area until her eyes landed on Kaysi, who was resting her head on Ben's shoulder. His head was tipped back, and his eyes were closed, so she quietly lowered herself into the soft cushioned seat. Exhaustion set in, and she knew she could easily drift off to sleep, but she couldn't let that happen. She needed to know that Kaleb was okay.

Her attention was pulled to two men in scrubs, walking quickly toward the reception desk. "…mass casualties. We have a chopper five minutes out with a GSW to the chest. I need you to assemble a team for their arrival and we'll need to return to the island to assess and triage." The metal door that she had come out of shut taking the rest of their conversation with them. She'd caught enough. Her chest tightened, and she couldn't suck in enough air. She closed her eyes, sending up a prayer and felt a hand squeeze her shoulder. Her head rolled to the side, and she saw Ben staring at her.

"He's fine. He should be here in a few minutes. They're getting everything turned over to the authorities." Ben slowly sat forward. "Are you okay?"

Relief washed over her. "Yeah. I am now." The buzz of the metal doors sounded again, and Eden quickly turned. Marissa locked eyes with her and hurried to where they were sitting.

"Any word?" Marissa asked as she sat next to Eden. Kaysi lifted her head, and Ben angled himself in his chair.

"Last transmission I got was they were with the ICMP wrapping everything up and turning things over to the local authorities."

Eden still had so many questions. "Who was shot?"

Marissa's eyes rounded. "Someone was shot?"

Kaysi's eyes flicked to Ben, and Eden could tell they knew something. "Malcolm was shot. I don't know who else."

"But you know Kaleb wasn't one of them?"

"He's been the one in my ear, jabbering this whole time, so I think he's fine."

The buzz of the doors pulled their eyes that direction, and Brant, Cody, and Mitch strolled through. Eden's eyes bounced between the men and the metal door. When it didn't open again, she voiced her obvious question. "Where's—"

Mitch held up his hand. "He's still ironing out some issues with the local authorities."

"He's okay?"

"Yeah, he's fine. A bit pissed when we left, so I hope he keeps his shit together and remembers he's in a foreign country, or he may get hauled in with Adam."

"What happened?" Kaysi asked as she and Ben joined the group.

Marissa shot up from her seat, alarm filling her voice. "They're taking Adam in? Why? What did he do?"

"He shot Victor, after Victor shot Malcolm," Brant said on a loud breath.

"What the hell? I thought Malcolm was on his side. I mean, I know he gave us some help getting in, but I figured that was more under duress than anything."

"No. Apparently, Malcolm had an attack of his conscience somewhere along our little journey and told Victor he was going to take him down. Victor didn't appreciate that, so he shot Malcolm and nearly took out Kaleb in the process, so Adam shot him."

Visions of Brant's words played out in Eden's mind, and she backed up to the chair and sat down as her body began to shake.

"So, they're taking him in for questioning. I'm sure it's standard procedure. Kaleb's boss is handling everything, so I doubt he will be there long," Mitch finished.

Voices were heard as the metal doors buzzed once again and Kaleb, along with Joe, April, and Ian burst through. "It's a good thing Quinten was there because I was ready to drop that—"

"He was just doing his job," Mitch huffed, immediately joining in on their conversation.

"He was being an ass, Mitch. Adam was

cooperating. He didn't have to be so rough."

"What did they do to him?" Marissa asked.

"They manhandled him. Bounced him up against the wall. He told them he was the one who shot Victor, handed over his gun, and they still treated him like he was resisting. It was unnecessary. He didn't do anything wrong. Victor was ready to take out anyone who stood in his way. Adam put a stop to it."

"And they took him in?"

"Yeah. They were getting ready to when we left. He was already in the car."

"Do you guys have to give statements?" Ben asked.

"We told them what happened, and Quinten is meeting the head of ICMP up there to give a full report. He said we need to hang out at the hotel until everything is hashed out."

His body was coiled tight as he swaggered farther into the room, and his voice held a rasp of agitation as he defended Adam. He was so animated when he was passionate about something. His arm movements and expressions sucked her in. She loved how he lived his life unapologetically.

Although everyone kept peppering him with questions, he didn't stop moving until he stood in front of her. She slowly stood, and he immediately wrapped his arms around her and squeezed her against his body. All the questions stopped, or at least she couldn't hear them anymore. He was there. He was safe. Her chest heaved as the panic finally began to subside. Sobs tore through her, and Kaleb tightened his arms and dropped kisses into her hair. She felt like all he ever did was comfort her, but when she finally tried to back away while she composed herself, he pulled her in tighter and laid his head on her shoulder. Then she heard him softly sniffle. Was he crying too?

He lifted her off her feet and she wrapped her legs around his waist. Her fingers threaded through his hair that was damp from sweat. She didn't care. She felt so safe pressed against him, and he smelled like her forever. "God, I was so scared. They said someone had been shot, and all I could think about was you. That I might never see you again. I've never prayed so hard in my life."

He finally lifted his head, letting his tear-filled eyes settle on hers. "I promised you I would come back to you. I don't break my promises."

"They said you nearly got shot."

"Then I guess it's a good thing you were praying."

"And Victor?"

Kaleb loosened his grip, and she slid down his body. "He didn't make it."

"Adam killed him?"

"Yeah."

"So, it's over."

"It's over."

****

Eden had come to hate being on planes because nothing good seemed to come of the last few flights she'd taken. Even though the mission was over and she was safe, panic still consumed her as she boarded. She was hoping this trip would be without issue and would make up for the rest.

Days had been spent giving statements to the local authorities and filling out paperwork to prepare to return to the states. Adam was finally released, but there was little time to address anything else before they were escorted to the airport.

Sliding into the cushiony seat, she watched as the others filled the aisle, and with each person that passed the lump grew in her throat. Men and women who weren't trained government agents, who lived normal lives, had put their lives on hold and were willing to risk everything to save someone they barely knew. She'd grown to love all of them, including Ben, who came off a little gruff but deep down was very caring and protective.

Kaleb entered, and her breath caught. He was wearing a pair of holey jeans and a bright, cobalt-blue T-shirt that made his eyes almost translucent. God, he was gorgeous. He plopped down in the seat next to her and stowed his backpack, then leaned over and gave her a chaste kiss. "How ya doing?"

"Oh, you know, feeling a bit panicked at the moment."

"Why?"

"I just don't have the best memories with planes."

Kaleb nodded knowingly, and Eden continued to replay the events of the past. "I can't believe it's finally over," she said after a minute.

"Well, it's not completely over. It's going to be a while sorting out everything and getting everyone off the island."

"What are they going to do with the compound?"

"It's hard to say. For now, it's locked down as well as Victor's house. They're crime scenes."

"How's Malcolm doing? Any word?"

"Last report he was still in ICU. His prognosis is good, and he's talking to the police, so hopefully that bodes well for him."

Adam came up the aisle, his fingers laced with

Marissa's. He ducked as he moved into a seat across from Eden. Marissa took the seat beside him.

"So, are you ready to come work at Grayeagle?" Kaleb asked while Marissa was digging in her carry-on.

Her eyes flicked to him. "Are you offering me a job? I haven't even interviewed."

"Do you like oil and gas?"

"Yeah."

"Do you know a lot about it?"

"Yeah."

"What about environmental management? Do you like that?"

Marissa giggled. "Yeah."

"Okay. Consider yourself interviewed, and you sound like a great candidate. So, you're hired."

"You're serious?"

"Hell yeah, I'm serious. I'm kind of in a situation here, if you haven't figured that out."

Marissa looked at Adam who smiled. "I think you got yourself a job."

"But what about—"

"I can go anywhere I want."

"But you love Canada. Your mom's place sounds amazing."

"And?"

She turned back to Kaleb. "Can I think about—"

"She'll take the job."

"What about us? I don't want you leaving everything behind for me."

"Who said anything about leaving it behind? Juliette and Eva will be moving there if I have anything to say about it. And that will give us a good reason to go visit." Marissa sat silently staring at Adam. "Take the damn job."

After a long minute, Marissa turned to Kaleb. "I'll take it."

Kaleb pumped his fist victoriously. "Yes. Can you start tomorrow?"

"Um…"

"I'm kidding. I honestly have no idea what day it is, so let's work out the logistics later."

Eden couldn't have been happier, seeing Adam and Marissa's lives blossom out of something so tragic, but the fact that their lives seemed to be falling into place made the questions surrounding hers more unnerving. She had no job, no place to go, and she was pregnant. And although Kaleb had said he loved her, she knew it could have been triggered by the dire situation they were in. Neither knew if they were going to be alive in the next few minutes.

Their lives had slammed together in a chaotic storm so crazy she wasn't sure she wasn't stuck in a nightmare that she hadn't woken up from. But she didn't want to wake up if it meant losing Kaleb.

Although she wasn't sure she'd ever known what love felt like, what she'd felt since she'd been with Kaleb was more intense than she'd expected. Her mind was calmed by him while her body felt like someone suddenly flipped the power on, and one by one each cell came to life. And if that's what love felt like, she was all in. She just didn't know if he felt the same way.

Shifting her attention to the clouds far below, she felt her stomach plummet as the uncertainty continued to play in her head.

"Eden?" A voice echoed through the menagerie of thoughts but didn't register. His breath against the shell of her ear was successful though and had all thoughts evaporating into thin air.

"What's going on in that pretty little head of yours?"

She turned to see him with one brow lifted, along with the corner of his mouth. She wanted to smile back, and she tried, but from the way his expression shifted she wasn't successful.

"Follow me." With those two words, he grasped her hand and dragged her from her seat to the back of the plane where there were a couple of rows that were empty. The plane suddenly shimmied and had Eden rocking back and forth holding onto the seats on either side of her to stay standing.

"Sorry, everybody. We are hitting a little turbulence. Might want to buckle up if you aren't," the pilot announced.

Eden stumbled into the seat beside Kaleb and latched the buckle. Her chest suddenly felt tight, and the butterflies in her stomach had decided to become angry hornets.

"Now, tell me what that was all about up there. One minute you were all happy and laughing with everyone, and the next you disappeared."

How was she going to figure out where he stood without making him feel obligated? She wanted his genuine answer, not one of his heroic do the right thing comments. With a deep shaky breath, she asked, "What are your plans when you get back home?"

His head tipped, and his eyes remained on her for a moment. "Well, I need to sit down with my parents and explain everything and hope my dad still thinks I can run the company someday. And if so, I need to get Marissa up to speed, because we still need to hire probably three more people. I need to follow up with Quinten and make sure all the loose ends are taken care of."

Her heart faltered with the observation that he hadn't mentioned anything that included her. It was becoming clear that although he'd probably be fine co-parenting, that might be all he would want. The plane dipped, and her fingers gripped the armrests. She really hated flying.

"And I'm hoping that Ben would be okay with us staying a little longer, until we can get our house put back together. I was thinking we could go ahead and decide on a theme for the nursery. April and Joe did a cool woodsy theme for AJ. Of course, with the house laid out the way it is, the baby is going to have to stay in our bedroom for a while. It's got that big sitting area though, and I think April could probably do something—"

"You want me to live with you?"

"Well yeah. Of course I want…wait. Is that what this is all about? Do you not want to—"

"No. I want to. I just wasn't sure…when…I mean, there was so much happening and…we didn't know if we were even going to make—"

"Eden, listen, if I'm being honest, I did lie to you a little bit when I said I had feelings for you."

Eden took a deep breath, trying to steel herself for what was about to come. "I get it," she said softly. "Having a baby is a lot. I know—"

"Eden."

"I barely got any sleep with Aurora, and I can't imagine—"

"Eden…stop." She hesitantly lifted her eyes to meet his gaze. "I'm obsessed with you. The past two years I have barely thought of anything else. You invaded my thoughts and even my dreams. I can't even guarantee it's healthy to be as obsessed with someone as I am with you." Now it was her turn to be confused. Her eyes widened and a shy boyish smirk appeared on his gorgeous face. "I wasn't actually planning to divulge that." He paused and stared up the aisle. "Anyway,"— his eyes swung back to her—"if you're good with that, I want to get married. I mean—"

Eden let out a snicker, and Kaleb tilted his head in that confused expression again, and Eden paused. "You're serious?"

"Why is it no one ever thinks I'm being serious?"

"Maybe because you have a tendency to drop crazy important information out of nowhere."

"I don't like wasting time."

Eden's thoughts went back to the bomb he dropped on her. "But...so...you really want to marry me?"

The plane shuddered and dipped, and Eden suddenly felt like she was on a rickety rollercoaster.

"Yes. Eden. I *really* want to marry you. I know I'm not down on one knee, but that's because I don't fit. And I don't have a ring, so I'm screwing this up royally—"

"Yes." Turned out she didn't like wasting time either, and she knew what she wanted her answer to be.

Kaleb's eyes opened wide, and a bright toothy grin filled his face. "You will?"

She matched his grin, nodding her head, then threw up.

Chapter Forty-One

Several months later

Kaleb could barely contain himself. It was a long time coming, lots of secrets to keep, and behind-closed-door meetings, but as he parked his truck he glanced over to Eden sitting in the seat next to him, her eyes covered by a black blindfold with a bit of a scowl on her face, and he grinned.

So much had changed in the months since the rescue. Although he was still kept abreast of the case, he was officially done with the Summit Agency and was working full time with his dad. Marissa slid into Malcolm's position and didn't miss a beat, taking over the audit and helping him with the new hires.

The last word he got from Quinten was that Malcolm had cooperated with the French authorities. The information he'd given them revealed just how far reaching Chalemaare's *Récolte* project spanned. It would be a while before the case could even go to trial because of the amount of work it was going to take to investigate the entire operation since it affected so many countries, including the US. All the victims had been rescued, and the compound was shut down. They had completed their mission without one civilian casualty.

It was still hard for him to believe how it all came together. He was glad to have the help of the ICMP, but it wouldn't have been a success without the help of his Dalton team. They all proved to be heroes.

His eyes drifted to the rearview mirror, which held a reflection of the mirror in front of the car seat holding a sleeping baby. Cadence Rose had made her debut a little over three weeks early. His eyes still misted over, thinking about how strong Eden had been throughout the pregnancy.

Although she'd had an early bout with morning sickness, it didn't last long, and it didn't slow her down. Once they were home from France, she pulled all the girls in to help her plan the wedding. She didn't want fancy, so within a few weeks everything came together and they were saying their "I do's" in a small glass chapel high up in the Arkansas hills in front of their family and closest friends. Quinten, Ian, and Kat had also come, at Eden's insistence. The only ones missing, were Eva and Juliette, who were still getting moved into Adam's mother's house. Adam graciously agreed to walk her down the aisle, and Kaleb had never been so awestruck. He had to give Victor credit. He had created perfection after all. She was everything he could have ever asked for.

They opted for a long weekend away for their honeymoon since he was still playing catch up at work. Marissa had been a life saver, immediately diving into the audit and performing miracles. She'd even convinced her friend, Marci, to jump ship from Peppin and join the team, and with a couple of other hires, his crew was a powerhouse.

Eden had talked about going hiking, and he immediately knew where to take her. Devil's Den. She wouldn't have found him without it. And it didn't disappoint. He had never seen her so happy, so full of life. Marrying her was the best decision he'd ever made. Even though they had been to hell and back, he wouldn't trade it for the world because he'd met her.

His parents quickly fell in love with her. He'd taken her with him when he finally revealed the secret life he'd been living, hoping she would be a buffer. Though his mom had scolded him thoroughly, they'd easily forgiven him since he was presenting them with a new daughter-in-law and their first grandbaby as a peace offering. His mom was eager to pitch in when it came to decorating the nursery.

They'd chosen to leave the gender a surprise, so April and Kaysi took a cue from Eden's passion and did the nursery in a musical theme, painting the focal wall a mint green with piano keys up one side and the lyrics to "Teddy Bear Picnic" in the center. Joe made shelves with treble clef and bass clef symbols for an adjacent wall that was painted a darker green with music notes scattered across it. Eden couldn't hold back the tears when they did the reveal.

Kaleb hopped out of the pickup and jogged around to the passenger side, opening the rear door. As he unlatched Cadence's carrier and lifted it out, he threw her baby bag over his shoulder. It had only been two weeks since she was born, and Kaleb was still in awe of his tiny daughter. In her little pink onesie with the words "made from love," it was still hard for him to believe that she was a part of him and Eden. But she was. He was there when she entered the world.

Chuckling to himself, he recalled singing, "we're having a baby" into Eden's ear when the doctor told her to push. And through gritted teeth she responded, "I still think we're crazy." And when he heard Cadence cry for the first time as the doctor laid her on Eden's chest, there was no holding back the tears. His prediction was spot on. She was the most beautiful baby in the world.

As he moved to Eden's door, he saw her fingers drumming on her leg. She was nervous. He hadn't given her much to go on. "Please tell me we aren't flying somewhere," she said as he tugged the door open. "I really don't think Cadence is old enough and—"

"No. We aren't flying anywhere." He could practically see the wheels turning in her head.

Most of the snow had melted with the warmer temperatures, although there were still a few piles where the snowplows had come through. He held her hand and let her slowly step out of the truck.

Setting the carrier down, he helped Eden step up onto the sidewalk, and once she was settled he said, "Don't move." He dug his phone from his pocket and sent off a text.

"What are you doing?"

He didn't respond until he was in position. "Okay. You can remove your blindfold."

He snapped a few pictures as she carefully untied it and let it drop. Her mouth fell open slightly and her eyes darted, taking in everything. Confusion drew her brows together.

Before her stood the old run-down building that she told him she'd fantasized about when she first arrived in Dalton. A huge sign on wheels sat in front of it, with the words "thank you" written in big red letters.

"What is this?"

"I wanted to get you something for a wedding present, but everything happened so fast. This is better anyway because now I can say thank you for marrying me and making me a daddy. You have made me the happiest man on earth." With the last word, he pushed the sign away, to reveal a completely remodeled storefront with a sign on the new windowpane that read Eden's Garden of Music. "Joe's been working on this for months to get it ready. I hope you—"

Before he could even get the words out, Eden had her arms wrapped around his neck and her lips pressed to his. "I can't believe you did this for me. I was so disappointed when Kaysi told me it had been sold. I figured my dream would have to wait. How did I miss Joe's truck?"

"He was being careful since it was supposed to be a surprise. And unfortunately, you will have to wait a little bit longer because I had no idea what you would need to get started. You still have a little while to recover, so you can use the time to decide. Do you want to see the inside? April and Kaysi hit it out of the park."

"Of course."

Kaleb opened the door, and the smell of fresh stain penetrated his senses. "Adam left it kind of an open concept in here and said he and Joe can adjust it to your needs."

"Adam worked on this?"

"Adam and Joe designed it and worked on it together. This is the waiting area." Kaleb pointed. "Over there is the coffee bar and office. Straight back is a small concert hall with a stage. Upstairs are several practice rooms."

"I-I can't believe it. It's perfect."

"Oh, you haven't seen the best part." Kaleb picked up Cadence's carrier and led Eden down the hallway. He could barely keep from giggling as he opened the door. Flipping the light on, he stepped inside. Eden's expression transformed from confused to overwhelmed as she took in the ruby red walls and the state-of-the-art equipment.

"This, this is a recording studio."

"That it is. You said it was something you wanted in your music studio."

"I meant something simple to record my students. I don't know anything about recording music."

"You don't need to. Cody's sound guy, Matt, is phenomenal. He's the one who helped me figure out what equipment to buy and said he'd be willing to offer his expertise for recording projects, in exchange for use of the studio."

"Well, that's a no brainer."

"Yeah. I thought it was a great opportunity for both of you. Cody's band has several original songs, so this would give them a chance to record them."

Eden wandered around the studio, letting her fingers run along the buttons and faders of the large, multi-channel mixer, then she sat in the leather cushioned chair and stared up at the black curtain in front of her. A huge grin spread across Kaleb's face as he waited for her to ask. "What's behind the curtain?"

"That's the sound-proof room. Open the curtain and I'll flip on the lights."

She stood. The grating sound of the rings against the metal bar added an edge to Kaleb's already jittery nerves. He flipped the lights, and the darkened room was illuminated and filled with all her friends holding a huge sign that read "congratulations." And standing in the middle were Eva, Juliette, and Bill.

Kaleb pinched his lips together as he watched the realization fill Eden's face. She turned quickly to him; her mouth moved without making a sound. Her wide eyes returned to the group, then to Kaleb, then back to the group.

"You can go in there, you know." He turned the knob and opened the door. Eden ran out, and Kaleb lifted Cadence's carrier and followed. She wrapped Eva in a tight hug first, then moved to Juliette and finally to Bill, who was leaning on a cane.

"I thought you were dead."

"I thought I was too. It was touch and go there for a while, but I'm too stubborn to die, I guess."

"What happened?"

"Let's just say I wasn't as sneaky as I thought, and I caught a couple of bullets for it."

"Are you okay?"

"Things are getting better every day."

"How'd you find me?"

Bill tipped his head and chuckled. "You do remember what line of work I'm in, right?"

"Oh. Yeah, I—"

Bill's eyes shifted and he nodded. "I think I have your husband and his team to thank for that. They found me. I got paid a visit while I was in rehab in London. Adam called me with the news, so I thought I would come see what all the hubbub was about."

Like Cadence knew she was being talked about, she started squirming in her carrier.

"Can I hold her?" Juliette asked tentatively.

Kaleb unbuckled her and gently placed her in Juliette's arms. Bill leaned in close, and Kaleb wondered if they'd somehow met each other. Apparently, Eden had noticed too.

"Wait. Do you know each other?"

"We met on the way here. Adam flew us all in together."

An arm wrapped around Kaleb's shoulders from behind, yanking him off balance. He flipped around to see Ian with a mischievous grin on his face.

"What the hell are you doing here? I thought you were in Colorado making snow angels."

His eyes shifted to see Quinten and Kat across the room.

"Just tying up another loose end to the case." Ian slapped him on the back then hugged Eden. His eyes drifted to Cadence then lifted to Eva's and he nodded and winked. A shy smile spread across her face. Kaleb raised a brow, letting Ian know that he'd seen everything. Ian cleared his throat. "You did good. I'm happy for you guys."

Kaleb's mind drifted back, thinking about when Quinten got the call from ICMP about the missing scientist and what had transpired in the years since. He took in all the faces in the room. People laughing and chatting. People who were willing to give up their lives for Eden and him, and he knew he'd do the same for them. And he had. Many had faced their own nightmares and come out on the other side. And he'd been there for them. Friends and family. Some who'd known him since he was born and some only a short time.

Juliette beamed, as she gazed down at Kaleb's new daughter, and he'd never seen a bigger smile on Eden's face as she scanned the room. This was his life. He breathed deep. Eden glanced back at him then closed the distance between them. "You okay?"

His fingers laced with hers as his lips pressed to her forehead. "Never better. You doing okay?"

Eden lifted her head and glanced around the room. "If you would have told me this is what my life would be like three years ago, I would have laughed in your face. Who knew all my dreams would come true."

"Funny. I was just thinking the same thing."

A word about the author...

DeDe Ramey is a Texas girl transplanted in the heart of Oklahoma. Her vivid imagination and love for people watching gave her a passion to write romance novels filled with swoon worthy heroes, smart, sassy heroines, unexpected nail biting suspense and a good helping of steamy, heart melting romance.

She grew up in the beautiful historic town of Georgetown Texas. Her crazy life experiences with family and friends helped develop her rich colorful imagination. In elementary school she started writing pages of poetry which transformed as a teen into writing and performing her own original songs. As an adult she wrote skits and plays, some short stories, and even a script for a TV series.

Before deciding to write full time, DeDe received a degree in sound engineering and broadcast telecommunication but soon realized those jobs were hard to come by. She took a job as an apartment manager then later settled into the job of domestic affairs manager, raising two amazing kids. Once the kids left home to start their own lives, she revisited her passion for writing.

When she is not reading or writing, she enjoys lifting weights at the gym, finding breathtaking waterfalls while exploring the national forests and parks, or searching for adventures in new cities, visiting thirty-one of the fifty states so far, and going to concerts of old rock bands with her husband Keith, her very own devastatingly handsome hero of over 35 years.